14

THE ORGAN TAKERS

Also by Richard Van Anderson

The Final Push: a short story of surgical suspense

THE ORGAN TAKERS

A novel of surgical suspense

Richard Van Anderson

WHITE LIGHT
PRESS

Copyright © 2014 by Richard Van Anderson

Cover design by Visual Quill.

This book is a work of fiction. References to real people, events, establishments, organizations, or locales are intended only to provide a sense of authenticity, and are used fictitiously. All other characters, and all incidents and dialogue, are drawn from the author's imagination and are not to be construed as real.

Library of Congress Cataloging-in-Publication Data

Anderson, Richard Van.
    The organ takers : a novel of surgical suspense / Richard Van Anderson.
        pages cm. – (The McBride trilogy, bk. 1)
    ISBN: 978-0-9907597-0-6 (hardcover)
    ISBN: 978-0-9907597-1-3 (pbk.)
    ISBN: 978-0-9907597-2-0 (e-book)
    1. Sale of organs, tissues, etc.—Fiction. 2. Black market—Fiction.
    3. Surgeons—Fiction. 4. Revenge—Fiction. 5. Grief—Fiction.   I. Title.
PS3601.N5449 O74 2014
813`.6—dc23

For Kathleen. Thanks for your love and support.
—and for my mother, Shirley, who really did see
monkey-faced people pop up through the floor.

Author's Note

Surgery is a technical endeavor. As such, this story is laden with surgical terminology. Taken in context, the meaning of these terms should be clear. If, however, you are interested in expanded definitions, photos of surgical instruments, X-rays and CT scans of pertinent pathologies, and links to videos of the ER thoracotomy described in the opening chapters, please visit the glossary on my website: rvananderson.com. I encourage you to take a look. Gaining familiarity with the subject matter will enrich your reading experience, and the glossary is interesting in its own right. Thank you, and enjoy the story.

Beginning in the early 1990s, stories of inebriated men waking up in hotel bathtubs full of ice, with surgical incisions on their sides and notes telling them their kidneys have been stolen, repeatedly surface in multiple cities. These occurrences are attributed to urban legend.

In 1999, a human kidney is posted for sale on eBay. Bids reach $5.7 million before company officials pull the ad.

In 2004, the New York Times *documents the sale of a kidney by a Brazilian slum dweller to an American woman. An Israeli organ trafficker brokers the sale. The illegal operation takes place in Durban, South Africa.*

In 2009, Newsweek.com posts an article titled "Organ Trafficking is No Myth." The article describes an international black market that recruits residents from the world's poorest slums and guides them to "broker-friendly" hospitals where their organs can be transplanted into paying patients from the developed world.

- 1 -

Fate, indifferent to the suffering of men, had dealt Michael Smith a bad brain. But it was his fellow man who went beyond indifference into the realm of cruelty, who conspired against Michael without conscience, who stripped him of his humanity when they violated his body for their own gain and on a frozen January morning, discarded him as if he were a bag of trash. It was his fellow man who left him in a dark alley in Midtown Manhattan, left him to wake up alone, freezing under a wool blanket, a pain in his side, a severe pain he didn't have before.

Before what?

Before when?

He couldn't remember. He had lost a chunk of time somewhere.

He tried to sit up. A ripping sensation tore through him. He screamed, clenched his eyes tight and lay there, balled up like a fetus, wondering if he'd been stabbed. He fumbled with the zipper on his coat and felt his shirt.

Dry.

He went limp with relief. Probably a broken rib. He'd cracked one a year ago and it hurt like hell, but not this bad. Maybe he broke two. He put his hand on the ground and tried again to push himself up, made it this time, sat against the wall with legs drawn up and breath held, tears streaming down his face. It felt as if someone had taken a swipe at him with a sword.

After several moments he relaxed, took a shallow breath, and another, then lifted his head and looked around. He was deep in the alley. To the right, a dead end. To the left, the open end. An overflowing Dumpster blocked his view of the street. He tried yelling for help but choked on the pain. He listened for cars passing or people talking but heard nothing. New York City was quiet—four a.m. quiet. He was on his own.

He carefully touched his ribs, feeling for a bulge. There *was* something there, but it was soft and didn't hurt. He blew into his hands, opened and closed them a few times and worked the buttons on his shirt, struggling with numb fingers. Not much light, but he could see a bandage taped to his side. White gauze. White and clean like the brightly lit room. He'd been strapped to a bed. For hours? For days? People in hooded baggy suits had done things to him, monitored him with instruments, mumbled but never spoke. He peered at the gauze with dread.

Wide strips of tape secured it in place. Using his thumbnail, he peeled up a corner and pulled. The skin tented up, felt like it was going to rip. He let go, rolled up more of the edge, pinched it tight and yanked.

He blinked, squinted, struggled to focus through the tears and murky light, and what he finally saw drew a wave of nausea up from the pit of his stomach. He shut his eyes and fought the urge to vomit. The pain caused by heaving would be unimaginable. His mind raced, tried to comprehend, but what he had just seen was incomprehensible. Staples. A line of them starting on his side and disappearing around his back. When he looked again, he saw a long cut stapled together the same way the ER doctors had fixed a gash on his leg some time ago.

Con Edison. They did this. They'd been following him for years, their blue vans and trucks parked all over the city, everywhere he went, watching him, the men in hardhats peeking out of manholes, cameras and listening devices hidden in their steam stacks. The baggy suits in the white room were blue like the Con Ed trucks. They had implanted a tracking device inside him. Now they'd be able to follow him without all that equipment. He had to get to Bellevue. Whatever Con Ed put into him, the Bellevue doctors would take it out. He buttoned his shirt and zipped his coat. If he could stand, he could get to the street. If he could get to the street, he'd find help, or help would find him. He shuffled his feet under him, put a hand on the cold ground, and, clutching his side, he stood.

He tried to stand up straight. Pain doubled him over. He teetered backward, his butt hitting the wall, then he felt dizzy and nearly toppled forward. He waited a moment for the dizziness to clear, then slowly straightened and took a step, then another. Every movement sent ripping jolts through his midsection, and after four or five steps he stopped, the pain intolerable, the shivering uncontrollable. He wanted to sit, but he'd never get up.

He made it to the mouth of the alley and leaned against the corner of the building. Except for a plume of steam rising from a manhole cover, the street was empty. No Con Ed trucks, no steam stacks. Lights were on in some apartments, but the buildings all had stoops. He tried yelling for help, but the effort was feeble. He looked up and down the block, to the avenues at either end, but he had nothing left. Time to give up.

He relaxed. The shivering eased. His eyelids drifted shut.

A clatter startled him awake. A flurry of yellow cabs passed through the intersection to his right, a hundred feet away. If he could just get there …

He staggered up the sidewalk, his legs heavy, then heavy legs became dead weight, and black curtains lowered over his eyes. As he fell, he reached for the rail at the base of a stoop. He missed, smashing his face into the steps.

- 2 -

The ambulance pulled away from the all-night diner and drove south on Lexington. Traffic was light—garbage trucks, delivery trucks, taxicabs. Paramedic Tom Burnett steadied two cups of coffee as his partner, Freddy Ramirez, maneuvered the box-shaped vehicle around the potholes at 34th and Lexington. They were headed for Bellevue Hospital, their home base.

They turned left onto East 26th Street, then crossed Third Avenue. As Burnett sipped his coffee something caught his eye. He snapped his head to the right, but parked cars blocked his view. He spun to look out the rear windows, but the glass dripped with condensation. "Did you see that?" he asked Freddy as they crossed Second Avenue.

"See what?"

"A body on the sidewalk."

"Probably a homeless dude sleeping one off."

"Doubt it. When it's this cold, homeless dudes find a shelter or die. Besides, he's facedown with nothing covering him."

Freddy switched on the flashing lights and circled back. Moments later they were inching along East 26th.

Burnett pointed. "There, by the trash cans." He radioed their status as Freddy parked, then they hopped out, unloaded the gurney and equipment, and trotted up the sidewalk.

The man seemed homeless—ratty clothes, tangled hair—but he wasn't sleeping one off. His arms and legs were splayed as though he'd lost consciousness first, then fallen. Freddy dropped to his knee and pressed his fingers into the man's neck. "Weak pulse. Let's log-roll him."

They pulled on latex gloves and tucked the man's arms by his sides. Freddy crouched above the head and held it like a basketball. Burnett knelt down and grasped the shoulder and hip. The move required perfect coordination. If they rotated the torso before the head, or the head before the torso, a fractured cervical spine could slice through the spinal cord. They had no idea what had happened, so they had to assume spinal injury until proven otherwise.

Freddy counted, and on three they rolled the man onto his back. Congealed blood covered his face. A jagged laceration extended from the left eyebrow to the hairline. They'd worry about that later. Right now, the ABCs of trauma resuscitation—airway, breathing, circulation—had priority.

Freddy unzipped the man's jacket and put a stethoscope on his chest. "He's breathing, but his respirations are agonal."

Burnett opened the equipment box, handed his partner a laryngoscope and an endotracheal tube. On his first try, Freddy slid the plastic tube between the vocal cords and into the trachea. He inflated the seal, attached the oxygen bag, and started squeezing.

Burnett slipped the man's arm out of his jacket and checked his blood pressure. "Sixty systolic. We need to get some fluids going." He tied a tourniquet above the elbow and tapped the fold of the arm. No veins, the dim light not helping. He stabbed blindly with a large-bore IV needle. Nothing. Changed the angle and tried again, and a third time. There, a red drop from the end of the needle. He advanced the catheter into the vein, connected the tubing, and started the IV fluid wide open.

Once the endotracheal tube and IV catheter were secured, Burnett checked the pressure. "Ninety systolic. He likes the fluid. I'm gonna hang another liter and we should scoop and run."

"No primary assessment?" Freddy asked.

"We're a block away. Let the ER docs do it."

With the ABCs established—the patient had a stable airway, Freddy was helping him breathe, the blood pressure was rising—

immobilization and transportation was now the priority. Burnett placed a C-collar around the neck to immobilize the cervical spine, then strapped the man to a backboard to stabilize the thoracic and lumbar spines. Using the backboard, they lifted him onto the gurney, pushed the gurney to the ambulance, and loaded him inside. Burnett climbed in, attached the heart monitor, and took over the oxygen bag. Freddy jumped in the driver's seat and headed for Bellevue, lights flashing and siren blaring.

Burnett bagged with one hand while patting the man's pockets with the other. No wallet. No surprise there, but in the left front, something hard and flat. He slipped a finger into the pocket, hooked a ring, and pulled it out. Burnett braced himself as Freddy laid on the horn and turned sharply onto First Avenue. Once the ride settled, he opened his hand to find a piece of plastic, about two inches square, a key ring with no keys. Inside the plastic, a head-and-shoulders photo of a young girl. She appeared to be eight or nine, had pigtails, a missing tooth, and wore a frilly dress with a lacy bow tied at the neck. On the back it said, "Third Grade, October '99." Given to her father at a time when he needed a key ring. Burnett thought of the trinkets and keepsakes his young daughter had given him, and now, the dirty and feculent-smelling man was no longer human waste. He was somebody. He was a father.

They wheeled the man into the ER. The waiting area overflowed with homeless people, many faking illness to get out of the cold. More lay on stretchers lining the hallway. As they passed the triage desk the nurse hollered, "Trauma One, guys. Any ID?"

"A John Doe," Burnett said.

They rolled into the first trauma bay. Nurses and technicians swarmed. George—a male nurse sporting tattoos up both arms—helped move the man onto the ER bed. Freddy removed the oxygen bag and stepped aside as the respiratory therapist connected the endotracheal tube to a ventilator. Clothes were cut off with shears. More IVs were placed. Blood samples were drawn. A urinary catheter was inserted through the penis into the bladder. As Freddy maneuvered the gurney out the door, Burnett waited to give report.

A voice boomed above the clamor. "What's the story here?"

Dr. Paul Hacker, chief surgery resident, had entered the room. He was short, stocky, and bald to a sheen under his surgeon's cap. The sleeves of his white coat were rolled up to his elbows as if he'd been working on a car. Blood spatter dotted his shoe covers and scrub pants.

Burnett emerged from the corner. "Freddy and I brought him in."

"Tommy, good to see you. What's it been, an hour?"

Before Burnett could answer, George interrupted. "Dr. Hacker, you might wanna check this out. Appears the patient recently had an operation."

A line of surgical staples coursed around the man's left side.

"A major operation," Hacker said. "Probably a kidney procedure, and look at his belly. He's bleeding internally."

The man's abdomen protruded as though he were six months pregnant.

The alarm on the cardiac monitor sounded. A woman's voice cut through the noise of the room. "He's coding."

Burnett glanced at the screen. Ventricular fibrillation.

Hacker moved to the head of the bed. "Charge the paddles. Push one amp of epinephrine. Get six units of O-negative STAT, and open a thoracotomy tray in case we need to crack his chest."

One intern pumped on the sternum as a second intern rubbed the defibrillator paddles together, smearing the conductive jelly. "Charged to two hundred joules."

"Shock him," Hacker said.

The intern yelled, "Clear!" and fired.

A loud pop. The man's spine arched like he'd been shot in the back. Burnett checked the monitor. Fibrillation.

"Charge to two hundred and hit him again," Hacker said.

Another pop and arch of the back. Still fibrillating.

"Three hundred, quickly."

No change.

"Okay, let's crack him."

Let's crack him—three simple words that sent a shock wave through the ER. Three words that invited every surgery resident, internal medicine resident, medical student, respiratory therapist, lab tech, blood gas tech—and even the housekeeping staff—to flood into the room, hoping to witness the most dramatic procedure, the greatest spectacle, in all of medicine: the emergency room thoracotomy.

Hacker shed his white coat, threw on sterile gloves, and grabbed a scalpel as a nurse doused the patient's chest with Betadine solution. With one long swipe, Hacker sliced through skin and muscle from the left side of the sternum to the left shoulder blade. The tissues barely bled. With a second swipe he entered the chest cavity. He placed a rib spreader and cranked it open. Ribs crunched and snapped. The lung billowed out of the incision like a pink balloon, inflating and deflating as the respiratory therapist squeezed and released the bag. Hacker stuck one hand deep inside the thorax, and with the other, guided a vascular clamp to the same spot and snapped it closed. "The aorta's cross-clamped," he said.

With a pair of scissors, he opened the pericardial sac and exposed the heart. It was dark blue and quivering like a sack of worms—the hallmark of ventricular fibrillation. He squeezed it between his palms in a rhythmic fashion.

For thirty minutes Hacker pumped John Doe's heart. Multiple units of blood were transfused using a fluid warmer. Bicarb, epinephrine, and calcium were administered intravenously. Shocks were repeatedly delivered with internal paddles. Nothing worked. Hacker called the code at 5:02 a.m. The respiratory therapist stopped bagging. The tattooed nurse turned off the IV infusion pumps. Hacker removed the aortic clamp and rib spreader and started closing the chest with an intern.

Burnett left the room and took a seat in the nurse's station. He wondered if he or Freddy could have done anything differently. He recalled their actions in the field, particularly their assessment, or deferment of, and decided no, they had met the accepted standard of care. If anyone was a candidate for a scoop and run, it was John

Doe. And if an ER thoracotomy, performed by a general surgery chief resident in a level-one trauma center couldn't save him, nothing could.

Freddy set two cups of coffee on the counter and sat down. "How's he doing?"

Burnett reached for his. "Didn't make it."

"That sucks."

Burnett sipped his coffee and peered at his partner over the rim of the Styrofoam cup. It didn't bother him that Freddy's response to the death of a raggedy homeless man was "That sucks," because it did. Anybody who'd been in the room would agree. What did bother Burnett was the lack of connection of "That sucks" to any discernible emotion. Freddy was the most capable partner Burnett had worked with, but for a young guy who hadn't had time to burn out, he was also the most detached. Maybe too much *Grand Theft Auto* on the Xbox. Whatever it was, Burnett thought about mentioning the twenty-two- or twenty-three-year-old girl who had just lost her father and would never know it, but decided to save his breath.

Several minutes later Hacker entered the nurse's station. Blood covered his scrubs. Sweat soaked his cap, neckline, and armpits. As he approached, he dried his hands and forearms with a towel, his face expressionless.

"Sorry, guys. Couldn't get his temperature up. Can't defibrillate a cold heart."

"What do you think happened?" Burnett asked.

Hacker folded his clean arms across his bloody scrubs. "I think he recently had a kidney resection, probably an impacted or infected stone. A ligature came off a good-sized artery and he bled out internally. You saw how distended his abdomen was."

The triage nurse gave Hacker some forms. Hacker thrust the forms at an intern and said, "Death certificate for the John Doe in Trauma One. Call the medical examiner's office. Tell 'em the patient died in the emergency department. They'll decide if they want to do an autopsy."

The intern scurried away.

Burnett picked up the thread of the conversation. "You said he recently had surgery."

Hacker removed his cap and wiped his shiny scalp with it. "Within the last few days. That was a fresh incision."

"Would a homeless man be discharged so quickly?"

Hacker shrugged. "Beds get tight. A guy four or five days out from a kidney resection is in better shape than a lot of the others. Doesn't mean he's ready for discharge, just means he's less likely to bounce back."

Burnett wanted to point out that John Doe had bounced back in a big way, but they'd had that discussion, people sent home too soon, the paramedics hauling them back in. Hacker was a resident. He didn't want to hear it. He had a service to run, junior residents to teach, attending surgeons to please. He had no time to worry about the ills of the health care system, so Burnett let it go.

From the hallway came the sound of vomiting. The smell of stale beer and stomach acid followed. That one wasn't faking it. Burnett's eyes burned. Freddy gagged. Hacker looked annoyed. The paramedics jumped up, thanked Paul Hacker for his efforts, and gathered their equipment.

- 3 -

Dr. Brian Steinberg, associate professor of psychiatry, was sitting across the nurse's station from Dr. Hacker and the two paramedics when the inebriated patient in the hallway emptied his gastric contents onto the floor. As Hacker and the paramedics dispersed, Steinberg followed, stepping outside to the ambulance bay and continuing around the corner to an isolated loading dock. He stood in the dark and the cold, shivering under his white physician's coat, a coat—and a title—of which he was no longer worthy. He slipped an unlit cigarette between his lips and reached into his pocket for the TracFone.

His hands trembled as he entered the number. He told himself it was the cold, but it wasn't. It was the dead man who lay on the table in Trauma One, an unfortunate soul who had suffered from a dopamine-glutamate imbalance in his brain since the age of twenty-five. Michael Smith had trusted Brian Steinberg, and to gain the trust of a paranoid schizophrenic was no small feat. But Steinberg had abused that trust, and now Michael Smith's blood was on *his* hands as surely as it was on the hands of the surgeon who stole Smith's kidney, and on the hands of the depraved piece of shit who forced that surgeon to desecrate another man's body. He pushed the send button.

A tired voice answered. "What did you find out?"

"He died."

"How?"

"The chief resident suspects it was internal bleeding from a recent kidney operation. They opened his chest in the ER and tried to resuscitate him but were unsuccessful."

"Did they call the medical examiner?"

"The resident told an intern to do it."

Silence.

The thrum of traffic over on the FDR seemed to be building ahead of the morning rush hour.

A siren signaled the arrival of another ambulance.

Then, "Anything else I need to know?"

"No," Steinberg replied.

The phone went dead.

Steinberg lit the cigarette, pulled the tar and nicotine into the deepest alveoli of his lungs, and prayed for the day when his obligation would be met and he'd be finished with all this.

- 4 -

Dr. Andrew Turnbull connected his browser to the proxy server and opened an anonymous e-mail account. There were two unread messages, both from Mr. White. The first was routine, a new contact number for White, a number that changed daily. The second was marked "Urgent."

Turnbull leaned his chair back and pondered the convoluted path he'd been forced to take in order to achieve his destiny. Anonymous e-mails, disposable cell phones, an NSA spook called Mr. White—all part of a grand design to propel him to greatness, to establish himself as one of the supreme thinkers of the ages. By his own measure, he possessed the greatest medical mind of the twentieth century, the young twenty-first century, and perhaps the centuries to follow. And if he accomplished his goal, history would have to agree. As would the Nobel Prize committee. He had no doubt his current trajectory would carry him to medicine's most prestigious prize and the public adoration that came with it, but first he needed money.

In just under two years, his company—NuLife Corporation—had burned through all of its start-up venture capital, as well as a second round of funding, at an astonishing rate of seventy-five thousand dollars a week. Unfortunately, accepting a third round would cost him control of NuLife, and therein lay the greatest threat to his destiny. Without a significant influx of operating capital, his life's work would come to an unceremonious halt, and he, as a transplant surgeon, biomedical researcher, and company executive, would be irrelevant. He'd prefer terminal esophageal cancer over irrelevance. He tilted his chair forward and opened the e-mail marked as urgent.

> The first donor died in the Bellevue Emergency Department this morning at approximately 5:00 a.m. Chief surgical resident on duty attributed cause of death to internal bleeding related to recent surgery. Medical examiner's office notified. Please contact to discuss.

Turnbull slammed his fist on the desk and backhanded the phone onto the floor. The donor bled to death? Donors don't bleed to death. In his fifteen-year career, his personal mortality rate for live-donor kidney harvests was zero. Not a single death. Not one. He leaned on his elbows and squeezed his head between his hands. Nobody was supposed to die. Dead people drew attention—even derelicts. Leave a dead homeless person on the sidewalk, nobody gives a shit. One of them dies in the hospital, somebody's gonna start nosing around. Goddammit. What kind of hack kills a donor? Turnbull checked the mahogany of his desk for scratches, picked the phone up off the floor, and buzzed his secretary. A moment later she entered.

June was a small woman, the only NuLife employee shorter than Turnbull. She had brittle gray hair, a smoker's rasp that seemed even more grating this morning, and a face subdivided by a complex of fissures and chasms, all by-products of the constant flood of nicotine bathing her tissues. A fifty-year-old encased in a ninety-year-old body.

"Tell Sam I need to see him immediately," Turnbull said. "And another thing. How long has that bubblehead Denise been working here?"

June crossed her arms and straightened her spine, adding a couple of inches to her frame. "Three months. Why?"

"It's her job to keep the conference room in pristine condition, and she can't handle it. I'm constantly finding fingerprints and food residue and cup rings all over the table, particularly where

Abercrombie sits. The trash can's always full. The chairs are never lined up."

June put her hands on her hips. "Ms. Westgate has her fair share of responsibilities, and she handles them as good as anyone. Don't worry about your room. I'll see that she moves it to the top of her priority list. Anything else?"

"Get Sam in here … please."

While he waited for his chief financial officer, Turnbull went over to the windows and stared out at the rolling hills of northern New Jersey—the gray sky, lifeless trees, and dead undergrowth. No, not dead, but in a cold-induced state of suspended animation, like a human organ in a bucket of ice. He wondered how many lives had been saved by ice, by the use of cold to suspend life just long enough to save the dying. And he wondered, if there was a God, how He felt about it, hydrogen and oxygen—His elements—bound together in their solid form and used to upstage Him, to interfere in His business, the business of life and death. As a practicing surgeon, Turnbull had found it amusing when family members would say "It's in God's hands now," as the patient disappeared behind the OR doors. When it came to replacing useless organs and saving lives, the outcome had rested not in God's hands, but his. God had never been in any operating theater where Turnbull had worked.

There was a knock on the door. Before Turnbull could answer, Sam walked in and sank into one of two leather chairs facing the desk. He ran his fingers through dark hair that had grown considerably since his ouster from Corporate America, then clasped his hands on top of his head. "The furrow in your brow, it's as deep as anything on June's face. What's up?"

As Turnbull made his way to his desk, he reconsidered mentioning the donor. He needed Sam and could not afford to panic him. He also valued Sam's loyalty and did not want to risk losing it by leaving him out of the inner circle. Samuel Keating—no relation to Charles Keating of the Lincoln Savings and Loan plunder in the 1980s—had been a Wall Street wunderkind. He knew how to move illicit funds, first offshore, then back again as venture capital. Without that capital NuLife Corporation would meet an early demise. As it stood, the company was already circling the drain. Turnbull knew tissue engineering and organ fabrication, not the intricacies of Corporate America. "Our donor died," he said.

Sam's face went slack. He sat up. "How?"

"Bled to death, probably the renal artery. Whatever it was, Jugdish botched it."

"Jugdish? Who the hell is that?"

"Our so-called surgeon. I don't know his real name. Mr. White found him, squatting in a hovel with a towel wrapped around his head for all I know, but it doesn't matter. He's history."

Sam slumped deep into the chair. "Jesus Christ, this is murder."

"Keep it down. June's a lurker. Besides, it's not murder. It's an unfortunate complication of a surgical procedure."

"Call it what you want, but if we don't remove his kidney, he's not dead. In my book that's murder, and I can't be a part of it."

Turnbull sat forward and planted his elbows on his desk. "First of all, murder implies intent. Secondly, a hundred yards from here is another man who can urinate for the first time in five years. Do you have any idea what that means to him? He's no longer tethered to a dialysis machine. He can be a father to his young children. He can contribute to society." Sam opened his mouth. Turnbull raised his hand. "Homeless paranoid schizophrenics offer nothing to society. The way I see it, we did this one a favor. We gave his life a level of meaning that otherwise would've been impossible. We relieved him of a lonely, meaningless existence and spared him a lonely, meaningless death. And we allowed him to leave behind a legacy that will help countless others."

"Tell that to the judge."

"I won't have to. There's no way to trace the donor to us."

"Someone did."

"One of the ER nurses is under the long reach of our thumb. He recognized the man and called White. White called Steinberg. Steinberg got there and made a visual before they tagged and bagged the guy. White's the only person who connects everybody, and to them, he's nothing more than a phantom voice on the phone."

"How'd he react? Steinberg, I mean. Is he gonna bail?"

"He can't. White has his head in a vise."

"And how about White? He's said all along he won't tolerate any deaths."

"If he wants me to grow a kidney for his daughter, he'll tolerate this one." Turnbull sat back and leveled a gaze at his young CFO. "What about you? Still in?"

"I don't know," Sam said, shaking his head. "No matter how you label this man's death, we caused it. We kidnapped him, he died. That's a capital crime. We get caught, it's not like doing thirty-six months in Rochester Correctional for pick-pocketing your investors. It's hard time, for a long time—Attica, Five Points, Sing Sing."

"We won't get caught."

"Won't or can't?"

"Can't. There are too many layers between us and the harvest team. If any of them go down, they have no idea who is on this end."

Sam stared into his lap, then looked up, his expression pleading. "Why don't we go back to the venture capitalists for a third round of funding, operate above the table instead of under it?"

"I've already given forty-nine percent of the company to the VCs. I give away another one percent and we'll have a bunch of snot-nosed Harvard MBAs calling the shots."

"That's how a lot of companies are run."

"Not this one. I have no patience for idiot investors who repeatedly ask inane questions while failing to understand the brilliance of what I'm doing."

"What if you give me access to those notebooks locked in your safe," Keating said. "If we reveal how close we are to a real breakthrough, I think we'd be able to squeeze additional funding out of our current investors without having to give up any more equity."

"Forget it. Nobody knows how all the research fits together except me. No one—not you, the scientists, or the investors—has enough information to form a complete picture of what we're doing here. And that's by design."

"That's what nondisclosure agreements are for."

"Nondisclosure agreements are only as good as the people who sign them, and most people can't be trusted, not with something of this magnitude. So, in or out?"

Sam Keating closed his eyes and ran his fingers through his hair.

Turnbull leaned forward. "May I remind you that you are an ex-con? What're your options beyond NuLife? Managing a McDonald's? Running a Dunkin' Donuts? Do you want to return to the real world as one of the gray people, or do you want to make history?"

Sam opened his eyes, took a long breath, and sighed. "Okay. I'm in. What do we do now?"

Suppressing a smile, Turnbull leaned back. One could always rely on the seven deadly sins to motivate others. Greed in this case, perhaps with a little pride thrown in. "We need a surgeon who can harvest a kidney without killing the donor."

"Have anybody in mind?"

"A former resident, who we should've used from the beginning."

"Let me guess. The guy who helped you manipulate the liver-transplant waiting list. What's his name—McClellan? McLaughlin?"

Turnbull narrowed his gaze, taking exception to his CFO's choice of words. He preferred to think of the waiting-list incident as a restructuring, not a manipulation. "His name is McBride," Turnbull said. "David McBride."

"So why didn't we use him from the beginning?"

"Because blackmail is more efficient than bribery. With Jugdish, the simple threat of deportation was enough. Fast and easy. McBride will be a tougher sell. Short of threatening bodily harm to him or someone close to him, we don't have any leverage. We'll have to offer him something he really wants or needs, and that means surveillance, gathering information. All those things take time."

"And money."

"Yes. Bribery is more expensive than blackmail."

After his CFO left the office, Turnbull opened the cabinet behind his desk. Inside was a safe. Within the safe, a pay-as-you-go TracFone, purchased with cash and anonymously activated online through a proxy server. Turnbull entered White's new contact number and waited. A single beep prompted him to leave only a time. Turnbull admired Mr. White's thoroughness. He would've made a fine surgeon.

- 5 -

For once Dr. David McBride did not have to worry about getting caught in the cross fire of a good drug deal gone bad. The streets of the Lower East Side were empty, the bitter cold driving the neighborhood vermin under their rocks. As he rounded the corner to his street, an icy gust of wind slammed into him. He put his twelve-pack and Chinese food on the sidewalk, pulled his stocking cap down, his wool scarf up, grabbed his stuff and moved on.

He approached his building, held the door as a bundled-up woman exited, then quickstepped into the lobby before the wind caught the door, and the door caught him. At the mailboxes he fished his keys out of his scrub pants and retrieved the mail. More credit card offers. He was sick of them, one or two a day, five or six a week. The letters tacked onto his name used to get him laid. Now they only brought in junk. At the bottom of the stack hid the only real piece of mail, addressed to David McBride, MD, return address the University of North Dakota School of Medicine, Department of Surgery. He stared at the envelope, his pulse bumping up a few ticks, then stuck it in his back pocket.

The monotonous beat of *Boyz n the Hood*–era gangsta rap hammered him as he climbed the stairwell to the fourth-floor landing. At 4-A the shrieks of the perpetually crying baby cut through the rap music. Poor guy probably had colic, but the dim-witted mother wouldn't know colic from cauliflower. At 4-C the stench of fried fish seeped under the door, as it did every night. At 4-E he took out his keys and turned the first of three locks.

A frenzy of vicious barking and growling exploded from the pit bull across the hall. David jumped, his heart racing as the noise blasted up and down the corridor. Claws digging at metal made his teeth ache. "You pink-eyed albino son of a bitch. Where were you last week when 4-H was robbed?" He'd love to get the hideous monster into the lab and perform a laryngectomy. He gave the dog the finger.

Once his heart rate dropped out of the death zone, David turned the second lock but hesitated before turning the third. This moment—walking through the door and facing his dad—was the hardest part of each day. He loved his father, but tension between David the compassionate son and David the detached caregiver was wearing him down. Hal McBride had gone from larger-than-life hero to demented five-year-old, and David didn't know how to handle it. Medical school had prepared him to deal with disease, but not when it lived under the same roof. He promised himself that tonight the compassionate son would rule, not the frustrated caregiver. He turned the key and went inside.

David disliked clutter and disorder, which meant he disliked their apartment. The place was small—a tiny bedroom for his dad, a microscopic kitchen, a glorified Porta-Potty of a bathroom, and a front room with an alcove just big enough to fit a desk. Boxes of medicine, surgery, and nursing textbooks were stacked in corners. A sleeper sofa filled the longest wall of the front room. A chest of drawers blocked the lower half of the only window. There were no keepsakes or knickknacks. The walls were white, dirty, and bare. David didn't aspire to live in a palace, but he did need a retreat at the end of the day, a sanctuary from the chaos of the outside world, and this wasn't it. But more than that, his wife deserved a home, a place to bear her personal touch. He owed her as much. He hung his coat and scarf and went to the kitchen. Cassandra was putting his father's plastic dishes into the cupboard. She was still in scrubs, so she hadn't been home long.

She gave him a smug grin. "The dog get you again?"

"Yeah, the bastard. I don't know why he never barks at you."

"Because I don't threaten to surgically remove his vocal cords."

"I guess. Anyway, how's it going?"

"Fine, except I'm starving."

"Got it handled." He lifted the bag of food. "There's a carton of mu shu pork in here with your name on it."

"Oh, David, I said moo goo gai pan, not mu shu pork."

"Hah—just fuckin' with you."

David kissed her, catching a hint of the lingering perfume molecules still adhered to her skin. He took a quiet breath and savored it, then handed her the twelve-pack and stepped back so she could open the refrigerator. As she put the beer away, he noticed more than a few wavy gray hairs entwined among the straight black ones. And maybe it was the fluorescent light reflecting off stark white walls or the long shifts in the OR, but her face looked washed out, and the skin around her eyelids seemed a deeper hue of purple.

Her hair and her eyes, they had drawn him to her. As an intern he had spent hours during long surgical cases doing nothing but tugging on retractors. When Cassandra was the scrub nurse on those cases, he'd wedge his retractor into place, rest his arms on the patient, and watch her. At first he saw a skilled nurse who passed instruments with confidence and conducted herself with grace. Then he started paying attention to the young woman behind the mask. He studied her brown eyes and the flawless skin that surrounded them. He anticipated those moments when long strands of hair escaped from under her hat, and the circulating nurse would tuck them back in. Most of all, he looked forward to the end of the case when the wound had been dressed and everyone removed their masks. While he wrote the post-op orders in the chart, he'd watch and wait, and, sure enough, someone or something would make her smile.

Now the pallor of her skin intensified the brown of her eyes and the dark circles around them, casting her sockets in shadow. At a glance, her eyes appeared recessed, sunken as with illness or unhealthy weight loss. She was not ill or too thin, but these were not the eyes of a twenty-eight-year-old woman. She was aging too soon, too fast. Their small life, lived in a small space, with small choices, was draining her youth, and it was his fault.

He kissed her again, this time with more intensity than the typical how-was-your-day peck on the cheek.

"That was nice," she said. "Everything okay?"

"Yeah, mostly. I'm gonna go check on my dad."

David went to the bedroom. His father was in his chair, a beat-up recliner with a sagging footrest. He was wearing flannel pajamas, a blue terry cloth robe, and fur-lined slippers—the same stuff he wore at breakfast. Either the nurse hadn't bothered to change him, or he had refused. Probably the latter. There had been periods as long as a week when David was unable to get his father to change clothes or take a shower. He would insist he had showered, and if David tried to convince him otherwise, a catastrophic reaction—the medical term for a nuclear hissy fit—would erupt. Once, and only once, David forced him to bathe, and it did not go well. The guy screamed for help, repeatedly yelling that he was being robbed. David called an agency the next day. The nurses they'd since hired had been more successful with the clothes and hygiene. Perhaps Hal McBride *was* robbed that night—of his dignity. What other outcome was possible when a son had to bathe his own father?

His dad greeted him with a wide grin, which meant he recognized David, but he wanted to know the name of the lady in the front room.

"Cassandra," David answered. "She's my wife, your daughter-in-law."

"No ... your wife ..." His father picked at the nylon border of his blanket. "Isn't she the one who's here all day?"

"That's Wendy, the nurse. She looks after you while Cassandra and I are at work."

"Oh. So how'd it go today? Do any transplants?"

It was a good day when his father thought his son had completed his surgical training and was now a transplant surgeon instead of a lab tech. "Yes," David said. "I put a new liver in a nineteen-year-old girl with autoimmune hepatitis."

His dad smiled. "Most folks don't save lives when they go to work in the morning."

"No, they don't," David said in a barely audible voice. He fluffed his father's pillows and pulled his blanket chest high. "Maybe we'll watch a movie later."

"The one about the boxer?"

"Yes, the one about the boxer."

As David turned to leave, his father said, "Uh, David, did you speak to the monkey-faced people downstairs? They're still popping up through the floor."

Last week they were chickens, this week monkeys. What member of the animal kingdom would next week bring? "Yes," David said with a weariness born of watching a mighty rock crumble. "Shouldn't happen again."

Cassandra had dinner waiting on the coffee table—the food thoughtfully arranged on real plates, a cold beer, a glass of ice water with a slice of lemon. Even though she had little to work with—a Barbie doll kitchen, a meager budget, frequent carryout—she always managed to present a nice meal. "You are the maestro of turning chicken shit into chicken salad," he said as he sat next to her.

"A compliment? Breathe in too much formaldehyde today?"

"Nope. Just hit myself with fifty micrograms of fentanyl before I locked up."

Cassandra turned sharply. "Don't even joke about that. Hardly a year goes by without a nurse or pharmacist or anesthesia resident getting fired for stealing vials of fentanyl or Demerol."

"Ampules of IV narcotics are the enriched uranium of the drug trade," David said. "If I formed an alliance with one of our street-corner entrepreneurs, you and I would be looking at mansions in Scarsdale by year's end."

"You're scaring me, David. I know you have access to the lab's drug cabinet. Please tell me you'd never do that."

"*Moi?*" he said with mock surprise.

He bit a fried dumpling and nodded toward the TV. "You care what we watch?"

"Not really."

He held out his hand. She slapped the remote into his palm as if they were in the operating room, then deftly used her chopsticks to pluck a moo goo off her plate of gai pan.

"Any interesting cases in the OR today?" he asked, already knowing what she'd say.

"Routine stuff," she replied.

Her standard answer. He had been exiled from medicine and surgery for two years now, sentenced to a life of operating on rats, and she always took care not to stir his resentment.

"Any exciting developments in the lab?" she asked between bites of chicken and button mushrooms.

"Yeah, if you enjoy watching glaciers move."

She reminded him that he was performing important work, making a contribution to medical research that would improve people's lives.

He did not remind her that he was a grunt, a surgical gun-for-hire. If the research led to any meaningful conclusions, the primary investigators—the guys who stopped by the lab once a month—would write the paper and list their names on the first page. He'd merely be thanked for his technical expertise in the acknowledgments, in a tiny font tacked onto the last paragraph.

"What do you think of the new nurse?" David asked. Wendy had been with them for a few days, hastily hired when her predecessor unexpectedly quit.

"I don't know. She's out the door as soon as I walk in."

"Odd isn't it? The last one at least stayed long enough to tell us how the day went."

"She's always in a hurry," Cassandra said, "like she has another job or something."

"Maybe she does. We're paying half what we paid Maria. After the agency takes their cut, can't be much left."

David took a bite of kung pao chicken and got one of those skinny black peppers mixed in. A blast of ammonia pierced his sinuses and lodged in the base of his brain. When his eyes stopped watering and his tongue started working again, he mentioned the letter from North Dakota.

"And?" Cassandra said.

"I didn't open it. I know what it's gonna say: 'Thanks, but no thanks.'"

"Then let's get it over with."

David pulled the envelope out of his back pocket and reread the return address. He'd spent the last two years applying to every surgical training program in the country and had received only rejections, so there was no reason to believe this was any different. He ripped open the flap and read the letter aloud. "Dear Dr. McBride, thank you for your interest in our general surgery program, but it is not our policy to offer residency positions to any resident fired from an accredited program." He wadded the paper into a ball and dropped it into the pool of soy sauce in the dumpling pan.

"Maybe that's for the best," Cassandra said. "Maybe it's time to move on."

"To what? Career rat surgeon? Physician's assistant? I'm not cut out to be someone's lackey."

"I'm a lackey, and I don't have a problem with it. If you want to use your surgical skills, those are your options."

"Well those options suck."

"Life sucks, David. What entitles you to get everything you want?"

"I'm smart. I work hard. I'll do whatever it takes to accomplish something. People like me get what they want."

"Unless they make a mistake and lose it all."

David stared at his plate, took a long breath, and slowly shook his head.

Cassandra flicked a mushroom with her chopsticks.

After several moments she stopped flicking and looked up. "You know what first attracted me to you?"

"How good my butt looked in scrubs?"

"Well, yeah, there was that," she said with a hint of a smile, "but mainly it was your passion. I saw it early on, from your first days as an intern. It didn't matter if you were assisting on a brain tumor or amputating a gangrenous toe, you loved being in the operating room. You loved cutting things out and sewing things back together, creating order out of disorder—your words. Even draining an abscess was a big deal."

" 'A surgeon is at his finest when he's draining pus'—William Stewart Halsted, the father of American surgery."

"Yes. You used to tell me that. At first I thought it was weird, but when I saw how you believed in yourself and what you were doing, I understood. So find that passion and apply it to your research. I know working with rats isn't the same as working with humans, but you're still making a contribution."

"I'm not making a contribution," David said. "I make no decisions. I have no input. I remove the heart from one rat and sew it into another. There's no glory in that."

"There's no glory in the life we're living, either. I'm doing my best to accept our situation, and it would help if you weren't stuck in the past." Cassandra picked up a clump of broccoli, then dropped it and looked at him. "You have a skill, and you're able to apply it to something you're interested in. Accept the fact that you are a medical researcher, embrace it, and let's move forward. Your worst day is a lot better than most people's best day."

David glared at his plate. "I'm a lab tech, not a researcher."

"Jesus, David, it doesn't matter." She turned and faced him squarely. "The job doesn't make the person, it's how the person approaches the job. You see it all over the city, people who take pride in what they do despite how trivial or menial it seems to the rest of us."

He turned and faced her squarely. "They don't know any better. They've never cut a failing heart or cirrhotic liver out of a dying patient, sewn in a new one, and watched that patient walk out of the hospital two weeks later."

"No, they haven't, yet they still find satisfaction in their lives."

He held her gaze for a moment, then grabbed his beer and took a drink.

Cassandra finished dinner and went to change. David cleared the table, fixed a cup of hot tea, and opened a new beer. When he returned, she was sitting on the couch with her legs pulled up, thumbing the pages of a nursing journal. He set the tea in front of her.

"Thank you," she said. "Listen, I'm sorry about the letter, but things don't always work out in this shitty world. Just remember, whatever happens, I'm in your corner."

"I know, and I appreciate it." He searched for something profound to say, but he was as good at expressing sentiment as he was at knitting. "Mind if I hang out with my dad?"

"No. I'm going to sleep soon, anyway."

After he helped her make the sofa bed, he carried the DVD player into his father's room. They watched *Rocky* again, his father lucid enough to tell boxing stories from his days in the navy. David had heard them all, but it was good to see the man so talkative.

His dad had spent eight years in the service, boxing his way around the country, then throughout Europe and anywhere else the U.S. Armed Forces were stationed. He fought Army, Air Force, Marines, and his fellow seamen. He compiled an impressive win-loss record and avoided the rice paddies of Southeast Asia. But he also took countless blows to the head and demonstrated signs of dementia at age fifty-two, well before the typical age of onset of sixty-five to seventy. The doctors debated whether he had developed early-onset Alzheimer's, or was suffering from Dementia Pugilistica, more commonly known as recurrent traumatic encephalopathy. The final classification made no difference. The pathophysiology was the same—abnormal tau proteins forming fibrous tangles in the brain. And the clinical course of both diseases was identical—relentless degeneration of cognitive and motor function resulting in a dehumanizing, hideous death. There was no treatment for either affliction, only custodial care, like living with your son and daughter-in-law and eating off plastic dishes. So David savored times such as these, when his dad emerged from his mental fog bank long enough to tell stories and enjoy himself. But the cruel irony of the situation—his father's few remaining memories were of those things that had stolen his memory—always left David feeling bitter and alone, aching for the days when he was a kid, his father was clearheaded and vital, and his mother was alive.

Taking care not to wake Cassandra, David climbed into bed and rolled onto his side, his back to hers. He was facing the radiator that jutted out of the floor about eighteen inches from his head. In the dark, the rusty heat exchangers resembled prison bars.

He was slow to fall asleep most nights, and as he lay awake to the sound of clanking pipes and a hissing steam vent, he'd journey into the deep folds of his mind, into the troubling thoughts and unwanted emotions he had suppressed during the day. Tonight he was plagued by what Cassandra had said at dinner. She was right, of course. She hadn't signed up for the life she'd been dealt. She was a beautiful woman who could've had anyone, deserved everything, and was getting next to nothing. She should have had a house up in Westchester by now with a master suite, a four-poster bed, and a separate wing for his father and a private nurse. Instead, she was sleeping on a pullout sofa in a shithole apartment, sharing space with her sick father-in-law who languished in their lives, creating hardship and uncertainty. He never understood why she didn't ditch him two years ago when his career imploded. He had witnessed flagrant violations of moral standards and medical ethics, then succumbed to intimidation and coercion when he should've come forward, and it cost them their dreams. Hardly a day passed that he did not mourn what could have been, the transplant surgeon and his scrub-nurse wife spending their days at the operating table, Cassandra handing him the instruments he'd use to give someone a new life. Restoring life was a privilege bestowed upon precious few. They would have shared that privilege.

He turned and faced her. In the dim light he studied her silhouette under the blankets and followed it to where her hair draped the pillow. He ran a finger through several strands and wondered if she mourned the loss of the dream as much as he did. She hadn't said so, but he could sense the resentment building. Part of him knew he had to let go of the dream. He had to move forward and redefine himself, not only for Cassandra's sake but because it was futile not to. But part of him clung fiercely to the idea that he was still a surgeon. He was not a lab tech. He was not a researcher. He was a surgeon, and he'd sell his soul to once again open someone's abdomen and lay hands on their organs.

- 6 -

David ignored the gangsta rap reverberating up and down the hall as he passed the shrieking baby and waded through the fried-fish stink. Four-D was quiet again, three days in a row of no barking and snarling, but his own door stood wide open. A wave of apprehension rippled through him.

Cassandra flew into the hallway. "Your dad's gone."

"How long?"

"Fifteen, twenty minutes? I don't know. I just got home."

"What about the nurse?"

"She was in the bedroom watching TV and thought he was in the front room napping on the couch."

"Dammit. Call 911."

David raced down the hall, the stairs, onto the sidewalk. The last time his father wandered, David found him a block away on E. Houston, attempting to cross four lanes of traffic. David ran north on Ridge Street, trying to remember what his father had worn at breakfast. Probably the faded-blue bathrobe he wore most days, but he wasn't sure. He came to Houston but couldn't decide, left or right? Stay on this side or cross the street? This was lower Manhattan, and it was cold, windy, and dark. The possibilities were infinite, the impossibility paralyzing.

Then it came to him—Grand Central Station. The neurologist said dementia patients didn't wander aimlessly. They usually had a destination in mind, ventured out, then got confused and disoriented. The one lucid thought that consistently emerged from his father's disintegrating brain was the impulse to go home, to get on the Metro North and return to Poughkeepsie. Think, like someone addled by Alzheimer's disease. The shortest distance between two points is a straight line. In this case, the next best thing would be three straight lines with only two turns. West on Houston, north on First Avenue to 43rd Street, west on 43rd to Lexington and Grand Central Station. Not the shortest route, but the simplest: left, right, left.

David joined the rush-hour pedestrians moving west on Houston. He pushed through long coats and wool scarves, drawn-up shoulders and frosty breaths. He studied gaits on both sides of the street, looking for the odd man out, the one shuffling along at half speed, or stutter-stepping in panic mode.

Heading up First Avenue he took an elbow to the ribs and a what's-your-problem-asshole every couple of blocks. He choked on bus exhaust, flinched at honking horns, and shivered against the bitter cold piercing his cheap coat and thin scrubs. Horrific images forced their way into his head—his father lying crumpled under one of those buses, or bouncing off the hood of a cab, or being preyed upon simply because he was feeble. He ran faster, pushed harder, apologized profusely.

Between 2nd and 3rd Streets he spotted the blue terry-cloth robe and matted salt-and-pepper hair of a man who'd been reclining on the couch one minute, and decided to get up and go home the next. Anger overpowered relief. He caught up, jerked his father's arm and spun him around, ready to spew years of fear and frustration, anger and resentment and self-loathing, but he didn't. He couldn't. His father cowered, seeing at first a stranger who wanted to hurt him, then, slowly, someone he knew but wasn't sure how. David let his shoulders drop and his face soften, and he hugged his father. But the man just stood there, arms limp, like a boy in the embrace of a distant relative.

David rubbed the corners of his eyes with the heel of his palm. "Let's go home," he said.

He took his dad by the hand and led him down First Avenue, like a man leading his child over uncertain terrain.

- 7 -

David tucked his father into bed and covered him with an electric blanket. "This'll warm you up in no time. If it gets too hot, kick it off." He set the control to medium. "By the way, where were you going?"

His father pulled at the edge of the blanket. "The nurse said I should go for a walk to get some exercise."

"You mean she said the two of you should go for a walk."

"No. She told me to go and she'd have hot chocolate for me when I got back."

David was startled by his father's clarity. His father was often forgetful and confused, but he had never confabulated. He had never invented a tale or a fib out of the blue. David wondered if confabulation was a harbinger of advancing disease. He'd have to look it up.

Wendy stood as David entered the front room. She glanced at him, then the floor. Her hands were joined at her waist, her fingers restless and fidgeting. Her eyes met his. "I'm so sorry. Is Mr. McBride okay?" Her gaze returned to the floor, and back to him.

"He's cold, but he'll be fine. So what happened?"

"I went into the hall to use my phone. When I came in, I guess I forgot to lock the door."

"Forgot to lock the door? Isn't that chapter one in *Alzheimer's For Dummies*? Make sure they can't turn on the gas, hide the matches, and keep the doors locked?"

Her eyes glossed over with tears.

"Every New Yorker, even those without an Alzheimer's patient living under their roof, keeps the door locked at all times. I can't believe you'd make such a basic mistake."

"It won't happen again."

David folded his arms and gave himself a moment to calm down. "He says you told him to take a walk and you'd have hot chocolate waiting when he returned."

She kept her gaze fixed on the floor and spoke just above a whisper. "I would never do that. It doesn't make sense."

"No, I don't suppose it does."

David sent Wendy on her way and went to the kitchen for a beer. Cold one in hand, he leaned against the wall and watched Cassandra beat a piece of flank steak with a wooden mallet. It seemed like she was trying to kill it, even though it was already dead.

"Seems we got what we paid for," he said.

Cassandra hit the meat harder. Blood dotted the counter and the front of her scrub shirt.

"Don't you want to cover that with wax paper?" he asked. "Cut down on the splatter?"

She glared at him. "We don't have waxed paper. You wanna do this?"

She thrust the mallet in his direction, which, now blood-soaked, reminded him of a barbaric surgical instrument called a Lebsche knife. The Lebsche knife resembled a small hatchet and was the only knife in the surgeon's armamentarium that required repeated blows from a mallet to do its job. It was primarily used to split the sternum when a saw wasn't available.

"No thanks," he said. "It's been a while since I've swung a hammer."

He took his beer over to the couch and sat down. Cassandra sprinkled seasoning onto the meat, put it in the oven, and joined him. She let her head fall back and stared at the ceiling, the look on her face saying she wished she were someplace else.

Then she abruptly sat up and turned toward him. "What are we going to do about this?"

"The nurse or my father?"

"Your father."

"I don't know." Then, more to himself than to her, he said, "Maybe we could chip him."

"Chip him? What does that mean?"

"I read an article on implanting GPS microchips in the forearms of Alzheimer's patients, you know, the way they inject ID chips into cats and dogs. Your loved one wanders off and you OnStar him like he's a stolen car."

Her face contorted with disbelief. "Jesus, David. Your father doesn't need to be chipped. He needs stimulation and supervision, particularly supervision. Even if we could afford the best nurse from the best agency, there are too many hazards in this place. He needs to be in a proper facility."

"I know, but we're not any closer to affording it now than we were the last time we had this discussion. Nobody pays for custodial care—not the VA, not Medicare, my insurance or your insurance."

"We can ask my family for help."

David shook his head. "They don't have the kind of money we need. All of the assisted care facilities I researched were three thousand a month or higher. Besides, your father used to think I was the Second Coming of Christ. Now I'm trailer trash. I'll euthanize my dad before I ask yours for money."

Cassandra jumped up. "You'd euthanize your own father. Nice. You know, one of these days you're gonna have to let go of that useless pride of yours."

She went back to the kitchen and started slamming cupboard doors. That was the problem with this goddamned place. It was so small there was nowhere to go when pissed or sad or whatever, and it was growing smaller by the day, by the moment.

He drained his beer, went after another, and returned to the couch. While Cassandra tossed a salad, he thought about what he had just said. He'd said it for shock value, and he hated himself for it, but the issue of euthanasia had been edging into his thoughts recently. Maybe it deserved serious consideration. After all, it was only a matter of time until his father would be better off dead.

Right now he was in the sixth stage of Alzheimer's disease. He had short- and long-term memory loss. He needed help getting dressed, using the toilet, and, from time to time, remembering he had a son. He suffered urinary and fecal incontinence and was a risk to wander, as he had just demonstrated. But he was still manageable and felt some joy in his life, even if those moments were short-lived.

At some point, though, stage six would give way to stage seven, the final stage, the end. He'd lose his capacity for speech. He'd lose his ability to walk, then sit, then hold up his head, then swallow. Reflexes would grow spastic. Muscles would become rigid. His father would be reduced to nothing more than a collection of vital organs, housed in an unyielding shell, governed by a malfunctioning nervous system, and he could exist in such a state for years. Financially, stage seven would be catastrophic. Emotionally, stage seven would be devastating.

As a resident, David had watched families agonize with the decision to pull the plug on a comatose loved one who had no chance for recovery. They were most often heart surgery patients who'd been resuscitated from a postsurgical cardiac arrest but had suffered irreversible brain injury. The heart had been fixed. The brain was dead. In many of these cases, it was common practice to order morphine drips. They'd run the morphine at a rapid rate, suppress the respiratory drive, stop the breathing. The family could then go home and mourn, relieved of the interminable waiting. For them, morphine represented pain relief and comfort. For David, it represented euthanasia. He wrote the orders, in effect pulling the plug, but it never bothered him. In the midst of all the pain and sorrow, he saw enormous burdens lifted.

David took another sip of beer, felt the cold aluminum in his hand, and squeezed the sides of the can, making it click. He pictured his father, unable to hold up his head, aware of nothing but pain and discomfort, the ability to experience joy lost forever. He imagined an IV in a well-hidden vein, a syringe full of potassium chloride. He'd push down on the plunger. The syringe would empty. The potassium ions would flood through the bloodstream and into the cells of the heart muscle, depolarizing them, causing them to fibrillate. The fibrillating heart can't pump blood, the brain dies, the person dies, and just as the criminal justice system relieves itself of convicted killers, David would relieve his father of his misery. He'd tell the paramedics his father died in his sleep. The medical examiner would have no interest in performing an autopsy on a stage-seven Alzheimer's patient. If he did, it wouldn't matter. Potassium and chloride were two of the most abundant electrolytes in the body.

If it were anybody else, ending such profound suffering would be a no-brainer, but when he personalized it, when he pictured his father's eyes rolling back in his head the moment his heart stopped, he wasn't so sure. He loved the man enough to want to end his suffering, but actually pushing the plunger would require a level of strength, conviction, and compassion that he wasn't sure he possessed.

Cassandra came out of the kitchen with two plates and sat next to him. "Quite the pensive look. What are you thinking about?"

David shook her off. "Just stuff."

He sipped his beer and peered into the black hole of the can.

The bed shook, waking David from a fragmented half sleep. He raised his head to find Cassandra curled in the fetal position, her back to his, and she was crying, her sobs coming in muted spasms. He propped himself onto an elbow and asked what was wrong.

"Nothing," she said.

"Must be something."

She turned toward him. "I said it's nothing."

Even in the dark he sensed her glare. "Alrighty then," he said in a you'll-tell-me-when-you-want-to tone. Then he rolled over, his face inches from the clanking, hissing radiator.

He couldn't remember the last time Cassandra had cried. When really upset, she entered her stoic OR-nurse mode, which was impenetrable. She had been tense all night, but he attributed that to his father's solo trek up First Avenue. He wondered if something else was going on, if something major had happened that she had decided not to share with him, or maybe the cumulative effect of everything was finally bearing down on her. It was the latter, he suspected, and it sickened him to think he had put her in this position, that he had smashed her dreams with a single error in judgment and sentenced her to a life of hardship.

- 8 -

David shuffled into the bathroom and squinted at the naked bulb. Cassandra stood at the sink, dressed in scrubs, putting on her makeup. He squeezed past her and lifted the toilet seat. He was still half-asleep and weaving, the sound of his urine changing pitch as the stream hit water, then porcelain, then water.

"I'm sorry about last night," she said in a flat tone devoid of all sincerity.

"Is everything okay?"

"No. Everything is not okay."

He caught her reflection in the mirror. She dabbed powder on the dark skin under her eyes, her face revealing nothing.

"I don't mean to bring this up and then go off to work," she said, "but I won't get through the day unless I tell you."

He was awake now, and hardly breathing.

She grabbed a bottle of capsules and handed it to him. He read the label, an iron sulfate, folic acid combination—prenatal vitamins!

He stared at her.

She stared into the mirror. "I had the lab run a beta-HCG. It's positive."

He flushed the toilet and watched the vortex suck the last remnant of his idealized life down the pipe. "This can't be happening," he said.

"Well it is, and I don't want to talk about it right now. We'll discuss it tonight."

"Are you high? You can't tell me you're pregnant and then walk out the door. Let's get it out there and start dealing with it."

She turned and faced him. Her eyes sparkled with tears. "What is there to say? What should be one of the happiest moments of our lives is one of the worst. I envisioned a nursery filled with sun every morning, Cat-in-the-Hat murals painted on the walls, a mobile hanging over a beautiful crib, a rocking chair in the corner. That's my dream, David. But instead, we'll be tripping over a hand-me-down bassinet, always worried about money for food and diapers and doctor bills. And who's going to help when I go back to work? I never thought I'd be in this position."

"I know, but we're two able-bodied adults. We'll figure it out."

"Two able-bodied adults buried in debt who have to support a baby and an old man with Alzheimer's disease. This is how people end up on welfare and food stamps."

David said nothing, his impotence and worthlessness hanging in the void between them.

Cassandra applied one more dab of powder, dropped her compact into the drawer and gave him a peck on the cheek. "I'm sorry. I have to go."

He climbed in the shower, turned on the hot water and lay down in the tub. They loved kids, wanted kids, but not now, not until their lives were in order. The spray hit him like a million tiny needles.

- 9 -

David placed his scalpel on the abdomen of the recipient rat and pulled, with the lightest touch. Too much pressure on the thin tissues, and the blade would plunge into the liver, colon, spleen, and anything else in the way. He carried the incision from sternum to pubic bone, about three inches, and it was perfect. He glanced into the open chest cavity of the donor rat. The beating heart remained vigorous, but the lab was cold, and it wouldn't require much of a temperature drop to trigger fibrillation. He increased the setting on the warming lamp. Rapid cooling was the small animal's biggest enemy.

He returned his attention to the recipient animal, carefully positioned a retractor, and exposed the aorta and vena cava. In the human, these vessels were twice the diameter of a garden hose. In the rat, they were a quarter the diameter of a drinking straw, and paper-thin. To excise the heart from the thorax of one rat and implant it into the abdomen of another required extraordinary skill, skill he possessed, skill wasted on rodents.

He thought of Cassandra, wondered how she was doing.

Pregnant! That bomb had dropped forty-eight hours ago, and it still seemed inconceivable. A new baby, a sick old man, no money, and days spent shrouded by the odor of rat piss—not the life he had envisioned. He'd lost control of his own fate, and he wanted it back. He wanted to be the man Cassandra had married and the kind of father his kids would be proud of. He wanted to raise them in a neighborhood filled with children and trees, not hookers and drug dealers. He wanted to take better care of his dad, and he wanted to use his considerable skill on humans, not rats.

David climbed from the musty warmth of the Delancey Street subway station into the freezing wind of lower Manhattan. Rush-hour traffic crept along Delancey, heading up and over the Williamsburg Bridge. Brake lights flickered as the column of vehicles traveled a few feet and stopped, traveled a few more feet and stopped. Plumes of condensation billowed from tailpipes. Horns honked. Like his fellow pedestrians, David lowered his head, leaned into the wind, and started home. He moved quickly, his nylon parka and cotton scrubs no match for the mass of arctic air that had stalled over the Northeast.

He came to his building, pulled the door hard against a gust of wind, and stepped inside, savoring the heat of the lobby. At the mailbox he thumbed through tonight's offering—a credit card bill, the phone bill, a letter addressed to David McBride, MD, return address, the State University of New York, Downstate Medical Center, Department of Surgery. He felt a twinge of excitement, but then his shoulders slumped under the weight of an instant depression. SUNY Downstate had always impressed him. Their training program was highly regarded. They had a busy transplant service that offered a fellowship, and the primary teaching hospital was a short train ride away at the University Hospital of Brooklyn. It would've been perfect, for him *and* Cassandra. He wouldn't have to relocate her to North Dakota or some other godforsaken wilderness. She would have been close to her family, had help with the baby. But all of New York, particularly the faculties of the city's academic medical centers, were acutely aware of the waiting-list scandal and its sordid details. He couldn't imagine that any New York City–based surgical residency would be interested in him.

He slid his finger under the flap and ripped open the envelope. There was no reason to wait until he went upstairs. The mood had been sour enough the past couple of days, and another rejection would only deepen their funk and add to Cassandra's resentment. He unfolded the page.

> Dear Dr. McBride,
>
> It is my pleasure to offer you a position in our general surgery training program. If you are willing to repeat your fourth year of residency and all goes well (a rehab assignment, if you will), we'll advance you to the chief-resident year and potential certification by the American Board of Surgery. You will, of course, need to sit for an interview to discuss your past ethical violations. If you are forthright regarding those events, we will reward you with a second chance to pursue your goal. Please call my office to schedule a meeting.
>
> Sincerely,
> Juan Carlos Valenzuela, MD, F.A.C.S.
> Chairman, Department of Surgery, SUNY Downstate Medical Center
> Chief of Surgery, University Hospital of Brooklyn

He stared at the letter, held by shaking hands he hardly recognized as his own. He had done it, persevered, never stopped believing in himself, and two years of unending remorse, regret, and self-hatred disappeared with the unfolding of a single sheet of paper. He bounded up the stairs, no longer giving a shit about the rap music, the crying baby, the fishy stench, or the barking pit bull. He felt a lightness in his feet as if they had pulled free of the muck and mire of lost hopes and dreams.

David found Cassandra in the kitchen, sprinkling something onto skinless chicken breasts. He couldn't contain his grin. She wiped her hands on a dishtowel and smiled.

"What?" she said. "You been dipping into the fentanyl again?"

He waved the envelope in her face. "SUNY Downstate offered me a spot. They want me to call and set up an interview."

She arched an eyebrow. "Are you messing with me?"

"It's right here." He slipped the letter out of the envelope. "Read it and weep."

She held the page, her eyes widening as they moved from line to line. "Oh my God," she said. "This is unbelievable."

He grabbed her and gave her a big kiss.

As they parted, she said, "Do you think you'll have any problems with the interview?"

"No. I'm a strong applicant. I turned in a stellar performance day after day for four-and-a-half years and had only one blemish. Granted, it was a large blemish, but if I'm totally honest about the Turnbull debacle, they'll understand why I did what I did."

"Any idea what they might pay you?"

"About the same as before. Maybe a little more, figuring in two years of cost of living raises. Not enough for a house up in Westchester, but at least we'll get out of this shithole." David patted Cassandra's stomach. "I'm sorry *this* guy won't have a sun-drenched nursery, but his little brother or sister will." And then it occurred to him: this was the first time he had touched his wife's pregnant belly and referred to the tiny being growing inside.

David climbed into bed and spooned Cassandra. Her body was warm, her skin soft, and each breath he drew carried the scent of freshly washed hair. He closed his eyes, but knew sleep would not come for a while, and that was okay. He was content to lie there and bask in the afterglow of a dream resurrected. It still seemed impossible, his fate back in *his* hands, his identity restored. He was going to be a surgeon. He'd once again have the opportunity to open an abdomen and lay hands on the organs within, and he didn't need to sell his soul to do it. His body tingled with the realization that the future he had always envisioned was within his grasp.

- 10 -

David forced himself to relax while Dr. Juan Carlos Valenzuela read the documents held in a manila folder. Valenzuela was probably in his sixties and completely bald with a perfect oval for a head. His eyes were oval as well, and shaded with a deep brown. His nose was full, straight, and rounded at the end. A gray, neatly trimmed beard softened the angles of his jaw. His face lacked hardness and angularity, as did his corpus. In short, the man resembled a brown-eyed teddy bear in a white coat. But David knew better than to judge a department-of-surgery chairman by his appearance. Many of the surgical high achievers David had known harbored pockets of psychopathology within their psyches that could erupt with the slightest provocation.

Valenzuela peered over the top of his frameless eyeglasses. "The impressiveness of your application is no less diminished with a second reading. Valedictorian in high school, *summa cum laude* in college, third in your medical school class." He looked down at the folder. "You scored in the ninety-fifth percentile or higher on the MCAT, all three sections of the medical licensing exam, and each of the five times you took the American Board of Surgery in-training examination. And most impressive?" He removed his glasses and locked eyes with David. "Despite being censured by the university's ethics board, banned for life by the United Network for Organ Sharing, fired from your residency, and relieved of your state medical license, your department chairman and the chief of the division of transplantation both wrote you exceptional letters of reference."

With a contemplative stare aimed right at David, Valenzuela let his eyeglasses swing from his fingertips like a pendulum. David couldn't tell if he was supposed to respond, or if the man was pondering this great mystery.

Valenzuela sat forward and shuffled through the papers in the file, coming up with three stapled pages. He held them up. "This is the letter from your chairman. Have you read it?"

"No," David said.

Valenzuela angled his head back so he could see through the lenses of his glasses. "The first page states the academic accomplishments I just mentioned and goes on to describe your outstanding skills as a diagnostician, the superior technical ability you displayed in the operating room, and a tireless dedication to the postoperative care of your patients." Valenzuela glanced at David as he flipped the page. "The rest of the letter details the events that led to your ... fall from grace, if you will.

"In summary, Andrew Turnbull accepted millions of dollars to move patients up the transplant waiting list. You unwittingly helped him by managing these patients while they were in the hospital, and by drawing blood samples from them and delivering the samples to his lab, whereupon he manipulated the test results. When you became aware of what he was doing, you failed to notify your superiors. Ultimately you did speak up, and an investigation followed. When questioned by the panel, you said the delay in coming forward was the direct result of coercion on the part of Dr. Turnbull. When questioned, Turnbull said no such coercion had occurred."

Valenzuela lowered the document. "So, Dr. McBride, did Andrew Turnbull coerce you to stay quiet?"

"Yes," David said, trying to repress the long-standing shame and embarrassment of allowing himself to be intimidated. "With Dr. Turnbull's support, I had been awarded the department's transplant fellowship. When I asked him about the waiting list, he told to keep my mouth shut or he would not only revoke the fellowship, but he'd see to it that I washed out of the general surgery program with only six months to go."

"And you believed him?"

"I did. He's an intense, driven man. He said the research he was funding with the illegal payments was going to win him the Nobel Prize and cement his place in history as one of the great medical thinkers of the ages. And he said if I came between him and his destiny, he'd crush me." David glanced at his hands folded in his lap, at the knuckles laced so tightly they were white with lack of blood, then back at Valenzuela. "I was a resident. He was an attending surgeon. In that context, the balance of power overwhelmingly favors the attending."

Valenzuela held up the letter. "It appears your former chairman believed you. And I quote: 'I never doubted that Andrew Turnbull was solely responsible for the egregious violations of the institutional policies, and the ethical and moral standards that govern the fair allocation of donor transplant organs. Moreover, all faculty members of the department of surgery, including myself, firmly believed Dr. McBride had, in fact, been coerced by Dr. Turnbull into not reporting said violations. Dr. Turnbull vehemently denied the accusation and claimed Dr. McBride remained silent out of loyalty to his mentor and a willingness to pursue a greater good. Unfortunately, Dr. Turnbull's denial left the panel with conflicting stories and no direct evidence to determine who was telling the truth. The panel, therefore, had no choice but to recommend the termination of both individuals.'"

Valenzuela turned the page and continued. " 'As the proceedings came to a close, the panel made clear to Dr. Turnbull that if he would assume full responsibility for the transgressions, they would recommend that McBride be allowed to retain his residency position with a censure from the ethics committee and a period of probation. Dr. Turnbull refused.'" With a disapproving shake of the head, Valenzuela set the letter on the desk, leaned back and folded his arms across his chest.

This last statement—*Dr. Turnbull refused*—stung David, dredging up two years' worth of bitterness and resentment. He had known about the offer, and despite all the pain and misery he suffered during the investigation, it was Turnbull's refusal that had hurt him the most. The panel was willing to pardon him for his mistake if the man he'd once revered and emulated would've simply admitted guilt. Turnbull was going down anyway. He didn't have to take David with him.

"So," Valenzuela said, "your conscience gets the better of you. You speak up. Turnbull follows through with his promise to crush you."

"Yes."

"And if you find yourself in a similar situation?"

With a tremor in his voice he couldn't control, David recited the answer he had rehearsed countless times. "For two years I've lived with the consequences of a moment of weakness that resulted in a costly error in judgment. If there is a next time, I will not cower to intimidation."

The men held each other's gaze, David trying to project conviction rather than hatred for his former mentor, Valenzuela pondering another man's future while doing the pendulum thing with his eyeglasses.

David finally gave in, looking down as he shifted in his seat and adjusted the lapels of his jacket. He had last worn the suit eighteen months ago when he sat before the state medical board and had his license stripped, a process no less nerve-racking than this.

Then Dr. Juan Carlos Valenzuela leaned forward. "Okay," he said. "A formal acceptance letter will go out in a few days, and a contract will be sent in the spring. You'll start on July one, with the incoming group of new residents. For the first year you will practice under an institutional license. If your record remains unimpeachable, you'll be eligible for reinstatement of your New York State license, pending a hearing with the state, of course."

David stared into his lap for a moment, fighting off an overwhelming surge of joy and relief. After a long, hard blink he looked up. "I'm very humbled by the opportunity to redeem myself, and I promise not to squander it."

"I don't doubt that. In fact, I figure *you* will be the hardest working resident this program has ever seen."

Valenzuela said this without a wisp of a smile, and David took it as a directive, one he fully intended to honor.

"I do have a question, if you don't mind," David said.

"Not at all."

"I applied to every surgery residency in the country. I sent them the same documentation, but I did not get a single offer for an interview. Why were you interested?"

"First of all, the majority of residents applying for a fourth- or fifth-year position are damaged goods. They've been through drug rehab, or they've been fired for incompetence. You have baggage, but you are not damaged. Big difference. Secondly, and most importantly, I know Andrew Turnbull, and in a profession populated with arrogant assholes, he is an ass among asses. He was your mentor. It was his job to protect you, and when he had the chance to do so, his arrogance would not let him. Were you wrong by not coming forward immediately? Yes. Should you be condemned for the remainder of your professional life for that decision? No. I believe you deserve a second chance."

A second chance. David had waited two years to hear these three simple words. "Thank you," he said, and he stood and offered his hand to his new chairman.

The #2 train clattered and clanked as it whisked David under the East River toward lower Manhattan. He rested his head against the glass, shut his eyes, and tried to bring order to the chaos of emotion swirling inside his skull. Happiness and relief dominated, of course. He could now close a bleak chapter in his life and begin moving forward. He would refashion himself in the form of the old David, the surgeon who enjoyed the aesthetics of his craft and the satisfaction of restoring health to the sick and dying. He would resurrect the David who Cassandra had married, a man passionate about his work, life, and future. And he'd rededicate himself to his father, providing him with the care he needed, and savoring—before it was too late—every moment they could communicate and understand each other. Above all else, he looked forward to experiencing the miracle of Cassandra's pregnancy without the relentless stress of financial uncertainty and a strained relationship.

Yes, happiness and relief dominated, but there was also a negative undercurrent tempering his joy. Despite having been a highly accomplished adult—a physician, a surgical resident, a husband and son—he had allowed himself to be bullied like a child, putting his own well-being above that of his patients, and for that, he felt shame. He supposed that over time he'd wall off the memory of his shameful actions the way the human body walls off a sliver of glass under the skin or a bullet lodged in muscle—layers of dense, fibrous tissue laid down until the object is encased in scar, like an oyster forming a pearl around an irritating granule of sand. The feeling would still emerge from time to time, often at first, but less and less as the years passed, finally becoming part of a life left behind. By then the new David McBride would have fully formed, and as a father, he'd tap into this dark period in his life to instill within his children a moral and ethical framework. We learn from our mistakes, he'll tell them. Just don't make the same mistake twice, and always consider giving others a second chance.

- 11 -

The rush-hour throng jostled David as he made his way up the steps of the Delancey Street station, but he didn't give it a second thought. The SUNY Downstate acceptance letter had arrived, his return to the gilded halls of medicine and surgery was official, and he was in a state of euphoria—or maybe mania. Cassandra was glowing with happiness, the monkey-faced people had not popped up through the floor in over a week, and the David of old—the David with a purpose, and the motivation and means to pursue that purpose—had returned from exile. On this night, not even a crowded, stenotic stairwell could dampen his mood.

At the top of the stairs he zipped up, covered up, and took his usual route home—two blocks north, four blocks east, past the Samuel Gompers housing projects. As he approached Jacob Riis Park a man drew his attention. He was standing beneath the only light in the park, backlit by its halo, nothing more than a silhouette of overcoat and fedora. He seemed oddly out of place, sinister in his stillness. David pulled his stocking cap lower, his wool scarf higher and picked up the pace.

The man called out. "Dr. McBride, may I speak to you please?"

David stopped, turned toward him. "You talking to me?"

"Yes, Doctor. A moment of your time, if I may?"

David peered between the steel bars that served as a fence. "Do I know you?"

"No. My name is White, Mr. White. I've come to offer you a job."

"Here? In single-digit temperatures? Unconventional, isn't it?"

"My offer is unconventional."

"Sorry, but I'm currently employed." David started to go.

"Yes, but this could be quite lucrative for someone in your position."

David turned around. "And what position is that?"

"A physician living in this neighborhood speaks for itself, does it not?"

"Look—" David paused while a couple, bundled up and moving as one, passed by. "I don't know who you are or what you want, but I'm not interested."

The man held out his hands in a welcoming manner. "Please hear me out. What I have to say has profound implications not only for you, but for your wife and father as well."

"What the hell is this? What do you know about me or my wife or my father?"

"You've been facing financial difficulties for some time. Logic would dictate this has had an impact on all members of your family."

"Who are you? A mobster? Drug dealer? Government agent? You've discovered my weakness and now you're here to exploit it?"

"Let's just say I'm a recruiter of sorts, and I'm here to offer you generous financial compensation in exchange for your surgical skills."

"Surgeons are not recruited from city parks. Besides, I'm a lab tech, not a surgeon."

Mr. White gestured toward a bench. "Thirty seconds. If you're still not interested, I'll send you on your way."

David turned to go, then hesitated. He was both creeped out and pissed off by the intrusion into his personal life, but the guy had done his homework, and something told David he'd keep pushing. "Okay," David said. "Thirty seconds."

David joined the man in the halo of the streetlamp. He was tall, six one or two, an inch-or-so taller than David and slender underneath his overcoat. A scarf covered the bottom half of his face. His hat rode low on the upper half. His eyes were light, like his skin, as though he were at home in the cold. He put out a hand sheathed in a tight leather glove. David offered up his frumpy nylon mitten. Puffs of frosty breath filled the space between them.

"Thank you for your time. I won't keep you long." Mr. White slipped his hands into his pockets. "I represent a group of entrepreneurs who are opening a kidney-transplant clinic, and they would like to hire you as their procurement specialist."

David folded his arms and swayed from foot to foot, the cold burrowing deep. "Mr. White, transplants are performed by teams of doctors in medical centers, not in clinics run by businessmen."

"Of course. Perhaps surgery center is a more apt description. Our clients will include patients with kidney failure who are too ill to linger indefinitely on the waiting list. We'll match them with donors, bring the parties together, and execute the operation."

"You'll be paying these donors."

"Yes."

"In other words, you'll be buying organs from the poor and selling them to the rich?"

"Your summary is crude but accurate."

"Surely, your entrepreneurs realize this is illegal."

"And may I remind you, Doctor, that tens of thousands of patients die every year waiting for cadaver organs, while the world teems with healthy people willing to sell a redundant body part?"

"So your incentive is humanitarian as well as financial?"

"Dr. McBride, I did not come here to debate the legal and ethical issues surrounding organ transplantation."

"Apparently not, seeing how what you're proposing is illegal, immoral, and unethical. Anyway, I'm assuming you know I was fired from my surgery residency two years ago, and since then I've done nothing but sew rat aortas together."

"Yes, and our only concern is that prior to your termination, you received the necessary training to harvest a kidney. We believe you did."

A Boar's Head Meat truck rumbled down the street. David pictured Andrew Turnbull, the surgeon responsible for most of that training, standing in front of it. Its brakes squealed as it stopped at the end of the block.

"Regarding the illicit nature of our endeavor, I can assure you the level of risk is extremely low. Multiple layers of security will keep the clinic, its clients, and its personnel hidden. You will be well-paid for accepting the small risk to which you'll be exposed."

"And what is well-paid?" David asked.

"Twenty-thousand per harvest."

"Jesus. What does a kidney go for on the black market?"

"Suffice it to say, when the wealthy stare death in the face, the cash flows."

David slowly nodded his head. "It's a compelling proposition, but I'm not interested in getting involved with illegal organ trafficking, regardless of what you're willing to pay."

"Maybe you should take some time and think about it."

"Won't make a difference."

"Then perhaps you should consider this. If you refuse my offer, your immediate supervisor—Dr. Roy Fitch—will be informed that you've been stealing vials of fentanyl from the laboratory's drug cabinet. You have sole possession of the key, control of the logbook, and I have a recorded conversation where you say, and I quote, 'Ampules of IV narcotics are the enriched uranium of the drug trade. If I formed an alliance with one of our street-corner entrepreneurs, you and I would be looking at mansions in Scarsdale by year's end.'"

"How did you—?" Adrenaline surged through David, ratcheting his muscles into steel cords, curling his hands into fists. "That's taken out of context, and you know it."

"It doesn't matter. If even a whiff of controversy finds you, you'll lose that coveted residency position you recently landed. And if that's not sufficient motivation, we always have these." Mr. White pulled an envelope out of his jacket and offered it to David.

David slipped out of his mittens and grabbed it. The envelope was thick, the contents stiff and unbending. He opened it. Photos. Hundreds of them. Cassandra walking down the street, standing at an ATM, entering their building, exiting their building, leaving work, grocery shopping at D'Agostino's—pictures of her everywhere she went, even her gynecologist's office. He thumbed through the stack, his heart pounding harder with each photo. They had been following her for weeks.

He sat hard on the park bench, the icy slats biting through his scrub pants. Mr. White sat down on the other end. David turned and faced him. "Why didn't you just show me these when I first walked up? Why all the bullshit about clinics and entrepreneurs and twenty-thousand-dollar payments?"

"Because blackmail is less savory than proper compensation. We would have preferred you come on board as a willing participant. Money and opportunity are more palatable than threats of violence."

"Do you hear what you're saying? You're not only threatening a woman, but a pregnant woman. Are you a fucking animal?"

Mr. White rested his arm along the top of the bench and turned toward David. He dropped his head for a moment, then looked up, his eyes pleading even though he clearly had the upper hand. "Dr. McBride, you have to believe that it pains me deeply to stoop to such a low level, but what's at stake here is larger than you can possibly imagine, far beyond selling organs to rich people. So please, do as we ask. Harvest a few kidneys over the next couple of months, and we will send you on your way without incident. Nobody wants to see you or your wife come to any harm."

"Nobody ever wants to harm anybody," David said, waving the envelope in front of Mr. White. "Just business, right?"

"Yes, it's just business. We are not murderers or thugs, but what we're trying to accomplish is of great significance. The stakes are very high, so we will resort to any means necessary."

"Why go through all this trouble? Why doesn't your surgeon harvest the organs himself? If you know how to implant one, you sure as hell know how to take one out."

"There are a number of reasons, none of which concern you."

"And when all this is over, you're gonna let me walk off into the horizon?"

"Yes."

David shook his head in disbelief. "It doesn't make any sense."

Mr. White pointed at the photos in David's hand. "That," he said, "is the only thing that needs to make sense."

David looked away, at the walkup tenements across the street. Lights were on behind many of the windows, the shades drawn on most. On the stoop of the closest building sat two men, big men, and they said nothing to each other, focused instead on what was happening in the park. Embers glowed as they took drags on their cigarettes. David gave a single nod in their direction. "Yours?" he asked, his throat so dry he croaked out the word.

"Yes."

"And you bugged my apartment."

"We've been monitoring all of your communications."

"By 'all' you mean phone, e-mail, conversations, everything."

"At home and at work."

"What are you, some kind of spy?"

"Let's just say I'm a highly capable eavesdropper." Mr. White looked at the men on the stoop, then at David. "If you decide to involve any law enforcement agencies, local or federal, I'll hear about it. If you seek help using any mode of communication, I'll know about that, too. And if you think a crowded bar might be a good place to talk to someone, we'll be a few tables over listening in. So, once again I ask you—I implore you—please accept our offer, keep what you learn to yourself, and in the end, your life will return to the way it was fifteen minutes ago. I would also suggest you don't bring Mrs. McBride into this situation. Pregnant women are often emotionally labile and unpredictable." Mr. White stood, as did the two men. "Any questions?"

David shook his head and quietly said, "No."

"Good. Now go home and think this through. I will be here tomorrow evening. If I don't see you, I'll take that as your answer." Mr. White gestured for the envelope. "I'll need those back."

David handed it to him.

Mr. White tucked it inside his coat and left the park, fading into the crystalline night.

- 12 -

David sat at the desk, with Cassandra sleeping peacefully a few feet away. The evening had been long and difficult. She'd sensed he was not himself and had asked what was wrong. He told her it was nothing, just the craziness of the past two weeks finally catching up. All the while, the encounter with Mr. White had raged within. And it was still raging, unabated and extreme now that the apartment was quiet and held no distractions. He listened to Cassandra's breathing. Rhythmic and slow, unlike his, which was erratic and shallow, fear constricting his chest. He wondered if he should ignore Mr. White's warning and go to the police. Would they believe him? Set up a sting in the park? Ask him to wear a wire? Wait until the first harvest, then come busting through the door right before the skin incision? Doubtful. In all likelihood they'd blow him off, another conspiracy-theorist nut job with a bullshit story. And if Mr. White became aware of David's attempt to enlist outside help, there'd be severe consequences. Whoever was pulling the strings had invested considerable time and energy scouring his private life, mining his personal information, tracking him, and following Cassandra. They were methodical, patient, intent on getting what they wanted, and therefore, exceptionally dangerous.

In surgery, the decision to operate was based upon the risk/benefit ratio. If the risk was high and the planned operation offered little benefit, nonsurgical treatments were implemented. If the risk was low and the potential benefits were great, it was a no-brainer. Right now, involving the police carried great risk while providing little or no benefit, so, until he had something concrete to offer, the path of least resistance seemed the wise choice. And besides, if Mr. White was being truthful—and granted, that was a big if—they wanted David to perform a finite number of harvests on individuals who had consented to sell a kidney. If consenting adults were willing to swap organs for cash, who was he to get in the way? From a personal standpoint, he didn't see it as a huge moral dilemma. Was it wrong to pay for organs? Illegal, yes, but not necessarily immoral. A number of groups were pushing for the legalization of paid organ donation, a policy that could save countless lives.

David pushed back from the desk, stretched his arms and enjoyed a small measure of relief in having made a decision. He'd go to the park tomorrow night, give Mr. White an affirmative answer, and would not involve the NYPD until the benefits far exceeded the risks. Now, he had one last question. Should he tell Cassandra? Again, the risk/benefit ratio. He could not think of a good reason why she needed to know, but he had three compelling reasons for not telling her. First, the less she knew, the safer she was. Second, she might take it upon herself to get help. And third, severe stress was no friend of the developing fetus. Chronic exposure to high levels of the stress hormones cortisol and epinephrine resulted in low birth weight, decreased head circumference, and a host of other developmental abnormalities. For the next few months he'd just have to put his best acting foot forward and deliver an Academy Award–winning performance.

And then something occurred to him. While in the park, he'd briefly thought about Andrew Turnbull. David wondered if Turnbull might be one of Mr. White's so-called entrepreneurs. Turnbull was clearly a sociopath. His blatant disregard for the moral and ethical guidelines that govern medicine and surgery were well documented. And he knew everything about David—his personal background, the status of his training at the time of dismissal from the program, his financial problems relating to his father, Cassandra. But would he break international law through the buying and selling of human organs?

David pulled himself back to the desk, turned on the computer and Googled NuLife, the company Turnbull had started after having been fired by the university. David clicked the link and was taken to a slick homepage that explained how NuLife, a leader in the field of tissue engineering and organ fabrication, was on the threshold of solving the world's shortage of donor organs. The blog posts, media reports, and excerpts from scientific journals seemed to justify their claim. Andrew Turnbull had indeed made some major advances since his days at NYU, and it seemed doubtful he would jeopardize his life's work—not to mention a shot at the Nobel Prize—by involving himself with black market human organs. David put the thought out of his mind.

- 13 -

What a difference twenty-four hours can make, lamented David as the rush-hour crowd carried him up and out of the Delancey Street station. This time last night he was living the dream of all humankind, the dream of self-determination, the unassailable right to have a say in one's future. Tonight he was entering into a nightmarish scenario where his free will had been stripped away, where soon he'd be forced to perform illegal organ harvests with total strangers, in a facility he had never seen, on patients he knew nothing about. He marveled at the capacity for those with power to shed all moral responsibility and exploit those who lacked recourse. He also reminded himself that throughout history, the abuser of basic human rights often met with untoward consequences. David hoped that would be the case here, and if he had a hand in such an outcome, all the better. He hit the street and headed north.

At Jacob Riis Park, on the same bench, under the same light, sat a solitary man in an overcoat and fedora. David went over and joined him.

"I'm in, as if I ever had a choice," David said. "Now what?"

Mr. White pulled a not-so-smart-looking cell phone and power cord from his coat pocket.

"Each evening between six and eight p.m. have this with you, fully charged, and if you're out and about, frequently check to see that it has a strong signal. If we have a donor lined up, I'll contact you. No call means no donor, and you are free to go about your business." He handed the phone to David. "We will schedule the harvests for the early morning hours so the implantation team can start by eight a.m."

David recalled the many late-night, early-morning harvests he'd done as a resident. "I suppose when you said I'd get paid you were blowing smoke up my ass?"

"A crude analogy, but no. As an act of good faith, we will pay you commensurate with our original offer."

David tried to read Mr. White, but the scarf covered everything except the eyes and the bridge of the nose, and his voice was controlled and unwavering.

"How do I know you can be trusted?" David asked.

"You don't. It's up to you—your instincts—to decide if you can trust me. But let me reiterate, we do not want to harm anybody. Just do as we ask, don't cause any problems, and you will walk away with a tidy sum of cash and nothing more than a bruised ego." Mr. White stood. "So, unless there are additional questions, we're finished here."

"Just one," David said as he also stood up. "Why didn't you check me for a wire?"

"No need to. If you had traipsed into your local precinct, told them what was going on and asked them to set you up with a hidden listening device, I would have known about it before they had your shirt off. Please don't underestimate my ability to see and hear everything you are doing and saying. Now, is there anything else?"

"No," David said.

"Good. Expect to hear from me within the week."

- 14 -

The scientists took their seats around the mahogany conference table. Turnbull brimmed with satisfaction as Denise made sure each had a coaster under his or her coffee, orange juice, or whatever their early-morning beverage of choice happened to be. Dr. Cynthia Evans, a paragon of fitness, had her usual protein bar and seaweed drink. Dr. Jeffery Abercrombie, the antithesis of fit, had two bear claws and a Double Super Big Gulp Mountain Dew Code Red—at five thirty in the morning. Abercrombie was fat and lacked nearly all hygiene and social skills, but he was one of the finest biochemists in the country. With great effort Turnbull had lured him away from a steady paycheck at Merck with the promise of academic fame and stock-option fortune. Turnbull could only hope the guy fulfilled his potential before he keeled over with a massive coronary.

Mr. White entered the room, taking the seat to the right of Turnbull. The scientists had come to know him as the newest addition to the scientific advisory board. Sam Keating was the last to sit, on Turnbull's left. Sam's hair was more unkempt than usual, and he appeared distracted, his greetings to the other conference attendees generic and unfocused. Turnbull wondered if his chief financial officer was holding it together. It seemed he'd been unable to shake off the news of the first donor's death.

With everyone seated, Turnbull called the meeting to order. "I'd like to begin with the liver group. This week we moved from ferret to porcine scaffolds."

"Yes," said Cynthia, lead investigator of the group. "The pig livers responded nicely to the detergent bath, yielding a completely intact extracellular matrix. We then infused five hundred million progenitor cells and three hundred million endothelial cells per organ. Initial seeding was in the high sixty-percent range. We actually had trace levels of enzymes, albumin, and bile, but the seeding stalled and then regressed to about thirty percent, and we lost all evidence of function."

"What did the histology show?" Turnbull asked.

"The thirty percent that grew early on and then stopped was necrotic, presumably the result of ischemic injury. The remaining thirty percent was healthy, viable tissue."

"So, all of the cells take off out of the gate, but half die from lack of blood."

"Exactly," Cynthia said. "The histology revealed well-developed arterioles, venules, and capillary beds in the viable tissues, but only rudimentary vascular components in the necrotic areas."

"Simply stated, then, the tissues are outgrowing their blood supply. If blood supply could keep up with cell demand, there is no reason we couldn't achieve a seed rate of one hundred percent and come away with a fully functional organ."

"Yes," Cynthia replied. "The lack of a mature vascular tree is the Achilles' heel of this procedure."

Turnbull had nearly identical exchanges with the lead investigators of the kidney, lung, pancreas, and heart groups. They all agreed that the lack of a quickly maturing vascular system was the most significant hurdle standing in their way. He turned to Abercrombie, who was starting in on the second bear claw.

"Jeffery," Turnbull said, "where do we stand with the modified VEGF?"

Turnbull was certain that vascular endothelial growth factor—known by its acronym VEGF, and pronounced veg-f—was the key to NuLife's organ-fabrication success. VEGF was one of the platelet-derived growth factors that played a central role in both vasculogenesis, the formation of the embryonic circulatory system, and angiogenesis, the growth of new blood vessels from pre-existing vasculature. The value of VEGF could not be overestimated. In fact, without it, the fabrication of bioartificial organs would not be possible. But it was not getting the job done fast enough, and simply adding more to the organ-growing broth didn't help. What they needed—as the results just presented had made abundantly clear—was a super-modified version of vascular endothelial growth factor. They needed to ramp up the speed of VEGF-induced blood-vessel proliferation. They needed Jeff Abercrombie to figure out how to amplify the effects of VEGF many times over. Thus, the very success of NuLife, and of all the young scientists seated around the table—indeed, Turnbull's date with the Nobel committee in Stockholm—rested on the shoulders of a guy who was washing down his second bear claw with a slug of Code Red.

When he finished swallowing, Abercrombie said, "Maybe instead of speeding up the growth of the blood vessels, we need to find a way to keep the cells alive while they're waiting."

"We've tried that," Turnbull said, leaning forward. "We've increased the oxygen tension in both the perfusate and the broth, and it hasn't made a difference."

"I'm not talking about oxygen delivery. I'm talking about generating the energy for cellular metabolism in the absence of oxygen."

"Impossible. Only anaerobes and plants can do that. Mammalian cells require oxygen to live, and blood delivers that oxygen. This is the most basic requirement for animal life on this planet, and there is no way around it."

"Maybe there is," Abercrombie countered.

"That would be like discovering how to turn off gravity."

"Exactly. I need to look up a few more articles, and I'll bring what I have by your office."

"When?"

"How 'bout an hour from now?"

"Make it happen."

Keating and White followed Turnbull into his office. Turnbull locked the door as the two men settled into the leather chairs.

"Translation please?" Mr. White said.

"The oxygen-delivery stuff?" Turnbull took a seat behind his desk. "It has to do with cellular energy production. Adenosine triphosphate, or what we call ATP, is the basic unit of energy in the body. It's like a single molecule of gasoline in your car. Every cell generates its own ATP, but they must have oxygen to do it. The lungs take in oxygen, it's absorbed into the bloodstream, the blood travels through vessels to the tissues, the oxygen leaves the blood and diffuses into the cells where it is used to make ATP. No blood, no oxygen. No oxygen, no ATP, and the cell quickly runs out of gas and dies. This is the basic pathophysiology of a heart attack or stroke, and the reason why we can't grow anything larger than a ferret organ."

"So, in your estimation," Mr. White said, "if the blood-vessel problem is solved, the last hurdle will have been overcome."

"Absolutely." Turnbull leaned forward and rested his elbows on the desk. "We've grown functioning, ferret-sized organs from human stem cells. We've learned how to produce those stem cells from each potential recipient so rejection will not occur. That leaves size as the only limitation. If we can find a solution to the blood-supply issue and accomplish a one-hundred-percent seed rate in a porcine scaffold, we will have fully functional, adult-sized, rejection-resistant organs ready for human implantation."

Mr. White started to say something. Turnbull raised his hand and said, "I know time is of the essence, and I certainly understand your daughter's dire condition. All I can tell you is if Abercrombie has a real solution to the problem, we'll be very close, weeks to months. If he has nothing, we are back to tinkering with VEGF. Is that what you wanted to know?"

"Yes," Mr. White said.

Sam Keating cleared his throat, shifted in his chair, and said, "Not to diminish Mr. White's predicament, but it sounds like we're planning to transplant the world's first bioengineered kidney off the books, before we have FDA approval."

"There's no other way," Turnbull replied. "A multi-center FDA trial could take five years and thirty million dollars."

"So when do we start doing things aboveboard around here?"

Turnbull laced his fingers and glared at his CFO. The pesky little worm was becoming a big thorn in his ass. "We made a deal with Mr. White, and we have to honor that agreement. Without his unique set of skills, you and I would be spending all of our time on the road, scraping up a few dollars here and a few dollars there from dickhead investors who want to seize control and steal our ideas."

"Yeah, we've had that discussion. I'm just saying, at some point we need to become legitimate, you know? Get all the skullduggery behind us so we can take this company public."

"I couldn't agree more, but until our war chest is full of cash, skullduggery is our only option." Turnbull held Keating's gaze, then said, "Any other questions, comments, concerns?"

Sam Keating said, "No."

- 15 -

An hour and twenty minutes later, Abercrombie dropped a stack of research papers on Turnbull's desk and then plopped into one of the leather chairs. Turnbull thumbed through the stack, reading the titles. Low-level laser therapy—a topic unfamiliar to him—was the dominant theme. He looked up at his senior biochemist.

"A lot of stuff here on the treatment of hair loss," Turnbull said, amused that Abercrombie's ever-enlarging girth didn't seem to bother him, while unrelenting hair loss did.

"Yeah, well, my disdain for going bald may have provided us with the breakthrough we've been looking for."

"How about the nutshell version," Turnbull said as he resumed his perusal of the articles.

"Okay. First of all, the 'low level' reference in the titles really means low energy. These lasers use infrared light, which has a biostimulatory effect as opposed to the destructive effect associated with the types of high-energy lasers used to vaporize tumors and coagulate spider veins."

Abercrombie went on to describe a laundry list of biologic effects seen at the cellular and intracellular levels, including increased cell proliferation, increases in protein synthesis, activation of immune cells, and improved blood flow to tissues secondary to dilatation of capillaries, arterioles, venules, and lymphatics. When he mentioned ATP production in the absence of oxygen, Turnbull stopped reading and looked up. "How?" he asked.

"No one knows for sure," Abercrombie said, "but the final cytochrome complex in the electron transport chain has long been known to act as a photoreceptor, and it absorbs light of the infrared wavelength."

"So, if there is no oxygen present to drive electron transport and ATP formation, photons of infrared light can substitute and ATP production continues?"

"That's one possible mechanism, but it's very speculative."

Turnbull rocked forward in his chair. "But if that's the case, if cells can be induced to generate energy without oxygen, do you realize the implications?"

"Of course," Abercrombie said. "They're enormous."

"Enormous is right. Forget what *we're* doing and think about two of the biggest killers in medicine—heart attack and stroke. They kill by the same simple mechanism. Blood flow is blocked, the oxygen supply is cut off, cells die, the organ is damaged beyond repair." Turnbull leaned back and formed his fingers into a steeple. "So imagine if we could keep a majority of those cells alive until blood flow is restored, which is exactly what we need to do to get our organs to grow."

"Yeah, I know. It's a hot topic. There's a private company in San Diego already developing a device to treat acute myocardial infarction and stroke."

Turnbull reached for the stack of research papers. "Have they published anything?"

"No. I found their website as part of my search, but they don't disclose any of their techniques or data. They say they've done some human studies, but there's no mention of an FDA trial."

"Keep looking, and find out if anyone else, private sector or university affiliated, is doing this kind of work. By the end of the day I want every paper that's been published on low-level laser therapy. I want the name of every company exploring low-level laser therapy as a treatment for anything, and I want you to tell me how we can use it to grow our organs." Turnbull leaned forward and leveled a stern gaze at his biochemist. "If we are the first to use infrared light to manufacture bioartificial organs, that's proprietary information that can be patented, so don't tell anyone about this, not even your colleagues within this company. Remember, you've signed numerous nondisclosure agreements covering everything that might leave your mouth."

Abercrombie gave his boss a lazy nod. "I know, I know."

- 16 -

David held his father by the arm as they turned the corner at Avenue D and East 10th Street. Despite the bitter cold, their Saturday afternoon walk was going well. Hal McBride was slow and his gait stiff, but his balance was good. David hoped the stiffness was due to inactivity, or the cold, and not early motor dysfunction. Degeneration of motor skills was a bad sign, a harbinger of end-stage Alzheimer's—stage seven. The previous nurse knew the importance of physical therapy. She had put his father through a number of strength-training and range-of-motion exercises each morning. Wendy didn't do squat. In fact, he wasn't sure what she did all day.

Across the street, a white Escalade pulled up to the curb at the Jacob Riis housing projects, the chrome wheels still spinning even after the vehicle had come to a full stop. Four scowling black kids of various heights, sizes, and ages piled out of the back. A tall, lanky black guy, wearing a powder-blue New York Yankees stocking hat and an oversized down coat, climbed out of the shotgun seat— Tyronne Pradeaux. Tyronne spotted David, gave him a slight nod, then hobbled into the complex of towers with a gait that was part pimp roll and part shortened femur.

David met Tyronne Pradeaux—pronounced pray-dew, not pray-doh, or pray-dex—when David was chief resident of the trauma service at Bellevue Hospital. Tyronne had come in with six large-caliber gunshot wounds to his torso and limbs, and after the trauma team and orthopedic surgeons finished with him, he had lost the lower lobe of his right lung, the left lobe of his liver, half his pan-

creas, and his spleen. Numerous holes in his large and small intes-
tines had been closed, two holes in his stomach patched, and his
right femur pieced together. Ten hours after being rushed into the
operating room, Tyronne Pradeaux had emerged with a temporary
colostomy and a right leg that was two-and-a-half inches shorter
than the left.

Not only had David and the team saved Tyronne's life that
night, but David had spent more than a month supervising his
recovery. And most important, before Tyronne was discharged,
David had taken him to the OR and performed a colostomy take-
down, thus restoring the continuity of his colon. Tyronne never had
to set foot in the hood with a bag of shit hanging off his side, and
for that, Tyronne Pradeaux was eternally grateful.

David wasn't sure how much influence Tyronne and his crew
wielded, but for the two years he and Cassandra had lived on the
Lower East Side, not one street punk or gangbanger had given them
an ounce of crap. Maybe Tyronne had something to do with it, or
maybe it was luck, but David knew one thing: as a resident, he had
treated every patient—shot-up gangbangers included—with the
same care and respect he would have given a member of his own
family.

David and his father turned right onto 6th Street and ran head-
long into an icy blast of wind. Despite the stocking cap, his brain
ached as if he'd gulped a slushy drink at a convenience store. And
in the midst of his brain freeze, the irony of the situation hit him
like a steel-toed boot to the groin. He had endured twelve years
of primary education, four years of college, four years of medical
school, almost five years of a brutal residency, had saved a few lives
and touched many others, and while Tyronne and his boys were all
warm and cozy in their arctic-expedition down jackets, he—David
McBride, MD—was freezing his skinny ass off in a flimsy old ski
parka.

It was all a matter of income to debt ratio, he figured. Tyronne
lived in public housing, had no family to feed, no loan payments,
and the overhead to run his street-corner pharmacy consisted of a

cell phone bill. So while his debt seemed low, his income appeared quite large, judging by the white Escalade and the down coats.

By comparison, Cassandra's modest income and David's poverty-level paycheck were no match for their student loan payments, medical bills, nursing care, cell phone, grocery and utility bills, and the ludicrous amount of rent they paid to reside on the island of Manhattan. Yes, rents dropped the farther outside the city one was willing to live, but Cassandra had never learned to drive. As a result, she'd be forced to traverse the Bronx, or countless other dangerous places, in an isolated subway car, by herself, whenever she worked late-night shifts or got called in at three in the morning for an emergency case.

This would all change in July if—and this was a huge if—Mr. White was true to his word. David was willing to show up, do the work, keep his mouth shut and the blinders on. All he wanted in exchange was Cassandra's safety and his unimpeded matriculation into the SUNY Downstate surgical residency program on July 1st. Anything less than this, and he'd make it his life's work to find those responsible and deliver some untoward consequences of medieval proportions.

- 17 -

Standing on the street corner in the early-morning darkness, David hugged himself, swayed foot to foot and willed the car to hurry. A few minutes later, a dark-blue Lincoln Town Car pulled to the curb. It was an older model, boxy with square lines, from the mid-1990s, he guessed. The driver climbed out and introduced himself as Aleksandr. He had an Eastern European accent and appearance—squarish face, prominent jaw, thick dark hair—but his English was clear. He opened the rear passenger door and gestured for David to get in.

Traffic was sparse along West 14th Street. They were catching green lights, moving at a decent clip, and except for an occasional chassis-jarring pothole, it was a quiet ride to wherever they were going. Mr. White had said nothing more than when and where to meet the car. Aleksandr would only say they were going across town, so David rode in the backseat, alone with his anxiety.

It had been a week since he first met Mr. White in the park—a week filled with apprehension, a week filled with anticipation. He'd spent his nights waiting for the phone to ring, and his days reminding himself he had no choice. He'd wondered how well he had maintained his technical skills by operating on rats, and worried that he'd forgotten much of what he knew about kidney surgery. He moved dusty boxes from their corners, reviewed his textbooks and operative reports, and realized he had forgotten very little. He went to the Columbia medical library and read the latest transplantation journals. No major advances in the past two years, his fund of knowledge still current. And although he gained confidence in his abilities, he carried the burden of guilt. He had lied to Cassandra, told her they'd started a new study using pigs, that he'd have to go to the lab in the early morning hours, on short notice, to administer postoperative care. This would involve getting the animals to walk and take deep breaths, he told her. If they didn't do this, the pigs would get pneumonia and die. He said it might take several hours, or longer, and he hoped he wouldn't have to do it more than once or twice a week. She praised his dedication and told him she was proud. He convinced himself that in time he would deserve her praise.

Now, as he traversed Manhattan Island at one a.m., his heels drumming the floorboard, he lay his head back, closed his eyes and focused on the task at hand, visualizing each step of the operation he was about to perform, from skin incision to skin closure, just as he had done a thousand times over the preceding days.

They turned south off 14th and after a right and a left, drove down a street of decay and renewal, a patchwork of old and new. One- and two-story meatpacking warehouses mingled with renovated lofts and boutiques. They passed Diamond Meat Packers on the left, and on the right, Weichsel Wholesale Beef and Lamb. Next to Weichsel, an apartment building under construction, and on the opposite corner, a wine shop, its shelves still empty. On the next block stood a dilapidated warehouse. To David's surprise they stopped in front of it. Aleksandr entered a number in his cell phone and spoke to someone in what sounded like Russian.

The two-story brick structure occupied the middle of the block. Five graffiti-covered roll-up doors stretched from one end of the lower level to the other. A flat awning on the verge of collapse hung over the doors. Bolted to the awning was a faded pig-shaped sign, R&K PORK PROVISIONS. There were no windows or lights at ground level, but the upper floor had windows, complete with bars, and the lights were on. The glass was opaque with filth.

"You sure this is the place?" David asked.

Aleksandr nodded. "Yes, Doctor."

It seemed impossible. The building was a ramshackle piece of shit. You can't operate on the human body in the midst of squalor.

One of the corrugated panels rumbled open. They drove in, parked beside an identical Town Car, and as David climbed out, a large figure standing in the shadows lowered the door, pulling hand over hand on a rattling chain. The scent of stale blood hung in the air, like an OR after a messy operation. Rows of fluorescent bars dangled overhead, but only a few were on, casting hazy islands of illumination. Except for the cars, the first floor was empty, and cold. David could see his breath.

He flinched as the metal door slammed shut, then walked around the back of the car toward Aleksandr. "There must be a mistake," David said. "You can't perform surgery in a place like this."

"No mistake," Aleksandr replied. "You will see."

They went to the freight elevator in back. The man from the shadows joined them. David recognized him as one of Mr. White's goons from the stoop. Like Aleksandr, he had a square face, prominent jaw, and black hair, but he was much taller with a thick neck, broad shoulders, and a big chest, apparent despite the overcoat. David wasn't short—a tinch over six feet—but this guy had at least five inches and maybe fifty pounds on David, making him feel like a dry twig. And the man's eyes were disturbing, unlike any David had seen. They were set deep in his head, below a thick ridge of bone, and in the dim light seemed black—no pupils, no irises, no whites— just black, steely orbs stuffed into sockets.

Without uttering a word, the big Russian jabbed the button. The elevator began its noisy descent from the upper level, clanking and moaning as it dropped. David was seized by a sense of foreboding as he anticipated the chamber of horrors waiting above.

The cage clattered to a standstill.

Aleksandr slid the gate open. "Please, Dr. McBride."

Feeling like one of his rats, David entered the cage, followed by the two Russians. As they ascended, David stared at the worn planks beneath his feet.

The elevator jerked in spasms until it leveled itself with the second floor. The big Russian pulled back the gate and motioned for David to exit. He stepped out, turned a corner and stopped, dazzled by the sight before him. A gleaming white box—a room within a room—stood amidst the dingy concrete and grimy brick. An operating theater had been constructed in the middle of the second floor. It had four walls and a ceiling, a swinging door, a stainless-steel sink mounted on the front, and a window above the sink. Cartons of disposable hats, masks, and Betadine brushes filled the windowsill. It could have been any OR in the city.

David went over and looked inside. In the back, two nurses were preparing for the operation. One of them, a young Asian woman already in her sterile gown and gloves, was organizing a tray of instruments atop a Mayo stand. She would be the scrub nurse. The other, also Asian, and also young, was peeling open suture packs and dropping them onto the tray. She would be the circulator. In the center of the room, a slender, brown-skinned man stood at the head of the operating table, aspirating solution out of a vial with a syringe—the anesthesiologist. Cabinets, shelves, and a counter lined the wall to the left. Stands holding suction canisters and the control box for the electrocautery were sitting against the back wall. A pair of disc-shaped high-intensity lights hung over the table. Aleksandr tapped David on the shoulder and offered to show him where to change.

In the rear of the building they approached an alcove containing a gurney, an IV pole, a basic monitor, and a space heater. The recovery area, David figured, but it was only large enough for one patient, and it wasn't enclosed. It looked more like an oil change bay than a place to care for a transplant recipient, or a donor for that matter. In a proper facility, recipients received immunosuppression drugs during the operation. They recovered in an isolation room with a laminar airflow system, and a sink for frequent hand washing. They needed sophisticated monitoring equipment and a lab, blood bank, and food service.

Aleksandr pointed beyond the alcove. "Surgical scrubs and lavatory around there."

"Yeah, thanks, but hold on a minute." David gestured toward the rudimentary setup. "What is this?"

"Recovery for the donor."

"How about the patients receiving the kidney? Where are they supposed to go after surgery? How are they going to be fed? And what about the lab and blood bank? What exactly is happening here?"

"My boss will be here soon. He can explain."

"You mean Mr. White?"

"No, I don't know who that is. My boss brings the donor."

David wasn't going to wait. A better source of information was already in house. He changed into scrubs, went back to the OR, and after slipping a hat on his head and tying a mask over his face, went in.

The anesthesiologist stood at the head of the bed, writing on a clipboard. David introduced himself.

"I'm Veejay," said the anesthesiologist without taking his eyes off his paperwork.

David leaned in close. "Maybe you can tell me what's going on here."

"What do you mean?"

"This place is not equipped for a kidney transplant. At best, you could do a harvest, but even that would be pushing it."

Veejay looked up. "I just pass the gas. I don't know anything else. Don't want to know anything else." He glanced past David, then down at his clipboard, fear gripping his face.

David turned to see what had spooked him—the big Russian, glaring through the window, now wearing scrubs and putting on a hat and a mask. He was coming in. He stuck his head in the room. "Donor is here. He fights and needs anesthesia fast."

Fighting? That didn't make sense. David wondered if he had heard correctly.

Veejay looked at David. "Can you assist me if the donor is in fact combative and I have to use rapid induction?"

"Yes," David said. But rapid induction was used to anesthetize someone with a gunshot wound who had bled out most of his blood volume, or a drunk trauma patient who was flopping around on the table and throwing punches at the nurses—anyone who needed to be put down quickly. It was not used on patients undergoing elective procedures.

"Veejay, why would he be combative?"

The anesthesiologist ignored the question and focused on de-airing his syringes, holding them up one at a time and flicking them as solution streamed from the needles.

The ascending elevator moaned and clanked.

David familiarized himself with Veejay's set up. IV supplies were laid out. A bag of Lactated Ringer's solution hung on the IV pole. Drugs had been drawn up in labeled syringes. An endotracheal tube and laryngoscope were ready. The ventilator was on.

The door swung open. The big Russian pushed the gurney into the room, maneuvered it parallel to the operating table, and what lay before David horrified him—a weather-beaten man with wild hair, an unruly beard, and tattered clothes, tied down with four-inch leather straps across his chest, arms, and legs. He wasn't exactly combative, but he was agitated, writhing against the restraints, trying to sit up. His eyes were open but glassy. He tried to talk, but his speech was slurred. David smelled the man's breath, checked his arms for needle tracks. No marks. No alcohol.

David looked at Veejay. "What the hell is this?"

Veejay nodded at the window. "Ask him."

A hulking man peered in. He was fat and sweaty. Pendulous jowls hung from an oversized jaw. Flakes of dandruff clung to his oily hair and the shoulders of his undersized, navy-blue sport coat. He took out a handkerchief and blotted his forehead.

David pushed through the swinging door, slamming it into the metal scrub sink. The warehouse filled with the sound of a gong. "What the fuck is going on here?"

The fat man casually turned his bulk toward David.

"This man is drugged," David said. "He's not voluntarily selling a kidney."

"Not for you to worry about, Doctor. Do your job, keep your mouth shut, everything is good. Make problem and bad things happen."

The fat man pulled an envelope out of his jacket and held it up. It was the same one Mr. White had given David in the park. "Maybe you need second look."

David didn't answer. He couldn't. His throat was constricted as if a hand were clamped around his trachea. He stood silently as the fat man walked over to the changing area.

- 18 -

David turned on the scrub sink faucet and opened a Betadine brush. The hot water felt good, the warehouse drafty and cold. As he spread the yellow-brown soap from fingertips to elbows, his nose ran and his eyes burned. The iodine. It had always bothered him. He used the pink soap when he was a resident. Easier on the eyes, nose, and skin. He washed each finger and watched the activity in the OR.

The donor lay in a right lateral decubitus position—right side on the table, left side up, legs bent, arms folded, back slightly arched. A blanket covered him from the waist down. He was naked and scrubbed clean from the waist up. An endotracheal tube protruded from his mouth like a giant straw, connected to the ventilator by corrugated plastic tubing. EKG electrodes sensed the rate and rhythm of the heart, a procession of spikes and dips marching across the monitor. IVs dripped fluid into arm veins. An arterial catheter measured the blood pressure. The donor was ready—bound, gagged, violated. The sooner he was under the drapes, the better. Detachment was easier when everything was covered, the human reduced to a patch of skin.

Veejay recorded vital signs and other data on his flow sheet. The circulating nurse, who he now knew as Amy, opened a pack of Ray-Tec sponges. Touching only the outside of the carton, she dropped them onto the Mayo stand without contaminating the instruments. The scrub nurse, Meiling, attached sterile handles to the lights and adjusted them until the surgical field was maximally illuminated. She painted the upper abdomen, chest, flank, and back with an undiluted iodine solution. The fat man sat in the corner reading a Russian-language newspaper, his XXL scrubs about to split open at the seams.

Aleksandr came up to the sink, now wearing scrubs, a hat, and a mask. He opened a Betadine brush and started washing his hands.

David cocked his head back. "You're scrubbing in?"

"I am your assistant."

"As in surgical assistant?"

"Yes. In my country I was a surgeon. I do not have experience with kidney transplants, but I know the abdomen well."

"Huh, driver and surgeon."

"I do what they tell me."

"And if you don't?"

Aleksandr said nothing, just scrubbed his arms as if trying to take off the skin.

"Looks like they got their hooks into you, too."

"Hooks? What is that?"

The toilet flushed and the big Russian exited the bathroom, still tying the string on his scrub pants. David and Aleksandr stared into the sink.

David finished and backed through the OR door, holding his arms up in front of him so the excess water would run toward his unwashed elbows instead of his clean hands. He exchanged glances with Meiling as she handed him a sterile towel. Her eyes revealed nothing. Like Cassandra, she was stoic. He finished drying off and slipped into the gown she held open. Amy moved in behind him and tied the gown as he shoved his hands into latex gloves. He went around to the other side of the table, and with Meiling's help, draped the surgical field. No words were spoken. None were needed. She knew what she was doing.

Aleksandr entered the room, dried off, and gowned and gloved himself without Meiling's help. Donning your own sterile garments was not easy, indicating he had at least a modicum of experience in the OR. He came to the table, across from David. David was glad to have him.

The preparations complete, Meiling picked up a scalpel and waited. The room was still. Only the beeping of the heart monitor and the blowing of the ventilator broke the silence. David held out his hand. It trembled. The scalpel hit his palm with a snap. He put the blade on the skin but could not apply pressure. Instead, he just stood there, heart racing, rivulets of sweat collecting on the small of his back. He was going to remove the left kidney from a man he knew nothing about, with people who were not what they seemed, for reasons beyond his control. No rational person would do it.

The newspaper ruffled. "Problem, Doctor?" asked the fat man.

David thought of Cassandra's photos, her vulnerability, the brazen arrogance of those behind them. "No ... no problem."

He pushed down and pulled. The blade sliced through the skin and into the subcutaneous fat. He carried the incision from the spine, parallel to the twelfth rib, forward to the midaxillary line. Red blood from the subdermal capillaries spread over the yellow fat, turning it a beautiful shade of pink. He took the electrocautery device, cauterized the larger bleeders, then used it to divide muscle and fascia. Wisps of smoke rose from the wound, carrying the smell of cooked meat, a smell that was not unpleasant. The instruments felt good in his hands. He had all but forgotten the sublime pleasure of dividing human tissue. How he desperately wished the circumstances were different.

The kidney had been resected, flushed with preservative solution, sealed in sterile plastic bags and packed in ice. The fat man had taken the ice chest and left the building, his spot in the corner now filled by the big Russian. The remainder of the operation consisted of drying up any residual bleeding, and closing the wound. David removed a wad of blood-soaked laparotomy sponges from the space previously occupied by the kidney. Aleksandr suctioned fresh blood and old clots with one hand, and pinched arterial and venous bleeders with DeBakey forceps held by the other. David buzzed Aleksandr's forceps with the electrocautery device, the current traveling down the shaft and arcing from tip to tip, searing the vessels within the forceps' grasp. Pops, crackles, and wisps of smoke rose from deep inside the abdomen.

After ten minutes of sucking, blotting, grasping, and zapping, the wound was dry and ready for closure. Twenty minutes later, the muscle layers had been reapproximated, the skin closed, the dressings placed. Fifteen minutes after that the donor had been weaned off the ventilator, transferred onto the gurney, and wheeled over to the recovery area in the alcove.

Aleksandr went with the donor. David stopped at the scrub sink, leaned against it, and peered into the black hole of the drain. He was relieved the procedure was over and satisfied with how well it had gone. He'd been focused, meticulous with his surgical technique, and efficient with his time. On occasion he'd felt rusty, but for the most part, his hands had done what he wanted them to do—unlike now. They trembled as they had at the beginning of the case. His scrubs were soaked with sweat, and the muscles in his neck and back ached from prolonged tension. He had violated the body of another man against that man's will and had removed a life-giving organ without consent. David could think of no greater violation of human dignity, and it left *him* feeling less than human.

He wondered if the others felt remorse. The fat man and his muscled sidekick were nothing more than hired goons ruled by greed, but what about the rest of the group? Clearly, Aleksandr had been a competent surgeon in a previous life. In fact, the whole team had performed well. They possessed skill, knowledge, and experience. But where were they from, and how did they land in this decrepit warehouse? They spoke English with facility, so they were not fresh off the boat. Did they have families under threat? Were they desperate for money? Did they face deportation?

Aleksandr joined David at the sink. David started washing his hands.

"You did nice work," Aleksandr said. "When you change, Yuri will drive you home."

"The big guy?"

"Yes. That is Yuri."

David craned his neck and looked around. They were alone. "I'd rather have you take me home."

"I cannot. They want me to stay here."

"Who are 'they'?" David fought to keep his voice down. "Who's really running this show? The fat guy doesn't look smart enough."

In a hushed tone, Aleksandr said, "I don't know any more than you do."

David dried his hands and threw the paper towels into the bucket. "What about the man we operated on? Where did he come from? Who's going to manage his post-op care?"

"I know nothing about the patient, but I will be in charge of his recovery."

"He's staying here?"

"Yes."

David looked around again. "You know as well as I do this man should recover in a hospital, with physicians and nurses caring for him."

"You have done your job, Doctor, now let us handle the rest. I will see that he gets appropriate care."

"You're not going to tell me anything, are you?"

Aleksandr's eyes met David's. "I have nothing to tell, and it is best if you stop asking."

David walked over to the alcove. Veejay sat at the patient's bedside, checking vital signs.

"Doesn't it bother you that you're administering general anesthesia to someone you've never met before?" David asked. "You don't know his medical history, or if he's had an adverse reaction to anesthetic agents in the past."

Veejay jumped up. "Of course it bothers me. It bothers me a great deal, but I can do nothing." He looked past David to make sure they were alone. "They have threatened my wife and kids, so I will do what the bastards say. I give the best anesthesia I can and hope to avoid complications. I have treated these first two patients as if they—"

"Wait a minute. What did you just say? There's been two patients?"

"Yes. This is the second harvest we have performed, but I don't want to talk about—"

"Who did the first one? Who was the surgeon?"

"His name was Anil. Based on his dialect, I believe he came from southern India."

"What happened to him?"

"I don't know, but he was a hack, and very slow. I am not surprised they replaced him. Now, please stop with the questions."

"Just one more," David said. "What are those for?" He pointed at two surgical gowns hanging on hooks just outside the alcove.

The gowns themselves were standard—long, baggy, blue—but they were paired with hoods that completely covered the surgeon's head and neck. Plastic eye shields allowed the surgeon to see out but kept the microbes in, thus decreasing the incidence of postoperative infection. They were used primarily by orthopedic surgeons during total joint replacements.

"We don't use those types of gowns for what we're doing," David continued. "And they're no longer sterile now that they're hanging on the wall."

"We have been told to put them on when the patients wake up, so our faces are hidden. And we are supposed to be liberal with the IV morphine to keep them confused and disoriented."

"Jesus," David said.

Veejay glanced past David, then abruptly sat down.

David turned. Aleksandr and the big Russian were coming toward him, with the fat man a few steps behind.

"Please, Doctor," Aleksandr said as he approached. "Yuri waits to take you home."

The big Russian stepped up to David. "But first, this is for you." He drilled David in the solar plexus with his cinder block of a fist.

David dropped to his knees, clutching his midriff, unable to draw a breath. Then a shock wave hit the side of his head and sent him sprawling across the dirty floor. When he opened his eyes, the fat man was standing over him.

"You ask more questions, your wife suffers worse than you. Understood?"

David slowly nodded his throbbing head.

- 19 -

Detective Kate D'Angelo wanted to know how long Rodney's chief clocker, Strike, would be able to treat his stomach ulcer with vanilla Yoo-hoo before it ruptured or bled. She was wedged into the corner of the couch, pillow on her lap, Richard Price's *Clockers* on the pillow, a glass of white wine on the end table, the TV and all of the lights off except for the table lamp just beyond her shoulder. No distractions. Even the sounds of rush hour rising up from West 33rd Street were muted. Vanilla Yoo-hoo. She'd have to ask her father.

For Kate, having her father a phone call away was like having a direct line to the National Library of Medicine. Raymond D'Angelo had obtained his MD degree from Montefiore Medical Center in the Bronx, had completed Montefiore's forensic pathology residency, and had spent most of his professional life in the office of the New York City medical examiner, a fair portion of which he served as chief medical examiner. As a result, he had seen nearly every disease process and traumatic injury the human body could suffer, and that meant Kate always had an encyclopedic knowledge of medicine at her fingertips.

Just as she turned the page, her phone rang. She had already fielded her father's daily call, so she figured it was departmental business. She put down her book, went over to the kitchen counter, and checked her iPhone. She was right. The front desk of the 13th Precinct.

"D'Angelo," she said, picking up.

"Kate … Morales. Sorry to bother you at home, but I got a nurse from the Bellevue ER on the line, says you'll remember her from last summer. Name is Carla Espinoza."

Of course Kate remembered. Her partner at the time, Frank Deitz, had been shot in the upper abdomen and was bleeding to death. They cut open his chest in the ER, put some kind of clamp in him, pumped him full of blood, and rushed him to surgery. Even though a surgeon had done the cutting, Carla had essentially run the show, maintaining the focus of everyone in the room, thus keeping the procedure from degenerating into a ghoulish spectacle.

"Nurse Espinoza, how are you?"

"Doing well, Detective, but I'm afraid I have a favor to ask."

"What can I do for you?"

"It's about a patient I'm taking care of, but the doctors don't want the NYPD involved. In fact, I'm violating any number of HIPAA privacy policies just by calling you."

"Consider yourself a confidential source. What do you have?"

"We're seeing a twenty-nine-year-old man with paranoid schizophrenia who claims he was drugged and forced to undergo surgery against his will. He has a large incision on his left side that's no more than three or four days old, and he doesn't know how it got there."

"Why would that raise a red flag, coming from a paranoid schizophrenic and all? Maybe he had a legitimate operation and just doesn't remember."

"That's what the docs think. There's nothing in our records, so they figure he had the procedure somewhere else and they failed to keep him on his psych meds."

"And you don't agree."

"This guy is one of our regulars. I've seen him when he's on his meds, I've seen him when he's off. Right now he seems mostly rational to me, like when he's on them."

Kate went back to the couch and sat down. "I have to tell you, a paranoid schizophrenic claiming he was abducted doesn't sound that far out there. Actually seems tame for Bellevue."

"I know, but something bothers me. The man is homeless. Private institutions don't operate on these folks. They come here or go to one of the other city hospitals. Somewhere in the HHC database there should be records for a major procedure like this, but I found nothing."

That made sense. Kate had been to Bellevue plenty of times, and the place was always crammed with homeless people. "The incision on his side, what types of surgery would it be used for?"

"Removal of a kidney, most of the time."

"And kidneys are removed for?"

"Tumors, chronic infection, chronic obstruction, transplant."

"What do the doctors think?"

"In a homeless man? Infection or obstruction from an untreated kidney stone."

Kate sipped her wine. "Did the docs consider why someone might drug him and operate on him?"

"No. They blew that off. We're swamped tonight. They want him out the door. His temperature is normal, wound looks good, blood work is okay, so the intern gave him a scrip for pain meds and told to come back in a few days to get his sutures out."

"Did the patient give any details of the abduction or the operation?"

"Quite a few, actually, but then he mentioned people in spacesuits and the docs bailed."

"And you didn't?"

"No. I mean, I realize it's a crazy story, but the guy is scared. He just wants to know what happened. If you'd talk to him, tell him you'll check it out even if there's nothing to check out, it'll make him feel better."

Kate glanced at the time. Seven thirty and off duty. The last thing she wanted to do was schlep herself over to Bellevue and listen to another abduction story from some nut bag. Then she thought of Frank Dietz's brush with death, and how the Bellevue doctors and nurses had saved his life. And now Frank Dietz was retired on full disability, spending his days with his teenage daughters. Carla Espinoza had played no small part in that.

"Okay. I'll talk to him, see if I get the same vibe you're getting. Where will he be?"

"The intern is writing up discharge orders, so I'm gonna send him to the coffee shop on the ground floor and have him wait for you there."

"Sounds good. What's his name, and what does he look like?"

- 20 -

Carla Espinoza was right. Jimmy Gray was the only white guy in the place with a big, woolly Afro. He sat in the far corner, back to the wall, adjacent booths empty. Kate crossed the room, and as she approached the table, Jimmy appeared to be praying. He had his hands clenched in front of him, his head hanging down, and was speaking to himself in a hushed tone.

"Mr. Gray?" she asked.

He looked up, startled, then relieved.

Kate held out her shield. "Detective D'Angelo."

"I 'pologize for not getting up," he said. "Still hurts to stand."

"It's okay." She slid out of her overcoat and tucked it into the corner.

As she was taking a seat, she thought of the story of Dorian Gray—she hadn't done that since college—and wondered if Jimmy ever studied himself in the mirror and tried to recognize the once handsome young man under the nappy hair, unruly beard, and sand-paper skin.

"Appreciate you coming to see me," he said.

"Sounds like you had a long day in the ER."

"Yeah … long day."

He slipped a cigarette out of a crumpled pack and put it in his mouth.

"They're not gonna let you smoke in here."

"I know."

He put the cigarette away, laced his fingers, and planted his elbows on the table. The hands were weathered, the fingertips thickened and worn, and even though his fingers were locked together, his hands undulated with a fine, wavelike motion.

Carla had said Jimmy was twenty-nine, which made him ten years younger than Kate. He looked twenty years older. There but for the grace of God go I, she thought, but she didn't really believe it. This was not about the hand of God, or fate, or some other nebulous entity. This was about biology and luck, the countless near misses that start as soon as the sperm pokes its head into the egg. A bad gene, a little too much of this brain chemical, or not enough of that one, and you were Dumpster diving for your next meal instead of eating New York strips in an Upper East Side penthouse. "Mind showing me the incision?" she asked.

Jimmy grimaced as he shifted his body and pulled up his shirt. A razor-thin line started on his left side, just under the ribs, and curved around almost to the spine. There were no stitches or staples, but parallel to the incision, half-inch segments of suture, resembling dark-blue fishing line, intermittently appeared on alternating sides of the wound. An inch or so beyond the end of the incision, a small knot of the same material protruded through the skin.

"The ER doc said whoever closed me up did nice work, like a plastic surgeon."

"Looks painful."

He let his shirt fall over the wound. "It is. Any movement, coughing, deep breath, feels like someone's trying to pull you in half."

"I can only imagine," Kate said. "They gave you pain medicine, right?"

"A scrip for Vicodin. Be ready in the next hour or so."

"Okay. Good. Why don't you tell me what happened?"

Jimmy looked to his right, sized up three young men in scrubs and white coats a couple of tables away, then spent about thirty seconds trying to get comfortable, moving his butt one way, then the other, shrugging one shoulder, followed by the other, clutching his side the whole time, grimacing and grunting. Once he settled down, he leaned in close, stared at the table as though he could see something in the design of the Formica, then spoke just loud enough to overcome the clinking dishes and muffled conversation.

"I stay next door when I can, at the old Bellevue psychiatric hospital. They turned some of the wards into a homeless shelter, but you gotta line up every evening 'cause they only take so many. It's safe and warm and close to the clinic where I get my meds." He briefly made eye contact with Kate, then scanned the room as if protecting the location of a secret fishing hole. "The other night, Doc Steinberg—he's my psych doctor—he finds me in the hall and tells me he got the results of some blood work done a few weeks ago. Says one of my kidneys might be bad and I need more tests. He has this cup full of liquid he wants me to drink, then he's gonna send me downtown to a hospital that specializes in kidney diseases."

A young Filipino woman came over to take their order.

Jimmy sat back and repeated the can't-get-comfortable routine.

Kate asked for two cups of coffee.

Once the server left, Jimmy slipped another cigarette from the pack and glanced at Kate. "Can't help it," he said. "Feels like there's a million cockroaches crawling inside my body." He stabbed the cigarette into his lips. "Won't light it, but pretty soon I'm gonna have to go outside."

"Does smoking kill the cockroaches?"

He shook his head with a quick burst and plucked the cigarette out of his mouth. "There aren't any roaches. Just feels like it. Doc Steinberg says it's the meds. They cause restlessness and tension. The nicotine helps with that. On a typical day it takes about two packs to keep me from jumping off the Williamsburg."

"The bridge."

"Yeah. That's why so many of us psychotics stop taking our medications. We're trading one horror for another."

The irony and acuteness of the situation was not lost on Kate. The guy was a ball of nerves—fidgeting, trembling, squirming, pain contorting his face with every movement, eyes darting around the room when he wasn't staring at the table, and when he did make eye contact with Kate, he'd quickly divert his gaze as if he had glanced at the sun. Kate felt like she had cockroaches crawling inside her. But she had no desire to stand outside the front door, in the bitter cold, amongst a mob of smoking patients and staff, while Jimmy Gray calmed himself with a reeking stick of tobacco.

"We'll try to get through this quickly," she said. "You were saying your doctor wanted to send you downtown for kidney tests."

"Yes," Jimmy said, tapping the filtered end of the cigarette on the table. "I asked him is it an emergency. Why do I have to go at night? Why don't we just go to the main Bellevue hospital? It's a block over. He says if we didn't handle it right away I could end up on dialysis." Now tapping the unfiltered end on the table. "Then I remembered there was a hospital on Second Avenue strictly for bones and joints, and another one downtown called the eye infirmary, so I figured there probably was a hospital for kidneys."

The specific detail and logical train of thought impressed Kate, and she knew Bellevue was capable of treating nearly every affliction known to medicine, so why would he need to go somewhere else? Maybe it was benefit-of-the-doubt time. She took her notebook and digital voice recorder out of her coat pocket.

"Mind if I tape our conversation?"

"Okay with me."

Jimmy shut his eyes and rubbed his temples as Kate positioned her recorder. She turned it on and said, "So you decided to follow the doctor's order."

"I've known Doc Steinberg for a long time and I trust him, so yeah, I drink the stuff in the cup, and he takes me to the parking lot and puts me into a car with two men. Then, while we're heading downtown, I start to get real panicky, and I'm feeling kinda drunk, and one of the men says don't worry we're almost there. And that's the last thing I remember until I wake up in a strange building, surrounded by concrete walls just a few feet from the bed, and I got a terrible pain in my side like somebody gashed me open with a knife."

Kate jotted "Dr. Steinberg/shrink," "kidney hospital," and "drugged?" in her notebook.

"The stuff you drank, did it taste like anything?"

Jimmy shook his head. "Water."

"You ever had a kidney test before?"

"No."

"When you came to, I assume you weren't alone."

"I wasn't, but all I could see were these blue shadows moving around, people in baggy suits with hoods, and plastic windows over their faces. A bare light bulb was hanging over me, glaring in my eyes, and I was all groggy. Made 'em look like spacemen."

"Do you think they were spacemen?"

A quick shake of the head. "No. They had human faces, but with the glare, and me being drugged, they looked like they were wearing spacesuits, you know? Like when the astronauts landed on the moon?"

The server returned with two coffees. Kate stirred a Sweet'N Low into hers and watched as Jimmy carefully brought his to his mouth with thick, shaking hands. He was a likeable guy, and she wanted to believe him, but damn, he had to start talking about people in spacesuits. After he set down his cup, she said, "Did they speak to you, the people in the moon suits?"

"No. I asked what the hell is goin' on, where am I. Mumbles and whispers was all I got."

"Okay. Then what?"

"For a number of days, can't tell you how many, they took readings off their machines and checked my temperature and blood pressure, looked at the stitches, poked their fingers in my belly. They fed me pretty well. Soup at first, then regular food, deli food."

"Did you see any bags or cartons, recall any names?"

"No."

Kate jotted a few more notes and told Jimmy to continue.

"Then one day they put my clothes on and hauled me out of the cubicle on a stretcher. Now, I'm still groggy, like I'm in a dream, but I remember something really weird. The building we were in was old and dirty, like some kinda warehouse, but we passed by a room that was all white and shiny. Can't recall anything else except how clean and new it was compared to the rest of the place. Next thing I know, I wake up in an alley, freezing to death. My side feels like it's about to split open, so I get up and walk to Bellevue. Longest two blocks of my life."

"You told all this to the ER doctors?"

"Word for word."

"What did they say?"

Jimmy moved closer and held Kate's gaze, his jaw tight, his eyes moist. "I wait half the day to get in, then wait the other half to get seen by some intern. He tells my story to the resident doctor, who tells it to another resident doctor, and that one says to give me a prescription for pain pills and send me out the door. The intern tells me to stay on my psych meds and try real hard to figure out where I had my operation and go back there for follow up. I know it sounds crazy, Detective, but I'm tellin' the truth here." He pointed at his side. "This is real. I didn't imagine it. I know they took something out of me. I just know it."

His pleading eyes said he believed what he was saying, but wasn't that the definition of a delusion? A person clings to a false belief even though it goes against all reason? Kate wanted to say she believed him, but that would be a lie. The story was shaky at best, with the moon-suit thing tipping the balance.

Jimmy finished his coffee and stuck the cigarette between his lips, which were now trembling as well.

Kate said she had a few more questions, and they'd be done. Jimmy had no idea where the men had taken him. The car was big and old, like a Lincoln or Cadillac, and it was dark in color, blue or black. He couldn't recall any details that might distinguish the building, or any noises or smells or lights coming from outside. Steinberg's first name was Brian.

"You ever had any kind of kidney disease?" Kate asked. "Stones or infections? Anything like that?"

"No. Except for my psych problems, I've been pretty healthy."

"Ever had surgery before?"

"Hernia, a while back."

"At Bellevue?"

"Yeah. That's the only place I go."

"You have paranoid delusions very often?"

"Not for a while. I've been keeping up with my meds."

"Ever have delusions about doctors or hospitals doing bad things to you?"

"No." Jimmy gave his cup a forlorn look, probably thinking, *Here we go again ... the big blow off.* "They usually involve the military. Last time, they were trying to force me to breathe in a germ being tested for use against the terrorists. I actually made a surgical mask out of tinfoil."

"What about the two men?"

"Those guys I remember. The driver was huge, like NFL-lineman huge, and ugly, with these creepy black eyes set deep in his skull like a caveman."

"And the other one?"

"Fat and sweaty. Kept wiping his forehead with a handkerchief. And he spoke Russian to the big guy."

"Anything else?"

"No. My memory went hazy real fast once I got in the car."

"The alley you woke up in, you know where it is?"

"Off East 29th, between Third and Lexington. The cold air had me clearheaded by then."

Kate noted the address. "Okay," she said, putting away her notebook and recorder. "That pretty much wraps it up."

"What do you think?" Jimmy asked. "Just another whack job with a crazy-ass story?"

"To be honest, it's hard to imagine something like this happening, but I've seen some bizarre things during my time on the force." She grabbed her coat and stood up. "I can't make any promises, but I'll ask around, do some checking."

"If you find out anything or come up with more questions, I spend most of my time in the park across the street."

She leaned over the table and shook his hand, and that's when Jimmy fell apart. His brow quivered and his eyelids fluttered as he tried to fight off the tears. Despite his effort, a few streamed down his ruddy cheeks. Back in the day she would have taken a moment to comfort him. Tonight, she turned and walked out. She was abandoning a scared and lonely soul and felt like shit for doing it, but as a cop, she collected pieces of human misery every day. The bin was getting full.

- 21 -

Kate paused in the lobby of her building, coiled a wool scarf around her neck, buttoned her overcoat, and slipped into a pair of gloves. Two degrees in Central Park, she'd heard on the morning news. And forget about finding a cab. This time of day they'd stick to the avenues, looking for fares heading uptown or downtown. They wouldn't want to fool with someone going nine blocks across town, so she covered her face with the scarf and joined her fellow commuters on the sidewalk.

As she headed up West 33rd Street toward Seventh Avenue, she skirted frozen mounds of grime-coated slush, dodged the occasional patch of black ice, glimpsed a thin strip of blue above, the crisp sky contrasting sharply with the mid-winter gray of the city. And fifteen eye-burning, nose-stinging, brain-numbing minutes later, she stepped into the 13th Precinct.

The second-floor squad room was empty except for Detective Mike Scarpelli, who was on the phone. He gave Kate a perfunctory nod as she hung her coat on the rack near the door. She nodded back, then made her way to the command log at the other end of the room. She signed in, went to her desk and sat down, scarf still wrapped around her neck, arms crossed as if she were hugging herself. With his sleeves rolled up and tie loosened, Scarpelli didn't seem cold, but he was a big man with more flesh on his bones than she had. About a hundred pounds' worth, Kate figured, putting him in the two-twenty to two-thirty range. He gave her a look that said, *What the fuck, Princess? You cold?* She uncoiled the scarf and stuffed it in her desk drawer.

As she flipped through a case file, Kate wondered if Jimmy Gray had survived the night without incident. He probably had. When temps dropped into the single digits various agencies swept the city, gathered up all the homeless people they could find and put them into shelters. It was possible he stayed in the hospital, hunkered down in the ER waiting area or patient registration.

After returning home last night, Kate had mulled over Jimmy's story, and something about it had nagged at her, made her reconsider blowing him off. At first, she'd been impressed by the abundance of vivid detail, the logical sequence of events, and the presence of a definable beginning, middle, and end. Those were the characteristics of any coherent story. But then she recalled how some of the paranoid delusions she'd heard on the job were better told than many of the psycho thrillers she'd read over the years. So, after reviewing her notes, she concluded that Jimmy probably did have a bad kidney, that his doctor did send him for additional tests, and he did, in fact, undergo a legitimate procedure. At some point during his hospitalization, fear kicked in and his faulty brain circuits invented a detailed abduction scenario—complete with sinister Russians and nurses in moon suits—to deal with the stress. The thing that bothered her, though, was the lack of records in the HHC database. Why would a homeless man have a major operation outside the Health and Hospitals Corporation system when Bellevue, the flagship institution of that system, was a block away? Kate understood why Carla Espinoza had seen a glimmer of credibility in Jimmy's story, and she decided to give Jimmy Gray's tale of abduction and forced surgery passing consideration.

By eight thirty, the other seven detectives had logged in, poured coffee, and taken their seats. Kate went over to the pot, poured a cup for herself and turned to face the room as she stirred in a Sweet'N Low. The detectives' squad room was nothing more than a glorified corridor. To the left, a hodgepodge of wood and metal desks sat in clumps of three along an electric-blue cinder-block wall. To the right, two more desks were sandwiched between the door to the interrogation room and the bars of the holding cell. Three north-facing windows that caught no sun in winter filled the wall behind her. Duty rosters, team rosters, wanted posters, and shift calendars covered the walls. Stacks of manila folders and piles of paperwork covered the desktops. Even when it was empty, like at two in the morning, the squad room was cluttered and confining. With the day shift fully assembled, it was claustrophobic. Not so, over at Manhattan South Homicide. They had space, and clean white walls, and file cabinets that didn't catch. Everything was new. Everything was organized.

She cleared her throat, and when she had everyone's attention, she said, "Anyone ever heard of a person getting abducted and having a body part stolen?" She expected a bunch of half-assed noes, but leave it to Scarpelli to pry.

"Why? What you got?" he asked.

"I interviewed a man last night, a homeless paranoid schizophrenic who says he was drugged, kidnapped, and forced to have surgery. One of my sources at Bellevue thinks the guy had a kidney removed."

Scarpelli leaned back and chuckled. "C'mon, Kate. Why you wasting your time? Next thing you know, you'll be investigating alien abductions. Even if you prove aliens exist, Santa Claus is real, and paranoid-schizophrenic conspiracy theories sometimes come true, you ain't gettin' to Homicide any faster."

Kate's face sizzled. She wanted to kick Scarpelli in his dickless crotch. "Yeah?" she said. "At least I still have a chance to get there. How many times have they passed you over?" Under her breath, she muttered, "Fucking sexist dinosaur."

Scarpelli sat forward, slowly folded his arms and sneered. "Good thing you're a woman—excuse me, I mean female."

Kate stared him down, matched his contemptuous glare dagger for dagger.

In the back of the room, Clarence Murphy cleared his throat with an okay-boys-and-girls emphasis, then said, "I've heard of men in Vegas casinos who get all liquored up at the tables, and they go upstairs with a hooker and wake up in a bathtub full of ice with a note telling them to call 911, their kidney's been stolen."

Kate let her shoulders and face go slack as she turned away from Scarpelli and toward Murphy. It seemed as if Murphy *himself* had just flown in from Vegas. He was a tall, handsome black man who wore a three-piece suit to work every day, always with color-coordinated handkerchief in the vest pocket and gold watch chain dangling—a gentleman, he looked and acted the part, the complete opposite of Scarpelli.

Standing at the battery charger, Dan Austin said, "Those Vegas stories are urban myths, but a guy tried to sell his own kidney on eBay a few years ago. The bids reached five or six million dollars before they yanked the ad."

Tommy Li said, "In my country, you can buy kidneys from executed criminals." Grinning, he added, "Still warm when you get 'em."

Wayne DeSilva caught her eye and nodded for her to come over. She took a seat at her desk, which faced his.

"I have something that might interest you." He dug through a stack of files, pulled out the thinnest one, and slid it across to her.

"You guys are a pile of information this morning." The file held a couple of typewritten pages and an autopsy report.

"Not much there." DeSilva leaned back and clasped his hands behind his head. "A few weeks ago I get a call from the Medical Examiner's office. They have an adult male on the slab who died in the Bellevue ER. Paramedics found him facedown on the street. No ID. Homeless by all appearances. Turned out he recently had a kidney removed. A clip fell off a large artery and he bled to death. Now, the ME, he's pissed. Says whoever did the surgery botched it, didn't do anything right. Said even the skin incision was a hack job. So he wants to ID the corpse, find out where the operation was performed, and bring the hammer down on the surgeon. You know, complain to the hospital or the licensing board, whatever it is you do to bring the hammer down on a doctor."

DeSilva leaned forward, grabbed his coffee and sipped it. "Anyway, they ran prints, matched them to a Michael Kerwin

Smith, no known address, no next of kin, a big dead end. That's when the assistant ME handling the case called me. Seems I owed him a solid. So we checked the private hospitals and queried the HHC database. Lots of Michael Smiths, but only one with the middle name Kerwin. He'd been into Bellevue a number of times, mostly psych-related stuff and some ER visits. No major surgeries, no kidney removal, no help for the ME's office."

"Mind if I borrow this?" Kate asked.

"All yours. Let me know if you find anything."

She began with the autopsy report. The patient's ID was listed on the top left of the first page: Michael Kerwin Smith, white male, date of birth 7/6/70. The top right listed the autopsy number, date and time of the procedure, and the examining physician: Associate Medical Examiner, William Roberts, MD. Good. She liked working with Bill. The final pathological diagnoses followed: I. Status post left nephrectomy. II. Acute fatal hemorrhage secondary to left nephrectomy. III. Status post left thoracotomy (in emergency department) and attempted internal cardiac resuscitation.

"What's a nephrectomy?" Kate asked DeSilva.

"Removal of the kidney." He grinned and shook his head. "Daddy didn't teach you that one?"

She shrugged. "He probably did, at some point."

Kate had attended a fair number of autopsies, both job-related and with her father, and as a young girl she often studied his pathology books, but most of the Latin root words she'd picked up along the way had escaped her.

Paramedics, the report said, had found a John Doe lying face-down on the sidewalk about fifteen feet from the mouth of an alley on East 26th Street between Second and Third Avenues, at approximately 4:10 a.m. They resuscitated him at the scene and rushed him to Bellevue. He died in the ER less than an hour later. The autopsy revealed a surgical wound on the left flank, four to five days old, closed with staples. The incision was of poor quality with jagged edges.

Staples. Jagged edges. Kate thought of Jimmy Gray's wound—
the clean, razor-thin line, the use of sutures instead of staples.

The incision, the report stated, had been placed too low, most
likely resulting in difficulty exposing the kidney. The kidney bed
and retroperitoneal space contained a large volume of fresh blood,
indicating acute, massive hemorrhage. Of note was a large clip
adhered to the renal artery by a few strands of tissue. DeSilva had
written "renal artery = the artery that supplies the kidney" in the
margin. According to Roberts, accepted standard of care was to
ligate the renal artery with two separate sutures, usually heavy silk
ligatures. Using a single clip to ligate a large artery constituted gross
negligence. He went on to speculate that because of the errant location of the incision, the surgeon likely had difficulty exposing the
renal artery and therefore had found it easier to clip it rather than
properly ligate it with two sutures. The final opinion: the victim
died from massive hemorrhage as a direct result of poor surgical
technique.

Even over the phone, Bill Roberts still sounded pissed. "Please
tell me you've ID'd the hospital. I want to get the incompetent ass
who clipped a major artery."

"Sorry," Kate said, "no ID, but I am taking a fresh look at the
case and just wanted to know if you've had any new developments
on your end, or maybe another botched surgery similar to this one?"

"We've had a few surgical deaths, but nothing caused by poor
technique or negligence. I don't think we have anything new on
Smith, either, but if you'll excuse me a moment, I'll pull up the file."

Kate sipped her coffee. Moments later Roberts came back on
the line.

"I stand corrected," he said. "We do have a new development,
and quite compelling it is. The toxicology was finally completed,
and at the time of death, Michael Smith had Rohypnol in his
blood."

Kate felt a jolt of excitement, what she called her process-of-discovery adrenaline hit. She wrote "roofies" on the report and under-

lined it three times, her pen nearly cutting through the paper. "Any chance Rohypnol was one of his psych meds?"

"Check with a shrink, but I'd say no. Its abuse potential is so high, it's rarely prescribed in this country, and it's expensive. I can't think of any reason why he'd have it in his system."

Kate knew all about Rohypnol, street name, roofies. Pill for pill the drug was ten times stronger than its cousin, Valium, and was often mixed with alcohol, marijuana, or cocaine to produce a rapid and intense high. Unfortunately, because it lowered inhibitions and induced a state of amnesia, it was the perfect date-rape drug. On her way to becoming a precinct detective, Kate had done an eighteen-month stint with the Special Victims Division. During the assignment, she had investigated the case of a nineteen-year-old girl who claimed to have been repeatedly raped and sodomized. The medical exam confirmed that prolonged, forceful, vaginal and anal penetration had occurred, and semen from three different blood types was recovered, but the young woman admitted she had willingly taken the drug, along with two girlfriends, neither of whom were raped. No charges were filed.

Kate forced the image of the girl's ravaged pelvic area from her mind, thanked Bill Roberts for his help, and hung up the phone.

- 22 -

Kate had a case, a potentially high-profile case that could move her a step closer to Homicide. She grabbed another cup of coffee, turned on her laptop, Googled "kidney theft" and came up with over eight hundred thousand hits in 0.11 seconds. She took out her notebook, turned to a clean page and wrote, "Who?" "What?" "Why?" "Where?" and "How?" She figured she knew the "Why?" and decided to start there. She went to CNN.com and a few clicks later found what she was looking for. The headline: "Online Shoppers Bid Millions for Human Kidney." The date: September 3, 1999.

An eBay post for a fully functional kidney had drawn bids as high as $5.7 million before company officials intervened to block the sale. The seller, from Sunrise, Florida, had posted, "Fully functional kidney for sale. Buyer pays all transplant and medical costs. Of course only one for sale, as I need the other one to live." A spokesman for the company said it was impossible to tell if the offer was genuine, or if the bids were serious, and reiterated that, "eBay has zero tolerance for illegal items on the site." The article went on to state that trafficking in human organs is a felony, punishable by a minimum of five years in prison and fines of $50,000 or more.

Under "What?" Kate wrote, "Someone stole a kidney from a paranoid schizophrenic." Next to "Why?" she drew a bifurcated arrow and wrote, "Why steal a kidney? The oldest reason in the world—money," and, "Why steal it from a paranoid schizophrenic? Because nobody will believe him." She returned to Google to figure out the who, where, and how.

A link for an urban-myth website caught her eye. Several clicks later she was perusing a list of topics that started with cannibalism, ended with traffic tragedies, and included such eye-catchers as fatal vanities, insect manifestations, malicious mayhem, and murdering madmen. She clicked on "grave robbery" and was linked to e-mail propagated stories of drunk college students succumbing to the advances of party girls, weary business travelers accepting drinks from women in hotel bars, and Vegas gamblers heading upstairs for "play-for-pay hanky-panky."

Invariably, these men woke up naked in bathtubs full of ice with notes scrawled in lipstick on mirrors or across their chests saying, CALL 911 OR YOU WILL DIE. A phone was always within reach of the tub, with a well-informed EMS operator on the other end who advised the victim to climb out and check his back in the mirror. He would, only to find two nine-inch slits on his lower back. She'd tell him to get back into the ice immediately and wait for the rescue team.

According to the e-mails reporting these stories, they were "documented and confirmable," corroborated by a sister-in-law who worked for a lady whose son lives in Houston and this happened to a neighbor of his. Or the wife of a Vegas firefighter/EMT who said the crime ring was to be taken very seriously, because the same thing happened to the son of a friend of a fellow firefighter.

The website, dedicated to debunking urban legends, said there was no evidence such incidents had occurred. The Las Vegas Police Department had launched a formal investigation and came up empty. The Houston PD stated no such occurrences had been reported in that city. UNOS, the United Network for Organ Sharing, along with the National Kidney Foundation issued formal statements declaring that these so-called warnings were not only hoaxes, but detrimental to legitimate organ donation.

Seemed Dan Austin was right. The waking-up-buried-in-ice stories were just that, stories. Kate then linked to an article in the Augusta Chronicle Online and found what she'd been searching for—a jump from urban legend to the real world. According to a

UNOS spokesman, when kidneys are donated, the network checks its database for a patient with a matching blood type, and then distributes the organ to the person who is at the top of the list and lives closest to the donor. There is no incentive to steal kidneys, said the spokesman, because hospitals will not use stolen organs.

"But," asked the author of the article, "suppose there were these bad doctors, and suppose they had their own hospital and had access to the network's computer files. And suppose there were wealthy individuals on the list who did not want to wait and were willing to pay for a new organ. Would kidney theft then be a possibility?"

A medical anthropologist at Smith College in Northampton, Massachusetts said it would undoubtedly be profitable. He went on to say that despite it being illegal, people have been paid to donate kidneys. There were documented cases in England. And in South India, impoverished villagers had sold kidneys and eyes.

Bad doctors with their own hospital, transplanting kidneys into wealthy patients. Kate wrote this next to "Who?" and drew an asterisk at either end.

She followed another link to the *New York Times* website and almost spit out a mouthful of coffee when she saw a 2004 article titled, "The Organ Trade, A Global Black Market: Tracking the Sale of a Kidney On a Path of Poverty and Hope."

The story chronicled the paths of a desperately ill, forty-eight-year-old Brooklyn woman, and a thirty-eight-year-old Brazilian slum dweller, one of a prostitute's twenty-three children. The article described how Brazilian and Israeli middlemen had recruited the man and paid him $6,000 to fly to Durban, South Africa, and donate a kidney. The Brooklyn woman, aided by a middleman in Israel, paid $60,000 dollars and went to Durban to receive the kidney. The donor did not realize that what he was doing might be illegal until he was asked to sign a document stating he and the recipient were cousins, even though the woman was white, he was black, and neither spoke the other's language. The donor and recipient met at St. Augustine's Hospital, which according to investigators had adopted a don't-ask, don't-tell policy, and the transplant was performed. The operation was a success. The woman's health steadily improved, and she returned to Brooklyn. The Brazilian man went home and upon arrival was robbed of his $6,000.

As a result of an ongoing investigation into the international trade in black market organs, the two middlemen in Brazil had since been jailed. The "Mr. Big" of the Israeli organ brokering syndicate faced charges of tax evasion, and seven individuals from the Durban hospital were arrested. The ring had been dismantled, but, according to experts, it was only a matter of time before a reorganized version emerged in some other country. The only question was which one.

It didn't take long for Kate to find out. In a 2009 article at Newsweek.com, a UC Berkeley anthropologist disclosed the results of more than a decade of undercover work, tracking the worldwide sale of human organs. She had posed as a doctor in some locations, a potential kidney buyer in others. She had immersed herself in an underworld of surgeons, gangsters, and common citizens eager to buy and sell whatever body parts could be bought and sold. She found markets for kidneys, half livers, eyes, skin, and blood. According to the article, an elaborate criminal network spans continents, connecting buyers and sellers, who are then guided to "broker-friendly" hospitals in any number of cities around the world, including New York, Los Angeles, and Philadelphia. A prominent transplant surgeon interviewed by the anthropologist stated that, while they are in the minority, medical centers that adopt a don't-ask, don't-tell policy toward illegal transplants certainly exist in the United States.

There it was—evidence of bad doctors and bad hospitals transplanting organs into those willing to pay, and it was in *Newsweek* and the *Times*. Buzzing with adrenaline, Kate folded her arms and leaned back in her chair. She loved this stage of a case. It was like picking up a book, finding yourself hooked by the end of page one, and you can't wait to find out what was going to happen next. This case had set its hook, and Kate was ready to make the story unfold.

- 23 -

Kate checked her watch. Quarter after two. The doctor, fifteen minutes late. Not so bad for someone in his position. Scarpelli, go figure,
was already annoyed, slumped in his chair with arms crossed and a
pissy expression on his face. Kate got up. She wanted to put as much
space between her and her partner as she could, so she stepped
behind the doctor's desk for a better look at the diplomas and cer-
tificates hanging on the wall. Dr. Ambrose Daniel Perry, Bachelor of
Science, State University of New York, Buffalo. Doctor of Medicine,
New York University. Residency in general surgery, also NYU.
Fellowship in transplantation, University of Pittsburgh. Professor
and Chief of Transplantation Services, New York University
Medical Center.

The obligatory Perry family eight-by-ten was perched on the
corner of the desk. The Mrs. wore a low-cut, black-with-gold-lace
blouse over enhanced breasts. Two teenage boys in dark blazers
and red power ties stood on either side of their mother. Judging
by the flawless skin extending from cleavage to hairline, Mom had
not taken much of a hit bearing and rearing two boys. Kate figured
even if she had a baby tomorrow, breast implants the day after, and
started a regimen of weekly facials, she wouldn't look half as good as
the doctor's wife when her child was sixteen or seventeen.

As she studied the picture, a twinge of regret caught her by
surprise. It had somehow escaped from the maternal-instinct area
of her brain, an area that had been sealed off since her undercover-
hooker days in vice. After arresting hundreds of seemingly normal
married men, many of them in the market for extraordinarily lewd

sex acts, trusting the male species enough to marry one and have his children had fallen off her to-do list.

"Good-looking family," she said.

"Yeah? And?"

Jesus. Typical Scarpelli. He'd been pouting all afternoon, pissed off because the lieutenant had assigned him to such a lame case and made her lead investigator. But it was more than that. Their differences ran deep. She was a woman. He hated women. She was a college graduate. He hated college-educated cops. Her father, as Chief Medical Examiner of New York City, had built the Crime Scene Unit into an elite division of the NYPD and staffed it with detectives, unlike most of the CSUs around the country, which used technicians. For that, her father held great esteem among the investigative branch of the department, and Scarpelli hated anyone who garnered reverence or respect.

But most of all, Scarpelli just couldn't get over the fact that Kate had made Detective 2nd Grade in half the time it had taken him. He called it affirmative action and nepotism, as did the other old-school jerk-offs in the precinct. She called it working hard and being recognized for her efforts. He had said more than once that if it weren't for her father, she'd still be trolling for perverts on West 42nd Street. If she ever did have children, she wouldn't know what to hope for, a boy who might grow into an uninformed pinhead, or a girl who'd have to deal with the uninformed pinheads of the world.

Kate came out from behind the desk and browsed the bookshelves covering the wall on her side of the room. Lots of journals and textbooks, including two authored by the good doctor himself, and, lo and behold, a copy of her father's book, *Wound Patterns and Violent Injury*.

With a rattle of the knob, the door swung open and Perry entered, a lean man in a starched white coat over shirt and tie, steaming white cup in left hand. An air of authority followed him into the room, but not the arrogant I-don't-have-time-for-this kind of authority. More like the confidence-instilling kind. Part of it was the full head of graying hair. Even though the gray was premature—

the doctor's skin looked almost as good as his wife's—it still gave him a soothing grandfather quality. If you were lying in a hospital bed with a flesh-eating disease, Dr. Perry was the type of man you wanted to see walk through the door. While Scarpelli took his time getting up, Kate initiated the handshakes and introductions.

Perry gestured at the cups sitting on the edge of the desk. "I see you both have coffee. Good." He hung his white coat in the corner, sat down, buzzed his secretary, and told her to hold all calls except for Dr. Hacker, to put *him* right through. "One of our liver-resection patients from earlier today is bleeding and will have to return to the OR as soon as they get a room set up." He said this to Kate, giving the impression he had already sized up Scarpelli and wasn't interested in dealing with the guy.

"I'm sorry to hear that," Kate said. "We'll try to move along quickly."

"We'll be fine. My chief resident is very capable. He can start without me." Perry sipped his coffee, then folded his arms on the desk. "So, Detective D'Angelo, your father is Dr. Raymond D'Angelo?"

"He is."

"I'm a big fan. As a resident, I considered a career in trauma surgery. I read his textbook on violent wounds several times and attended a number of his seminars. My favorite was the presentation on impalement injuries. At the time, his collection of photos was the most comprehensive in the world."

"Still is, and he continues to add to it."

"So he hasn't retired?"

"Semiretired. He left the Medical Examiner's office a few years ago. He teaches forensic pathology at Montefiore Medical Center up in the Bronx."

Scarpelli shifted in his chair and let out a half grunt-half groan, his standard response to any discussion of Kate's father. The utterance was not lost on the doctor. A nearly imperceptible grin creased his lips as he took another sip of coffee and sat back in his chair. Bowing to the impatience of the spiteful ass sitting next to her, Kate took the notepad and recorder from her suit jacket. "We should get started. You mind if I record our conversation?"

"Not at all."

Kate recounted Jimmy Gray's story, then told Perry about Michael Smith and the toxicology screen that was positive for a well-known date-rape drug. He leaned on his elbows with hands clasped, riveted by every word. When Kate finished, he asked if she'd be able to find Jimmy Gray and get him to come in for an examination.

"Shouldn't be a problem," Kate said. "So you think we have something here?"

"It definitely sounds suspicious, worth following up. I'll send for Jimmy Gray's medical records, and I'll check with the lab. They hold blood specimens for a few days before discarding them. Maybe we can still do a tox screen."

Kate jotted "Perry – records and blood work" in her notebook and said, "Now, shifting gears a little, are you aware of the urban myth regarding the drugging of men in hotel bars and Vegas casinos, and they wake up in bathtubs full of ice with notes telling them their kidneys have been stolen?"

"Yes. In fact, a few years ago I helped prepare a statement issued by the American Society of Transplant Surgeons characterizing the stories as e-mail propagated rumors."

"But, if they had the expertise and proper equipment, could an individual or individuals do something like that?"

The doctor shook his head. "The whole idea is preposterous. To begin with, it would be impossible to turn a hotel room into an OR. It's not big enough, it's not clean enough, the lighting wouldn't be adequate, and it would be extremely difficult to perform abdominal surgery on a hotel bed. And the bathtub full of ice is ridiculous. There is no reason to cool someone after surgery. We go to great lengths to warm patients and keep them warm. If you submerge a person in an ice bath, the core temperature drops until their heart fibrillates and they die."

As Kate scribbled "urban myth" and drew an X through it, Scarpelli said, "How 'bout a legitimate hospital, Doc? Could you transplant a stolen kidney without raising suspicions?"

Perry leaned back in his chair. "Not likely. It would require a conspiracy among many individuals, not just those actually doing the operation. No single OR exists in a vacuum. It is part of a larger system with checks and balances."

Kate said, "I read an article about a Berkeley anthropologist who believes there are hospitals in the United States that have adopted a don't-ask, don't-tell policy toward illegal transplants."

"I've read it. She has indeed amassed a large body of information linking medical centers around the world to black-market organ buyers and sellers, but her data has been criticized for being anecdotal, based upon verbal reports and field interviews. She has failed to produce any hard evidence. Personally, I don't believe that what she has reported is possible in this country."

Scarpelli said, "Could someone build their own hospital, like a mini hospital?"

"I suppose, but the logistics would get very complicated. At a minimum you'd need an operating room, an ICU-type bed for the recipient, and a ward-type bed for the donor. You'd also need a lab and a blood bank. And I haven't even touched upon the process for matching donor and recipient, which is exceedingly complex. Even on a small scale, to harvest and transplant kidneys outside an established medical center would be a daunting endeavor."

The phone rang. Perry leaned forward and checked the caller ID. "My chief resident. I'm sorry, but I need to take this." He picked up the receiver. "What's going on, Paul?"

Perry listened attentively for a moment, then his face filled with blood and became grossly distorted as if someone had driven a nail into his temple. He screamed, "Who's in charge over there, you or the anesthesiologist?"

Kate shrunk into her chair. Scarpelli sat up and straightened his tie.

"That's right, you are. You're a surgeon, so act like one and tell anesthesia not to wait for me, to go ahead and put the goddamned patient to sleep. I'll be there when I get there. I can't believe we're even having this conversation."

The doctor placed the phone back in its cradle as though he had just confirmed a dinner date with his wife. As the natural color returned to his face, he smiled and said, "Every once in a while you have to hand these guys their asses so they don't forget who they are."

Kate returned his smile with an awkward one of her own, unsure of what to say. Cops were no strangers to verbal conflict. It was part of their daily existence whether they were shouting at each other, shouting at perps, or getting yelled at by their superiors, families of victims, or girlfriends of suspects. But something about Perry's outburst made her uncomfortable. He was a mature man of education and stature verbally beating the shit out of a younger man of education and stature when the younger man was doing what was expected of him, playing by the rules, staying loyal to the system. Kate had always believed that the medical profession was loftier than all others, that it rewarded good intentions and loyalty. Maybe she was wrong.

Scarpelli cleared his throat. "As operations go, is this one—the removal of the kidney—is it difficult to perform?"

"You mean the harvest? No. Not if it's a procedure you do often. There are pitfalls, of course. You have to ligate sizable arteries and veins to remove the organ, and there's the risk of uncontrolled bleeding if the ligation is not done carefully."

"Could somebody other than a surgeon do it—a medical student maybe?"

"No. Not a medical student, but a fourth- or fifth-year resident with transplant experience would possess adequate technical skill."

"What's the minimum number of people required for a kidney transplant?" Kate asked.

"For the surgery itself you'd need a surgeon, a surgical assistant, a scrub nurse, a circulating nurse, and an anesthesiologist—so five individuals. For post-op care you'd need a nurse or two and some ancillary staff to do lab work and the like."

"What about the harvest?"

"The same."

The phone rang again. Kate braced herself for another Hulk mutation.

Perry picked up the receiver. "Hello, Donna."

No facial contortions. No bursting capillaries. It appeared Donna was not going to get her ass handed to her.

"Of course I'm aware of the new policy. I helped write it. Don't worry. I'll be there before he's ready to cut skin." Perry hung up and said, "I'm sorry, but they're waving their policy B.S. in my face. Is there anything else I can tell you?"

Kate thumbed through her notebook, quickly reviewing the who, what, where, how, and why. The who: experienced surgeon, or properly trained resident, and five to ten others. The what: victims given a date-rape drug, kidneys stolen. The where: unclear but not a hotel room or legitimate hospital. The how: many complex steps requiring a conspiracy among individuals with significant resources. The why: money.

"I do have one last question," Kate said. "A few years ago, a man put one of his own kidneys up for sale on eBay."

Perry nodded. "Yes, I remember."

"Are there people who'd pay millions of dollars for a kidney?"

"I don't see why not. If I'm slowly dying from a relentless, progressive disease and I have the cash, I'd certainly fork it over as long as I know the organ is good and the surgeon is competent." He stood and reached for his white coat. "Have Jimmy Gray come see me. And I'll follow up on that tox screen and get back to you."

- 24 -

David backed through the OR door, holding his dripping hands out in front of him. Meiling gave him a towel, and after he dried off, she helped him gown and glove. The victim had been prepped and draped, the instrument stand positioned near the surgical field. Aleksandr waited at the operating table. In the corner, the fat man read a newspaper. Other than the ruffle of turning pages, the beeping of the heart monitor, and the blowing of the ventilator, the room was quiet, a snapshot of the first harvest. Everyone had assumed their positions, and a calm efficiency had replaced the turmoil of subduing an agitated homeless man and putting him under general anesthesia.

As David waited for the go-ahead from Veejay, he felt his own pulse, measuring his heartbeat against the slow beeps of the monitor. His heart rate was slightly faster, but much slower than one would expect for someone in his position—a position forcing him to violate a human body, a position so inconceivable that the only way to accept it was to shut off the higher centers of the brain where fear, guilt, and anger originate, and function on a lower level, a level governed by rote and reflex.

He peered over the drape. Veejay nodded. David took the scalpel from Meiling, pushed it into the skin just below the twelfth rib, and pulled, gently curving the incision as he drew the knife toward himself. Without looking up or saying a word, he exchanged the scalpel for the electrocautery device, dried up the bleeding, and dissected through the subcutaneous tissues.

With each buzz of the cautery, wisps of smoke curled from the wound and passed through his mask, filling his nose with the smell of liquefied fat, and then charred muscle, the latissimus dorsi. Each layer he divided would cause pain. Every movement, even breathing, would remind the homeless man of the cruelty one person can wage upon another, and for that and many other reasons, David had to find a way out of this nightmare. He'd thought it over countless times in the days since the first harvest, but came up with nothing. He couldn't walk away. That would put himself and Cassandra in danger. He couldn't call the police. That would serve up his team, not the person or persons pulling the strings. He had to follow the kidney, right into the hands of the implanting surgeon. But how?

He inspected the ends of the divided muscle, buzzed the persistent bleeders, then grasped the lumbodorsal fascia with a Kocher clamp. Aleksandr placed a second Kocher an inch from the tip of David's, and they both lifted. With the cautery device, David burned a hole in the fascia, giving him access to the retroperitoneal space. He enlarged the incision, cauterized everything that bled, and placed a self-retaining retractor. He worked the blades of the retractor deep into the wound, pushing back fat and bowels and anything else that encroached into the space.

David knew he couldn't follow the kidney in the Hollywood tradition, in a car, hanging back, darting in and out of traffic. The fat man would leave with the organ as soon as it was packed in ice. It could be halfway to its destination before David had the wound closed and the patient off the table. And there was something else to consider. Once on ice, kidneys can survive outside the body for up to twenty-four hours. It was entirely possible they were flying it out of state, or to another continent for that matter.

With his index finger, David bluntly dissected a thin layer of retroperitoneal fat, exposing Gerota's fascia. He cut through the dense, fibrous Gerota's with a pair of scissors and resumed the blunt dissection of another thin layer of fat. He recalled performing nephrectomies on the overweight and obese. Many of those patients had layer upon layer of fat surrounding their abdominal organs, making exposure complicated and risky. Unfortunately, his steady forward progress in this case was due to poor nutrition.

Using both sharp and blunt dissection, he freed the kidney of its soft-tissue attachments. With the organ now fully mobilized, he identified the renal artery and vein, and the ureter. He placed two clamps on the ureter, cut it with scissors, and tied off the ends with silk ties. Aleksandr then lifted the kidney, putting the artery and vein under tension. This was the crux of the operation. Too much tension and the vessels could tear, resulting in massive hemorrhage. Not enough and David would have a difficult time exposing them. Aleksandr had a soft touch. He kept the vessels under perfect traction as David trimmed away the fat and encircled them with red Silastic loops. The kidney was ready for explantation.

Meiling handed David a long vascular clamp. He opened the jaws, positioned them above and below the artery, and started to squeeze but stopped. He silently pleaded for a merciful twist of fate to intervene, a phone call saying the organ was no longer needed, but nothing disturbed the stillness. He had no choice. He snapped the clamp shut and put another on the vein. Meiling placed a pair of scissors in his hand, and with a squeeze of his thumb and first two fingers, David divided the artery, then the vein. Aleksandr lifted the kidney out of the wound and set it in a pan. They looked at each other for the first time since the procedure began. Everything was covered except their eyes, but that was all they needed to exchange looks of sorrow.

They had stolen their second kidney in as many weeks. Soon they'd be forced to steal a third and a fourth. David had to do something. As a surgical resident, he had held the conviction that violating the human body was a privilege, and except under lifesaving circumstances, that privilege could only be granted by the inhabitant. Nothing had been granted here. These men had been raped and pillaged not only of body parts, but also of dignity, trust, and perhaps their lives. He had to know where the organs were going. He had to follow the next kidney. But that would be a thousand times more difficult than following an Alzheimer's patient through the streets of Manhattan.

Unless ... he could chip it.

Of course. A GPS chip.

If stolen cars and Alzheimer's patients can be tracked by satellite, why not a kidney?

- 25 -

Andrew Turnbull's jaw tightened with enough force to crack a walnut. He had exited the glass doors of the main building and started across the parking lot when he saw it. The one thing that could spike his blood pressure. The one thing he dreaded every time he parked his car. A door ding. He interrupted his quick pace and stopped beside the Porsche, then moved slowly, up and down, front to back, using the low angle of the morning sun to delineate the full extent of the damage. It was deep, easily noticeable, but the paint wasn't chipped, making it a candidate for paintless dent repair. It must've happened the other night at the Elbow Room in Newark—the last time he had parked in an unprotected spot. What really pissed him off wasn't the two hundred dollars he'd have to pay, or the time out of his schedule. It was the fact that door dings were completely avoidable if the idiots of the world had respect for the property of others. He took a last look and headed for the gym, shaking his head.

As he walked along the perimeter of the basketball court, the hard soles of his dress shoes sent clicks and clacks echoing among the rafters and walls. One of the researchers, Cynthia, by the looks of her smooth stride and bobbing ponytail, passed overhead on the running track. He appreciated those employees who used his facility to stay fit, and detested anyone who defiled their body with toxins and inactivity. The elegant design of the human organism was unparalleled, and it disgusted him to think that a growing proportion of the population was abusing the gift of good health and encasing itself in fat. If there was anything he hated more than stupid people, it was fat stupid people. The sight of them standing in line at a fast-food restaurant was enough to make him want to shout at them and tell them they were a pathetic lot, wasting oxygen that the gifted and intelligent people of the world needed.

The one exception, of course, was Abercrombie. Yes, he was fat, but he was far from stupid. In fact, if his insights into alternative ATP metabolism were to prove correct—and they'd have an answer soon—he would not only have saved NuLife and launched Turnbull toward his date with greatness, but it would be one of the greatest discoveries in the history of medicine and physiology.

On the far side of the gym, he entered a carpeted hallway that led him past a racquetball court, a combined weight room and cardiovascular studio, and the men's and women's locker rooms. At the end of the hall stood a windowless metal door. He swiped his ID card and entered a code on the keypad. The lock clicked open.

A short corridor led to another set of locker rooms. In the men's, Turnbull put on scrubs, shoe covers, and a hat. He then exited through the back and entered the OR anteroom where he leaned against the cold steel of the scrub sink and looked in the window. The patient, a twenty-two-year-old kid from Dubai with polycystic kidney disease, was prepped and draped. Jill, the scrub nurse, was organizing her instrument tray. Dr. Daniel Harris, the anesthesiologist, was de-airing syringes. On the back table sat a metal basin of iced saline. Submerged in the saline was an AB+, six-antigen-match kidney with a six-million-dollar price tag. A six-antigen match despite the rare blood type—the organ would be worth every penny to the boy and his family.

Turnbull tied a mask over his face, tore open a Betadine brush, and started to scrub from fingertips to elbows. Seeing him at the sink, the circulating nurse, Stephanie, put down the carton of Ray-Tec sponges she was about to open. She looked at Jill, then Dr. Harris. They each nodded. She came out and joined Turnbull at the sink.

"Everything okay?" he asked.

"Yes, but there's something we wanted to ask you. We thought maybe we should do it now before the case starts, so, you know, there aren't any distractions."

"Of course. What is it?"

"This is our third transplant … and … well … it's just that …" She nervously glanced through the window.

He knew what she was going to ask but gave her a moment to frame her question. He could not afford to lose his OR team now. It had taken time to find, screen, and recruit them, time and effort he did not want to replicate. He wondered if he should appeal to their sense of duty or just barge into the room and level threats. He rather enjoyed watching subordinates succumb to pressure, observing the internal struggle as they weighed equally undesirable alternatives. But he also understood the utility of positive motivation and instilling a sense of control, real or perceived, in one's ancillary staff.

Stephanie turned from the window. "It's just that we need to know how many more transplants we'll be doing. In the beginning you said three or four."

"Yes, I did. Why don't I finish scrubbing, and I'll speak with all of you?"

Stephanie thanked him and went back to her sponges.

He scrubbed each finger a few more times, rinsed off, and backed through the door. After gowning and gloving, he moved to the right side of the table. Jill rolled her instrument stand to the left side. Neither nurse made eye contact.

Turnbull peered over the raised drape that separated the operative field from the anesthesia machine, and checked the monitors. Heart rate, 57. Blood pressure, 110/66. Oxygen saturation, 100 percent. All consistent with deep anesthesia. He grabbed the sterile handles of the three overhead lights and converged the beams upon the surgical field—the right lower quadrant of the abdomen.

Turnbull asked for the knife, told Dan Harris he was starting, and made a linear incision two fingerbreadths above and parallel to the groin crease. A big incision for a young man, but this was a kidney transplant, not plastic surgery. He traded the scalpel for the electrocautery device, dried up the bleeding in the subcutaneous fat, and started dividing the abdominal wall musculature. The kid's muscle tissue had the tensile strength of warm butter, as was often the case with a chronic, protein-wasting illness.

With the incision completed, Turnbull asked Jill to bring over the basin containing the donor organ. She set the basin on the draped area of the upper abdomen and held it steady.

"Daniel? Stephanie? May I have your attention for a moment?"

Stephanie came up behind Jill. Daniel looked over the drape.

"While I was scrubbing, Stephanie posed a question. I'll get to it in a minute, but first I want to show you something." He formed a cradle with his hands, lifted the kidney from the iced saline, and held up the fist-sized organ the way a nurse holds up a newborn for the mother and father. "I realize none of you have degrees in transplant immunology, so I'll keep it simple. This is an AB+ kidney. The young man under the drapes is AB+. The six major antigens expressed by this kidney match the six major antigens expressed by the patient. We call this a six-antigen match. The only perfect match is between identical twins. When transplanting organs between nonidentical twins, siblings, parents and their children, or unrelated donors and recipients, the six-antigen match is as close to perfect as we can get." He glanced at each of the three faces as if he were lecturing medical students. "Are you with me so far?"

They said yes.

Turnbull put the kidney in the basin, had Jill move it to the back table and asked her for the Bookwalter retractor. She handed him an oval-shaped, stainless-steel ring. He positioned it on the abdomen, centered the wound within the ring, and attached a couple of three-inch blades. "So, what does a six-antigen match mean to this young man?" He laid a folded lap sponge over a layer of fat. "First, with his rare blood type, the odds of receiving a six-antigen match through the proper channels is essentially zero." He placed one of the retractor blades on the lap sponge, maneuvered the tip of the blade deep into the wound, and secured it to the ring. "Second, the greater the number of antigens matched, the smaller the chance of rejection. The smaller the chance of rejection, the lower the level of immunosuppression drugs required. In other words, he'll be spared the scourge of high-dose steroids, the toxicity of cyclosporine, and the plethora of opportunistic diseases that attack immunosuppressed patients."

Turnbull positioned another retractor blade over the inguinal ligament and identified the femoral canal. "Now, what does this have to do with Stephanie's question?" He crimped layers of lymphatic tissue with medium and large clips, and divided the fat-like tissue with scissors. "We've developed a unique screening process that allows us not only to match donors and recipients who have rare blood types, but also to match the six major antigens. For this to happen under the UNOS system is nearly impossible. Here in our clinic, the six-antigen match is something we can guarantee." He stopped dissecting and looked up. "I'll say that again because it's important. We can guarantee a six-antigen match for patients with rare blood types." He resumed his dissection. "As you can imagine, we can command a significant fee for this service, so as long as we have donors willing to sell and recipients willing to pay, we'll carry on until NuLife Corporation has the operating capital it needs to accomplish its mission."

He listened for sighs, grunts, groans, or other sounds of dissent. He heard nothing but the slow beeping of the heart monitor and the crescendo-decrescendo blowing of the ventilator. "Now, if the ethics, morals, and legalities are a problem, consider this. We all know the buying and selling of human organs is illegal. Many activities between consenting adults are, but that doesn't necessarily make them morally or ethically wrong."

Turnbull finished dividing the last of the lymphatics and started to dissect the sheath of connective tissue encasing the iliac vessels. "In fact, there's an ongoing debate over paid organ donation. Many ethicists are in favor of it. And regarding morality, the long-term benefit of what we're doing has resolved my moral dilemma, and should ease yours as well, if you have one."

The kid was thin, which made for quick mobilization of the vessels. Turnbull passed red Silastic vessel loops around the artery, blue around the vein, and snapped hemostats onto the ends of the loops, then looked up. Stephanie was still standing behind Jill. Daniel had turned his back and was pouring isoflurane into the vaporizer. Turnbull folded his arms across his chest and began to recite parts of a speech he had given to a group of venture capitalists not so long ago. If they had funded him without demanding controlling shares in his company, he would not be standing over a kid from Dubai. "All of the money generated by this endeavor is going directly into research that will solve one of medicine's most daunting problems. The technology that will emerge from this laboratory will save countless lives around the globe. It will cause an epic shift in the battle against illness and death. It will eclipse the discovery of penicillin. Now, even though personal issues led each of you here, you are a key part of this effort. Through your presence here today, you're contributing to one of the great breakthroughs in medical history."

Daniel turned toward the surgical field. "Yes, we know this is for the greater good, and we're all thankful to be part of it, but we're also concerned that the more of these cases we do, the greater our exposure. It's like surgeons contracting hepatitis C or HIV from infected patients. On a per case basis the risk is small. Do enough cases, the risk grows."

"We've taken measures—very sophisticated measures—to minimize our exposure."

"But the risk is not zero."

"No, and I never promised it would be. I said the risk would be negligible."

"Okay. Whatever. But still, you led us to believe that after three or four transplants we would have fulfilled our obligation."

"As physicians and nurses does your commitment lie with me? Or to those who suffer from end-stage organ failure? I suggest it lies with the hundreds of thousands of patients waiting for replacement organs, and the second chance at life those organs afford, and by funding this lab, you are fulfilling that commitment."

"That's all fine and good," Daniel said, "but here in the real world, we had an agreement, and now you're telling us you are not going to honor it."

"Maybe I need to remind you that once our association ends, you'll be able to pay off your mortgages, put your kids through college, care for your aging parents, and retire young. If you decide to take an early leave, all of that will be sacrificed. And, have you considered the individual circumstances, or should I say difficulties, that brought each of you here in the first place? If one isn't careful, these problems can be magnified to the point where the money becomes meaningless." He looked over the drape. "Is that real-world enough for you, Dan?"

Each man held the other's glare, surgical masks and hats partitioning the eyes from the rest of the face. The heart monitor beeped. The ventilator cycled. The instruments clinked as Jill rearranged them. Finally, Daniel Harris turned away, flipping switches on the anesthesia machine that did not need to be flipped.

Turnbull looked at Stephanie. "Any other questions?"

She shook her head.

He turned to Jill.

She said no.

"Good. Now let's implant this kidney and get out of here. Stephanie, scrub in so Jill can help me sew these vessels together."

While Stephanie scrubbed, Jill spread out an icy lap sponge near the wound and moved the basin onto the field. Turnbull removed the kidney from the pan, wrapped it with the icy lap, and examined it. The artery and vein had been meticulously cleaned of connective tissue and fat, and divided close to their origins on the donor aorta and vena cava, giving Turnbull plenty of length to work with. To his delight, the ureter had *not* been skeletonized of its connective tissue—a common mistake made by resident surgeons. Instead, the surrounding tissue had been nicely preserved. Once again, David McBride had done exemplary work.

Turnbull hadn't seen McBride in over two years, and until the last few weeks, hadn't given him much thought. Sure, their association did not end well, and given the chance, David would put a bullet in his back, but Turnbull still felt pride in having produced a would-be world-class talent. If only McBride had shared Turnbull's vision: a world where an endless supply of human organs are grown in the laboratory, thus ending the mismatch between donor organ supply and demand. The realization of this vision was within reach, and Turnbull would finally receive the worldwide attention and acclaim he deserved. He'd stand above the rest of the medical profession as one of the titans of his era, and if McBride had kept his mouth shut, he could have gone along for the ride. Unfortunately, David McBride turned out to be one of the gray people, a mere mortal of average intelligence, unable to see the utility of bending a few rules to serve the masses. He had to adhere to the notion of right and wrong, and in the process, he fucked himself.

Stephanie returned to the room, and as she gowned and gloved herself, Jill moved the Mayo stand over the patient's chest, then assumed the assistant's position. Turnbull trimmed the end of the donor vein, clamped the recipient vein, and started sewing the two together.

- 26 -

The GPS transmitter in the back pocket of David's scrub pants was a bit smaller than a pack of cigarettes and about one-third the thickness. The guy who sold it to him said the battery would last ten days. David needed less than twelve hours. He tied a mask around his face and went into the OR.

Veejay and the nurses were making their usual preparations. The fat man was on the way with the donor. Aleksandr was changing. The big Russian was smoking somewhere in the warehouse. David went around to the back of the room, got down on his knees, and slid the ice chest out from under the instrument table. He made sure the top was latched and flipped it over. The sound of shifting ice caught Meiling's attention. She came to the table and peered down at him.

"I need a scalpel," he said, "something big, a ten blade, and a Weitlaner retractor."

"What for?"

"No questions. Just get 'em."

She stared at him for a moment, then retrieved the instruments. He took them in his bare hands without touching her sterile gloves, put the retractor on the floor, and used the scalpel to make a three-inch incision in the base of the cooler, in line with one of the walls.

"What are you doing?" Meiling asked, glancing at the door.

"Yes," said Veejay, "what exactly are you doing?"

David raised himself higher on his knees and looked out the window. Nobody there, but Amy and Veejay had joined Meiling. Too many people in one spot. They'd call attention to him. He grabbed the retractor, placed the teeth inside the cut plastic, and spread the edges apart. Without looking up, he said, "I'm gonna find out where this kidney is going. Now, go back to what you were doing before someone comes." With the scalpel, he cut out a rectangular chunk of Styrofoam.

The elevator groaned to life. David couldn't remember which floor it was on, if it would go down before coming up, or if it was already ascending. Veejay and Amy hurried away.

Meiling stayed. "Please, David, don't do this. Twelve people depend on me."

"She's right," Veejay said. "You don't know who you are dealing with. Do not make any problems for us, or yourself."

David pushed the GPS unit into the hole. It didn't fit. "Listen," he said as he scraped the bottom of the pocket with the scalpel. "I've tried to get answers from the three of you, but you either don't know anything or won't say anything, so I'm gonna get my own answers."

The elevator clanked to a halt. David tried the transmitter a second time. It still protruded by a half inch. He wiped sweat from his brow with his sleeve and gouged out more Styrofoam, but he couldn't get the chunks out of the hole.

The elevator started again. It was coming up.

"Meiling, DeBakey forceps, quickly."

She did as he asked. He plucked the pieces out of the pocket and inserted the transmitter. A perfect fit. He popped the retractor loose. The memory of the plastic brought the edges back together. The incision would be visible if someone flipped the thing over and carefully examined the bottom, but they'd have no reason to do so. David turned the ice chest upright, pushed it under the table, and stood just in time to see the big Russian in the window, tying on a mask.

And then he remembered. He hadn't activated the device.

The door opened halfway and stopped, the gurney not properly lined up. The buffoons, they were stuck. David waved at Veejay and loudly whispered, "Buy me some time."

Veejay froze, then hit a couple of switches, setting off two alarms. David dropped to his knees and grabbed the ice chest. Veejay blocked the door, said something about a gas leak. David flipped the cooler, picked up the retractor he'd left under the table, and opened the incision in the plastic. With the forceps, he removed the transmitter. With a single tip of the forceps, he poked a tiny button inside a hole in the case. A red pinpoint of light began flashing.

While Veejay argued with the big Russian and the fat man, David slid the transmitter back into the pocket, and as quietly as he could, turned over the cooler.

He stood as the Russians bullied their way into the room. They said the donor was fighting, and they didn't care about gas. Veejay gave up and switched off the alarms. The fat man looked David up and down. David gave himself the once-over. Sweat had soaked through his scrubs at the armpits and chest, and probably the rim of his cap.

"You were on hand and knees, Doctor," the fat man said. "Lose something?"

David held up the Weitlaner retractor and DeBakey forceps. "They fell on the floor. I was picking them up so Amy could re-sterilize them in the autoclave."

"So much exertion for two little pieces of metal?"

"They went way under the instrument table. Very hard to find."

The fat man held David's gaze as the big Russian positioned the gurney next to the table.

With the conclusion of the stare-down and the departure of the fat man, Veejay caught David's attention and pointed at the gurney. David looked over, and what he saw sickened him beyond revulsion. On the stretcher lay a boy, no older than fifteen or sixteen. The boy's head was too small for his body, and his eyes were set far apart. His ears sat low, his jaw underdeveloped, the bridge of his nose broad and flat. The boy looked up at David with big brown eyes and smiled. Sadly, or perhaps mercifully, it was the smile of an infant, a smile not based in happiness or pleasure but a mere reflex triggered by the presence of a being with like features standing over him. David laid his hand on the boy's arm, and his smile widened, and he verbalized a soft mewing sound, like that of a cat. David's mind raced back to medical school and his pediatrics rotation, to the myriad genetic syndromes he had either seen on the wards or studied in textbooks. Many presented with microcephaly, wide-set eyes, low-slung ears and profound mental retardation, but only one exhibited the soft cry of a kitten—the *cri du chat* syndrome.

David pushed through the OR door, slamming it into the metal sink and filling the upper floor with a metallic boom. The fat man and the big Russian turned around as David stormed toward them, but before he could open his mouth, he found himself lying in a heap on the floor, unable to take a breath, his abdominal wall on fire where the big Russian had landed a blow with his cinder-block fist.

When his diaphragm started moving again, David pushed himself into a half-sitting position and looked up at the two men towering over him. "I will not steal a kidney from a profoundly retarded child," he said.

The fat man slipped the white envelope out of his coat pocket and said, "Yes, Doctor, you will," as he flicked photos of Cassandra at David the way one flicks playing cards into a hat.

- 27 -

The ride home was nauseating. David slumped in the backseat, loathing himself for what he had just done to a helpless child, seething with hate for the big Russian, the fat man, and their boss, whoever that was. The only bright spot? He'd soon be sitting in front of a computer, tracking the kidney right into the hands of the sick, demented fuck who was waiting to sew it into the recipient.

He climbed the stairs two at a time and started down the hallway on the balls of his feet. All was quiet, as it should be at four in the morning, but the degenerate pit bull in 4-D was known to go off at any time, day or night, with little or no provocation. He passed the dog's door with a pounding heart and a light step. The calm remained undisturbed. He approached his own door with trembling fingers and sweaty palms. There was no way to quietly turn the locks that kept the scum out and his father in, so David took a moment to settle himself. He wiped his hands on his pants, carefully inserted the keys, and minimized the clinks and clanks as the cylinders turned and the bolts opened. Cassandra was a deep sleeper, and this week she was working the three-to-eleven shift, but still, this was one night he did not want to wake her.

David let himself in and locked the door as quietly as he had unlocked it. After shedding his coat and shoes, he went over to the bed. Cassandra's breathing was slow and deep, and as far as he could tell in the low light, her expression was that of stillness and peace.

After squeezing between the foot of the bed and the TV stand, he sat at the desk, swiveled the monitor away from Cassandra, turned off the speakers, and turned on the computer. The machine was old and slow—maddening, in fact—so he went to the kitchen and grabbed a beer. After bunching a dishtowel on top of the can, he slid his finger underneath and popped the top. He took a long drink, a deep breath, another long drink, and returned to the desk.

He opened the browser and typed hiddenwitness.com in the address bar. The home page appeared, and he signed in. The next page gave him a personal welcome and offered such options as "my account," "products," "security alerts," and "GPS tracking." He clicked "real-time tracking" and waited, and waited. He sipped his beer and drummed the hardwood floor with his heels. Real-time tracking. He could hardly believe that in a moment he'd know, to within a ten-foot radius, the kidney's location. An odd combination of giddiness, satisfaction, and fear overcame him. He felt like a kid playing a spy game, and took satisfaction in the fact that he had been forced into an intolerable situation, and by his own hand, was about to get himself out of it. He'd lost control, he was taking it back.

But he was also afraid. He was thwarting the efforts of a well-organized, far-reaching conspiracy. Reprisals would follow if they figured out he brought them down. He looked over at Cassandra's silhouette and asked himself once again if he was doing the right thing, and once again the answer to his question was *I don't know, but I have no choice.* He could not invade the body of another drugged homeless man, or a developmentally disabled fifteen-year-old, or whatever the sick bastards had planned for next time.

The monitor flickered. David turned to find a street map of Manhattan. He studied it, then sat back and marveled at the technology. From downtown to midtown, a red line traced the route of the transmitter, each stop marked, time in and time out, five minutes here, ten minutes there. The route went north, south, east, and west, seemingly at random, and after an hour of going in circles, the line crossed through the Holland Tunnel and into New Jersey.

His feet drummed faster as he enlarged the map and zoomed in on the leading end of the red line. Every few seconds, a pulsing cursor jumped ahead several millimeters. He was following the kidney in real time, right to the transplant facility and into the hands of the implanting surgeon.

He lifted his beer to his mouth and noticed how badly he was shaking. Even in the early days of his internship, when doing his first surgical cases with the most malignant attending surgeons, he never shook like this.

The cursor approached Jackson Township on State Route 677. He zoomed out to a more expansive view. Route 677 connected a succession of small towns in the north-central part of the state. By the looks of the map, there wasn't much else in the area. He zoomed back in. The line had moved past Jackson Township and was heading for Edwardsville.

From down in the basement came the faint clanking of pipes. The heat had kicked on, and it wouldn't take long for the banging and hissing to climb four floors to their apartment and the radiator a few feet from Cassandra's head.

The cursor had passed Edwardsville and entered a section of winding road, making a number of sharp turns, then it stopped. It didn't turn left. It didn't turn right. It didn't move forward or go back. It just sat there, pulsing.

The pipes banged louder as the head of steam worked its way up the walls. Cassandra stayed still. The line didn't budge. The car was sitting on the road, or beside it. Maybe they had blown a tire. Maybe another vehicle was coming to meet them.

The steam reached their floor. The radiator clanked. The valve hissed. The cursor pulsed. Cassandra turned, but her breathing remained rhythmic and deep. A dialogue box opened in the middle of the screen. Blinking red letters informed David that communication between the GPS unit and the satellite had been interrupted, the signal lost. David shuddered. They had found it. They found the transmitter and turned it off. And they'd know he put it there.

Down on the street a siren blared. Cassandra lifted her head and peered at him through bleary eyes.

"David? What are you doing?"

"Nothing. I'm logged onto the lab computer, reviewing blood work on one of the sheep."

"I thought you were working with pigs."

"No … I mean yes. I meant to say go back to sleep."

"What time is it?"

"Almost four thirty."

She murmured something, and her head fell into the pillow. He checked the cursor. The pulsing had ceased. He sat back and tried to think. Maybe he needed to give it a few minutes. Maybe hills or valleys or atmospheric phenomena had interfered with the signal the way they interfered with FM radio stations. He convinced himself to relax, let his arms hang loosely from his shoulders, stopped his heels from pounding the floor.

A ring sliced through the silence. He jumped, then sat paralyzed. The phone rang again, Mr. White's cell phone. He picked it up and said hello, the word meek in his dry throat.

"Dr. McBride," Mr. White said. "I have to say, I'm impressed by your ingenuity. Unfortunately, the ice chest containing the organ you so expertly harvested tipped over as the car travelled a serpentine stretch of road. When the driver stopped, he noticed the slightest irregularity on the bottom of the overturned chest—a very thin slice in the plastic, something only a surgeon could do so cleanly."

Cassandra climbed out of bed and came toward David. He fumbled with the mouse and minimized the screen. She shrugged her shoulders, mouthed, "Who is that?" and passed into the bathroom. Once she closed the door, he took the phone to the kitchen, and in a hushed tone he said, "Sorry, Mr. White, but I don't know—"

"Come on, David. Of course you know what I'm talking about. Fortunately for you and your wife, your services are still very much needed, so we will let this incident go. But heed my warning: If you try a similar stunt in the future, the consequences will be severe."

The line went dead. The toilet flushed. David hurried back to the desk.

Cassandra exited the bathroom. "What was that all about?"

"I had to call the lab and tell them to run the blood STAT."

"But someone called here."

"Uh ... yeah, I called them first and got voice mail. I asked them to call me back."

David put his fingers to his lips and gestured for Cassandra to sit on the corner of the sofa bed. He took a pencil and a legal pad from the desk, and across the top he wrote:

We are in serious danger.
Don't make a sound. Don't say anything.
They are listening.

Cassandra scrunched her face in confusion. David held up a finger, requesting she give him a minute, and with painstaking effort proceeded to write out everything that had transpired since he'd met Mr. White in the park four weeks ago. He described the initial meetings, the photos of her, the threats and invasion of their privacy, the homeless men, the severely disabled teenager, and the three kidneys he'd stolen from them. He told her how he had planted the GPS tracking device and that his effort had failed, thus the phone call a few minutes ago, and as she read the pages, fear drained the color from her face and the steadiness from her hands.

She took the pad and pencil and asked why he hadn't called the police.

He didn't know who was pulling the strings, he explained, and therefore faced certain retribution should he try to seek outside help and fail.

She asked what he was going to do next.

He had no idea, he replied, but he wanted her to go away for a while.

No way, she wrote. She wasn't going anywhere. She'd follow her regular schedule, stick to well-traveled routes and public places, and she'd be okay.

He reiterated that he wanted her somewhere safe, but he knew she had already made up her mind, and he'd be unable to change it.

- 28 -

Kate leaned back in the industrial gray chair and glanced at her watch. Five fifteen p.m. She thought back to her school days and tried to recall the rules. If she remembered correctly, you waited ten minutes for assistant professors, fifteen for associate professors, and twenty for full professors. But what about the chief of the department? How long did you wait for a guy who could take out your old liver and put in a new one?

Scarpelli wandered over to the bookshelves, removed her father's book on traumatic wounds and thumbed through the pages, then stopped, disgust contorting his face. "Holy Christ, there's a kid in here with a pool cue going up his nose and coming out the top of his head, and he has a dumb grin on his face. That ain't right."

Kate knew the photo and the story behind it. A twenty-something-year-old was playing pool in a bar and leaning on his cue when a brawl erupted. Someone was thrown onto the man's back, and the cue was driven up his nose and out his skull. "What's not right, the dumb grin?"

"No, that he's alive. The stick must've gone through his brain."

"It did, but it traversed the frontal lobes and missed the vital areas. He ended up with a brain abscess, and his emotions were out of whack, but he eventually recovered."

Scarpelli closed the book and looked over at Kate. "You have a knack for this stuff. Why'd you drop out of medical school, anyway?"

Kate turned in her chair. "I didn't drop out."

"You got accepted and decided not to go."

Heat climbed her neck and invaded her face. "It's not the same thing."

"It is the same thing. I mean, what the fuck, Kate? You could be making six figures and living in Westchester. And doctors don't get shot ... well, not as much as cops."

"I never intended to be a doctor. I wanted to be a detective since I was thirteen and saw my first autopsy—a murder case. The only reason I went through PreMed was to prove to my father I could get accepted into medical school."

"Who doesn't wanna be a doctor, especially if it's laid out on a silver platter?"

"I don't, and nothing's been laid out for me. I've worked for everything I have."

Scarpelli started to open his fat mouth. Kate was about to put her fist into it. A muffled voice outside the door, followed by a click of the knob, stopped them both.

Dr. A. Daniel Perry entered. Kate composed herself as she stood, said hello and gave him a quick handshake.

Scarpelli returned the book to the shelf. "Hey, Doc. Hope you don't mind."

"Not at all. See anything interesting?" Perry set his coffee on the desk, hung up his white coat and took a seat.

"Plenty. Why did you pass up all that gruesome stuff for transplants?"

"Bad hours. Most trauma hits the door late at night or early in the morning, and a great deal of it is alcohol, drug or gang related. In general, it's an unsavory group of patients."

Perry sat back and laced his fingers on his chest. "Sorry to rush you over so late in the day, but I have some very interesting findings to report."

"It's actually early for us," Kate said. "We're working the four-to-one shift."

"Good. I'll start with Mr. Gray."

Kate pulled out her notebook. Scarpelli did likewise.

"I saw him in my clinic this afternoon, and I have to say, he tells a compelling story. He gives no history consistent with chronic urinary tract infection, kidney stones or tumor, nor does he recall undergoing a workup for those conditions. And the lab had enough blood to run a tox screen. It was positive for Rohypnol."

Kate felt the process-of-discovery buzz kick in. She wrote "healthy kidneys" and "roofies" in her notebook.

"I also spoke with one of our psychiatrists. He said Rohypnol is a sedative hypnotic and has no role in the treatment of paranoid schizophrenia. So, bottom line, if Jimmy Gray is a reliable historian, and I believe he is, there were no surgical indications for the removal of his kidney, nor was there a medical indication for the presence of Rohypnol in his system." Perry leaned back and paused, seemingly for dramatic effect. "Now, for the big break detectives are always searching for. I examined Mr. Gray's incision. Whoever closed it used an unusual technique, a technique I've seen before, in this institution."

Kate gave Scarpelli a look that said, *I knew this wasn't a lame case.*

"Some surgeons would staple a wound like his. Others might use a subcuticular closure."

"A sub what?" Scarpelli said with a half-befuddled, half-annoyed look.

"Subcuticular. It's a continuous stitch that runs beneath the skin. As the wound heals, the suture material dissolves. No staples to remove. Leaves a nicer scar."

Kate said, "Jimmy Gray's suture was under the skin, but came out every few inches."

"Exactly. Mr. Gray's incision was closed with an unusual variant of the running subcuticular, and I'm aware of only one person who would close an abdominal wound this way." Perry sat forward and leaned on the desk. His expression intensified as if he were about to impart a great secret. "Two years ago we had a resident in our program named David McBride. During his fourth year of training he spent a couple of months on the plastic surgery service, and when he resumed his general surgery rotations, he began closing abdominal wounds with a stitch he had learned from the plastic surgeons. They use this technique on the face to minimize scarring. McBride decided he'd use it for all his wound closures."

Kate wrote "Find David McBride" and underlined it twice.

"If it's good for the face, why not the rest of the body?" Scarpelli asked.

"On the abdomen or chest, the difference in scar formation between a standard subcuticular stitch and the plastic surgery variant would not be noticeable. On the face of a fourteen-year-old girl, the difference is huge."

"So why was he doing something that wasn't necessary?" Kate asked.

"You'd have to know David. He was bright and possessed surgical skills beyond those of his peers, but there came a time when he resented having to adhere to the dogmatic norms of the profession. He often believed he had better ways of doing things, like the plastic surgery wound closure, or the way he sewed in drains or placed dressings. Sound techniques, just different."

"Where's McBride now?" Scarpelli asked.

A troubled look came over the doctor, like he was about to tell someone they had inoperable cancer. "David was one of our finest residents. He was slated to enter our two-year transplant fellowship after he finished his general surgery training, and by every indication, was on his way to a brilliant career. Sadly, in his final year, he and one of our attending surgeons, Andrew Turnbull, were fired for manipulating the liver-transplant waiting list."

"I remember that," Kate said as she scribbled "Andrew Turnbull" in her notebook. "It was all over the media. If I recall, test results were switched?"

"Yes. Turnbull and McBride took blood from status-one patients—they're the sickest and in greatest need of an organ—and relabeled the tubes with the names of status-two patients. When the results came back, it appeared the status-two individuals were deteriorating, so they were changed to status-one and moved up the list.

They received livers sooner than they should have, and Turnbull was paid a million dollars per patient."

"How many did he move?" Kate asked.

"Six that we know of, probably more."

"What did he do with the money?"

"At the time, Turnbull was a leader in the field of tissue engineering and organ fabrication." Kate started to ask but before she could, Perry said, "He was using stem cells to grow human tissues and organs. But federal funding for stem-cell research dried up, and Turnbull needed cash. He devised the waiting-list scheme to fund his lab."

"What was McBride's role?" Kate asked.

"He drew the blood from the sicker patients and delivered it to Turnbull's laboratory, believing the specimens were part of a clinical study. Turnbull replaced the labels and sent the tubes to the hospital lab."

"McBride didn't know about the switch?"

"Not at first, but he noticed a trend. Turnbull would admit a status-two patient who didn't appear sick enough to warrant hospitalization. He'd tell McBride to draw their blood, and that person was subsequently moved up to status one."

"But he didn't blow the whistle," Scarpelli said.

"Only after the sixth patient did McBride come forward."

"Why'd he wait so long?"

"It took the first three for McBride to spot the trend, and when he mentioned it, Turnbull gave him a sermon about serving the greater good, then threatened to fire him if he said anything."

"Really?" Scarpelli said. "An educated man? Smarter than the rest of us? Knows the difference between right and wrong? And he keeps his mouth shut?"

Perry nodded. "When you are in the final months of a five-year residency and a senior attending surgeon threatens to ruin your career, you take that threat very seriously."

"The authority of the mentor-student relationship," Kate added.

"Yes," Perry said. "And to fully comprehend such a relationship, you have to understand the mentality of the surgical resident." He explained how surgery residents are like Marines, broken down and stripped of their identities in the intern year, then rebuilt in the image of their mentors. For five years, he said, they are deprived of sleep, isolated socially, abused mentally, and stretched to the limit physically. As junior residents they quickly learn to fear the attending surgeons. As senior residents, they drag the blunt traumas, gunshot wounds, and GI bleeders back from the brink of death under the guidance of those same attending surgeons. These shared experiences, often under great stress, breed hubris among the residents and their mentors, and the residents come to regard their mentors as godlike, to be feared and respected. "And if God tells you to keep your mouth shut," Perry said in conclusion, "you do it."

"But eventually, McBride decides to speak up," Scarpelli said.

"Yes, and following a lengthy, painful investigation, both men were fired." Perry finished his coffee and set the cup on the desk. "What else can I tell you?"

"Just a few more questions," Kate said. "Routine stuff. Were either of these men odd, antisocial, in any kind of trouble—substance abuse, money, women?"

"Andrew Turnbull was an insufferable prick." Perry looked at Kate with mild embarrassment. "Pardon my language, but I can think of no description more apt than that."

"Quite all right," Kate said. "Please, go on."

"Turnbull had a huge ego, probably a compensatory mechanism for his five-foot-six stature. His nickname was Andrew, don't-call-me-Andy, Turnbull. He worked out every day, wore perfectly tailored Armani suits, and required a special parking space for his two-hundred-thousand-dollar, custom-built Porsche so no one could park on either side of it. He dumped his first wife the day after medical school graduation and treated her replacement like an accessory." A grim smile creased Perry's lips. "Regrettably, that description fits half the surgeons on our faculty."

Scarpelli chuckled.

Kate wanted to jab her ink pen into his jugular vein.

"Turnbull wasn't quite antisocial," Perry continued, "but he did not get along well with his colleagues or the staff. He thought of himself as a genius, and he probably was. He was supposedly reading novels at the age of three, graduated college at nineteen and medical school at twenty-three—top of the class both times. He treated his patients as though they were lucky to have him as their doctor, and he viewed himself as superior to the average practicing physician. As you can imagine, this rubbed everyone the wrong way. Otherwise, no personal problems I was aware of."

"And McBride?" Kate asked, shifting in her chair, her butt starting to hurt.

"Other than his father's illness, he had no personal issues. He was highly regarded by the patients, staff, and faculty. We were all shocked when news of the scandal broke. There was a great sense of tragedy and loss when he was fired."

"What're they doing now?" Scarpelli asked.

"Both lost their licenses to practice medicine. Turnbull took his lab personnel and started a private research facility in New Jersey—NuLife Corporation. McBride joined the surgical research lab at Columbia. I think he's still there."

The phone rang. Kate braced herself. Perry picked up, said "Yes," followed by "I'll be right out."

"One of my residents is outside with an abdominal CT scan in hand. He's working up a patient who may have a fractured liver and torn hepatic vein. I'll be just a minute."

Perry left the room.

Scarpelli said, "You figure both Napoleon and the kid for this?"

Kate turned to face Scarpelli, sized up his neck, figured she'd never get a ballpoint through all that fat. "I do," she said. "We have two surgeons who've had falls from grace. We have two paranoid schizophrenics missing kidneys, and one of them has a stitch on his side commonly used by one of the surgeons. As far as motive, Turnbull ran out of money once before and came up with a creative solution. Why not another scheme to fill the coffers? McBride goes from surgeon to lab tech. Takes a big cut in pay. Needs cash. Regarding means? They build a facility they can hide, recruit staff who'll stay quiet. And opportunity? The city is crawling with schizophrenic homeless men."

"How 'bout McBride as a rogue, selling his skills to a black-market organization, and Turnbull's over in New Jersey minding his own business?"

"Possible," Kate said, "but my gut's telling me Turnbull is deep in this. He's a sociopath, steps on everyone. He's the mastermind, and he recruits McBride. I don't see McBride staring at runaway credit card bills and saying 'I gotta link up with one of those organ-snatching rings so I can make my payments.'"

"Either way, seems we got enough to pay 'em both a visit and rattle the cages."

Perry came back in and sat down. "Sorry, but the patient needs to go to the operating room now, so I only have a few minutes. Is there anything else?"

"Would these guys use human kidneys for their research?" Scarpelli asked.

"No," Perry answered.

"Do you think McBride removed Mr. Gray's kidney?" Kate asked.

"I can't say he removed it, but I can say there's a high probability he closed the wound. In all my years of working with surgical residents and attendings, I've seen only one person use that stitch on the abdomen, and that person was David McBride."

- 29 -

Kate wanted to tell Scarpelli to slow down but figured he'd just sneer and push harder on the accelerator. She tightened her grip on the door handle as he maneuvered the Ford Taurus around some hairy turns. A steep hill rose from the left side of the road. A sharp ravine fell to the right. The utter darkness of northern New Jersey stretched beyond the reach of the headlights.

She checked the dashboard clock. Almost seven. They had just passed through Edwardsville, the last town before NuLife, which was another ten minutes down the highway. She hoped Turnbull was still there. According to the Passaic County Sheriff's Office—which had routed their chopper over the NuLife parking lot at five thirty and again at six forty-five—the Porsche was on the grounds. She also hoped DeSilva and Murphy had located McBride. There was general agreement that Turnbull and McBride remained tight and would tip each other off, given the chance. They also agreed each man would be interviewed as opposed to interrogated, thus giving the impression they were sources of information rather than suspects.

The landscape flattened. The road straightened. Kate relaxed her grip, and a few minutes later, a well-lit, one-story building interrupted the lightless void of countryside. It stood off to the right, set back in the trees. A small sign marked the turn.

After a hundred yards, they pulled up to a guard shack that was no more than a glorified phone booth. While Scarpelli displayed his shield, Kate noted the compound-like nature of the facility. A twelve-foot hurricane fence, topped with coils of razor wire, enclosed the grounds. Floodlights illuminated what turned out to be two buildings. The one she had seen from the road was single level, utilitarian red brick, probably built in the 1940s or '50s. The second was relatively new, a tall, windowless structure resembling a warehouse or small aircraft hangar. Neither building was quite what she had imagined for a cutting-edge biotech firm.

The guard hung up his phone. The gate opened. Scarpelli drove through.

Kate said, "Kind of odd that whoever was on the other end of the line—assuming it was Turnbull or someone who had his ear—didn't ask what this was about. I mean, two New York cops all the way out here?"

"Like he's expecting us."

They drove another hundred yards to the parking lot, and there it was, Andrew Turnbull's $200,000 Porsche. The spaces on either side had been painted over with white hash marks and contained small potted trees. Kate didn't know how it felt to own a car, and she certainly didn't know how it felt to own one worth that kind of money, but if she did, she'd probably treat it the same way. Compared to the Porsche, the other cars in the lot seemed tired and unloved.

An icy gust of wind whipped Kate as she climbed out of the Taurus. She and Scarpelli threw on their overcoats and headed for the main building. Turnbull was waiting, and there was no doubt it was him. He was short, wore a perfectly tailored suit, and his tie was still cinched. He pushed open one of two glass doors. They entered, along with a rush of air that mussed Turnbull's perfectly coiffed salt-and-pepper hair.

Turnbull followed them in and was about to introduce himself when the wind slammed the door. The bang echoed down the stark hallway of white cinder block and gray linoleum.

"Sorry about that." He ran the fingers of his left hand through his hair and offered his right to Kate. "Andrew Turnbull," he said.

His handshake was firm, his smile warm. He was handsome and personable, and showed no outward signs of irritation or annoyance.

In fact, he struck her as more of an Andy than an Andrew. She held out her shield. "Kate D'Angelo. This is Detective Mike Scarpelli."

Scarpelli displayed his badge. The two men shook hands.

"I'm surprised, perplexed actually, that two of New York's finest have business in the wilds of northern New Jersey."

"We got a few questions about a former associate," Scarpelli said. "Won't take long."

Turnbull led them to a nondescript door and held it open as they passed through. The disparity between the aged exterior of the building, the barren hallway, and the posh suite of offices was striking. The glassed-in conference room with its mahogany table, high-backed chairs and array of audiovisual equipment rivaled anything on Wall Street. "The staff's gone for the day," he said. "There is coffee, but it's old."

Scarpelli declined, as did Kate.

Turnbull gathered their coats and motioned toward his office. "Please …"

Kate and Scarpelli sat down in overstuffed leather chairs. Turnbull took a seat behind his desk, also mahogany. Everything— the furniture, the Persian rug, the wood paneling—was far nicer than the university-issue laminates and Naugahydes in Perry's office. Like Perry, Turnbull had a wall of books. Unlike Perry, there was no eight-by-ten of the wife.

"Kinda isolated out here," Scarpelli said.

"Yes, it is. The Army built this place in the early forties as part of a biological warfare research program. They studied anthrax and smallpox right down the hall. Nixon folded the program in the early seventies, the Army dumped the facility a few years ago, and here we are."

Kate said, "So the government, in all its wisdom, thought it was safe to study two dangerous diseases fifty miles from one of the world's largest cities?"

Turnbull shrugged. "Guess they had faith in the containment system."

"Interesting," Kate said, "but maybe we should get started. We don't want to take up too much of your time."

"Not a problem. What can I do for you?"

The detectives opened their notebooks. Kate said, "We're gathering information on a former student of yours, David McBride."

"There's a name from the past. Is Dr. McBride in trouble?"

"Not sure yet," Scarpelli said. "When's the last time you saw him?"

"Going on two years. I haven't seen nor heard from him since our days at NYU. I assume you're aware of that story or you wouldn't be here."

"We've heard the tale," said Scarpelli.

"Then you know as much as I do about McBride. Following his dismissal, he joined a research lab at Columbia. After I lost my faculty position, I started this company and put New York behind me. That's all I can tell you."

While jotting a couple of notes, Kate said, "But the two of you were close, weren't you?"

"Within the bounds of an attending surgeon-resident relationship, yes. It was no secret I was grooming him to join the faculty once he finished his transplant fellowship."

"So, despite that relationship, after you parted ways you severed all ties."

"You know how it is when you share an intensely negative experience with someone. You don't want to associate with the person anymore. You don't want the daily reminder. That's how I felt, and I'm sure if you asked David, he'd tell you the same."

Kate knew the feeling. A Taser to the base of the neck would befit her ex–significant other. She said, "Hate to dredge up past difficulties, but it will help us get a better understanding of McBride if we could talk about the trouble you had at NYU."

"It's all a matter of public record."

"But it helps to get a personal perspective."

Turnbull nodded. "I suppose it does. What would you like to know?"

"Why move people up the list?"

"It was a simple idea. Antiabortion activists effectively cut off federal dollars for stem-cell research. I needed to fund my work. I was going to make the transplant waiting list obsolete with money from those on the list. I thought it was poetic. The hospital administration didn't."

Simple idea? Poetic? Did he really say that? Kate was appalled that a member of the medical profession could be so cavalier about manipulating the lives of the sick and dying. Her ears had just confirmed what her gut had been telling her. This man, devoid of a social conscience and lacking all moral responsibility, was more than capable of stealing kidneys from mentally ill homeless men. And if McBride was involved, he was being paid, blackmailed, or bribed. Thankfully, Scarpelli spoke up before her silence turned into an awkward moment. They still needed Turnbull to believe the three of them were on the same side.

"What about McBride?" Scarpelli asked. "Why did he go along with your scheme when he knew it might jeopardize his career?"

"He shared my vision."

"But your vision cost him big time, did it not?" Kate asked, perhaps with too much edge in her voice.

Turnbull leaned forward, and in a deliberate manner, planted his elbows on his desk and laced his fingers. "David McBride was solely responsible for his career, both in its formation and destruction. He was an independently functioning adult who made his own choices. Unfortunately, he made errors in judgment that cost him dearly."

Kate searched Turnbull for any sign of emotion—remorse, regret, responsibility, anything—but saw only a man unfazed by a rather nasty period of his life. She said, "Did he have any personal problems? Drugs, booze, gambling, women?"

"No. He was a good person and an excellent surgeon. He would've been a fine addition to the faculty."

Scarpelli turned the page in his notebook. "When he was fired, did he know how to remove a kidney?"

"Yes. He was quite proficient at harvesting organs of all types."

Turnbull sat there, waiting for the next question, patient as a rock. Kate figured it was time to step on a nerve. "The reason for our visit is we believe McBride may be stealing kidneys for a black-market organ-snatching ring."

Turnbull cocked his head and assumed a look of confusion. "David McBride? Are you sure?"

"We're not sure of anything, yet. This is preliminary, but we think he's taking them from homeless men."

Scarpelli added, "The evidence suggests he's working for an Israeli organ broker."

Turnbull shook his head with thoughtful deliberation. "I'm shocked. I can't imagine David McBride getting involved with anything as sinister as black-market organs."

Turnbull's response struck Kate as measured. He acted surprised, but not riveted, as Perry had been. This was big news, someone stealing kidneys out of humans, particularly if you had trained the chief suspect. On the other hand, he wasn't looking into his lap, fidgeting with a pen or breaking a sweat. She said, "Can a surgeon remove a kidney by him- or herself?"

"No. Not possible."

"Could you perform a harvest in a hotel room?"

"If you are referring to the bathtub-full-of-ice urban legend, the idea is ridiculous."

"Could someone with enough cash build their own facility, maybe hide it in a larger building?" Like the one across the street, she wanted to say.

"The only place a surgeon can open an abdomen, excise an internal organ, and expect the patient to live is in a well-staffed hospital with properly equipped operating rooms and full support services. Donor nephrectomy is not a procedure performed by a Dr. Frankenstein wannabe in some half-assed basement OR."

"So, if McBride is involved, he's working for a group with significant resources."

"That would be my guess," Turnbull said. "The existence of a highly organized black market for human organs is well documented. They operate in countries all over the world, including this one, and they use hospitals that turn a blind eye. Sometimes they pay the donors. Sometimes they steal the organs. If David McBride is illegally harvesting kidneys, he is most likely working for such an organization."

"Any idea where one would begin to search for an organ broker?"

Turnbull leaned back in his chair and grinned. "Why, Google, of course. Just type in 'Kidney for Sale.'"

"Where would modern police work be without Google?" Kate said. She turned to Scarpelli. "Any more questions?"

"I'm good," Scarpelli said, moving to the edge of his seat, "but I wouldn't mind a quick tour, see what a tissue lab looks like."

"I can't go into too much detail without signed confidentiality agreements, but I can give you a general overview."

"Works for me," Scarpelli said.

As they stood, Kate said, "Oh … one last thing, if you don't mind."

"Not at all."

"Do you know a Dr. Brian Steinberg? He's on the psychiatry faculty at NYU and has a clinic at Bellevue."

Turnbull slipped his hands into his pockets and shook his head. "No. Why? Is he a suspect as well?"

"More like a person of interest."

"Sorry. Can't help you. NYU and Bellevue are huge places with many clinical services and large faculties, most of whom never cross paths." He gestured toward the door. "Shall we?"

- 30 -

Windows lined the hallway beyond the office suite. Behind the windows were a series of laboratories containing workbenches, ventilation hoods, things that resembled ovens, things that resembled refrigerators, a lot of stainless steel, a lot of glassware. Computer workstations stood along the walls. Some of the labs had alcoves with desks, or separate office space. And despite the late hour, numerous people clad in white coats—men and women of various ages and ethnicities—were sitting at tables, standing under hoods, and bellied up to benches. Turnbull explained how one lab worked with liver cells, another with heart, and others were developing kidney, pancreas, and lung tissues.

"No brain cells?" Scarpelli asked without a trace of expression.

Turnbull smiled. "No, but there are plenty among us who'd benefit from a new brain."

As they made their way down the corridor, Turnbull spoke of his mission to solve medicine's most daunting problem. "On any given day in this country," he said, "there are more than a hundred thousand people on waiting lists for kidneys, livers, pancreases, hearts, and lungs. In a good year, twenty-five percent will get organs, while the remaining seventy-five percent continue to wait. About half of those waiting will die, and most who survive have a poor quality of life." He paused, giving them time to appreciate the gravity of his words, then said, "I envision a day in the not too distant future when the world's supply of replacement organs are grown in the laboratory. It's an extraordinarily complex process, and there are significant hurdles to overcome, but right here, in this lab, we've taken a unique approach to the most difficult problems, and I believe we'll solve them before anyone else. When that happens, this technology will save hundreds of thousands of lives around the world, every year, and the improvement in the quality of life of those patients with nonfatal but chronic diseases will be immeasurable."

Kate figured these were excerpts from a pitch Turnbull had made many times, but he spoke with conviction, and the message was powerful. In fact, he exuded a charisma that hadn't been there while speaking about McBride. He certainly believed what he was saying, but Kate wondered if an element of megalomania was rearing its head. If he was on the path to a breakthrough of such magnitude, Andrew Turnbull, sociopath or not, was indeed a very important person. "That's a lofty goal," she said.

"Yes," Turnbull replied. "Right up there with discovering penicillin or realizing if you wash your hands and put on gloves before surgery, your patients won't die from postoperative infection. It's the rare person who can have that kind of impact on the human race."

The corridor ended in a *T*. To the left and right was more of the same. Every lab had windows, and Kate saw nothing that might function as an operating room. But when they came to the final laboratory, a surge of adrenaline sent blood whirling through her veins. The workers inside wore blue spacesuits with hoods and plastic face shields. With their slow, deliberate movements, they appeared to be walking on the moon. She glanced at Scarpelli, and he back at her.

"Why the special suits?" Kate asked.

"This is our nude mouse room. Nude mice lack immune systems, so we can transplant human tissue into them and there is no rejection. A great model for transplantation research. The downside is they easily succumb to infections. Those hooded gowns prevent contamination of the animals by their human handlers."

"Are they used in hospitals?"

"Orthopedic surgeons wear them during joint replacement surgery. Postoperative infection of an artificial joint is a disaster. These suits offer more protection than standard surgical gowns."

"So they're widely available?"

"Yes, from any medical supply company."

"Do you use them for transplants?"

"No. Transplant recipients are immunosuppressed to prevent rejection, but their immune systems still function to a certain degree. We take precautions, but we don't wear the hoods."

"Same for the donors?"

"Yes. The donors are giving organs, not receiving, so there is no rejection and no need for immunosuppression. The intraoperative and postoperative regimens are the same as for non-transplant surgery cases."

"Interesting," Kate said.

"Yes, it is. Transplant immunology is a complex, fascinating field." He looked at Kate, then Scarpelli. "If there are no more questions, you're probably anxious to get back."

"We are." Kate checked her watch. "We still have about four hours to go on our shift."

"This time of night you'll be back in the city in less than an hour."

They went to the office, picked up their coats, and Turnbull walked them to the entrance.

Scarpelli slipped his coat over his large frame. "By the way, what do you do in the building over there?" He pointed across the parking lot.

"That's our gymnasium."

"Looks new," Kate said.

"I had it built after I acquired the property. I insist my employees stay fit."

"Mind if we have a quick look?" Scarpelli asked.

"Not at all," Turnbull replied.

He held the door as they stepped inside. Three full-sized basketball courts stretched from wall to wall. A running track circled overhead.

"Impressive," Kate said.

"What's back there?" Scarpelli asked, pointing to the far recesses of the building.

"Racquetball courts, a weight room, a cardiovascular studio."

"I'd love to check out the cardio stuff, get some ideas," Scarpelli said. "My wife's been after me to drop a few pounds."

"I wish I could show it to you, but a group of our female Muslim employees reserved the facility for the evening. They'd be quite upset if a man strolled through the door—you know, the exposed skin and all."

"Yeah," Scarpelli said, "I can see that being a problem."

The detectives thanked Turnbull for his time, and had taken a few steps toward the Taurus when he called out. They stopped and turned.

"By the way," he said, "what do you have that ties McBride to an organ-snatching ring?"

"Sorry," Kate said, "can't discuss an ongoing investigation."

Scarpelli waved as they passed the guard shack.

"So?" Kate asked.

"Too accommodating. Not arrogant enough. If Andrew, don't call me Andy, Turnbull has nothing to hide, he'd a been put out, annoyed by us dropping in."

"Scripted comes to my mind, like he was ready for us. He didn't so much as wrinkle a brow at any of our questions. And how about the spacesuits?"

Scarpelli turned onto the highway. "They're no smoking gun."

"But they prop up Jimmy Gray's story."

"I'll give you that."

"And my money says the gym isn't full of scantily clad Muslim women pumping iron."

"We need to get a look inside," Scarpelli said. "That's where the action is."

"Let's hope DeSilva and Murphy got something out of McBride, because none of this adds up to probable cause. The Passaic County Sheriff's Department isn't going to raid the place because a paranoid schizophrenic saw people standing over him in blue spacesuits."

Back in his office, Turnbull retrieved the TracFone from the safe. Mr. White answered on the first ring. "Grab McBride," Turnbull said. "Two NYPD detectives just stopped by, and I figure McBride's next, if their partners haven't already been to see him."

"They haven't," Mr. White said. "He came home from work, left thirty minutes later, and now he's sitting in an Irish pub drinking a Guinness stout."

"Any chance he put two and two together after his GPS stunt last night?"

"I don't think so. Today has been business as usual. He's made no attempt to communicate with anyone. What should I do with him?"

"Hide him. I just set up a thirty-million-dollar transplant. We need him one last time."

"Do the detectives suspect you?"

"I'm sure they do. They dropped in unannounced, asked bullshit questions, watched my reactions. I didn't give 'em anything, but the female cop reacted to the hooded gowns. It was subtle, but I saw it in her eyes. She also mentioned Steinberg. That means one of our donors is talking, which isn't unexpected. But somebody's listening, and that is unexpected."

"You don't sound concerned."

"Annoyed? Yes. Worried? No. Steinberg and McBride may be on the radar, but they don't know anything. If the NYPD decides to put us under surveillance, you'll hear about it. And even if they obtain a search warrant and launch a commando-style raid, an hour from now all they'll find is a primate research facility. All we have to do is get through one more harvest and transplant, and we're done."

"Who are the detectives?" Mr. White asked.

"Mike Scarpelli and Kate D'Angelo."

"I'll see what I can find out."

"And keep your ear trained on Passaic County as well. NYPD is out of their jurisdiction over here and can't make a move unless the locals are on board."

Turnbull locked the phone in the safe, and using the landline, called over to the gym to check the status of his patient. "Stable, and making lots of urine," said the nurse who answered.

"Good. Get him ready for transfer. We're shipping him out."

"Tonight?"

"Within the hour."

Turnbull hung up and dialed the paging operator at UMSNJ. "The University of Medicine and Surgery, New Jersey," she said. "How may I direct your call?"

"My name is Dr. Andrew Turnbull. Will you page Dr. Keith Rimes for me please?"

With the patient transferred, and every surface in the operating room and recovery area bleached, there was no way to distinguish this facility from any other primate research lab. All of the instruments, equipment, and supplies were as suitable for monkeys as they were for humans. Nobody—not surgeon, scientist, or cop—would be able to poke around and discern what had recently occurred. So, with the place all buttoned up, the OR personnel long gone, and the nursing staff just leaving, Turnbull decided to look in on the organs.

The organ room was the size of the gym floor above—three basketball courts side by side. Rows of waist-high lab benches stretched from one end to the other. Glass cylinders, three feet tall, two feet in diameter, and spaced a foot-and-a-half apart, lined the bench tops. Each was illuminated by its own track light, each was filled with fluid, and each contained a human organ grown from stem cells seeded onto a porcine extracellular matrix. The sight was breathtaking, like standing in the middle of a carefully planted farmer's field. No matter the line of sight, all rows displayed perfect symmetry.

Turnbull strolled up and down the aisles, nodding at the occasional technician, marveling at both the beauty and complexity of his creation. Silastic tubing came and went from the cylinders, passing through stainless-steel fittings in the glass and connecting to the organs inside. Red tubes delivered oxygenated arterial blood and nutrients. Blue tubes carried away deoxygenated venous blood and metabolic waste products. Specialized tubing aided functions unique to each organ type. Bile from the livers drained into small tubes sewn to the common bile duct. Smaller tubes cannulated the main duct of each pancreas, draining the pancreatic enzymes and digestive juices. The urine produced by the kidneys flowed down a segment of ureter before draining into a small Silastic tube.

The hearts and lungs were more problematic. For each heart, oxygen-rich blood needed to enter the left atrium, pass through the mitral valve into the left ventricle, and then get pumped by the left ventricle out the aortic valve and into the aorta. At the same time, venous blood had to flow into the right atrium, pass through the tricuspid valve into the right ventricle, then get pumped through the pulmonary valve into the pulmonary artery. The pressure in each pumping chamber had to closely approximate the physiologic pressures found in the human body, or the muscular walls of the heart chambers, and the valves that separated them, would not develop properly. Needless to say, the hearts looked like pulsating squids.

The lungs were a bit less complicated. Air had to cycle in and out at appropriate pressures and time intervals in order to ensure normal development. Thus, corrugated plastic tubing extended through the tops of the cylinders and into the fluid where it was sutured to the trachea and sealed with a physiologic glue. Benchtop ventilators moved a gaseous mixture of nitrogen and oxygen into and out of each pair of lungs, giving them the appearance of billowing pink balloons. Turnbull took a moment to appreciate the uniform pinkness of the organs. All of the adult lungs he had operated on were marbled with black pigment, a by-product of breathing the carbon-laden air of the post–industrial revolution. Only the lungs of newborns and young children were this pink.

He entered the glassed-in confines of the master control room. Compared to the tranquility of the organ room, the place was a beehive of activity. A multitude of computer screens and digital readouts illuminated the otherwise dark space. White-coated scientists and their assistants monitored hundreds of time intervals, oxygen levels, fluid outputs, and chamber pressures. The temperature of the organ-growing broth in each cylinder had to be maintained within a degree or two of the human core temperature or cell damage would occur. The inflation pressures of the lungs had to be just high enough to open the bronchioles, but not any higher or they'd pop. Those organs producing fluids and juices frequently needed their output tubes checked for obstruction. Any backpressure would injure the tissues. The complexity of the operation was supremely impressive, but what really struck Turnbull was how the human body had evolved its own internal monitoring system that governed interconnected organ systems with a vastly more complicated and intricate design.

He came up behind Cynthia and bid her a good evening.

She turned around, momentarily startled.

"How're things going?" he asked.

"No change. The livers are making bile, but only trace levels of enzymes and albumin."

"So we have growth but no function."

"Yes. Based on what I've observed grossly, I think we have a seed rate close to one hundred percent. Now it's just going to take time for the stem cells to fully differentiate into functional liver cells capable of synthesizing what they're programmed to synthesize."

"Of course," Turnbull said. "After all, embryologic organogenesis takes forty weeks, right? And these organs are no more than a month old."

Turnbull had similar discussions with the other scientists. The hearts were fully formed but could only pump against pressures half that of the human physiologic blood pressure. The lungs were pliable enough to accept normal adult tidal volumes, but they were not absorbing oxygen. The kidneys looked like kidneys but were not producing much urine or filtering waste products and electrolytes.

Turnbull wasn't concerned. Anxious for success? Yes. Afraid they might fail? No. All fear of failure—well, much of it—had been eased by Abercrombie's serendipitous discovery of low-level laser therapy, and the ingenious delivery system Turnbull himself had devised.

Abercrombie's review of the scientific literature revealed that most of the infrared lasers designed for clinical use employed gallium arsenide crystals, which emitted light in the near-infrared spectrum. The decision to use the same energy source had been an easy one. Light of this wavelength was not visible to the human retina, and therefore, remained invisible to the other scientists. Also, due to its low energy, it would not produce damaging heat within the developing cells and tissues. The first challenge that presented itself, however, had to do with delivery of the light to the organs. Turnbull wanted every cell of every organ exposed to photons of laser light, but it wouldn't have been practical to mount multiple devices around each glass cylinder. In addition, he feared that the superficial layers of cells would absorb most of the energy, while the deep layers would see very little or none at all. And this is when his considerable genius flexed its muscle.

If *macroscopic* gallium arsenide crystals could be mounted in a solid-state circuit and prompted to emit energy by applying electricity—the definition of a laser—why couldn't *microscopic* crystals of gallium arsenide be added to the organ-growing broth and the blood supply of the individual organs? Then it would simply be a matter of applying an electric current to the fluid in the cylinder, thus stimulating each crystal to emit photons of near-infrared light. Add billions of crystals, generate trillions of photons, and since the crystals were smaller than a red blood cell, they'd pass freely through the blood vessels and capillary beds, thus augmenting any oxygen-driven energy production. It seemed a perfect solution, the developing organs bathed externally by infrared light, while light-emitting crystals perfused the deeper layers of cells and tissues. The next step? Putting theory into practice.

They conferred with an optical physicist Abercrombie knew from his postdoc days. After studying the model Turnbull had proposed, the physicist agreed to join the company for a sliver of NuLife stock and promptly went to work implementing Turnbull's idea. And the result? It stood before him: an inexhaustible supply of human replacement organs and a legacy that would cement his place among the great thinkers of the ages.

- 32 -

The bartender at Kell's asked David if he wanted another beer. He checked his watch. Seven forty-five. His father was enjoying a blissful slumber thanks to a cocktail of antipsychotic medications, and Cassandra worked until eleven, so, yes, he had time for another. While he waited, he gazed out at Delancey Street. A cluster of cabs idled at a red light. Pedestrians leaned into the wind. He thought about texting Cassandra, just to say Hi, and ask her how her shift was going, but his cell phone was on the kitchen counter charging. He'd check in with her later.

When David turned back to the bar, a pint of Guinness stout awaited. He took a sip, savored the velvety liquid as it slipped over his tongue, then he blocked out the din of the moderate-sized Friday night crowd and studied the decision tree he had started at the apartment. As a medical student and surgery resident, he had often used lists, flowcharts, and decision trees to organize his thoughts, solve problems, and manage his workload. Now that he faced the mother of all problems, how to extract himself from a well-organized conspiracy, he needed the ultimate decision tree. Across the top of a legal pad he had written "What do I do now?" Then he decided he'd think more clearly with a cold beer sitting in front of him, so he checked on his dad, locked up, and two pints later had generated a page full of columns, arrows, and crossed out ideas.

Earlier this morning his attempt to track the donor organ had failed, and that left him with three options. If he anonymously called the police and told them illegal kidney transplants were being performed somewhere near Edwardsville, New Jersey, they'd want details. He wouldn't have any, and they'd blow him off. If he exposed the warehouse, he'd disrupt the conspiracy, but it would not lead the cops to the person or people behind it. He could drive to Edwardsville himself and look for a facility that might support an organ transplant. And if by chance he discovered something, then what? Knock on the door? Call the police? What if they found nothing? He planted his elbows on the bar, pushed the heels of his hands into his temples, and stared at the legal pad. There were three columns of notes, three possible actions, and three arrows pointing to one conclusion: if he meddled again and failed, he'd place himself and Cassandra in danger. He picked up his pen, drew one more arrow down the page, and listed his fourth and final option: "No choice but to go along."

To keep himself and Cassandra safe, he'd have to continue to steal kidneys for a deplorable bastard he'd never meet. To say it'd be difficult would be a gross understatement. He'd just have to distance himself from the victims, reduce them to patches of skin, and at the same time, do his best work and minimize the risk of postoperative complications—wound infection, bleeding, abscess—any of which could be fatal to the malnourished.

He sat back and rubbed his eyes. Thirty-six hours without sleep, and total exhaustion was setting in. He had worked a full day yesterday, performed major surgery last night, had threats of violence leveled against him and his wife early this morning, then lay awake in bed until it was time to go back to work, back to slicing open rats. He stretched, leaned on his elbows, and looked along the bar, at the sad-faced loners deep in thought and the couples absorbed in petty dramas. He'd give anything to be sitting here with Cassandra, discussing the problems that now paled in comparison to the deep shit through which he was wading.

David stopped at a corner store for two twelve-packs of beer, and headed home. As he approached his building a cigarette ember glowed from the passenger side of a parked car, a Lincoln Town Car, one of Mr. White's goon squads. But there was no way to harvest on consecutive nights. They could only recover one nephrectomy patient at a time. Mr. White had said as much. David slowed his pace and tried to get a better look inside.

A huge man in a black overcoat climbed out, left hand in pocket, right hand holding a cigarette to his mouth. He took a drag. The ember intensified. He stepped into the halo of a streetlamp. The yellow light gave his face a jaundiced pallor, and his eyes the appearance of black holes. He resembled the big Russian from the warehouse—his brother, perhaps. David's anxiety turned to fear. He started to walk past. The man flicked his cigarette away and expelled a frosty puff of smoke. David lowered his gaze and veered toward the lobby. With several quick steps, the Russian put himself between David and the entrance. David froze, heart pounding, muscles taut. The Russian stood squarely in front of him, not more than two feet away, the reek of cigarette smoke closing the gap. A gust of wind cleared the reek and sent a page from a newspaper tumbling down the sidewalk.

"My boss wants to see you," the Russian said.

The big ugly fucker was lying. Mr. White never deviated from his protocol. This was payback, the sending of a message, or worse. If they gave him a beat down for asking questions, something far more severe was in order for trying to track the kidney. He knew Mr. White had let him off too easy last night. He was not getting into that car.

"Sorry," David said, "I'm busy tonight." He put his head down and stepped to his right.

The Russian mirrored the move, blocking David.

"My boss insists." He pointed toward the Lincoln. "You have no choice."

Movement inside the lobby caught David's eye. A young Latino wearing a hooded jacket exited the elevator, then stopped, jerked on a leash, and out of the elevator emerged the albino pit bull from the apartment across the hall. David's heart rate jumped into overdrive.

He needed to buy himself three seconds. He said, "Why don't you tell me what this is about?"

"Just go to car. Do not make problems."

The door opened. The dog strutted onto the sidewalk. The Russian turned. David swung his arm in a huge arc and slammed a twelve-pack of beer into the Russian's head. The Russian reeled backward into the Latino and fell to the ground. Beer cans bounced and sputtered on the concrete. The pit bull exploded in a frenzy of vicious growling and clamped his jaws onto the Russian's arm, thrashing back and forth. The Russian screamed at the Latino. The Latino screamed at the dog. David heaved the second twelve-pack at the driver, now coming around the front of the car, and took off down the sidewalk. At the end of the block he looked back. The Russian was still on the ground with the pit bull pulling on one arm, the driver pulling on the other, and the Latino yelling in Spanish and yanking on the leash. David turned the corner.

The crack of a gunshot. A yelp. Silence.

David ran as fast as his legs would carry him. Adrenaline pulsed through his arteries, forcing his heart to squeeze harder and his lungs to breathe deeper. The frigid air burned his chest and sucked the moisture from his eyes. He took a left and then a right, frantically searching for a place to hide in the maze of apartment buildings. But there were no alleys, parking garages, basements, or unlocked lobbies, just deserted streets, parked cars, and empty sidewalks.

He ran until his hamstrings tightened into knots. He stopped at an intersection, clutched a signpost, gasped for air. The frozen metal stung his hand. He jerked it back. Behind him an engine whined. He turned around. Headlights, several blocks away and coming fast. He looked up at the sign, a black-and-white arrow pointing toward the speeding car. They were going the wrong way on a one-way street. It had to be the Russians.

David crossed the intersection and sprinted down a narrow side street. A stabbing pain gripped his side. His legs burned. He could not outrun a car. Seized by panic, he stood paralyzed in the middle of the road. If he crawled under something, maybe they'd drive past. He dropped to one knee and peered beneath a red sedan.

Light engulfed him, but it wasn't the Town Car. That was behind him. David jumped to the sidewalk as a black Escalade full of homeboys blew by, music thumping, the monstrosity barely clearing the parked cars. The Escalade rolled through the stop sign and turned right, into the path of the Town Car. Tires screeched. Horns honked. The Russians were blocked. They'd have to back up and circle around, unless they were stupid enough to take on a bunch of homeys on their own turf. It was the break David needed. The boys in the Escalade had bought him enough time to get to the Delancey Street subway station. It was large with multiple tracks and levels— his only chance.

David descended into the station two steps at a time, passing a young couple coming up. Maybe their train was still there. He pulled out his wallet as he neared the gate, swiped his MetroCard, and trotted onto the platform as a pair of red taillights disappeared into the darkness of the north tunnel. He groaned. It would be at least five minutes until the next train. He raced down two more flights of stairs, to the lower level.

Nothing. He bent over, hands on knees, chest heaving.

After a few deep breaths he lifted his head and studied the long corridor of gray concrete and white tile. He was alone, on his side. Across the tracks, an old woman in a tattered wool coat and rainbow-colored knit hat leaned on a cane. Not far from her, three Latinos in canvas jackets formed a tight, agitated circle, drank out of brown paper bags, and argued in Spanish. David walked to the north end of the platform, stood with his back to the wall and made himself as thin as possible. He watched the south tunnel, desperately hoping to see the black hole fill with light, glanced at the stairs … the tunnel.

A dark form exited the stairwell, but it was just a pasty-faced white guy in a down coat and Yankees hat, swaying to the beat of whatever his earphones were piping into his head. David clenched his eyes shut, drew in a deep breath, and let it out. When he opened them, a second person had appeared, a big man in a long overcoat, his right arm limp, his left hand grasping something in his pocket.

Their eyes locked. The Russian grinned. A menacing stare replaced the grin as he started toward David. David looked to the other platform. It was four feet high. He could jump down, cross over and climb out. With a bad arm, the Russian would have a hard time following.

David moved to the edge and examined the tracks. There were two sets, northbound on his side, southbound on the other. The electrified third rails, separated by a series of columns, occupied the space in between. He jumped, landed close to the wall, but before he took a step a loud clatter filled the station. The southbound train. The glass-and-steel behemoth rolled in and slowed to a stop, blocking access to the other side. David spun, one way, then another, like a rat in a maze. The Russian was now running toward the end of the platform, leaving David with one option—the black void of the north tunnel.

He ran down the track, out of the light into near darkness. He stumbled on uneven ground. His lungs struggled to move the dank air. His pursuer's footsteps grew louder. An explosion boomed. A shower of sparks erupted from the iron column next to him. He ducked. Two more shots rang out. He ran harder, searched for a place to hide, a passageway, a hole, anything. He saw nothing in the dim light.

A low rumble signaled the approach of a northbound train. High-intensity headlights turned night into day as the rumble built to a roar. Using a support post for balance, David hopped over the electrified rails and ran up the southbound tracks. Every muscle in his body tensed as he waited for a bullet to tear through his flesh or bore through his brain.

Movement off to the right. He turned. Against the far wall stood the Russian, legs spread, gun raised. Flame spit from the muzzle. The screech of steel on steel drowned out the sound of the shot. Searing heat ripped through David's right thigh. His leg buckled. He staggered and fell backward, smashing head and shoulders into the concrete wall. The Russian aimed again. David rolled into a shallow depression and buried his head under his arms. The concrete above exploded. Shards of cement dug into his scalp and neck.

The ground shook as the train roared past. Trash whirled in the turbulence. The smell of electrified heat permeated the air. David rolled onto his side, tried to get to his feet. The pain was unbearable and his leg useless, but he managed to claw his way to a standing position. He moved along the wall, hopping on one foot as the last of the northbound cars approached. The Russian would be waiting on the other side.

A bright light appeared in front of David. A southbound train rounding the bend and coming fast. He flattened himself against the wall.

The final northbound car passed. The Russian jumped over the third rails onto the southbound tracks, left arm raised, gun leveled at David's head, then he simply disappeared into the blinding light of the southbound train. There was no scream, no thump or thwack, only the furious roar of eight subway cars hurtling by less than three feet away. David squeezed his arms over his ears and fought off the wind. Grit pelted his face and hands. He choked on dust. The shriek of steel wheels skidding on iron rails pierced his eardrums like ice picks.

The train went by and grew distant before coming to a stop. David slid down the wall and sat there, head back, eyes closed, body shaking, unable to comprehend what had just happened. He was moments from death, yet here he sat, everything a blur, like a fragmented dream that lingers after awakening, and you try to make sense of it, but it's already distorted and surreal.

But the pain was real enough. His right thigh burned as if a red-hot poker had been driven through it. He pressed his fingertips into his inner thigh and pushed on the femur. No change in the pain. The bone was intact. He pulled the shoe and sock off his right foot, touched the tips of his toes and wiggled them. Sensation and motor function were intact. He found the dorsalis pedis artery on the top of his foot. The pulse was strong. Circulation was intact. He felt the warmth of fresh blood on his skin, but that didn't worry him. The major nerve, artery, and vein that supplied the leg were uninjured. He wasn't going to bleed to death. He had nothing more than a soft tissue injury.

But extensive soft tissue trauma carried the risk of a compartment syndrome. Damaged tissues swell. Swelling creates pressure. In the case of a brain injury, the rigid cranium traps the pressure, and when intracranial pressure exceeds systemic blood pressure, blood flow to the brain ceases, and the patient dies. Same with the muscles of the thigh. They were contained within an unforgiving space—a compartment of dense fascia—and if the swelling was extensive enough, the pressure would collapse the femoral artery and vein. No blood in. No blood out. The leg dies. Amputation. Longitudinal slits through the skin and fascia would effectively treat a compartment syndrome, but David was in no position to enter a hospital for a surgical procedure. Instead, he'd have to check the pulse in his foot whenever the opportunity presented itself, and hope to God it didn't disappear. He was now running for his life.

He struggled to get his sock and shoe back on. And standing was nearly impossible. Every movement sent bolts of pain radiating from his thigh—all those shredded muscle fibers trying to contract. By clawing his way up the wall, he finally stood, bearing just enough weight on the injured leg to maintain balance. Slowly, he hobbled down the tracks, the pain a nine on a ten scale.

- 33 -

"Ridge Street, right?" Scarpelli asked.

"Yes," Kate replied. "One fifty-five Ridge Street, Apartment 4-E." David McBride's last known address, according to DeSilva. He and Murphy had been up to McBride's apartment twice, no answer on the door, parked out front until about a quarter to eight, then had to abandon their vigil to investigate a shooting over on Orchard.

Scarpelli turned off of E. Houston onto Ridge and was met by an Animal Care and Control van obstructing the one-way street about a half block down. Two radio motor patrol units, lights flashing, were parked in front of the AC&C van.

"That's it," Kate said. "One fifty-five."

"Not good," Scarpelli replied as he pulled up to the van. They climbed out and threw on their overcoats.

Four uniforms were working the scene, one speaking to a seriously pissed off Latino, one watching AC&C technicians attend to a white pit bull lying on its side, and two others taping off the sidewalk. Beer cans littered the area. A few had popped open and spewed. Maybe an altercation over a twelve-pack—she had seen people killed for less. Scarpelli joined the officer talking to the Latino. Kate eyeballed the dog.

He lay on his left side, eyes closed, breathing reduced to a weak pant, tongue blue and dry. Near the top of the muscular shoulder, a thin rim of blood surrounded a dime-sized wound. Lower on the chest, close to the end of the rib cage, a quarter-sized wound oozed a bright red patch into white fur. Kate studied the relation of the wounds—the smaller entrance above, the larger exit below. The shooter had been standing over the animal, within a foot or two. There'd be a slug somewhere, but fired at close range into concrete, it would be mangled and useless.

"Is he gonna live?" Kate asked.

"Hard to say," answered the female tech. "We need to get him to the ASPCA hospital up on East Ninety-Second. They have a fully staffed ER and surgeons on call."

"Long trip," Kate said. "Hope you make it."

"We'll do our best."

Kate joined Scarpelli, a uniform named Vasquez, and the Latino. "Someone tried to take out McBride," Scarpelli said.

"Shit. What happened?"

Scarpelli fingered the pages of his notepad and recounted the Latino's story. When Scarpelli finished, Kate looked at Vasquez and nodded toward the Latino. "He ID'd McBride?"

"Yep," Vasquez replied.

"If he doesn't speak English, how does he know McBride's name?"

"Their mail is always getting mixed up."

"Was he able to describe what McBride is wearing?"

"Jeans, blue parka, dark-colored stocking cap."

"Height and weight?"

"About six feet. Not heavy or thin. Maybe one-eighty."

"And the other two?"

"The man on the ground, big, ugly, black eyes, black hair, over-coat. The shooter, average size, blunt features, overcoat. They were yelling the whole time. Sounded like Russian."

Scarpelli checked his watch. "If McBride's alive, he's been on the run for twenty-three minutes with his pursuers a minute or so behind. Problem is, he coulda gone any direction."

Vasquez's collar mic blurted, "All units in the vicinity of the Delancey Street subway station, we have a report of a man hit by a train in the north tunnel on the F track. Repeat, all units in the vicinity of the Delancey Street station, man hit by train, north tunnel, F track."

Kate glanced at Scarpelli. "You think?"

"A dark subway tunnel's not a bad place to hide," Scarpelli said. "Let's check it out. I'm going to the car to radio Morales, see if I can get Tommy Li or Dan Austin over here."

Kate said to Vasquez, "You call this in yet?"

"Right before you pulled up. Got a supervisor on the way."

"Okay, good. Control the scene until he shows."

She turned to go. The AC&C techs had put the dog on a sheet and were loading him in the van. He offered no resistance. Bad sign.

Kate stepped off the curb between two parked cars. From the gutter, a flash of yellow caught her eye. A legal pad. She picked it up, angled it toward a streetlight. Written across the top, "Attempted to track the donor organ and failed." And below that, "What do I do now?"

Holy shit. She was holding David McBride's notepad. She hurried to the car, placed it in a Ziplock bag, and as Scarpelli drove to Delancey, she scanned McBride's notes.

"Son of a bitch," she said over the blaring siren. "Turnbull *is* behind this, but McBride doesn't know it. He's being forced to steal kidneys, doesn't have enough to go to the cops, so he's trying to find a way out." Kate waved the pad at Scarpelli. "These are his options."

She read further. "McBride removes the kidneys in a warehouse of some kind, then they're taken to a second location for the actual transplant. He managed to track one of them as far as Edwardsville, the last town before NuLife, but something happened and he didn't make the connection to NuLife or Turnbull. So he runs through his options and decides the only way to keep himself and his wife safe is to go along with the scheme—to keep stealing organs."

"Then we knock on Turnbull's door," Scarpelli added, "and he thinks McBride *did* make the connection. We leave NuLife and within the hour, a Russian enforcer pays McBride a visit." He looked at Kate. "I got a feeling we're gonna be peeling him off the front of a train."

Kate studied the columns and arrows, the questions and answers filling the page. Every action and all possible ramifications were meticulously diagrammed out—an analytical mind at work. "Don't bet against the surgeon," she said.

- 34 -

David limped along the tracks as fast as the darkness would allow, grinding his teeth with each step, grunting a new obscenity every time his foot slipped into a hole or his toe caught the edge of a wooden tie. Every jolt sent pain surging down his leg and up through his hip to the lower back. His thigh burned. His eyes watered. His stomach churned. And he was slow. He held his watch next to a green lightbulb marking a utility box—8:43. Cassandra finished her shift at eleven. They had tried to abduct him and failed, so now they'd go after her. He had to get to Lenox Hill Hospital—more than eighty blocks uptown—before she walked out the door.

As he rounded a turn, the tunnel filled with light. He listened for the clatter of a moving train but heard only the drone of a PA system. Of course, a man had been hit. The section of track between Second Avenue and Delancey was now closed. A few minutes later the light became a glare, and a few minutes after that, the glare turned into two distinct orbs—the headlights of the parked southbound train.

Now that he could see, he stopped to reassess his leg. The exam he had performed in the dark was accurate. The bullet had entered midway between the knee and hip, passed through the outer aspect of the thigh—lateral to all vital structures—and exited the back of the leg. But both the quadriceps and hamstring compartments had been traversed by the slug, increasing the chances of developing a compartment syndrome. He loosened the shoelace on his right foot, slid a finger under the sock, and felt for a pulse. Still there, but for how long?

The bloodstain was close to what he had envisioned. A maroon splotch extended from mid-thigh to knee. He'd lost about half a unit of blood. Not a big deal. He could lose several units before becoming symptomatic. The stain itself, though, presented a huge problem. He couldn't exactly walk the streets of Manhattan with blood running down his leg. He needed to dress his wounds, and he needed clean pants. How to accomplish this? He had no idea.

David resumed his straight-legged gait, and as he scrutinized the ground for hazards it came to him, a remedy for the bloody pants. He kicked at the dirt between the track and the wall. Packed solid. He scraped his shoe along the base of the wall. Softer. Eddies of turbulent air had deposited loose dirt into the nooks and crannies. Keeping the injured leg straight, he bent over and scooped up a handful, then smeared it on the moist blood. It stuck, turning the dark-red stain into a cake of brown filth. He grabbed more dirt and rubbed it up and down both pant legs. When finished, he looked like he had spent the day digging a ditch.

As David neared the station, a rat scurried along the tracks ten feet in front of him. Both he and the rodent were conspicuous in the light of the parked train, but they were alone. The PA system repeatedly announced that the station was closed until further notice, to please find the nearest exit. The platform across from him, the northbound side, had already cleared. The train blocked his view of the southbound side.

He approached the end of the platform, which was even with the front of the train, and climbed the access steps. At the far end of the station, the conductor and a couple of transit cops stood at the base of the stairs, directing the last few stragglers up and out. David checked his pants. Fresh blood had seeped from the wounds. At first glance he was merely a dirty mess, but if anyone scrutinized his leg, the bullet hole and blood would be obvious.

In the second car of the train David found his ticket out. A middle-aged white man lay in a heap on a row of seats. David stepped into the car and jostled the guy's shoulder. The smell of urine clung to him. His clothes were filthy.

David shook him again. "Wake up, man. This is your stop."

His eyes opened into pink slits.

David shook harder. "Dude, this is your stop. Come on, I'll help you."

He raised himself onto an elbow and squinted at David. David pulled him upright.

His eyes now wide but glassed over, he mumbled, "I don't have a stop."

The remaining passengers had exited the station. The transit cops held their post. The conductor moved down the platform, checking each car, coming toward them.

"C'mon, man. We have to get you off the train. I'll count to three and you stand up."

He nodded sluggishly.

With all his weight on the good leg, David counted to three and tugged on the man's arm. Their efforts were timed perfectly. The homeless guy, bigger and heavier than David, popped out of the seat and into David's arms. David bear-hugged him and stutter-stepped to keep from falling backward. His thigh lit up with pain. His eyes watered. But they were standing. He positioned himself under the man's left arm.

"What's your name?" David asked.

The man lifted his head, slurred something resembling "Kevin," then let his chin fall back to his chest.

"Okay, Kevin, time to get out of here."

With David limping and Kevin shuffling, they made their way out of the car.

The conductor was twenty feet away. David checked the bleeding. The maroon stain had grown. He pulled Kevin close and pushed the bloody pant leg against Kevin's leg.

"Station's closed," the conductor said.

His head down, David nodded, and they staggered toward the exit and the transit cops.

As they passed the cops, the PA system announced, "All units in the Second Avenue station, be advised that witnesses report two men entering the F-track tunnel from the Delancey side, and only one accounted for. Repeat, two men entered the F-track tunnel from Delancey, only one accounted for. NYPD has been dispatched to seal all exits."

David tensed, expecting to hear the clicks and snaps of weapons being locked and loaded, or at least a stern command to stop, but heard nothing. He kept moving to the base of the stairs.

Four flights stood between David and Kevin and Second Avenue—two flights up to a mezzanine level, and two more up to the street. It might as well have been twenty. David considered leaving Kevin at the bottom, but the NYPD were looking for a single person. Having Kevin glued to his hip might be enough to throw them. Besides, the bloodstain was growing.

They climbed one step at a time, David's left hand pulling on the rail, his right arm steadying Kevin, his left leg doing all the work, his right leg bearing just enough weight for balance. Kevin supported his own bulk and stepped when David told him to, but his vestibulocochlear apparatus was toxic with alcohol. He rocked wildly every time he lifted a foot.

At the top of the first two flights, David stopped to catch his breath and contemplated the next two. Twenty-four steps remained, and he didn't think he could do it. Every sensory nerve in his body pulsed with pain. His stomach churned with the stench of filth and urine. Again, he considered leaving Kevin. Again, he abandoned the idea when a pair of uniformed NYPD officers started down the stairs. David tightened his hold on Kevin, fixed his gaze to the floor and hoped for a little luck.

They were about to take a step when a nightstick lodged against David's sternum.

"And where are you gentlemen off to?" asked one of the cops.

David briefly made eye contact. The one fondling his stick was young, and an asshole, judging by the look of disdain on his face. The other one was older, probably nearing retirement and had nothing to prove. David wanted to spill everything to the senior cop—the warehouse, the shooting, the danger to him and now Cassandra.

But where would that get him? He still didn't know who was behind the conspiracy. He'd find himself shackled to a bed on the Bellevue prison ward, while Cassandra was left to fend for herself. If he had nothing to offer the NYPD, they'd have nothing to offer him.

He bowed his head and spoke to the young cop's feet. "They ran us off, said the station is closed. We're looking for someplace warm to sleep."

The asshole cop jabbed Kevin with his stick. "What's wrong with him?"

Kevin nearly toppled. David struggled to hold him up. "Drank all the money he made on the train."

"Panhandling in the subway is illegal, right?" said the hard-ass.

"Uh … yes, sir. Maybe he should spend the night in a warm cell."

The cop nudged David with his club. "You gettin' smart?"

A siren echoed into the tunnel. David stared at the dirty concrete. "No, sir. Just not sure he'll survive the night in this condition, that's all."

The senior officer spoke up. "Last I heard, all the drop-in shelters are full, but Beth Israel has its ER waiting room open. No beds, but it's a warm place to sit."

Beth Israel Medical Center, New York Eye and Ear, and The Hospital for Joint Diseases were all within a few blocks of each other, but David couldn't remember the cross street. "Sounds good," he said, briefly looking up. "Beth Israel's on Second and …?"

"You'll want the ER entrance, which is on First and Sixteenth."

"Thank you. We'll be on our way, if it's okay."

"Yes," said the older man. "Be on your way now."

The cops went down. David and Kevin started up. At the top, two more officers blocked the entrance to the subway. They paid little attention as David and Kevin passed.

With Kevin held close to his side, David headed up Second Avenue. He needed three things: a safe place to deposit an incapacitated homeless man, dressing supplies for his leg, and a clean pair of pants for the trip uptown. He had one hour and forty-seven minutes to do all that and get to Cassandra.

- 35 -

Scarpelli held the flashlight while the medical examiner poked his latex-gloved finger into the dead Russian's temple. "It's like a bag of pulp," the ME said, then he kneaded the top and back of the skull as though it were a loaf of bread dough. He looked up at Kate and Scarpelli. "I doubt there's a piece of bone in there any larger than a poker chip."

Kate grinned. She loved working with the guys from the ME's office. They possessed a unique talent for turning grisly physical findings into vivid portraits of anatomical mayhem. Having grown up with a chief medical examiner for a father, she knew such morbidness came with the territory, a side effect of continued exposure to grotesque distortions of the human body, like the one that lay before her. The Russian's head resembled a medicine ball, his facial features obliterated by massive swelling, his neck twisted a hundred and eighty degrees, his limbs bent and angled in all the wrong directions. His clothes, skin, and muscle had burned away from his rib cage where he lay on the third rail, the blood draining from his ears and nose coagulated by the heat. The electricity had since been cut off, but the smell of high voltage and singed meat still hung in the air. Kate could almost hear the local rodent population sharpening its knives.

Scarpelli said, "What about that right arm, Doc? The way it's all shredded and torn up, would you say it looks like a dog got after it?"

"That's a fair assessment. Speeding trains crush organs. Third rails burn flesh. Vicious animals avulse soft tissue. I'll test the wound for saliva, but my working diagnosis is dog bite."

Scarpelli turned to Kate. "He's big, ugly, wearing an overcoat, right arm torn up. Any doubt in your mind?"

"No," Kate said.

A line of flashlight-bearing officers slowly moved toward them from the Delancey side, their beams sweeping back and forth as they combed the tracks for anything useful.

She added, "Witnesses see two men go in the tunnel. We have one body. Means McBride made it out. And being the smart guy that he is, he knows all hell's gonna break loose in Delancey when the train rolls in with Russian DNA smeared all over the front, so he keeps moving forward, to the Second Avenue station." She looked down the tracks. "Our next stop."

- 36 -

Despite Kevin's glass-eyed stare and David's grimace and limp, the two men were invisible as they tottered up Second Avenue. The bars, restaurants, and corner stores were doing brisk business in spite of the biting cold. People laughed in small groups, horns honked up and down the avenue, and those going inside, coming out, or waiting for others paid no attention to the spectacle of one derelict leading another up a busy sidewalk.

It seemed like every person they passed had a cell phone glued to their ear. David wanted to ask—no, beg—someone to borrow a phone, only for a moment, to make an urgent call. If he could just get a message into Cassandra's OR, telling her to stay put. But he quickly abandoned the idea. First, he'd be told to fuck off. Second, any such request would invite scrutiny, and scrutiny would result in a call to 911.

Between East 6th and 7th Streets he spotted one of the few remaining phone booths in the city. He dug through his pocket, found some change, but the receiver had been amputated from the cord.

By East 9th Street Kevin had become an insurmountable drag. It was now 9:40. David had an hour and twenty minutes to get uptown. He needed clean pants, he needed to dress his wounds, and he'd never make it unless he dumped Kevin. But the few homeless folks they had passed might as well have been cardboard cutouts. Nobody acknowledged them, let alone showed any concern for their well-being. An unconscious man would rapidly drop his core temperature, fibrillate and die, much like the rats in the lab.

David peered into Kevin's nystagmic eyes and knew the man's life now rested in his hands. He had dragged Kevin from the warmth to the cold. He was exploiting the man for his own gain. He couldn't just hand the guy over to chance and hope the cops or the Coalition for the Homeless found him in time. But that meant tipping the balance in favor of a stranger's well-being over his wife's. A bad decision, maybe, but as a resident he'd seen it all too often—"bumsicles" found unconscious on busy sidewalks, rushed to the operating room and placed on cardiopulmonary bypass so their blood could be warmed. Some lived, some died, but more than a few survived only to wake up with massive strokes. So yes, potentially a bad decision, but he was not going to leave a fellow human to freeze to death in one of the most densely populated cities in the world.

By East 14th Street the throbbing in David's leg was off the scale, and blood had seeped well beyond the dirt. The cold had perked up Kevin enough so he could consistently pick up his feet, but David still fought to keep the guy upright. His leg hurt. His back hurt. His arm hurt. His head ached. Even if he wanted to, there was no way he'd be able to haul an ataxic homeless man another seven blocks.

Thank Christ, he wouldn't have to.

The sidewalk on the north side of 14th was inlaid with subway-ventilation grates that blew warm air each time a train passed below, and a small community of homeless had formed. Some slept in boxes. Some lay on blankets. Some filled doorways. David led Kevin into a shallow entryway near a grate. Leaving a drunk person flat on his back was an invitation for him to drown in his own vomit, so David laid Kevin on his side and wedged him against the door. David thanked the oblivious man for his help and stuffed a ten-dollar bill deep in his pants pocket. And that gave David an idea.

He walked west along 14th Street, studying the men hanging out in boxes and lying on blankets. One of them would be close to his size. With his stocking cap low on his head, his shoulders hunched and his head down, David headed up Third Avenue. He had to find an ATM.

On the corner of 19th and Third he found what he needed. Three machines lined the wall of a locked enclosure, all three unoccupied. He swiped his bankcard. The lock clicked. A buzz followed, and the door opened. He inserted his card into the machine on the left and emptied the savings and checking accounts—about four hundred and fifty dollars—and waited as the inner workings hummed and counted. Then the lock clicked. The buzzer buzzed. The door opened behind him. He fought the urge to turn around, but he knew it was two young women. He could tell by their voices, the inane conversation. They went to the ATM on the right.

The right. Fuck! His bloody leg was fully exposed.

Their conversation ended abruptly.

His machine beeped, the cash and card waiting.

He half-turned as one of them hustled the other out the door.

He slipped the bills into his wallet, saw the girls step onto the corner across the street, one with a phone to her ear. They both wore short dresses, black stockings, and tall heels. Nobody makes a call with that much skin exposed to single-digit temperatures unless it's urgent. The girl with the phone looked over. Her eyes met his. Startled, she turned away. He pulled open the door and headed down Third Avenue, the way he had come, and away from the women.

At 18th Street he looked back. A cop car had stopped alongside the girls. He quickened his pace, swinging the bad leg in a big arc, while hopping with each step of the good leg. At 17th he looked again. One of the girls was leaning in the window, pointing at him. He had no choice but to run. The pain was excruciating, like someone driving nails into his thigh with every stride. He crossed 16th, heard the yelps of a siren, wanted to look back but he'd have to stop or risk falling. At 15th the siren went quiet. This time he did stop. One of the officers had jumped out and was now running down the avenue, the patrol car at a standstill in the Friday night gridlock. At 14th David rounded the corner, resumed as normal a gait as possible, tried to slow his breathing, and went straight to a refrigerator box he'd seen earlier. He dropped to one knee and crawled in, dragging his dead leg behind him.

A lump in a sleeping bag pushed him away and said, "What the fuck. Get outta here, asshole."

"Twenty bucks to keep your mouth shut and let me lie here for a moment," David said.

A black face, barely visible in the low light and cinched hood of a coat, peered out the top of the bag. "Forty bucks."

"Okay." David pulled three twenties out of his wallet. "I'll make it sixty if you'll spoon me and cover me with your sleeping bag."

The man snatched the bills from David's hand and unzipped the bag. David took off his stocking cap, rolled onto his side and scooted in close, stopping when his back was against the other man's chest. The homeless guy flipped the bag over them. "How long you say you need?"

"A couple of minutes."

"Fuckin' weird is all I got to say."

"Yeah, yeah. I know. How 'bout you pipe down."

David lay perfectly still, his heart hammering, his breathing labored. He covered his head with the sleeping bag, and the stench of unwashed clothes, body, hair, and feet made him gag. The sound of shoes scuffing along the concrete suppressed his urge to dry heave. Then, a burst of static, followed by, "I'm on Fourteenth between Second and Third, checking out the homeless camp. I'll meet you on Second."

The footsteps fell silent at the open end of the refrigerator box.

Three taps on the cardboard. "NYPD. Show yourself."

Both men lifted their heads. David stared into the flashlight, rubbed his eyes, gave his best impersonation of someone emerging from a deep sleep. The beam alternated from David's face, to the homeless man's, and back. The cop walked away.

David let his head fall onto the cardboard, but the relief was short-lived, interrupted by the pulsating pain in his leg and an elbow to the ribs.

"You can get out now."

David scooted out of the sleeping bag, moved up against the wall of the box and turned to face the homeless man. "Thanks for keeping quiet."

"Sixty bucks is sixty bucks."

"What's your name?"

"Larry."

"How would you like to earn another sixty dollars, Larry?"

"Make it eighty."

"You don't even know what I need."

"Don't matter."

"All right. Eighty bucks for your pants."

Larry leaned on one elbow. "You want my pants?"

"I'll give you mine, plus the cash."

"Those bloody things?"

"Tomorrow you can get a new pair at the Salvation Army and still have a nice profit."

"They gonna fit?"

"Good enough. And there's one other thing. I need you to run an errand for me."

- 37 -

The Lincoln Town Car crept along East 77th toward Lenox Hill Hospital.

"Let me out in front of the main entrance," Mr. White said to the Russian driver, Dimitri. "If you can find a place to park, go ahead, but not on this street, and nowhere near the subway station. If you can't park, circle around, but once again, stay off this street. Understand?"

Dimitri nodded.

"Wait for my call. I'll tell you where to pick me up."

Again, Dimitri nodded.

Mr. White jumped out, flipped up the collar of his overcoat, lowered his hat, and made his way to the sidewalk.

The Town Car turned left onto Park Avenue and disappeared.

- 38 -

David checked his watch. He'd been waiting for Larry for all of ten minutes, but it seemed like twenty. With the cold and pain settling deep in his core, he wouldn't be able to lie still much longer. And he had only thirty-two minutes to get to the subway, ride from East 14th to East 77th, and then walk another block to the staff entrance of Lenox Hill Hospital. He wondered if he should just go, forget the dressing supplies and clean pants, and take his chances. The answer was yes. He had to get moving or he was going to crawl right out of his skin.

He started to push himself into a sitting position when a plastic Duane Reade bag appeared in the opening of the box. Larry stooped down and handed it in to David. He checked the contents—two rolls of Kerlix gauze, two boxes of four-by-four gauze pads, a roll of cloth tape, a bottle of hydrogen peroxide. He moved the sleeping bag to the top of the refrigerator carton and set out the supplies. Larry sat cross-legged on the sidewalk and peered in.

Working fast, David opened a box of four-by-fours and made two stacks, each about an inch thick. He blew a warm breath on his cold fingers, then opened a roll of Kerlix and set it near the four-by-fours. He placed the tape and hydrogen peroxide next to the gauze. Everything was ready. Time to remove the pants.

He tried sitting up. The pain stopped him. He lay back on the cardboard, rested his head on the wadded up sleeping bag. "You mind popping off my shoes and giving my pants a tug?"

The cold felt like a hot iron against David's exposed skin. He propped himself onto an elbow, spread the Duane Reed bag under his thigh, and poured hydrogen peroxide into both bullet wounds. White froth boiled in the holes and instantly turned pink. His eyes watered. He groaned through clenched teeth. He drizzled more peroxide, muttered a string of profanities.

He'd need both hands to dress the leg, so he forced himself to sit up, grimacing with the added pain. He grabbed the first stack of gauze pads, placed it over the exit wound, and wrapped it tightly with Kerlix. He put the second stack on the entrance wound, wrapped it tight, then used the rest of the roll to go up and down the thigh. After blowing on his fingers, he tore three strips of tape from the roll and secured the end of the gauze to itself. The snug dressing would stem the bleeding, but the trade-off was increased pressure inside the fascial compartment. He felt for the pulse on top of his foot—diminished by at least half. Dammit. Either the dressing was too tight, or the swelling within the compartment had increased. Possibly both, but he could do nothing about it. Not now. Not with only twenty-four minutes to get to Cassandra.

"You done this before," Larry said.

"Used to be a surgeon."

"Me too. Then I got laid off … the wife left … you know how it goes."

"Actually, I do." David leaned back on his elbows. "Pants, please?"

Larry took off his boots and stood, upper body disappearing above the opening in the box, big toes protruding from holes in black socks. His belt slipped out of its loops. His jeans came off a leg at a time and landed in David's lap.

David worked his way into the pants—a good fit at the waist, about three inches too short—and had Larry help him with his shoes, and out of the box. Once steady on his feet, he looked up and down 14th. No cops.

He pulled two more twenty-dollar bills out of his wallet. "Forty for the coat?"

"Ain't you got no shame, totally exploitin' a homeless man?"

"Not tonight."

"Then let's make it sixty," Larry said with a toothy grin.

The men swapped jackets. Larry's was made of heavy green canvas lined with fake fur. It smelled as bad as the sleeping bag, but it was warm and had a hood that David would be able to cinch around his face. He stuffed the remaining dressing supplies into the pockets and held out his stocking cap. "You're gonna need this. And thanks for your help."

"No problem. If you're ever in the neighborhood—"

"Yeah, I know."

David cinched the hood tight enough so no one could see in and he could barely see out, then limped to the corner of 14th and Third. He was wearing another man's dirty pants and foul-smelling coat, but the clothes and his altered gait gave him a new identity. He now blended into the landscape of Manhattan's underbelly, was now a member of the urban netherworld. He glanced at his watch—10:42. Eighteen minutes to travel sixty-three blocks. If only the new clothes made him faster.

- 39 -

David clutched the pole as the 6 train barreled uptown. The rocking and the clatter and the repeated reminders to stand clear of the doors, along with the throbbing leg, the stench of the coat, and the fear—especially the fear—had his stomach twisting and turning. He needed to get out of this hole, get aboveground, and take a big breath of cold air or he was going to heave. With Grand Central behind them, the car had emptied considerably. A handful of Spanish- and African-Americans, probably on their way to Harlem or The Bronx, and a few Caucasians, probably not on their way to Harlem or The Bronx, were all that remained, giving him a corner to himself. He thought about sitting, but his thigh had turned to granite, and his knee would no longer bend, so he stood with most of his weight on the good leg and counted the remaining stops on the map. Four more to West 77th, but with every passing minute, his body's store of adrenaline and endorphins was depleting, and the pain was intensifying. He wondered if he'd be able to walk at all when he got there.

After what seemed like hours instead of minutes, the train pulled into the 77th Street station. The time—10:54. Grimacing with every step, he left the car and limped his way along the platform. He exited through a turnstile and bypassed the stairs up to the street, opting instead for the handicap elevator, which he finally found in a dark corner. He hit the button. The doors slid open. The stench of urine enveloped him, burning his eyes and nose. He reconsidered, but decided that breathing rancid piss for ten seconds was better than climbing thirty or forty steps. He got in and punched the up button.

The elevator opened onto the street, and David gasped for air like a kid coming up from the deep end of a pool. He filled his lungs several times, pumping new life into the gray matter of his brain. His nausea cleared. His senses sharpened. His focus returned. He cinched the hood of his coat and headed up East 77th Street. The hospital entrance Cassandra used was one block away, on the corner of 77th and Park Avenue. He'd made it.

He made his way down the sidewalk, hunched over and limping, bumbling along as if searching for a warm place to sleep or a garbage can to pick through. If Mr. White wanted him—dead or alive—the entrance to Cassandra's hospital would be a likely place for a goon-squad-in-waiting. Halfway down the block he stopped and hugged a tree rising from a square hole in the concrete. He peered out of the fur-lined tunnel of his hood, scanned the sidewalks and apartment-building entryways, the nearby cars. He saw nothing suspicious. He shambled thirty feet, hugged another tree, looked around. No silhouettes lurking. No cigarette embers glowing. No one sitting in a parked car.

A garbage can sat at the curb outside the hospital entrance. He went over, leaned against it and checked his watch—11:04. But it usually took Cassandra a few minutes to physically leave the building. She had to give report to the oncoming staff, collect her belongings, and ride the elevator down from the eighth floor. He'd made it on time. If she had left right at eleven, he would have seen her walking to the subway. He reached for the sky and stretched his stiff neck and back. The tension drained away.

A coworker of Cassandra's came through the revolving door. She moved fast, making a beeline for the subway. David couldn't remember her name. He hobbled after her.

"Excuse me," he shouted.

She kept going.

He caught up and grabbed her shoulder. "Excuse me," he said, huffing, puffing and grimacing.

She turned and recoiled in fear.

He pulled the hood off his head. "I'm David McBride, Cassandra's husband."

She stepped back, confusion replacing fear. "Dr. McBride? You're supposed to be at Bellevue undergoing surgery."

"Say again?"

"A detective from the NYPD called into the OR and told Cassandra you were shot during a subway robbery. He said you went to Bellevue for emergency surgery, and he'd take her there if she'd meet him in the lobby. She scrubbed out of her case and left."

"What? She left with him? Are you sure?" David looked up and down the street, bewildered, searching for a remnant of what happened, some clue as to what he should do next.

"I know she left early," the woman said. "That's all I can tell you."

"When—when did she leave?"

"About twenty minutes ago? Are you okay, Dr. McBride? You're pale, and you're sweating."

"I'm fine. I just—" David looked up and down the street again, then at the woman. "Do you have a cell phone?"

"Yes." She took it from her bag and handed it to him.

He dialed Cassandra's number.

A female answered. Janine Lieberman, one of the charge nurses.

"Janine—David McBride. How'd you get Cassandra's phone?"

"She forgot it in the OR. She was frantic when she scrubbed out. Are you all right, Dr. McBride? We heard you'd been shot. Cassandra left with a—"

"Yeah, I know. Uh, yes, I'm okay. I need to go."

He thrust the phone at Cassandra's coworker. "Thank you," he said absently as he formulated his next move.

Mr. White now had Cassandra. He'd be trying to call, to make demands or level threats or whatever the fuck they were up to. David's only option: go back to the apartment and get the TracFone.

- 40 -

Cassandra McBride sat huddled in the corner of the backseat, blotting her eyes with the handkerchief Mr. White had offered. After observing her and listening in on her conversations over the past couple of months, he had become quite fond of the young woman, finding many of the same qualities in her that his own daughter possessed, or had possessed before a chronic, debilitating disease robbed her of her vitality. He just hoped to God he could protect Cassandra McBride from the sociopathic Andrew Turnbull.

"Did anyone tell you about his condition? Is he stable? Critical? Where was he shot? What part of the body?"

"I was told he's in stable condition, and that's all I know."

"When you called into the OR, you said they took him for emergency surgery."

"Yes, but I don't think the injuries were life-threatening."

"Can't we go any faster? Don't you have one of those sirens you can stick on the roof?"

"No need to worry. We'll get you there in a timely fashion."

"If he's stable, why did they send two detectives to pick me up? Is that standard procedure?"

"Well, as it turns out, we have a special interest in your husband. We believe he's become mixed up with black-market organ thieves, and we've been keeping tabs on him lately."

Cassandra looked out the window for a moment, then back at Mr. White, her expression lacking any sign of shock or surprise at such a revelation. He knew McBride had told her.

"Do you think this is related?" she asked.

"It seems like a random mugging, but we'll look into the possibility."

At 47th Street the driver turned west off Park Avenue.

Cassandra spun and looked out the passenger window, then back at Mr. White. "Where are we going? Bellevue is on the east side. We should've taken a left on Forty-Eighth."

"Just a slight detour."

"Bullshit. What is this? What's going on?"

They stopped at a red light. Cassandra tried rolling down the window but couldn't, then started beating on the glass and screaming for help at the people standing on the corner.

Mr. White grabbed her head and shoved it onto the seat with one hand, and clamped her mouth shut with the other. He held her down as they drove crosstown and entered the Lincoln Tunnel, and the more she struggled, the tighter his grip, and the tighter his grip, the more his brutality shocked and sickened him.

She finally succumbed and lay still, but he kept her pinned down until they were north of Paterson, New Jersey, where the busy, well-lit byway had narrowed to a dark, less-traveled state route. When he released her, she wedged herself into the corner, putting the full expanse of the backseat between them. She pushed the hair out of her face, and with shaking hands wiped tears from her cheeks and spittle from the corner of her mouth.

"You're a fucking animal," she said.

Mr. White stared into his lap, squeezed his eyes shut, then looked up. "I'm sorry. It sickens me to think I am capable of such brutality, but these are extraordinary circumstances." He turned in the seat and faced her squarely. "I have a daughter about your age, and she's dying from end-stage kidney disease. Her prognosis is measured in months."

"So she needs a transplant, and if she's that sick, she should be at the top of the list."

"Yes, but she has already rejected two kidneys, and she's had so many transfusions over the years her blood is full of antibodies. Add to that her AB+ blood type, and it's been impossible for us to find a match."

Cassandra pushed a lock of hair behind her ear. "And that gives you the right to kidnap and assault a pregnant woman?"

"No, it doesn't. Nothing like this was supposed to happen."

"Well maybe you can tell me what *is* supposed to happen."

"We need David to perform one more organ harvest and we're done. Unfortunately, there was an incident earlier this evening, and now he's missing."

"An incident? What does that mean?"

"One of our enforcers deviated from the plan and chased David into a subway tunnel. The Russian is dead, but there was no sign of David down there, so we think he got out alive, and now we need to bring him in."

"Why didn't you just wait for him in front of Lenox Hill? You had to know that's the first place he'd go."

"That was our strategy earlier tonight, but things got a little messy."

"What if he's not okay? What if he's hurt? How do you know he's not somewhere in the tunnel dying? It's a maze down there."

"That's why we picked you up. If he has an ounce of life left in him, he'll do whatever it takes to help you."

"Risking the life of an innocent man, and brutalizing his wife is going to help your daughter live?"

"It's complicated, but yes."

"And she's okay with that, and when you're finished with us, and you dump our bodies in the Jersey swamp, she's okay with that, too?"

"I promise you, nothing like that is going to happen. Neither you nor your husband have been exposed to anyone of importance other than myself, and when this is over, I will simply disappear." Mr. White pulled a black cloth sack from his coat pocket. "We're getting close to our destination, so in order to keep my promise, I need you to put this over your head."

- 41 -

David crossed Park Avenue, stepped into the southbound lane of traffic and raised his hand. A cab veered toward him and slowed, but when the driver got a good look at the stained coat and dirty pants, he punched the accelerator and chiseled his way back into traffic. Five or six additional cabs passed before another pulled over, but that one blew him off as well. Figuring another descent into the feted hell of the subway would finish him off, David lumbered along 77th back to Lexington, went a half block south to the bus stop, and leaned against a Learning Annex box while he waited for the M101.

His heart was racing and his breathing labored—nothing new—but as he stood there at rest, the heart should have slowed and the breathing should've eased. They didn't. Tachycardia and tachypnea—rapid heart rate and shortness of breath—were the two most common symptoms of anemia. Maybe he had lost more blood than he thought. Or maybe he had bled into his thigh. The thigh was the largest muscle mass in the body, and it was possible he was still bleeding into all of that soft tissue. If so, he could do nothing about it. Even if he were hemorrhaging all over the sidewalk, it wouldn't keep him from going after the phone.

The bus screeched to a stop, followed by a rush of nauseating diesel exhaust, hissing air brakes, and the door whipping open. David hopped up the steps with his good leg, grabbed a pole, and braced himself for the long ride from the Upper East Side to the Lower East Side.

Thirty agonizing minutes later he disembarked in front of the Hamilton Fish Park on Houston. After the bus rumbled away—

leaving him gagging on more diesel fumes—he resumed the bumbling-homeless-guy act and gimped over to Ridge Street. Turning the corner, he stopped. A half block down, in front of the entrance to his apartment building, a sea of whirling red lights.

"Dammit," he mumbled through clenched teeth. Why were the cops still there? Muggings and other lowlife street crimes occurred in this part of the city every night, and the police usually wrapped up their investigations quickly. In the eyes of the NYPD, one person accosting another, gun or no gun, should look like nothing more than a drug deal gone bad, or any of the myriad other reasons one person shoots another. There was no way they would devote so much manpower to a run-of-the-mill street crime, even if animal cruelty was a factor. This level of attention meant one thing—the NYPD were looking for him.

David cinched the coat tighter, stooped a little lower, and was hobbling his way closer when a huge commotion erupted outside the entrance. He couldn't see what was happening, but what he heard filled him with horror—his father, in the grip of a massive catastrophic reaction, screaming and yelling, "They're killing me! They're killing me!" David rushed down the sidewalk and joined a small group of gawkers held back by an NYPD sawhorse and a uniformed cop. Not ten yards away he saw Hal McBride—Navy veteran and championship boxer, loving father and devoted husband—strapped to a stretcher like an animal. The paramedics loaded him into a Bellevue ambulance, slammed the door, and drove away, lights and siren blaring.

David grasped the sawhorse, his eyes brimming with tears. His father would soon be admitted to the Bellevue psych ward, getting poked and prodded by nurses, medical students and psychiatry residents. He'd be terrified and alone, suffering through a perpetual catastrophic reaction, his baseline confusion gone viral. David could only hope they quickly loaded him with Thorazine and tucked him away in a dark room.

He gimped his way back up Ridge Street to Houston, over to the bus stop at the Fish Park, and lowered himself onto the bench.

He let his head fall forward, squeezed his eyes shut, and wondered about Cassandra. Where was she? What was she going through? Would they harm her, or worse? The two most important people in his life, the only people in his life, and they were gone, taken away. He wanted to scream, beat on his bad leg, jump in front of a bus, but he couldn't allow himself to fall apart now. He needed to enter some kind of adrenaline-fueled, fight-or-flight hyperdrive. He needed to act. He needed to figure out what to do next.

- 42 -

Kate walked down the hallway leading to the office of Lieutenant Joseph Hernandez, commander of the 13th Precinct Detective Squad. She wanted to turn the kidney-snatching case into a media shit-storm by morning, and to do that, she needed her boss on board. It usually required a divine act to get any of the supervisors back to the station house after hours, but now that they had some solid leads, Hernandez had developed a sudden interest in the case. Kate sensed he was about to appoint himself the face of the investigation.

She waited outside the door while he paced back and forth, talking on the phone, seemingly unaware of her presence. Hernandez was tall and lean with nearly perfect olive skin and a full head of black hair combed straight back. Other than a few wrinkles at the corners of his eyes, and a touch of gray on his temples, he appeared remarkably young for a man in his position. He said, "This thing is about to get really hot, Robert."

Robert O'Callaghan, chief of detectives, Kate figured. The bosses liked to push the shit uphill to cover their own assess, just as she was doing now. No doubt the chief of detectives would hang up and call the chief of department, who would then call the deputy commissioner of public information, who would brief the commissioner in the a.m.

"The lead detective is standing outside my door."

Hernandez waved her in and pointed at one of two metal chairs in front of his desk. She went in and sat down, a fresh copy of McBride's notes in her hand, the original legal pad already dusted for prints and logged in as evidence.

"She wants to go public, tonight. Thinks the cutter is being coerced, and his life is in danger."

Hernandez looked at Kate, his face expressionless. She returned his gaze for a moment, then glanced past him at a collection of plaques and pictures on the wall.

"Okay," Hernandez said. "I'll see what she has and call you back."

He hung up the phone and took his seat. The springs in the faux-leather chair groaned and popped as he leaned back. "Big night, huh?"

Kate laid it all out—the meeting with Perry, the visit to NuLife, the chase of McBride into the subway, security cameras showing him exiting the Second Avenue station, the report of a man matching his description getting cash from an ATM, then ditching the cops near East 14th Street and Third Avenue. "And that's where the trail goes cold. The thing that worries me? The cameras show him sprinting into Delancey, then limping out of Second Ave. The girls at the ATM are sure they saw blood on the right leg of his pants."

"You think he's been shot?"

"I'd bet on it. We notified the ERs. If it's a significant injury we'll hear about it."

Hernandez pointed at the page of copied notes. "Let's see what you got."

Kate pushed it over to him.

"McBride's prints on the pad?"

"All over it."

"Why did he have prints on file?"

"Medical license application."

"They have a photo?"

"No," Kate said, "and his only driver's license was issued when he was sixteen. He moved into the city when he started college, probably sold his car and let his license lapse."

"Did you check the social media sites?"

"Yes, but found nothing. We Googled him and got a few hits, but no photos. We're checking with NYU to see if they still have an ID-badge photo in their files."

The lieutenant put on his glasses and read the page of notes. A couple of minutes later he tossed it onto the desk and removed his glasses. "I agree with you. Looks like McBride is an unwilling participant, trying to extricate himself. Interesting how, after he weighs all of his options, he decides to stop meddling and just go along, then he's chased into a subway tunnel."

"Yes," Kate said. "The timing fits with our visit to NuLife. McBride doesn't know who's manipulating him, but Turnbull thinks McBride does know, so Turnbull sends an enforcer to pick him up before we can get to him, and McBride panics and runs."

Hernandez nodded in agreement. "What else do we have besides a handwritten list of options and the account of a paranoid-schizophrenic homeless man?"

"Nothing. There is a Dr. Steinberg on the psych service, but he's gone AWOL. We've checked the alleys where the victims woke up, and canvassed the nearby buildings, but came up empty. The legal pad is the only hard lead we have."

"So what do you want to do?"

"First, we get McBride's photo, then go full court press with the media—TV, radio, morning papers, and as soon as we can get everyone out of bed, a press conference announcing a Crime Stoppers reward. We'll play up the connection between McBride and some kind of international black market, keep Turnbull out of the glare, let him relax while all this unfolds. Hopefully, we can put together enough probable cause to get Passaic County on board with a search warrant, then we'll hit NuLife."

The lieutenant nodded. "Okay. Get me everything you can on McBride and Turnbull before morning. I want to be standing on the steps of One Police Plaza, facing every news organization in the tri-state area, by eight a.m. And I want you standing next to me."

Kate walked down the hall, shaking her head. Goddamn climber. If he wanted face time in front of the cameras, so be it, but he didn't have to drag her along. She had better things to do than stand there, smiling and nodding and showing the public that women make good detectives, too.

- 43 -

David hesitated outside the revolving door. The Hotel Pennsylvania was not one of New York's finest hotels, but it was far from one of its worst. He reconsidered finding a flophouse over on Ninth or Tenth where he wouldn't stand out, but it was crucial that he clean his wounds, hydrate himself, eat something, and check the news. He needed his own bathroom, room service, and a television. He had attended a transplant surgery symposium at the Hotel Penn a couple of years ago, so the familiarity of the place gave him a small measure of comfort. And besides, he had no travel left in him. He'd gone from Lower East Side to Upper East Side, back to the Lower East Side, and now stood in Midtown. He'd been chased twice, shot once, had limped across half the city, ridden its nauseating subways and climbed aboard its toxic buses. He had to get off his feet and elevate his leg before the swelling pinched off his femoral artery and vein. He'd be of no use to Cassandra with a bloodless, dying leg. He went inside.

Luck was on his side. The lobby was mostly empty. He used the wheelchair ramp to bypass a set of steps and did his best to suppress his limp as he made his way to the check-in counter. The young woman staffing the desk looked him up and down, then turned and grimaced as the odor of Larry's clothes wafted behind the counter. He couldn't blame her.

"May I help you, sir?" she asked, with a great deal of sarcasm accenting the sir.

"I'd like a room, please."

"I'll have to check our availability."

The woman went into the back. A moment later, a thin man with a French accent appeared, seemingly annoyed that he had to deal with a derelict. His name tag identified him as Jean-Pierre. "I am sorry," he said, "but we do not have any rooms available."

"It's the middle of January, and this is a big place," David said. "I suspect you probably do have rooms available."

"Yes, but we reserve them for tourists and business persons, not street ruffians."

"I'll admit, I'm dirty and I smell—"

"And you have no luggage."

"I'm a freelance writer doing a story on New York's homeless population. I thought I'd live on the streets for a while, but it's too damn cold. I'm cutting the assignment short."

"Then perhaps you have a credit card and photo ID stashed upon your person."

"I have cash."

"Rates start at one-seventy-nine per night, but I'm certain those units are occupied."

David dropped ten twenties on the counter. "I'll take whatever you have."

Jean-Pierre glanced at the bills, then gave David a look that said, *You can do better than this.*

David added two more to the stack.

Jean-Pierre scooped up the bills with the deftness of a poker player gathering his cards. "I think we can accommodate you. Name, please?"

David hesitated for a moment, then said, "Lazarus, David Lazarus."

Jean-Pierre tapped the keyboard and peered at the monitor. "Room 1408," he said to the woman. Then he looked up at David. "We'll have your clothes laundered if you'd like."

"At this time of night?"

"This is New York. Anything is possible if you have the money."

"Isn't that the truth."

"Pardon me?"

"Nothing. How much?"

"Forty ought to cover it."

David handed Jean-Pierre two more twenties.

"I'm sorry the writing assignment didn't work out. Perhaps you can come back during the warmer months."

"Perhaps."

"Call down to the desk when it is convenient for us to pick up the clothes. We will have them back in your room no later than eight a.m."

Giving up his clothing seemed like a bad move, but the thought of taking a bath, then putting dirty clothes back on, was decidedly unappealing. "Sounds fine."

"And lastly, if you have sustained an injury, we do maintain an on-call physician."

"I twisted my ankle. I just need to get off it for a while. A physician won't be necessary."

"I'll have a bag of ice sent up immediately."

"Make it two, if you would."

Jean-Pierre handed David a card key. "The elevator is across the lobby on the other side of the partitions. Thank you, and welcome to the Hotel Pennsylvania."

- 44 -

The water was as hot as David could stand it, yet he was still having trouble scrubbing the clotted blood off his skin, particularly those beads of clot matted to the hairs. He doused his thigh with more hydrogen peroxide, tensing as it drained into the wounds and boiled. Reddish-brown foam dripped into bathwater the color of cherry Kool-Aid. He tossed a dirty washcloth in the corner, grabbed a clean one, and dabbed the entrance and exit wounds. With added pressure he rubbed the rest of the thigh.

The bathroom resembled a trauma bay in the Bellevue ER, the wastebasket full of bloody gauze, blood-soaked washcloths strewn over the white-tiled floor. The air smelled of stale blood and filth, much like an OR after operating on a homeless person who'd been shot or stabbed.

With his leg as clean as it was going to get, David emptied the tub and refilled it. He now had the proper conditions to fully assess his injury. The entrance wound was about a half inch in diameter, the exit about an inch-and-a-half. Small going in, large coming out. The slug had been a hollow point, or some other type of mushrooming design. Blackish-purple bruising encircled the wounds. The skin edges, and the macerated tissue beneath the skin, continued to ooze, but there was no heavy bleeding. The depths of the wound, and probably the entire path of the bullet, was filled with clot. He opted to leave it undisturbed. Clotted blood was a good thing. Flushing it out would only stir up more bleeding.

The right thigh was markedly larger than the left, and rock hard. With great difficulty, he bent forward and felt the pulse on his foot. Barely detectable, and the swelling hadn't finished. If he packed the leg in ice and kept it elevated through the night, maybe he'd be out of the compartment-syndrome woods by morning. And if not? If he woke up with a blue foot? He pushed the thought from his mind. To dwell on it now was a useless endeavor.

David had seen plenty of gruesome injuries as a surgery resident, but cleaning matted blood from his own skin and examining a through-and-through gunshot wound to his own thigh defied reality. If the slug had traversed any other part of his body—like the head, chest, or abdomen—he'd be dead. He hoped to God he'd somehow get one-on-one time with the detestable scumbag who had dragged Cassandra, himself, and his father into this freakish nightmare. He was not above trading an eye for an eye, and given the chance, he'd do a lot more than inflict a soft-tissue injury. He toweled off, dressed his leg, donned a white terry-cloth robe, and went to the other room where a cheeseburger, fries, and vanilla milkshake awaited him.

The smell of grease made his stomach lurch. Guess he wasn't hungry after all. He kept the shake, moved the tray into the hall, then propped his leg up on a chair. After burying his thigh with bags of ice, he turned on New York One, the city's own twenty-four-hour news channel. The lead story: a ninety-two-year-old woman—Miss Sadie Mitchell—had been killed by a stray bullet as she sat on the couch of her Bronx apartment.

Shaking his head, he checked the time. It was 1:38 a.m., and so far, no mention of an organ-snatching surgeon or a man hit by a subway train. Ongoing stories cycled around at the top of the hour. He'd wait for the two a.m. update, then try to sleep—*try* being the key word. He'd now been awake for over forty-two hours, but his leg was throbbing, his body ached, and his brain was scrambling for answers. Sleep was not going to come easy.

The two-a.m. hour led off with a homicide on Orchard Street, just a couple of blocks over from David's place on Ridge. The incident was newsworthy in that it appeared the shooter was a close friend of the victim—a college buddy. They'd been hitting the bars, got into an argument outside their apartment building, and the one guy pulled a gun and shot the other in the chest. An educated white guy packing a piece while bar hopping, and he used it on his friend. David shook his head in disgust. Innocent old ladies murdered by sociopathic punks. Friends shooting friends in the chest. Those ruled by greed praying on the mentally ill. Where was the humanity in this fucking world?

"And also on the Lower East Side," the anchorman continued, "a man was hit and killed by a train after chasing another man into a subway tunnel earlier this evening." According to eyewitness accounts—explained a female reporter, standing on the very platform from which David and the big Russian had jumped—one man chased another into the north tunnel of the F track at Delancey Street station where one of the men was hit and killed by a train. The whereabouts of the second man was unknown. The reporter went on to say the subway incident was apparently related to an earlier shooting on Ridge Street, where a dog was injured. The motive for the shooting and subsequent pursuit remain unclear, she said.

"Bullshit," David said to the television. The cops knew who he was and where he lived, and that meant the entire NYPD was now looking for David McBride, MD, the failed surgeon who had turned to stealing organs for a living. At least his face wasn't plastered across the screen. Not yet anyway.

He climbed onto the bed, elevated his leg with pillows, and repositioned the ice. He wasn't expecting quality sleep, but if he could keep his leg higher than his heart for several hours, the swelling might go down just enough to ease the pain and avert a compartment syndrome.

He closed his eyes. Murky images of Cassandra locked away in a dark room, and his father strapped to a bed on the Bellevue psych ward, immediately crowded into his brain. An overwhelming sense of longing and isolation followed, along with an aching desire to be with them in their dreary apartment, eating Chinese food, drinking water with lemon slices, and watching *Rocky*.

- 45 -

A slamming door jarred David awake. He sat up, disoriented, but the pain in his leg quickly reoriented him. He glanced at the clock—7:27 a.m. He'd slept more than five hours. He flipped back the bedding, found himself lying in blood-soaked sheets, but it wasn't fresh blood. The stain was thin and watery, serum from clot breakdown. That was good and bad—good that he wasn't bleeding, but if there was substantial clot in his leg, it could drain for days and soak a lot of dressings. He felt his pulse—still weak—but his toes were warm and pink.

He fell back into the pillows, stared at the ceiling, and made a mental list of priorities. Get out of bed before the laundry valet showed up. Clean and dress his wounds. Dispose of the bloody linens. Leave the building unseen. Get more dressing supplies, and if that weren't enough, he needed to figure out how to make contact with Mr. White, do whatever the fucker wanted in exchange for Cassandra.

He grabbed the remote and turned on New York One. The NY-1 icon in the lower left corner of the screen displayed the temperature as four degrees at 7:39 a.m. The forecast predicted a daytime high of ten degrees with gusting winds, dropping the wind-chill factor well into the subzero range. The top stories would lead off the hour.

Lowering his stiff leg to the floor as if it were a glass log, he slowly climbed off the bed. If the swelling had decreased while he slept, he couldn't tell, but the pain had diminished slightly, from a throb to a constant ache. It still wouldn't bend without sending bolts of electricity up his spine, but it could bear about a third of his weight. He put on the robe, left a five-dollar bill on the desk, and went into the bathroom.

He sat on the toilet with his leg outstretched and a towel underneath, uncoiled the gauze, and tossed everything in the wastebasket. Even though the dressings were soaked with bloody serum, the wound edges were clean and the bleeding had stopped. Using a washcloth, he drizzled warm, soapy water into the depths of the wounds, then gently dabbed the skin edges and macerated muscle. He followed that with hydrogen peroxide irrigation.

A knock on the door. David jumped. "Who is it?"

The muffled voice of a young male. "I have your laundry, sir."

David told him to come in, then panicked when the lock clicked open. He couldn't remember if he had pulled the blanket over the bloodstained sheets. He pushed the bathroom door to within an inch of being closed, and waited.

Plastic rustled and paper crinkled. The valet said, "I brought in your complimentary copy of the *New York Times*. Is there anything else I can do for you?"

David exhaled. "No. I'm good. The five on the desk is yours."

"Yes, sir. Thank you."

David wrapped his leg with clean gauze, washed up, and returned to the room, cinching the belt on the robe as he went. The clothes were on the bed—the coat and pants in a dry cleaner's bag, the other things wrapped in a brown paper bundle tied with string. The bloodstain was hidden under the bedspread.

The valet had placed the newspaper on the desk near the window. The headline read: "Suspect Sought in NYC Kidney-Snatching Case." And below that, a photograph of the suspect. A photograph of him.

He yanked open the blackout curtain, letting in more light. His NYU physician-ID photo, blown up about ten times, stared up at him. His entire body buzzed as if an electric current were passing through it, turning his skin clammy, beading his brow with sweat. He sat down and read the story.

A New York City man is sought in connection with a kidney-snatching scheme that preys upon mentally ill homeless
men. David McBride, a former New York University surgical resident, and presently a lab tech at Columbia Medical
Center, is believed to be involved with the theft of two kidneys from two separate victims. Evidence suggests the organs
have been sold to brokers who represent an international
black market. Investigators have linked McBride to a shooting that took place in front of his Manhattan apartment
building last night, and the subsequent death of a man in the
north tunnel of the F track at the Delancey Street subway
station. McBride's present whereabouts are unknown.

The television flickered in David's peripheral vision, and there
he was again, his photo in the upper-left-hand corner of the screen.
A high-ranking cop—a lieutenant, according to the graphic—was
making a statement from the steps of One Police Plaza. Next to
him stood a stone-faced female cop, lead investigator on the case,
Detective Kate D'Angelo. The lieutenant essentially repeated the
story in the paper, then opened up the conference to questions.

David became increasingly pissed off as he heard his name
repeated again and again, questions about his background, his mari-
tal status, was he dangerous, was he mentally disturbed, was this the
same Dr. McBride fired for manipulating liver transplants two years
ago? No mention was made of Russian mobsters or Chinese illegal
immigrants. He, and he alone, was the face of the kidney-snatching
scheme. He, and he alone, was preying on homeless men. He was
a sick, soulless ghoul, and now the entire city would be looking for
him, spurred on by a Crime Stoppers reward of $25,000.

He calmed himself and tried to focus. Only two people knew he
had checked in here, and hopefully, they were home in bed. On the
other hand, they might have seen the morning papers or watched
the news before turning in. They might have already called in to
report that the kidney-snatching ghoul was staying in room 1408 of
the Hotel Pennsylvania. He had to get dressed and get out.

- 46 -

The elevator took forever to get to the fourteenth floor. He was alone in the vestibule, but probably not for long. The Pennsylvania was a big place with a lot of rooms on each floor. Someone was bound to walk around the corner any second. He studied himself in the full-length mirror on the wall. The hood of the coat was cinched down tight, but if scrutinized in good light, he'd be recognizable. And there was plenty of reason to scrutinize him the way he was skulking around inside a major hotel, hidden inside his coat like a street thug.

The bell pinged. The doors opened. One person occupied the car, a man in a business suit, briefcase in one hand, the *Times* in the other. Engrossed in the front-page story, he didn't look up. David moved to the back.

The elevator stopped soon after it started down. David leaned into the corner and stared at his feet. Two more men entered. "Dude," one of them said. "Did you see the morning paper?"

"Yeah. Stealing kidneys? That's fucked up. Is there anything that can't be bought and sold?"

"Not anymore," said the man who'd been reading the *Times*. "That pretty much completes the list."

David closed his eyes. A new low in man's indifference toward his fellow man had been reached, and he was the face of it, coerced or not. Mercifully the bell pinged, the doors opened, and the men hurried out. David followed, his shoulders drawn up and his head lowered.

He stopped at the mouth of the elevator alcove and studied the lobby. It was a busy place, mostly businessmen and women in suits, moving with purpose, talking on phones, texting, e-mailing, reading documents or newspapers. The Seventh Avenue exit was at the far end, a mile away, it seemed. He started toward it, trying to minimize his limp, but any attempt to bend his knee was met with pain. Between his faded jeans, worn sneakers, heavy canvas coat, and dead leg dragging behind, he was convinced all eyes were upon him. He tried to keep his head down and face hidden but was forced to look up every few seconds for fear of running into someone or tripping over the edge of a rug. He passed by the front desk, busy with people checking out, the exit now twenty yards away. He was almost there.

From Seventh Avenue a siren wailed, and it was growing louder, coming toward the hotel. David wanted to turn and go the other way, but it wouldn't do any good. He stood out like Quasimodo and moved about as fast. If the cops were coming for him, it was all over. He lowered his head and quickened his pace, the exit now a few yards away.

He pushed through the revolving door, nearly spilling onto the sidewalk as the next panel came around and hit him from behind. An NYPD patrol car blew by, lights flashing, siren blaring. He took a deep breath and reminded himself that he was in New York City, and despite being one of the most densely populated cities in the world, it was also one of the easiest places to remain anonymous if one didn't call attention to oneself.

It also had to be one of the coldest. A frigid gust of wind knocked him back a half step. A bronchial spasm cut his breaths short, the body's way of protecting the lining of the lungs. He squinted at the strip of blue sky overhead, then looked across the avenue for the street vendors who worked Penn Station. A few were set up, and considering it was a bright, cloudless day with single-digit temperatures, he'd be able to find what he needed without any difficulty.

- 47 -

The wool scarf and cheap sunglasses covered what the hood of the coat didn't. David was now confident he was completely unrecognizable, like he could walk up to a cop and ask for directions. He stepped onto the escalator and descended into the warmth of Penn Station.

At the bottom of the escalator, a Hudson News store had the full complement of area newspapers on display. As expected, his mugshot-of-a-photo covered the front pages of the *New York Post*, the *Daily Mirror*, and the *Daily News*, as well as the *New York Times*. The *Daily Mirror*, the bottom feeder of New York papers, had already tried and convicted him. In huge block print across the top of the page: "Good Doctor Gone Bad." And in smaller block print down the left side of the page: "Disgraced Surgeon Stealing Kidneys From Homeless Men." He shook his head. What tripe. He was glad his mother was dead and his father was too gorked to read a paper.

He followed the concourse to a bagel shop. Mumbling through the scarf, he ordered a sausage-egg-and-cheese bagel and ate it as he walked. On the way out, he saw his mugshot again, on a fifty-inch TV hanging over a waiting area.

The escalator lifted David into the glaring sun and bitter cold of Seventh Avenue. Along the curb, a small crowd had gathered to watch the action across the street. He adjusted the scarf and glasses and joined them. A line of marked and unmarked cop cars were double-parked in front of the Hotel Penn, lights flashing, exhaust billowing from tail pipes, doors opening and slamming shut. Uniformed officers stopped everyone coming out. Plainclothes cops hurried in. From one of the unmarked cars climbed the female detective he'd seen on TV, Kate D'Angelo, the lead investigator. So they'd discovered the bloody mess, and thanks to Jean-Pierre, they knew that the man who inhabited room 1408 last night, the man whose blood was all over the bathroom and bedsheets, was the same man whose photo was spread across the front pages of all the papers. And he had a pronounced limp. Detective D'Angelo was tightening the net, and David had to get to the warehouse—the only link to Cassandra—before she snared him.

- 48 -

David gimped his way across Avenue D and stood before the massive Jacob Riis housing projects, a maze of nineteen redbrick buildings, most of which were thirteen or fourteen stories high. East 10th Street cut the complex in half and led to a circular drive within the labyrinth of walkways and structures. He knew Tyronne Pradeaux lived in the Riis houses, but he didn't know where.

He traveled the half block to the circle drive and sat on the first bench he came to. He'd ridden the #3 train from Penn Station to 14th and Seventh, transferred to the L line, taken the L east to First Avenue, and then walked south for five blocks. Not much of a hump by New York City standards, but with a fresh gunshot wound to the thigh, it felt like he had run a marathon and someone had hammered a sixteen-penny nail into his leg as he crossed the finish line.

The circle was void of all human presence, as were the footpaths, but he had no doubt that news of a lone white man sitting in the middle of a Lower East Side housing project would travel fast. Question was, what would happen first? Would he freeze to death? Get beaten to within an inch of his life for being in the wrong place? Get turned in for Crime Stoppers money? Or, could he somehow find Tyronne Pradeaux, and get Tyronne to deliver him from the aforementioned fates? He wasn't sure, but he had no other options. He couldn't go home, even though his apartment was only blocks away. He couldn't check into a hotel—no cash, and his credit cards were unusable—and he couldn't spend the night on the streets.

Across the circle, a young woman pushed a stroller covered with a plastic hood toward the M8 bus stop. He hoped the kid had a space heater under there. Down another path, three young boys, twelve or thirteen years old, hurried toward the drive. They were dressed like David, hooded coats and wool scarves, and they didn't seem too ominous, their eyes brighter than the usual menacing gaze or hundred-mile stare encountered in this part of the city.

David intercepted them not too far from the bus stop. "Excuse me, guys," he said.

The boys stopped, cocked their heads, and sized him up. He was well hidden behind his scarf and glasses, but enough white skin was exposed to raise suspicion—or was it contempt he saw in their eyes?

"I'm looking for Tyronne Pradeaux."

They traded glances, brows furrowed with the disbelief that a white man would venture into the projects, ask for a homeboy, and expect them to blurt out an address.

"I'm not a cop," David said.

"Never heard of him," said the shortest of the three boys.

"We know each other. I need his help."

"Still ain't never heard of him," said the short one, the obvious mouthpiece of the group. "But you give me yo' wallet, and I see if I can find him." He snickered and backhanded the shoulder of the kid standing next to him.

"I don't have time for this crap," David said. "Do you know Tyronne, or don't you?"

The mouthpiece puffed out his chest. "We got no time neither, so hand it over."

David should have been scared. Even the occasional twelve-year-old in this part of the city was known to a carry a weapon and use it on impulse, but he didn't have the adrenaline left to mount a fear response. He gave the boys a slow, disdainful nod. He'd be goddamned if he was going to let three jackals rob him.

"You guys want to know how I met Tyronne?"

"Don't give a shit. We wanna meet yo' wallet."

The other boys laughed.

"I'm the surgeon who put him back together when he came into Bellevue all shot up a couple years ago. I saved his life."

"Still don't give a shit," said the mouthpiece, impatience growing in his pre-teen voice.

"Well, maybe you will when you hear this." David fixed his stare on the shortest boy. "Imagine you're in Bellevue and you've been shot in the gut, and there's crap and undigested food floating around your belly, seeping into your bloodstream like poison, or maybe you've been stabbed in the chest and your lungs are filling with blood and you're coughing it up all over your clean shirt. Now let's say I'm the surgeon on call, the one who takes you to the OR to patch you up, and I look down at you lying on the table and it occurs to me, Hey, this is one of those little fuckers from the Riis Houses who robbed me. Then I say to you, 'Hey, you're one of the little fuckers from the Riis Houses who robbed me.' And the last thing you see before the anesthesiologist puts you under is me, standing over you with a knife in my hand, and a big grin on my face. Now, I know this sounds far-fetched, but if you all keep going around mugging people, you will end up at Bellevue shot or stabbed, and you will end up in my operating room. *And*, if Tyronne hears that you robbed me, he'll personally see to it you end up in Bellevue, but before he busts a cap in your colon, or a sticks a shiv in your pulmonary artery, he'll check with me and make sure I'm on duty." David held up his wallet. "So, you want it? Take it."

A bus roared into the circle. "Damn," the short kid said. "Looks like we outta time." He glanced at the other boys. "Don't wanna miss our ride on a cold day like this." They scampered over to the bus stop, where the short one pulled out a cell phone. David limped back to the bench and sat down. He'd had his fill of people fucking with him.

The stroller-pushing woman and the three jackals boarded the bus. It roared out of the circle the way it had come in, leaving David alone. He started to shiver. He would not be able to sit much longer—or stay out in the cold—and wondered if he should walk the paths, hoping to find someone who'd tell him where Tyronne lived. He stood, rewrapped his scarf, and looked at the pathways leading into the northern half of the Riis complex. Then he turned and peered into the southern half. A toss-up. He decided to go south.

He was about to enter the maze when two black guys in hooded down jackets rounded a corner. They were quiet, faces covered by scarves, gaits conveying a sense of purpose. And that sense of purpose was directed toward David. They were coming right at him. One of them was big, David's height and a lot thicker. The other, a few inches shorter and not so bulky. Could be a couple of Tyronne's boys, David figured. He'd be able to tell if they'd lose the scarves. He had come to know Tyronne's crew when Tyronne had been hospitalized for all those weeks, and had since seen them around the neighborhood. They stopped in front of David, shoulder to shoulder, blocking the path. He wished it were ninety degrees and the pathways were full of mothers, children, and housing cops.

The tall one said, "Let me see yo' face."

David removed the glasses and scarf.

"You the doc that saved Tyronne."

"Yeah."

"Appears you in some shit."

"I need his help."

"You worth twenty-five G's, we call Crime Stoppers."

"Is that what he wants you to do?"

A sneer. Then, "Follow me."

David took a few steps and stopped. "Hey," he said.

The two boys turned around.

"I need a ride, and I'm in a hurry. See if Tyronne can meet us down here."

Five minutes later the white Escalade pulled into the circle. The front passenger door opened, and Tyronne Pradeaux climbed out. David tried to stand tough against the overwhelming relief welling up as the isolation of the last fourteen hours lifted. He had never believed in divine forces, or karma, or any of that stuff, but five minutes ago he'd been alone, running for his life without anyone to help him, and now he had help. He had saved Tyronne's life. The favor would be repaid. Tyronne joined him on the sidewalk and gave him a single, expressionless nod. "You just topped NYPD's most wanted."

"Yeah," David said, smiling at the implausibility of such a statement. "It's a long story. I'll tell you about it on the way."

Tyronne nodded at the Escalade. "Hop in."

- 49 -

David told his tale on the way to the warehouse. R'Shaun, a large but soft-looking kid, drove. Tyronne had the shotgun position. Marcus, the big guy from the path, sat in the back with Jamar, the shorter kid from the path. Le-Vaughan, the thinnest and probably youngest of the group, sat between Marcus and Jamar, all three of them grim-faced and tight-lipped, not at all happy to be sharing their personal space with some white asshole. David had the middle row, back against the door, leg stretched across the seat. Tyronne had been nineteen when he came into Bellevue with multiple gunshot wounds. He was now twenty-one or twenty-two. David figured R'Shaun and Marcus for their early twenties as well. Le-Vaughan and Jamar were a lot younger, fifteen or sixteen.

"Motherfuckers got your wife?" Tyronne said. "Some cold shit, there."

"Yeah," David replied, already knowing that would be the extent of the conversation.

He shifted his butt and silently willed the Percocets to kick in. Before they left the Riis Houses, Tyronne sent Le-Vaughan upstairs for a bag of pills—Darvocets, OxyContin, Percocets—probably worth several thousand dollars on the street.

R'Shaun turned off 14th onto Ninth, and took the first right, onto West 13th. With the exception of a few parked cars, the street was empty.

Tyronne looked back at David. "What exactly we lookin' for, Doc?"

"Not sure. They have Cassandra, and I assume they want to trade her for me, but they don't know where I am, so I'm thinking there might be something at the warehouse. For all I know, there's a note taped to the door." David pointed. "That's it, the one with the pig sign."

R'Shaun slowed the Escalade to a crawl. David searched the façade of the building for anything out of the ordinary, something that stood out.

And there it was.

In the midst of the graffiti, large bulbous letters, spray-painted white with black outlines, said DAVID LOVES CASSANDRA, and underneath, in smaller red letters, a phone number.

Tyronne handed David a phone. Mr. White answered on the second ring and said hello as generically as if he were sitting at home reading the Sunday paper.

David's rage erupted. "My wife better be okay, you lying prick."

"Now, now, Doctor, calm down. She's fine. It's you we're worried about. Are you hurt?"

"What do you want, Mr. White? Am I a loose end? Are you gonna use Cassandra to lure me in so you can finish the job?"

"Nobody wants you dead. The NYPD were going to pick you up. We were going to hide you. When you resisted, the Russian deviated from the plan on his own volition."

"Whatever. Now why don't you cut through the bullshit?"

"All right," Mr. White said. "We need you to perform one more harvest. Once completed, Cassandra walks, you walk, we will provide you with a tidy sum of money, and if you like, new identities and help leaving the country. Cassandra has not seen anyone of significance and, therefore, does not pose a liability."

"That's it? One more harvest and we're finished?"

"Yes."

"Why should I trust you?"

"As I see it, you have no choice."

"I want to talk to her."

"She's not at this location, but I can assure you she's fine."

"I'm not agreeing to anything until I hear her voice."

"Come on, David. Surely you realize you're in no position to negotiate. We'll see you tonight, the warehouse at midnight, and after you've finished your task you can put this distasteful episode behind you. And finally—you know, I hate to even say it because it's so cliché—if you seek outside help, well, we have your wife, right?"

"The warehouse at midnight? You have my wife? This whole thing is one big fucking cliché."

"Yes," Mr. White said, "it has degenerated into melodrama, but let me reiterate that the stakes are exceptionally high, so I encourage you to show up on time, by yourself, do your job, and there will be no further complications."

The connection went dead.

David handed the phone back to Tyronne. "She okay?" he asked.

"I don't know."

- 50 -

Mr. White set the TracFone on Turnbull's desk.

"Is he okay?" Sam Keating asked.

"Yes. Plenty of fight left in him."

"Will he show?" asked Turnbull.

"He'll show."

"What did he say about his wife?"

"He wanted to speak to her. I assured him she was doing well."

"Make sure she continues to do well. We may need her. If anything happens to Cassandra McBride, I will personally cut the heart out of the person responsible."

"I'll pass it along."

"What about tonight? Should we proceed?"

Sam Keating let out an audible groan. "Are you kidding? This thing is way too hot. It's time to cut our losses and work with the cash we have. And when it runs out, we go after another round of funding."

Turnbull fixed his gaze on Keating. "First of all, what's left of our cash won't get us very far. Secondly, we don't have anything new for the venture capitalists. Yes, we have a room full of organs, but they aren't functioning, and until they do, they're useless. In the eyes of the VC's, we're just another high-risk biomedical company that could take a decade or more to turn a profit. And third, even if the organs do start to function, now is not the time to give away controlling shares in the company." Turnbull leaned forward and clasped his hands on the desk. "Look, if we do this last transplant, we'll have enough capital to fund an FDA trial, and once we acquire human data, our current investors will carry us all the way to market without demanding additional shares. What they already hold will be worth a sizable fortune, and they won't jeopardize it by trying to take a bigger bite."

Keating sank into the chair, ran his fingers through his hair and muttered something.

Turnbull looked at Mr. White. "How confident are you that we can pull this off?"

"Very, or I'd be packing my bags. I have no intention of spending the rest of my days in a federal supermax facility."

Keating turned toward Mr. White. "I just wonder if your emotional connection is clouding your judgment."

Mr. White gave Sam Keating an intense stare. "My judgment has never been clouded by emotion, nor will it ever be. My emotional connection to what we are doing has been compartmentalized and isolated, and will remain so until my mission is complete."

Keating countered with a glare of his own. "Two NYPD detectives were out here just last night, and you don't think that right now they're typing up a search warrant?"

"They don't have probable cause, and even if they did, my contact in the FBI has already called them off—no search warrants, no surveillance. Neither Passaic County nor the NYPD will make a move without going through the Bureau, and if they try, I'll hear about it."

"You're sure of that?" Turnbull asked. "There won't be a jurisdictional pissing contest?"

"The locals may push and posture, but they will not move unless the Feds give them the green light."

"So, back to my original question: Is it safe to proceed?"

"Yes."

Keating jumped up. "Well you can do it without me. I'm outta here."

"Sit down, Samuel," Turnbull said. "You're not going anywhere. Your paw prints are all over this thing. We either come out of this cleanly, or we all fall together."

- 51 -

The Escalade pulled to the curb on the south side of the Riis circle. The ride to the warehouse and back had taken less than an hour, but David's leg had stiffened considerably from the inactivity. The Percocets hadn't made an appreciable difference. OxyContin, an oral form of morphine, would definitely blunt the pain, but he couldn't risk feeling dopey when it came time to perform the harvest. Looked like he had a long day of suffering ahead of him.

David followed Tyronne and the others into the complex. Marcus walked about ten feet in front of Tyronne, R'Shaun alongside him. Jamar and Le-Vaughan brought up the rear. David didn't see any guns, but he knew they were all packing. Marcus and the two younger boys had made a point of flashing their gats at David several times, and they were ready to use them. The whole group was in a constant state of high alert, fight or flight—mostly fight—looking for any threat, believing it might be around the next corner. They had probably been developing these skills since childhood. In fact, in this neighborhood, those without such skill sets probably didn't make it out of their teens.

They moved through the web of walkways. The buildings appeared to have been plunked down in no particular order, some parallel to Avenue D, some perpendicular, others oblique. Maybe a pattern could be seen if one were flying overhead, but from ground level it seemed without order.

They came to a building that had a rusted "17" screwed into the brick above a gray steel door. A one-foot-square, wire-reinforced window provided the only glimpse inside. Marcus pushed open the heavy door and everyone followed him in. As David entered, Marcus gave him a sneer that said, *If it weren't for Tyronne, you'd be sucking gunmetal, Whitey.*

David was torn. Look down? Glare back at the guy? Marcus was no twelve-year-old punk, but white and weak didn't fly in the projects. David glared back, hoping Tyronne could reel the guy in if he had to.

The stench of urine filled the tiny lobby. Trash littered the floor. Graffiti defaced every bit of available space on the plaster walls, and tags were etched into the stainless steel of the elevator car. They all stepped inside and started up.

Tyronne and David exited at the fourteenth floor, the rest of the group getting off earlier. More graffiti extended down the hallway, as did the smell of urine. The Ridge Street apartment didn't seem so bad now. Tyronne's place was at the end of the hall. He unlocked three dead bolts, opened the door, and gestured for David to go in.

Straight ahead was a small front room. To the left, just inside the door, a tiny kitchen, and around the corner to the right, a bedroom and a bathroom. A giant flat-screen TV, connected to an Xbox, hung on the wall. A tattered metal blind covered the only window. Shafts of dust-filled sunlight partitioned the room. Tyronne pointed at a beat-up couch. "All yours."

David nodded toward a ratty chair. "Mind if I borrow those cushions?"

"Nah," Tyronne said.

David lowered himself to the couch—half on, half off—unable to lift his leg.

Tyronne placed the cushions at the foot of the sofa, then grabbed David's legs at the ankles. "On three," he said, "like you used to do for me."

David counted, and Tyronne lifted both legs onto the cushions. David wormed his torso in line with his lower body. "Thanks."

Tyronne gave a single nod. "What else you need?"

"A couple bags of ice, dressing supplies, and at midnight, a ride back to the warehouse."

Tyronne called R'Shaun, gave him the list, then sat down in the cushionless chair. After a few moments of reflection, he said, "What do we gotta do to get you and your wife outta this shit you're in?"

"If I perform one more harvest, Cassandra walks and I get the bad guys off my back."

"You believe that?"

"I have to. What else can I do?"

"Maybe it's time to get Five-O on board."

"The cops?"

"Yeah. You know, get 'em to meet you at that shitty old warehouse tonight."

"Won't work. The head guy never goes there. He stays away, and he'll keep Cassandra where she is. Even if I call the police and they bust everyone on this end, it still doesn't get Cassandra back, but that'll piss off the leader."

Tyronne nodded, contemplating. "How 'bout they follow the kidney to the main man. Get him and rescue your wife."

"It wouldn't be legal or ethical for the cops to sit by while a body part is stolen. And if they tried to send an empty ice chest, or a decoy of some kind and it went wrong, that puts Cassandra in danger." David shifted his butt on the couch. "I can't risk any dicking around by the NYPD or anyone else. My only option is to do what the fuckers want. Hopefully, they'll honor their end of the deal and let her go. And if it actually happens, and she's safe, then I'll worry about me. Either I turn myself in or spend the rest of my life running."

"No offense, Doc, but I don't figure you for the fugitive type. Maybe you get enough money and go hide in some cool country, but you still always lookin' over your shoulder."

"Yeah. I'm thinking I'll go to the cops, tell them everything, and face the consequences."

"Guy like you stands a decent chance in the criminal justice system." Tyronne stood. "R'Shaun will be up here with your shit pretty soon, then we see you 'bout eleven thirty."

David lifted his head and started to say thank you.

Tyronne waved him off. "No need, Doc." And he left, locking the door behind him.

David let his head fall onto the arm of the couch and stared at a brown water stain on the ceiling. He hated that Tyronne contributed to the insidious drug problem that eroded society and destroyed lives the way metastatic cancer eats away at tissues and organs, but he couldn't ignore the fact that the two of them shared a powerful bond, a bond forged by an unconditional loyalty that was largely nonexistent in the rest of the world. David had offered his loyalty to Andrew Turnbull, and Turnbull had abused it for his own gain. And when Turnbull had a chance to deflect the shit rolling in David's direction, he turned away. Tyronne, on the other hand, was willing to go to the mat for a white man, a doctor no less, merely because the white doctor treated him with the kindness and respect all patients deserve.

- 52 -

Kate and Scarpelli hung their coats, drained the coffee pot, and headed for their desks. The events of last night had bled into an early-morning press conference from the steps of One Police Plaza—featuring the announcement of a substantial Crime Stoppers reward—followed by a four-hour investigation of room 1408 at the Hotel Pennsylvania. They now knew David McBride had been shot in the right leg and was treating his own wound, and that was about all they knew. Room service had found the bloody mess around 8:20 a.m. It was presently 12:57 p.m. The trail had gone cold once again.

A few minutes later, DeSilva and Murphy checked in, poured cups of coffee, and joined Kate and Scarpelli at Kate's desk. Although the four of them were scheduled to work the four-to-one shift, time was of the essence, so they had agreed to pull a double.

Murphy, with legs crossed and arm draped on the desk beside him, said, "Every ER in the city has his photo. He keeps bleeding, he'll turn up."

DeSilva, leaning back with his fingers laced on his chest, said, "We got nothing from the apartment but two cell phones. One has Sprint as the carrier, McBride's name on the account. I got a request in for the records. The other is a TracFone throwaway."

"The wife's?" Kate asked.

"No," DeSilva said. "She has her own with Sprint. Same account as McBride's. Interesting thing about the TracFone, the only numbers stored were in the calls-received folder, all different and untraceable."

Scarpelli said, "They're doin' what the drug dealers do. Get a box of these things, use 'em a few times and dump 'em."

Kate said, "It's a means of one-way communication between McBride and his handler. They call him, give him his next assignment. If he tries to call back or gets the urge to turn the phone over to law enforcement, the number is already defunct. Anything on the computer?"

"Forensics has it," DeSilva said, sitting forward, "but I don't expect it'll be much help. If they're using untraceable phones, doubt we'll find a bunch of saved e-mails."

Kate looked at Murphy. "Has the father had any visitors?"

"Nary a one."

"What do the docs say?"

"Alzheimer's, most likely. They did blood tests and a brain scan. Nothing acute going on. They'll sit on him a few days, then start working on placement. If we don't find any family, they're going to send him to some kind of long-term care facility."

"Any family to be found?"

"Probably not. McBride's mother died some years ago. Hal McBride has no siblings, both his parents are dead, and our perp is an only child. Seems David McBride and his father are the last of the McBride lineage."

"The wife," Kate said. "She leaves work early with someone impersonating a detective, and disappears. That tells me the bad guys have her, and they'll use her to bait McBride. Anyone think Turnbull has her stashed at NuLife?"

"That would be a bonehead move," Scarpelli said, shifting in his chair. "After our visit last night, he has to realize he's under the microscope, and it's only a matter of time before we show up with a warrant."

"I think he's arrogant enough to believe he's untouchable out there in his little compound" Kate said. "In fact, I can picture Cassandra McBride all tucked away nice and warm in some unused office or lab."

232 | Richard Van Anderson

"He just might be untouchable," DeSilva said. "So far, I haven't heard anything that sounds like probable cause."

"And therein lies the crux of our case." Kate swiveled her chair sideways to the desk and leaned it back. "Unless we find McBride, NuLife is our only viable lead. We need to figure out how to get a search warrant."

And that, she knew, was going to require some creativity. Search warrants were not as easy to obtain as the TV cop shows would lead one to believe. It's not like the judge gave his blessing, and the cops busted in and thrashed around until they found something incriminating. Instead, the Fourth Amendment of the Bill of Rights mandates that a search warrant describe in detail the area to be searched, list the items to be searched for, and explain why the law-enforcement officer expects to find those items at that location. The officer's expectation equals probable cause. Suspicion by itself does not. So, unless they had strong reason to believe NuLife's computers held incriminating files, or their refrigerators were full of stolen kidneys, they couldn't just barge in and ransack the place.

"We saw the main building," Scarpelli said. "Other than the spacesuits, there was nothing suspicious going on. The gym's where the action is."

"Even if we found a state-of-the-art surgery facility tucked away in the gym, it still wouldn't add up to probable cause," Kate added. "According to Daniel Perry, Turnbull could claim it was used for large animal experiments, that he was using pigs or primates as test subjects."

"Then we need to get eyes on Turnbull and his building," Murphy said. "Catch him doing something he ain't supposed to be doing."

Kate said, "I'll speak to the lieutenant and see how many of the guys we can pull for surveillance detail."

"Zero," said a voice from the doorway. Lieutenant Hernandez walked into the squad room, dragging an aura that said things had not gone well in the sandbox. Even before he opened his mouth, Kate knew her case had been pulled, and so did the rest of the guys as evidenced by the drooping shoulders, folding arms, grunts and groans.

"The National Security Agency and the FBI have been watching Andrew Turnbull for a while, and they don't want us mucking around in their operation. I just got off the phone with the coordinating agent from the FBI, and he told me to give Turnbull a wide berth—no more questions, no surveillance, nothing that might spook him."

"Turnbull's the central player of our case," Kate said. "Why the hell are the NSA and the FBI interested in him?"

"The NSA flagged him for making multiple phone calls to several Middle Eastern countries. The agent I spoke with wouldn't elaborate on the nature of those calls, but they've piqued the interest of both agencies."

"What about McBride?" Kate asked. "They interested in him, too?"

"No, but Homicide is."

"Are you kidding me?"

"We have a dead homeless man, a Russian mobster smeared across the front of the F train, and an organ snatcher running loose who may have had a hand in both. That's more than enough justification for Homicide to take over."

Kate could tell the lieutenant was as pissed as she was. Climbers hated losing cases that promised substantial media face time. And Kate hated losing any case.

- 53 -

David checked his watch—midnight, as instructed. He banged on the roll-up door. Waited. Hit it again. Moments later the metal panels rumbled open. Yuri, the big Russian, was standing on the other side. David limped into the warehouse. Yuri dropped the chain. The door rushed down its tracks and slammed the concrete. He stepped in front of David, their faces inches apart, the stench of cigarette smoke rising from deep within the Russian's lungs. "You are dead man," he said, his black eyes glinting in the half-light. "That was my brother you kill in subway."

David held the man's menacing stare. He wanted to explain what had happened, that he was simply running for his life, but it would be useless. He dropped his gaze and headed for the elevator.

He hurried past the OR, locked himself in the bathroom, leaned over the sink and splashed cold water on his face. His hands trembled uncontrollably. The big Russian wouldn't do anything before the donor organ was on ice, but once the fat man left the building, the homicidal maniac would be waiting. And there was no way out. Steel bars covered all windows. Padlocked bolts secured every door from the inside, and Yuri had the keys. That left David with two options: kill the Russian first—ridiculous—or find a way out.

The only area of the warehouse he had not seen in detail was the far end of the lower floor. He was fairly certain there was a restroom, the companion to the one in which he presently stood. Maybe he'd get lucky and find a window or a large vent.

After donning scrubs, David unrolled a giant wad of toilet paper and dropped it in the toilet bowl. He used a hanger to stuff the paper into the pipe, packed a couple more wads on top of the first, and flushed. The bowl overflowed. He made sure the cuffs of his scrub pants were wet, then took what was left of the roll and walked out of the bathroom.

David paused outside the OR for a head count. The fat man sat in his usual spot. Veejay was intubating the donor. Meiling was arranging instruments. No sign of the big Russian. He was probably downstairs, smoking in the shadows. David would love to be the one to carve out the fucker's lung cancer in twenty years. One slip of the scalpel near the main pulmonary artery, and it would take all of thirty seconds for his entire blood volume to fill his chest and spill onto the floor.

Standing at the elevator, he was about to hit the button when the cage jerked to life, clanking its way up to his level. He fought the urge to walk away. He did not want to face the big Russian again, but it was good that he was coming up. David now knew his whereabouts.

The elevator arrived. Yuri slid open the gate and stood there, glaring, his bulk blocking David. David held up the roll of paper. "I have to take a crap, and someone plugged the toilet." He pointed down. "Spilled all over my goddamn shoes. So unless you have a plunger, I figure I'll use the bathroom on the ground floor."

The Russian stepped aside. David entered and pushed the down button. Halfway between floors his body started to shake.

He exited the cage, moved along the back wall, and checked the rear door. It was bolted and padlocked like the one upstairs. The room in the corner was, in fact, another restroom. He flipped the switch, but the bulb was burned out. It didn't matter. There were no windows. And the wall that extended to the front of the building was solid brick. No fans. No vents. No way out.

He went over to the Town Car, hoping to find keys hanging in the ignition. They weren't. He leaned against it, trying to conceive a plan B when he noticed a trough running lengthwise down the middle of the floor. It was about two feet wide and covered by steel plates laid end to end, each probably five or six feet long with finger holes at the ends. Of course. This had been a meatpacking ware-house. Hacking apart animals was messy, and they needed a high-volume drain so they could hose the place down. Somewhere along the length of the trough there'd be an outflow that communicated with the sewer, probably near the center of the room.

David stood over the midpoint of the trough and tried to kneel, but he couldn't bend his bad leg. He would need something long and rigid. He went back to the car and popped the trunk. It ech-oed like a rifle shot. He wiped sweat from his brow, rummaged through newspapers and other assorted trash until he found what he needed—a tire iron.

He jammed the beveled end into a finger hole and lifted the plate. It was lighter than he anticipated, and came up too easily. He tottered sideways, nearly fell, and lost his grip. The plate banged against concrete. The tire iron skittered across the floor with a series of pings. David froze, breath held, heart pounding. The elevator remained quiet.

After a few moments, he moved the plate with his foot, but saw only trough. He retrieved the tire iron and removed two more plates, finding the outflow under the third. The opening was rectangular and just large enough to admit a thin man, he hoped.

The elevator groaned to life. David repositioned the plates. The elevator stopped, and the big Russian jerked open the gate. "They need you. What takes so long?"

"Guess I haven't been drinking enough water."

- 54 -

The donor, another homeless man by all appearances, was anesthetized and ready to be prepped and draped. David hadn't seen Aleksandr and wondered who was going to assist. He supposed Amy could scrub in when it came time to tie off the vessels. As he turned to go out to the sink, Meiling approached. She glanced at the fat man, then spoke to David in a whisper. "I think you should look at the instruments," she said.

He wasn't sure why he needed to see them, but he followed her to the back of the room. When he neared the table, it took him a moment to make sense of what he was seeing. Lying among the scalpels, scissors, and forceps was a bone saw, a sternal retractor, and a cardioplegia needle. "These are cardiac instruments," he said, trying to control his voice. "They want us to harvest this man's heart."

The fat man lowered his newspaper. "Problem, Doctor?"

"Yes. A huge problem. When you cut out a person's heart, they die."

The fat man punched a number into his cell phone and motioned for David to come get it.

David put the phone to his ear and said, "What the fuck is going on here, White?"

"I figured you'd have questions regarding this evening's procedure."

"No questions, just a statement. I'm not cutting out a man's heart."

"And I have a rebuttal. We have a father who is willing to pay thirty million dollars for an organ that will save his dying son, and we have two potential donors. One of them is on the table before you. The other is here with me."

"You're lying. You wouldn't remove the heart of a pregnant woman."

"Her blood type is O positive, as is the recipient's, and the HLA panel reactivity is less than ten percent. That's a perfect match."

Mr. White was telling the truth. Cassandra was O positive, and if the recipient's panel-reactive antibodies were less than 10 percent, they didn't even need to do a crossmatch.

"Don't underestimate the power of money, David. Now, wash your hands and get started. When we receive the heart, we'll return Cassandra to the city."

The room felt like a sauna. Sweat had soaked through David's scrub top. He thrust the phone at the fat man and said he was going to change.

He locked the bathroom door, leaned on the sink, and stared into the blackness of the drain. He had no idea what to do, but he knew what he couldn't do. He could not cut the heart out of a living human. He'd done it before. He had performed a number of donor cardiectomies as a resident, but those patients were brain dead, and even that was unsettling. Maybe he could stay out of the OR until the body was draped, until the man was nothing more than a yellow-brown patch of skin. Then go in. Focus on the surgical field. Detach himself from everything but Cassandra. He could do it. He had to.

He changed his scrub top, returned to the operating room, and peered through the window. Meiling had finished with the drapes. Only the sternum was exposed. He scrubbed his hands, gowned and gloved with Amy's help, and positioned himself on the right side of the table. Meiling moved her instrument tray to the left side. The air hose for the sternal saw had been connected to a tank of compressed air, the cautery device plugged in to its console. Two liters of cardioplegia solution hung from an IV pole. Behind David sat a pair of defibrillator paddles, standard for any cardiac operation.

Veejay whispered over the drape separating him from the surgical field. "You are going to do this, right? These people know where I live, with my wife and kids."

David whispered back, "They *have* my wife."

Meiling held out a scalpel but made no eye contact. David took it in his hand, tentatively, without the usual snap. He pressed it against the skin over the sternal notch, but he could not push down with any force. He could not make an incision. He looked at Meiling, made eye contact this time. Her eyes were full of tears, and pleading with him. To do what? Hurry and get it over with? Don't do it? In the far corner, Amy pulled a blanket out of the warmer and wrapped it around her shoulders. In the near corner, the fat man slept on the stool, his newspaper hanging over his chest. On the other side of the drape, Veejay was drawing up a syringe of fentanyl, morphine's synthetic cousin but twenty times as potent. Fifty micrograms would drop the average-sized adult. A hundred and fifty would drop an elephant ... or a fat Russian. David remembered something Mr. White had said on the phone—they would return Cassandra to the city. That's it. They had her at the implant facility, somewhere in North Jersey, and he had a rough idea of the location.

He checked the defibrillator paddles, made sure the power was on, and in a near whisper, told Veejay to turn up the alarms on both the heart monitor and the pulse oximeter.

"What? Why?" he asked.

David whispered harshly, "Doesn't matter why. Just turn 'em up."

"This is no time to be a hero."

"Do it."

David lifted the drapes on his side of the patient, exposing the EKG leads on the chest and the pulse oximeter probe on the fingertip. He then charged the defibrillator to 400 joules—the highest setting—took a deep breath, and removed two of the EKG electrodes and the pulse oximeter. The heart tracing flatlined. The oxygen level hit zero. The monitors interpreted this as cardiac arrest and did what they were designed to do.

Both alarms sounded—loud pings from the heart monitor, a repeating series of three chirps from the pulse oximeter. David shouted, "The patient is coding. We're gonna lose him."

The fat man awakened and jumped to his feet in one swift move. "What is happening?" he asked.

"The patient's dying. Get over here and help. I need you on my side of the table."

David grabbed the defibrillator paddles and held them above the patient's chest.

The fat man bellied up next to David. "What do you want me to do?"

"Fibrillate and die, you fat fucker."

David pushed the paddles against the fat man's chest and fired. A loud pop filled the air. The fat man reeled backward, smashed into the wall, and fell to the floor unconscious.

Veejay yelled something about getting all of them killed. Meiling was screaming and crying. Amy ran out of the room, Meiling right behind her. The alarms were chirping and pinging. David was hyperventilating. He knelt down next to the fat man, who smelled of burnt scrubs and fried skin. Two paddle-shaped scorch marks were burned onto the scrub top. David felt his neck for a carotid pulse. It was strong. He'd wake up any second.

"Veejay," David shouted, "toss me that syringe of fentanyl."

He did, and David removed the cap from the needle. "How many micrograms in here?"

"Two hundred."

David stabbed the syringe into the fat man's thigh, burying the needle to the hub. The fat man flinched, opened his eyes, and groped at the sting in his leg. David batted his hand away and pushed hard on the plunger, pumped all 200 micrograms into his quadriceps muscle, then jumped back as he floundered around on the floor, glassy-eyed and confused.

The OR door flew open and smashed the wall. Before David could turn around, he had been picked up and heaved into the shelves, the impact ripping them off the wall. He lay in a pile of surgical supplies, the big Russian coming toward him. David was unable to get up fast enough. The Russian kicked him in his bad thigh.

David clutched his leg and bellowed a guttural scream. Veejay came up behind the Russian and hit him in the back of the head with a metal tray. The sound of a gong filled the room. The Russian backhanded Veejay and sent him crashing into the anesthesia machine.

David dug through the stuff on the floor, searching for anything he could use as a weapon. The Russian bent over and grabbed David's gown, but he couldn't grip the baggy material. David found a bottle of undiluted Betadine solution, flipped open the top, and squirted a stream of it into the Russian's eyes.

He grabbed his face and stumbled backward, knocking over the Mayo stand. It crashed to the floor, sending surgical instruments clattering everywhere. David struggled to his feet. Searing pain shot up and down his leg. The Russian came toward him, arms flailing, but he couldn't see. David stepped aside like a matador moving away from a charging bull. He yelled at Veejay, "More fentanyl. Fill the syringe."

Veejay tossed a syringe to David. David maneuvered himself behind the Russian and lunged, grabbing him around the waist and jamming the needle into his thigh. He groaned, jerked from side to side, and threw punches behind his back. David held on as if he were riding a bull, smashing the plunger with his thumb, taking hit after hit to the head and ribs. The syringe emptied. David let go.

The big Russian didn't go down immediately. He was a huge man and the fentanyl had been injected into a muscle, not a vein. It would take time for the drug to exert its full effect. Veejay and David left the room and watched through the window as he thrashed around like a wild animal, stumbling and crashing into things. David worried that the guy might fall onto the operating table and knock the homeless man to the floor, but he didn't have to worry for long. The Russian's legs buckled, he tripped over the fat man, and smacked the floor with his head.

David and Veejay went back in. David nudged each man with his toe, then felt for carotid pulses. The fat man's was slow and regular, and his chest was moving. Sleeping like a baby. Yuri's pulse was racing, but he was breathing. Veejay checked the homeless man.

"How's he doing?" David asked.

"Better than you and me."

Veejay was right. David's thigh was on fire. His back ached from where he had smashed into the shelves. His head and ribs throbbed as if he had just gone fifteen rounds.

"What do we do now?" Veejay asked.

"I'm gonna tie these guys up. You're going to wake our patient and get him out of here. How long until they come to?"

Veejay shrugged. "Each of them received very large doses, but they are big men with rapid metabolisms. I'm sorry, but it is hard to say."

David grabbed rolls of Kerlix gauze from the mess on the floor and tied the wrists and ankles of the Russians as tight as he could. Kerlix was strong stuff, but it wasn't rope, and David wasn't exactly well-versed in tying up humans. He looked at Veejay. "On your way out, give them each another hit of fentanyl. I need time to drive to New Jersey."

"Why are we not calling the police?"

"These guys are peons. They don't know anything. I'll call the police when I find my wife."

David dug through Yuri's pockets, found the keys to the Town Car and the warehouse doors, and took both men's cell phones.

- 55 -

With molars grinding and arms folded tight, Turnbull sat squarely in his chair and tried to read Mr. White's expression as White spoke to one of his Russian goons on a TracFone. It had been forty-five minutes and still no word from the warehouse, while across the parking lot a sixteen-year-old Yemeni boy lay on a gurney, waiting to be wheeled into the OR as soon as the heart was on its way—the thirty-million-dollar heart.

Mr. White closed the cover on the phone, the grim look on his face telling all. "The donor is gone, along with McBride and the rest of the team."

Turnbull sprang forward and slammed his fists on the desk. "Goddammit. I knew it. What about the Russians?"

"Tied up and drugged. Appears there was a major struggle."

"Why'd you hire those cretins, anyway?"

"Because they're ubiquitous, and they have no limits."

"Neither do I. If McBride wants to fuck with me, I'll fuck him right back." Turnbull grabbed the TracFone and punched in a number. Another one of Mr. White's Russian imbeciles picked up. "Change in plans. Get the woman and bring her to the OR, and stuff something in her mouth so no one can hear her scream."

"You aren't really going to remove a pregnant woman's heart," Mr. White said. "We were bluffing."

"That's exactly what I'm going to do."

"You're acting like a psychopath."

"America's boardrooms are full of psychopaths."

Mr. White took pause, then said, "Nobody will help you … myself included."

Turnbull leaned forward. "Everybody will help, and if you want a kidney for your daughter, *you* will personally see to it."

Mr. White held Turnbull's stare, then said, "Okay, but let me bring her over."

Mr. White arrived at the surgical supply room just as the Russian was unlocking the door. "I'll get her," White said to the man, and motioned for him to wait in the hallway.

Mr. White crossed a larger room to a small anteroom, unlocked the door, and opened it. Cassandra sat up on the edge of the cot, shielding her eyes from the wedge of light coming through the doorway.

"We need some chloroform, or something like it," Mr. White said in a hushed tone.

"What for?"

"I'm getting you out of here."

Cassandra jumped up and flipped on the lights. "Right there," she said, pointing to a shelf. "The brown bottle with the purple label that says Forane."

"What is it?"

"It's isoflurane, an inhalational agent used for general anesthesia. Much stronger than chloroform."

Mr. White grabbed the bottle, then glanced at the cot. Army type with a wooden frame. Good, he told himself.

Speaking just above a whisper, he said, "The Russian man who drove us here is standing out in the hallway. I'm going to hide behind one of those equipment racks out there, and I want you to start screaming, like you're resisting me. When he enters, I'll come up from behind him and hold a gauze full of this stuff over his mouth and nose. It works fast?"

"Very fast."

"Okay. When he passes out, take his keys and go down the hallway to the loading dock. The same car that bought you here is parked out there. Get in, crash the gate if the guard doesn't open it—"

"Hold on," Cassandra said. "I've never driven before."

"What?"

"I grew up in Manhattan."

"But you've watched someone drive a car, right? There's a pedal for the gas, one for the brake, the lever on the steering column that you pull down into drive?"

"Yeah, I know how all that works. I've just never done it."

"It's okay. You'll figure it out. Now, when you get to the highway turn left and follow it all the way to the city. I'll do what I can to stall at this end and give you a head start."

Mr. White put down the bottle, grabbed both of Cassandra's hands, and looked into her eyes. "And one last thing. I'm saving your life. Return the favor by saving my daughter's. No police. I will see to it that you and David are no longer part of this, just give me a chance to finish what I've started."

Cassandra nodded and said, "Okay."

Mr. White slipped into a pair of surgical gloves, and saturated a stack of gauze with isoflurane, turning away from the pungent odor. He then hid behind a rack just outside the anteroom and gave her a nod.

Cassandra started yelling and screaming and throwing things on the floor.

The Russian came in from the hallway. "What is prob—"

Mr. White jumped out from behind the rack, locked his arm around the man's neck, and clamped the gauze over his face.

The Russian jerked, twisted, and threw elbow punches.

Mr. White tightened his choke hold, clamped his hand tighter, and turned his face away from the noxious smell of the isoflurane.

A few moments later the Russian stopped fighting and went limp. Mr. White let him fall to the floor.

Cassandra rushed over just as Mr. White's phone rang. He flipped it open—Turnbull.

"Yes," Mr. White said calmly.

"What the fuck is taking so long?"

"You'd better come over here."

Mr. White took the keys from the Russian's pocket and thrust them into Cassandra's hand. "Go. Fast. Don't stop for anyone."

As she ran out the door, he ripped one of the wooden legs from the cot and smashed it into the Russian's forehead.

The man lay sprawled on the floor of the surgical supply room, just outside the anteroom. Turnbull stepped over him and picked up a wad of gauze sitting near the man's face. Both the room and the gauze smelled of a pungent chemical—Forane. An open bottle of the stuff sat on a nearby shelf. He turned to Mr. White. "Am I supposed to believe that a one-hundred-and-ten-pound woman overpowered a two-hundred-pound man?"

"I think she hit him with that when he opened the door." Mr. White pointed at the wooden cot leg. "And when he went down, she held the gauze over his face to make sure he was out."

Turnbull shook his head in disbelief. "Round up the rest of your idiots and find her." He called the guard shack. "Don't let anybody leave."

"Okay," the guard said, "but a young woman just drove out of here like a bat outta Hell in one of those old Town Cars."

"How long ago?"

"Three, maybe four minutes."

"Fuck!" screamed Turnbull, and he kicked the unconscious man in the ribs—twice.

- 56 -

David tightened his grip on the steering wheel as he took the Lincoln through a sweeping turn. The tires screeched. Tree trunks flashed in the headlights like a picket fence. He lifted his foot off the accelerator and slowed a bit. Just a bit. He had to get to Edwardsville, and he had to get there fast. The fat man and the big Russian were immobilized, but for how long? And even if they were still drugged, Mr. White would call them soon—if he hadn't already—to ask about the heart and get an estimated time of explantation so the recipient could be prepped. When the call went unanswered, the alarm would sound.

The road straightened. David glanced at the map. He was close, a couple of miles to Jackson Township, a few more to Edwardsville. The car he had tracked two nights ago had stopped just west of Edwardsville before the link to the GPS satellite was severed. The road he was on now would take him to the same spot. But then what? He had to believe he'd know what he was looking for when he found it—a commercial building, a small industrial park. He was out of the city now, past the suburbs, in the sticks. A structure capable of housing a surgical facility should jump out at him. He drove through Jackson Township, and minutes later was driving down the main street of Edwardsville. He went straight at the only traffic light and started out of town.

The two-lane road began to twist and turn as the landscape became hilly. He gripped the wheel tighter, turned harder, and hit the brakes often. Trees and scrub lined the road. To the left the hillside rose sharply. To the right it dropped off quickly.

A glare of light filled the bend. David clicked off the high beams and waited for the other driver to do the same, but the glare did not dim, and as he rounded the corner he saw headlights, stationary and grossly malaligned, one pointing into the sky like a searchlight, the other shining right at him. He slowed to a crawl and let his eyes adjust to the glare. A car—a Lincoln Town Car, just like the one he was in—had run off the road and sat angled up the hill, its front end smashed into a tree. The left front tire was off the ground and still turning. Steam hissed from under the crumpled hood. Water spewed down the frozen hillside and streamed onto the pavement. He stopped next to the car. In the driver's seat, a woman, slumped over the steering wheel.

Cassandra!

He drove past, cranked the wheel right and then left, trying to turn a long vehicle on a narrow road. Dug the front end into the bank. Backed up, tires screeching as the bumper hung up in the gravel. Pulled free, made the turn, and parked behind Cassandra. He jumped out and hobbled to her window as fast as his bad leg would carry him. She wasn't moving. He opened the door, gently pushed back her hair, and felt her neck for a pulse. Weak, but she had one.

She opened her eyes, and despite the grotesque deformity of the steering wheel crushing her chest, she was as beautiful as ever. Her eyes sparkled with tears. A dreamy smile parted her lips. "David …" Her voice was feeble. She gasped for enough air to form words. "So glad … it's you."

"Don't try to talk. I have to get you out of here."

"No … you have … to go."

"I'm not leaving you."

"They're … chasing me. Please …"

He tried moving the seat. The motor did nothing more than make a sick, grinding noise.

He pulled on the steering wheel. If he could relieve the pressure on her heart—

It wouldn't budge.

He wedged his shoulder against the seat and pushed, but couldn't generate any leverage with his injured leg.

He grasped her shoulders and tried to slide her toward him. She was pinned tight.

Tears filled his eyes.

"David … you have to …" She struggled with several small breaths, then her head fell forward.

He shook her. "Cassandra, please." Pushed his fingers into her neck, tried different angles, felt the other side, squeezed her wrists, but he could not find a pulse. He grabbed her and held her, tears pouring down his cheeks. And the hissing steam ceased. The radiator stopped draining. The tire went still.

Silence.

Pierced by the sound of squealing tires making sharp turns.

He didn't want to let go of her, but he did, and it felt as if his soul had ripped itself away from him to follow hers, his body hollowed out, dark and vacuous, on the verge of imploding.

He needed to hide the car, jumped in and pulled around Cassandra, the glow of headlights growing in his rearview mirror. There, a break in the guardrail. He turned the wheel hard to the left, rumbled down the embankment, slammed into a tree and came to rest at a steep angle, driver's side downhill, the tree pressing against the door.

He climbed up the seat, wormed his way out of the passenger side window and started up the hill. The ground was frozen, making it difficult to get a firm hold with either hands or feet. He grabbed shrubs and roots and pulled. His leg throbbed as he fought for every agonizing inch. His ribs ached from the beating he had taken from the big Russian.

From up on the road he heard cars stop. Doors open and close. Men speaking in hushed tones. He clawed his way up the bank, slowly, quietly, and was a few feet below the edge when another car rounded the corner—a sports car, a high-pitched whine to the engine. It screeched to a stop. The door opened and slammed shut. A voice boomed into the night air. "Is she dead?"

David froze, breathing suspended, ears trained on the road above.

"Goddammit! Is she dead?"

He knew that voice. Pressure exploded into his head. His heart pounded. His brain pulsated. His skull threatened to crack open like a hard-boiled egg that had been left in the pan too long. The sound of that voice was imprinted on his brain as permanently as his dead mother's. It evoked hatred the way Pavlov's bell made the dog drool.

Andrew Turnbull.

Turnbull's voice boomed again. "Get out of my way."

David crept up the last few feet and peered over the edge of the embankment.

Turnbull leaned into the Town Car and felt Cassandra's neck. "Dammit," he said, pounding the roof of the car with his fist. "The steering wheel caved in her chest. Now we've lost both donors. Get White on the phone. Tell him we have a body to dispose of."

Turnbull jumped in the Porsche, smoked the tires as he spun a U-turn, and disappeared around the corner.

Two men tried to pull Cassandra out of the car, yanking and jerking, her head flopping to and fro like a rag doll. David couldn't stomach the sickening display. He felt for the cell phone in his pocket, lowered himself down the hill and hid in the brush, where he called 911. He reported an injury accident—a possible fatality— gave the approximate location, and climbed back up the slope. He wasn't ready to give Andrew Turnbull to the cops, but at the same time, he was not going to let Turnbull's goons treat Cassandra like a piece of trash.

The plan worked. Within minutes, a siren. He reached the road in time to see Turnbull's buffoons take off, leaving Cassandra behind. A Passaic County Sheriff's cruiser arrived, and not long after that, a paramedic unit. Now her body would be handled properly. He wiped away the tears, said good-bye to Cassandra, and as he stared up at the black, starless sky, promised her he would kill Andrew Turnbull.

An hour and a half later, David was heading back to the city in R'Shaun's Escalade. Fresh blood from his bullet wound soaked his pants. Clotted blood from a scalp laceration matted his hair. Crusted blood had dried on the left side of his face. His leg hurt, his ribs hurt, his head hurt, and he was frozen to the core. He had bushwhacked his way down the hill for a couple of miles, falling countless times on frozen ground, and now he sat in the backseat of the Escalade in silence, void of all feeling except pain and hate.

They stopped at the Holland Tunnel tollbooth, paid the toll, and drove into a blur of pale neon light and white tiles. R'Shaun's eyes met David's in the rearview mirror. A thin smile creased R'Shaun's lips and he said, "You find out where the bitch lives, we'll cut him open and feed him his own kidneys. You know what I'm sayin'?"

David held R'Shaun's gaze. The kid who had initially appeared soft, and seemed out of place running with a gang from the projects, now had a gleam of suppressed violence in his eyes, violence in the eyes that was dissociated from the smile on his face. David had seen this look before, on both the prison and psych wards of Bellevue. "Yeah," he said, "I know exactly what you're saying, and I might just take you up on that." And he turned and stared out the window at the blur of lights and tiles.

- 57 -

Through the tinted glass of the Escalade, the grays of the head-stones, the browns of the dead grass and leafless trees, and the blacks of the overcoats were intensified, sharply focused, in high definition—resembling not a scene from real life, but a dream so vivid and disturbing the dreamer realizes he is dreaming and wills himself to wake up.

Over the past week David had existed in such a dreamlike state. He'd find himself sitting in Tyronne's chair or lying on Tyronne's couch, not knowing how he got there, how long he'd been there, or why he was there. Only after a few moments would the reality set in, like an amnesiac waking from a fugue state, the pain wash-ing over him and settling deep in his chest, his dilated failing heart about to stop pumping. Through the window he could see only the backs of the heads of Cassandra's mother and father, but he felt their pain as intensely as he felt his own. Their heads hung low and jerked, almost continually. Tears, no doubt, streamed down their faces. Disbelief, no doubt, dominated every attempt to form rational thoughts. Perhaps they were in fugue states of their own.

With all twenty to thirty attendees standing, David could not see the casket, but he had caught a glimpse of it when the Escalade carried him into the cemetery. It was high-gloss black and covered with dozens of red roses, as elegant as an evening gown and exactly what he'd have chosen. He wondered if that would have been Cassandra's choice.

Jesus! Twenty-eight-year-olds don't think about funeral arrange-ments. She didn't even get the chance to pick colors for the baby. He slammed his fist into his bad thigh, buried his face in his coat sleeve, and screamed until he was hoarse. Thankfully, Tyronne and R'Shaun were not in there with him. They were hovering over a nearby grave, a couple of homeboys lamenting the loss of a fallen brother, should anyone be watching.

After a few minutes he lifted his head and smeared away the tears with the heels of his palms. Never before had he felt such a vast emptiness. His wife and unborn child, dead. His freedom, stripped away. His father, shipped off to some psychiatric snake pit in Queens or Brooklyn. He had nothing, with no way to reclaim what had been lost. He buried his face in his arms and wept.

Then the sobbing stopped as quickly as it had started. Anger and hatred replaced grief and self-loathing. Yes, he was supposed to protect those he loved. And yes, he had failed. But he didn't abduct his wife. He didn't try to cut out her heart and force her to escape, to drive a car even though she had never driven before. Andrew Turnbull did, and now he was going to suffer.

Tyronne climbed into the front seat. "Gotta roll. We got Five-O lurkin' around out there, hidin' behind trees and shit."

"Yeah," David said. "I've seen enough."

David finished the latest set of laps, laid on the couch, and propped up his leg. It had been ten days since the gunshot wound to the thigh and subsequent beating by the big Russian, and as the leg healed and the contused ribs recovered, David had been doing an increasing number of laps around Tyronne's apartment. He would start at the window, take several steps to the counter that separated the front room from the kitchen, turn left toward the bathroom, and make another left into the bedroom. He'd then go around to the far side of the bed, turn, and retrace his steps. Every tenth lap he stopped and bent his leg at the knee and hip. The thigh muscle remained swollen and hard, and bending his knee greater than ten degrees caused significant pain, but he was walking better, and his leg could bear most of his weight.

A knock at the door. Tyronne. The locks opened in succession, the distinctive clinks and clanks ingrained in David's mind. He sat up and lowered his leg to the floor.

Tyronne came in and dropped into the cushionless chair in the corner. R'Shaun followed him in, slouched against the countertop on one elbow, and gave David a nod and a smile—that dissociated psychopathic smile of his. David nodded back.

"Got the call," Tyronne said. "AT is at a bar in Newark. He went up in there with a big-tittied blonde. This time of night, you be walkin' through the door in thirty."

"Big place? Small place?"

"Small, but let's scope it out. We can always bail, if we need to."

"You get the stuff I asked for?"

"Yeah, but I gotta ask, instead of druggin' the man, and risking havin' to haul his ass outta there, how 'bout we wait and jack him at his car?"

"No. I want him to experience what his victims experienced. He's in his ordinary world one minute, having drinks, thinking he's gonna get laid, then he wakes up in a nightmare. And when he awakens into that nightmare, I want to be standing over him. I want my face to be the first thing he sees when he wakes up, not the last thing he sees as he's forced at gunpoint into a car."

"Okay, let's get you ready, but before we do this there's somethin' needs to be said." Tyronne sat forward and put his elbows on his knees. "You know I'm down with this shit, whatever way you wanna go, but kidnapping is big-time, right? A capital offense? Could land you upstate for at least a fifty. And this nightmare you're plannin'? Not sure what it is? But I got a feeling it's a capital crime, too."

"Doesn't matter. I have nothing, and the man with nothing has nothing to lose."

"No offense, Doc, but I don't think you know what it means to have nothin'. Yeah, you lost everything, but you're educated and white, and those two things right there'll get you pretty far. So maybe you go to the cops, get yourself outta the hole you're in."

"Know what, Tyronne?" R'Shaun said, now standing erect. "If the doc wants to waste the muthafucker, or feed him his own kidney, that's what he oughta do. You go messin' up any of my folks, I'm gonna go all *Call of Duty: Black Ops* on yo' ass."

Tyronne gave R'Shaun a hard stare. "The doc? He ain't like you or me. He got a lot more goin' for him. He can still get out of this shit and get back on track. Me and you? We ain't even been on the track. We'll never be more than a couple niggas from the hood."

"Yeah, he ain't you or me. What he is, is a smart muthafucker who know what he's doin'. I say we be *his* crew for now, and we shut the fuck up and follow *his* orders."

Tyronne jumped out of the chair. "You sayin' I need to shut the fuck up?"

R'Shaun took a step toward him. "No, *Dog*. I'm sayin' the doc is smarter than the rest of us niggas put together, so we don't need to be talkin' him outta nothin'."

David pushed off the arm of the couch and stood up. "Look," he said, turning to R'Shaun, then Tyronne. "I appreciate what both of you are saying, but whatever happens to me doesn't matter. I made a promise to Cassandra when she was dying on the side of that road, and I'm gonna keep that promise if it's the last honorable thing I do. What about you guys? You're assuming the same risk just to help out a white doctor?"

"You saved my life," Tyronne said.

"I was just doing my job. I was the chief resident on call that night. If you would have come in the night before or the night after, someone else would've saved your life."

"But you the one that stuck with me. Treated me the same as the white Wall Street guy layin' over in the bed next to mine, got all busted up on his motorcycle. Don't think I noticed?"

"I treated everybody the same when I was a resident, but the legal system has a different view of race. You have prior arrests. You're black. If you get arrested for kidnapping the white president of a company, you'll get life."

"Risk I'm willin' to take, Doc."

"What about you, R'Shaun? Why do you want to do this?"

R'Shaun flashed his demented smile. "Sound like fun, fuckin' up one white man who fucked over another white man. Us niggas from the hood? We big believers in a eye for a eye."

"So you guys are full of good intentions. And the others?"

"They do what I tell 'em," Tyronne said.

"Just to make sure everyone's on board, how about I sweeten the pot? Close the gap between the risks and the benefits, so to speak."

"Come again, Doc?"

"I think I can get you five to ten boxes of IV fentanyl. Each box contains ten ampules, each ampule contains a hundred micrograms. My guess, it's worth a small fortune on the street."

Tyronne nodded. "You'd be guessin' right."

"I'm not sure it's still there, but if it is, it's all yours. And there may be other things, like Versed, maybe some Demerol."

"We take whatever you got," R'Shaun said. "We all be onboard with that."

David sat down on the couch. "Good, because I'm going to need all of you."

- 59 -

David spotted the Elbow Room, tapped the brakes, and studied the layout. The small structure sat about ten feet back from the curb with a strip of dead grass filling the space between the sidewalk and the brick façade. On the side of the building, a red canvas awning hung above two wood doors with oval windows. The only other windows stretched across the front. What a typical North Jersey relic. He could already picture the cocktail lounge—oak bar, walls, and ceiling. Leather booths worn from decades of use. Just enough ambient light to keep the servers from tripping over each other. The perfect place for a tryst. David had met Turnbull's wife. She was neither big-titted nor blonde.

He turned into the parking lot, bypassed the open spots in front, and drove the stolen Ford Expedition around back. And there it was, Andrew Turnbull's $200,000 custom-built Porsche 911, parked diagonally across two spaces. David pulled in next to it and eased the nose of the Ford up to a chain-link fence that bordered an abandoned lot. The cellulose skeletons of last summer's weeds swayed in the breeze, then vanished when he switched off the ignition and killed the headlights.

The Porsche's gunmetal-blue paint job glistened like cold steel in the xenon glow of the single lamppost. An image of Turnbull climbing from the Porsche, and beating the roof of the Town Car after failing to detect Cassandra's pulse, spiked David's hatred to a new high. He switched on the interior light, checked himself in the rearview mirror, and wondered, should they come face-to-face, would Turnbull recognize him. He wore a pair of black-framed twenty-dollar reading glasses, had leeched the color from his hair with peroxide, and cropped it to within an inch of his scalp so it would stand up straight. He hadn't shaved since getting shot and now had a thick growth of whiskers, also bleached white. And he was pale from losing a couple units of blood into the dirt of the subway tunnel and his thigh muscle. He might be able to fool his own mother, but not Turnbull. Turnbull will know the eyes. The two of them had spent countless hours standing across operating tables from each other, hats low on their brows, faces covered by masks. Turnbull will definitely know the eyes.

Trying to minimize his limp, David made his way to the entrance. He held the door as a white-haired man in a suit, and a giggling young woman in a short skirt and long fur coat staggered out, oblivious to his presence. The maître d' stand—unstaffed for the moment—stood across from the entrance. To the left, the clanking dishes and muffled conversation of the dining room. To the right, the live piano of the cocktail lounge. David went down the hall and around the corner.

The bar stretched along the wall to the right, and a glance to the left gave him the basic layout of the place. Two rows of round-top tables filled the center of the room. Booths lined the remaining three walls. Tiny hanging lamps cast halos of light over each table. In the far corner stood a piano. A bald man in a black tux was playing "Luck Be a Lady Tonight," a Sinatra standard. The place was dark, just as he had imagined, just as he had hoped. He made a conscious effort to not focus on any of the faces in the crowd. He was not yet mentally prepared to lay eyes on Andrew Turnbull.

The two stools at the near end of the bar were vacant. David took the seat next to the wall and draped his coat on the other. Acutely losing faith in his disguise, he stooped forward and fixed his gaze on the half-finished drinks in front of him—a strawberry daiquiri and something clear with a wedge of lime at the bottom. A stack of cocktail napkins, arranged in a spiral pattern, rose from the four-inch recession along the inside edge of the bar. A glass full of red straws sat next to the napkins.

Reluctantly, David looked up as the bartender approached. He was a young guy with sharp features and thick, dark hair combed straight back. He wore a light-blue dress shirt with the sleeves rolled up to the elbows. The knot in his red power tie was loose and the top button of his shirt undone. He efficiently removed the dirty glasses, wiped up the rings of condensation, and placed a clean napkin next to a bowl of miniature pretzels. "What can I get you?" he asked.

Above the surface of the bar, David was a picture of taut composure. Below the surface, his good leg drummed up and down on the rung of the barstool like a jackhammer. "How 'bout a Jack on the rocks. And make it a double, please."

While he kept his eyes fixed on the parcel of varnished oak he'd claimed for himself, he could feel Turnbull's presence. As a resident, David knew when Turnbull was about to turn a corner or walk into the operating room. The clip-clop of wooden clogs announced his imminent arrival and triggered an uneasy anticipation. That same feeling was bearing down on him now, only a thousand times stronger. He grabbed a handful of pretzels, tossed a couple in his mouth, and silently pleaded with the bartender to hurry.

Moments later the bartender set a tumbler of Jack Daniel's on the cocktail napkin and walked away. David emptied it in two quick gulps, the sour-mash whiskey scorching the epithelium as it washed over his tongue and plunged down the esophagus. He caught the bartender's attention and tapped the edge of the glass. The bartender nodded.

As David waited, he studied the people seated along the bar, glancing at them one by one, quickly returning his gaze to the empty tumbler. A grizzled old man sat alone at the far end. Couples filled the remaining seats, slouching over their drinks to varying degrees. No Turnbull.

The bartender delivered another glass of Tennessee's finest, and as he turned to go, he looked back, for maybe two seconds. A glint of recognition? David froze, eyes unblinking, breath shallow while he waited to see what the guy would do next. But he didn't rush to the phone, as David thought he might. Instead, with no obvious change in his demeanor, he went about the business of mixing cocktails and pouring beers. David waited for a crack in the façade, a waver in the fluidity of movement, but saw no cracks or wavers, just routine. Nobody who had come face-to-face with the most wanted man in the tri-state area could remain so steadfast. Maybe the guy was sizing him up, wondering what was going to happen when all that whiskey made its way through the bloodstream and into the brain cells. As far as David was concerned, it couldn't soak into his gray matter fast enough. He needed to relax or he was going to blow a cerebral aneurysm right in the middle of the Elbow Room. He pushed the bogus reading glasses up to the bridge of his nose and took a deep breath.

Now immune to the burn of the alcohol, David sipped his drink and shifted his focus to the sounds around him—the occasional adamant voice rising above the muffled din, an outburst of laughter interrupting the melody of the piano. He listened for Turnbull's self-assured discourse but heard nothing quite so obnoxious. As much as he dreaded it, the time had come to lay eyes on Turnbull. He took a swallow of Jack and swiveled his stool ninety degrees.

The four tables near the bar were occupied. Turnbull was not at any of them. David casually moved side to side to get a better view of the second row. Again, no Turnbull, but at the third table over sat a woman, by herself, with two drinks in front of her. She leaned into the light and checked her makeup with a small mirror. She was young, early twenties, long blonde hair, big dark eyes. A tight red sweater showcased her generous breasts. Turnbull's date. She had to be.

To his right, flashing through the farthest reaches of his peripheral vision, David spotted a man passing the far end of the bar, exiting the hallway that led to the restrooms. He jerked his head toward the man, catching only a glimpse, but a glimpse was all he needed. The sudden swell of hatred and revulsion told him he had just seen Andrew, don't-call-me-Andy, Turnbull. As the man approached the blonde, David had an unobstructed view of the audacious swagger and perfectly tailored suit, and all doubt was eliminated.

For two years he had been telling himself he hated Turnbull, but as David thought about his father, and Cassandra, and the bullet hole in his leg, and the victims who had suffered under the knife he'd been forced to wield, he actually *felt* the hatred for the first time. His body trembled with contempt. Repulsion seethed through his veins. Turnbull needed to suffer, the way burn patients suffer, or like those who have experienced the traumatic amputation of an arm or leg suffer. The absoluteness of such strong, negative emotion should have been horrifying, but David found it empowering. He now felt unencumbered, focused on his goal, truly unconcerned about the consequences. He realigned himself with the bar, sucked down the rest of the Jack, then put his hand in his pocket and rolled two roofies between his fingers. Now or never, he told himself. He summoned the bartender.

"I'll take a Heineken," David said. "And I just spotted a couple of friends at that table over there." David didn't point, but gave a slight nod instead. "I'd like to buy them a round. What are they drinking?"

"Vodka martinis for the man. White wine for the woman."

"Sounds good. And why don't I take care of their tab."

"No tab to take care of. He's been paying cash."

The bartender started to turn, and David said, "And one other thing. I'll take the drinks over myself. I'd like to surprise them."

"Whatever you say." The bartender tapped the bar with his finger and walked away.

Minutes later he came back with the drinks and left with three twenties. As David waited for the change, he took the roofies from his pocket and dropped them into the martini. The white tablets rolled down the funnel-shaped glass like tiny snowballs tumbling down a slope. They came to rest at the bottom, nestled among two olives, invisible unless one looked closely. The bartender returned with the change. David left a ten on the bar and said he'd be back for the drinks once he used the restroom.

After ten minutes of sitting in a bathroom stall, he returned to the bar and peered into the bottom of the martini glass. The roofies were gone, dissolved, the drink still colorless. He waited for the bartender to move to the far end of the bar, waved over one of the cocktail servers, and put a five-dollar bill on her tray. "Would you mind taking these drinks to the couple at that table?" He gestured toward Turnbull. "I'll join them in a moment, but first I have to make a call, and just tell 'em they're on the house. I want to surprise them." She said No problem, and he left his glass of beer on the bar, his coat draped on the stool, and headed for the parking lot.

David called Tyronne, told him the plan had been set in motion, and estimated leaving the bar within thirty minutes. Tyronne said they were ready. David turned off the phone, the call lasting all of twenty seconds. He needed to kill more time, but how much more he didn't know. He knew Rohypnol was a potent benzodiazepine. He also knew the average onset of action to be thirty minutes. What he didn't know, and what worried him most, was the effect of combining two milligrams of Rohypnol with an unknown number of vodka martinis. Human physiology was always a wildcard when it came to mixing drugs, and while David stood there thinking about it, two very powerful sedative-hypnotics were swirling through Turnbull's circulatory system, waiting for the chance to cross the blood-brain barrier and have their intended effect on each and every nerve cell. He decided he'd wait ten minutes, in the car, with the heater on.

Twelve minutes later he went back to the bar. Turnbull's martini glass was empty, and his head was bobbing up and down. David grabbed his beer and coat and headed for the table.

He approached from behind the woman, getting a good look at Turnbull, and what he saw shocked him. Turnbull's eyes were glassed over, and his head lolled forward while his torso tipped back and forth. David walked up and patted Turnbull's shoulder, doing his best to appear mildly surprised. "Andrew old buddy, how you doin'?" David smiled at the woman and extended his hand. "I'm Eric Johnson, an old friend of Andrew's."

She tentatively shook David's hand and said her name was Denise. A timid smile peeked through her mortified expression.

"Looks like my friend is in the midst of one of his legendary benders."

"Yeah, I guess, I don't know. I'm kinda worried about him. He was fine until a few minutes ago. Now he can barely hold his head up."

Turnbull wobbled. David pushed him against the chair and kept a firm grip on his shoulder. The man had lost all muscle tone. "I've seen this too many times. He pounds the martinis and seems alright, then hits a wall and he's out of it. Mind if I sit down?"

"No. Please. So he's going to be okay?"

"Yeah." David kept Turnbull steady while he sat down. "He just needs to sleep it off. How'd you get here?"

"We came separately, but he can't drive home like this."

"No—definitely not." David leaned closer, put his hand on Denise's forearm and spoke softly. "We both know he should've been home with his wife hours ago, so I'm going to do both of you a favor. I'll take him, and I'll tell her we ran into each other after work and things got out of hand. She's seen it before. She'll be pissed, and she'll have a few choice words for me, but I'll get over it. Now, if a beautiful young woman hauls him home … well, that just can't happen, can it?"

"No," Denise said, glancing down as if she had been scolded by her father.

"So, if you don't mind, I'll ask you to help me get him to my car. He has a tendency to turn into dead weight about halfway across parking lots."

Turnbull lifted his head and squinted at David. His eyes widened. Drool ran from the corner of his mouth as he uttered an incomprehensible sound.

"He's trying to say something," Denise said, "like 'muck' or 'mick.'"

David knew exactly what it was. McBride. Turnbull had recognized him. "It's drunken gibberish," David said, his impatience growing. "Let's get him out of here. You ready?"

She said yes, but it was meek, and she sat there looking perplexed.

"Denise, we need to go."

"It's just that I'm kinda nervous sending Andrew away with someone I don't know."

David leaned in and took her hand in his. Working hard to restrain the frustration in his voice, he said, "I get it, but I'm a friend, and I'm doing you both a huge favor. Has Andrew told you anything about his wife?"

"No," Denise said quietly.

"She is one of the most feared divorce attorneys in the state. If she finds out her beloved was here with you tonight, first she'll castrate him, then she'll blow your life apart. Understand?"

She nodded.

"Okay. Now let's go." David smiled to ease the tension, his and hers.

He nudged Turnbull and asked him if he could walk. The guy muttered more gibberish. A good sign, actually. His brain was still functioning, on some rudimentary level, anyway. David moved next to Turnbull, and with Denise's help, lifted him out of the chair. He supported his own weight but lacked balance, his equilibrium having been effectively extinguished by roofies and vodka. David and Denise each put an arm around Turnbull's waist, and once the three of them melded into a stable unit, David pushed the fake reading glasses higher on his nose and started for the exit.

They carefully maneuvered among the tables and booths, David repeatedly saying Excuse me and Pardon us. Behind the bar, the bartender had paused to watch the commotion, his hands raised in a What-the-hell? position. David shrugged, made sure Turnbull put one foot in front of the other, and hauled him out of the cocktail lounge of the Elbow Room.

- 60 -

The ride in from Jersey was uneventful—no high-speed pursuits, no roadblocks at the Holland Tunnel, Andrew Turnbull had maintained a steady pulse. After ditching the Expedition in a labyrinth of carbon-caked factory buildings, Tyronne updated David on the situation at the warehouse. Le-Vaughan, the skinniest member of the crew, had wormed his way through a roof vent and cut the lock on one of the doors. Marcus and Jamar had walked the surrounding streets and scanned the adjacent buildings, looking for cops or Russian thugs. As far as they could tell, nobody was watching the place.

R'Shaun turned onto West 13th and moments later, pulled into the warehouse. While Tyronne, R'Shaun, and Le-Vaughan loaded Turnbull onto a gurney, David went up to the OR to see what, if anything, was left of the operating room and equipment.

Nothing had changed since the last time he was there. Broken shelves and spilled supplies lay at the base of the wall. Surgical instruments littered the floor. The Mayo stand remained upended. The drapes that had covered the last victim were a wadded ball in the corner. As David surveyed the carnage, he was met with a profound sense of loss. For him, the operating room had always represented a temple of humanity, a place where dedicated individuals alleviated the suffering of others. The ability to open the body, navigate the intricacies of human anatomy and physiology, close the body and return the person to their former state of health was one of mankind's greatest achievements. But now, the temple had been stained by one of man's most despicable traits—greed. And he was no better. The instruments he had once wielded to help would now be used to hurt, used for the pursuit of one of man's other despicable traits—vengeance. He had discarded the last shred of his humanity, descended to Andrew Turnbull's level, and, sadly, he didn't care.

David opened the drawer of the anesthesia cart and found seven boxes of fentanyl and four of Versed—more than enough to compensate Tyronne and his boys. The thought of all those drugs hitting the street should have left David with at least a modicum of guilt, but he felt nothing. His life had narrowed to a single purpose. The junkies of the world no longer garnered his concern.

The elevator groaned its way to the second floor. David was on his way to the cage when the metal gate whipped open. "He's wakin' up," Tyronne said. "When we strapped his ass down, he started squirmin' and mutterin' like a bitch."

Turnbull's eyes were open but unfocused, and his speech slurred. He groped for the leather strap, which had been placed across his shoulders instead of his wrists. "Get him into the OR," David said.

While R'Shaun pushed, David steered the gurney alongside the operating table. He then told Le-Vaughan, "Look for a pair of big scissors in that pile of stuff over there and cut the right sleeve of the shirt, from cuff to collar."

Le-Vaughan glanced at Tyronne. "Why we takin' orders from this white motherfucker?"

Tyronne bitch-slapped Le-Vaughan. " 'Cause I say so."

Working quickly, David gathered IV supplies out of the anesthesia cart. The faster he could get Turnbull under and send these guys on their way, the better.

Le-Vaughan returned with the shears and cut the sleeve of Turnbull's shirt.

David wrapped a tourniquet around Turnbull's bicep and cinched it tight, the veins in the forearm distending with blood. David pinched an IV catheter like a dart and said, "When I stick him it's gonna piss him off, so be ready."

R'Shaun and Tyronne each held an arm, Le-Vaughan the legs. David stabbed the needle into a vein. As predicted, Turnbull jerked and moaned. When he settled down, David threaded the catheter all the way in, connected the IV tubing, popped the tourniquet loose, and started the flow of Lactated Ringer's solution. After securing the catheter with tape, he drew five milligrams of Versed into a syringe and slowly infused it through an injection port. David wondered if five milligrams was enough, or too much. Versed was more potent than its brother Valium, but not nearly as potent as their illegitimate brother the roofie. If five was the proper dose, Turnbull would pass out again. If five was too much, he'd stop breathing.

Moments later Turnbull went flaccid. David had the guys cut off the rest of the clothes as he hit a series of switches on the anesthesia machine, bringing it to life. The bellows moved up and down, emitting crescendo-decrescendo blowing sounds. A flat line appeared on the cardiac monitor. The pulse oximeter chirped and entered warm-up mode.

"Hey, Doc," Tyronne said, "what you wanna do with these?" He held a BlackBerry in one hand. A gold Rolex and a set of keys dangled from the other.

"I'll take the phone and watch." He'd be able to sell them on any street corner. "You can have the keys. They go to a custom-built Porsche parked behind the bar we were just at."

With Turnbull's clothing removed, Tyronne and the others slid him from the gurney to the operating table while David supported his head. David then grabbed a couple of blankets, covered Turnbull from the waist down, and proceeded to place the monitoring equipment.

He clamped a pulse oximeter over the tip of Turnbull's index finger and glanced at the readout on the screen. Oxygen saturation, 96 percent. Heart rate, 98 beats per minute. Perfect. He dialed up the volume so he could hear the chirps of the oximeter, and set the alarm to sound if the heart rate fell below 60 or the oxygen level dropped below 90 percent. He placed EKG electrodes on the chest and wrapped an automated blood pressure cuff around the left arm. He could now prepare for induction of general anesthesia and endotracheal intubation while using his auditory sense to monitor the patient.

David sat down on a metal stool, rolled his shoulders, and tried to relax. Tyronne said something about all this surgical stuff dredgin' up memories of some bad shit, and he left the room with Le-Vaughan in tow, to join Marcus and Jamar in their surveillance efforts. R'Shaun stayed next to the table in case Turnbull's sedation wore off. David drew anesthetic agents into syringes, prepared the intubation tray, and set up the suction. Everything was ready.

He connected a face mask to the ventilator tubing and held the mask over Turnbull's mouth and nose. With his free hand, he rhythmically squeezed the football-shaped ambu bag, blowing pure oxygen into Turnbull's lungs. The pulse oximeter chirped at a heart rate of 72—down from 98 thanks to the Versed—and an oxygen level of 97 percent. The cardiac monitor showed a regular rhythm. The blood pressure cuff read 134/76. He would place the breathing tube when the oxygen saturation reached 99 or 100 percent.

As he continued bagging, he studied the intubation tray, which consisted of an endotracheal tube and a laryngoscope. David had not intubated a human since his residency, and even then it wasn't something he did very often. But since that time, he had intubated countless rats. If he could slip a catheter the size of a cocktail straw into a rat trachea, he should be able to insert a tube the width of his thumb into an adult male.

The pulse oximeter read 99 percent. David handed R'Shaun a syringe of succinylcholine. This was the crux of the procedure. Succinylcholine was a neuromuscular depolarizing agent, and upon intravenous injection, it would paralyze all skeletal muscle, including the diaphragm and the musculature of the pharynx. If David did not get the tube inserted quickly, Turnbull would suffocate. He told R'Shaun to go ahead and slowly inject the solution into the IV tubing. About thirty seconds later, Turnbull's body began to twitch—the muscular fasciculations that herald total paralysis, the point of no return. Turnbull was now paralyzed.

David stopped bagging, picked up the laryngoscope, slipped the curved blade to the base of the tongue and lifted, hoping to see the vocal cords. He didn't. He repositioned the blade and lifted again. Nothing. He pulled harder, nearly bringing Turnbull's head off the table. Still no cords. He checked the pulse oximeter—94 percent—grabbed the endotracheal tube and made a blind attempt, inserting it where the cords should be, then connected the bag and squeezed. The chest did not rise. He listened with a stethoscope. No breath sounds. The tube was in the esophagus.

The alarm sounded. Oxygen saturation, 89 percent. Heart rate and blood pressure okay.

He removed the tube. Suctioned the pharynx. Looked again. Nothing.

The cardiac monitor started pinging. Heart rate, 110. BP, 84/52. Oxygen saturation, 79 percent. Cardiac arrest was imminent.

Then he recalled a trick he'd seen when he was a medical student. David grabbed R'Shaun's hand, placed it on Turnbull's Adam's apple and told him to push. The external pressure moved the larynx posteriorly toward the spine. The pearly white vocal cords came into view. David slid the tube between them, connected it to the ambu bag and squeezed vigorously. The chest rose and fell. The oxygen saturation climbed. The heart rate dropped. The systolic blood pressure hit 90. David bagged until all the numbers normalized, then connected the endotracheal tube to the ventilator and turned on the isoflurane canister. Inhalational anesthetic was now traveling directly to the lungs.

IV access had been established, the airway secured. The life-sustaining physiologic functions were being monitored, and could be altered with the push of a syringe. David now had complete control over Turnbull, the ultimate in bondage and submission, the power of life and death. He sat down and wiped his forehead on his sleeves, then looked up at R'Shaun. "The maneuver you just performed is called cricoid pressure. It saved the bastard."

"Why you sweatin' over it, Doc? Who cares if the muthafucker dies?"

"I care. I need to have a little one-on-one with the motherfucker before I send him into the white light."

R'Shaun smiled, his eyes gleaming with violence. "Right on, Doc."

With R'Shaun's help, David positioned Turnbull for a right flank incision—right side up, left side on the table, legs slightly bent, arms folded across the chest. He then strapped Turnbull to the table and taped his eyes closed. David thanked R'Shaun and said he'd holler when he needed help. R'Shaun left the room, leaving David alone with Turnbull.

After checking the monitors, David went and put on scrubs, a hat, and a mask. When he returned, he uprighted the Mayo stand, opened a basic instrument tray—scalpels, clamps, needle holders, retractors—placed it on the stand, dropped several suture packs onto the tray, and switched on the electrocautery device. He then prepped and draped Turnbull, and gowned and gloved himself.

Turnbull was ready. David was ready.

Just as David picked up a scalpel, Tyronne came through the door, stopping short as soon as he entered. "So you are gonna feed him his own kidney," he said.

"They're both coming out."

"Ain't that gonna kill him?"

"Yes. Without dialysis, it's a death sentence."

David rested the scalpel on Turnbull's skin, pushed hard, and pulled toward himself. The blade sliced through dermis and fat and into muscle, an amateurish move one would expect from an intern, but in this case, a move driven by a wanton desire to destroy—cells, tissues, the organism, the man. The wound quickly filled with blood. David grabbed the cautery device with one hand, held the suction in the other, and went to work zapping bleeders.

"How long will it take?" asked Tyronne, his voice now a few inches away.

David looked up. Tyronne was standing on the other side of the drape, next to the anesthesia machine.

"How long will it take him to die?" Tyronne asked.

"Hard to say exactly. Four hours, six hours, maybe ten. Depends on how fast the potassium and hydrogen ions build up in his blood. The kidneys remove excess amounts of those things, so without at least one kidney to do the job, potassium builds up, the blood turns acidic, and the heart stops beating."

"That's some cold shit, Doc."

David resumed suctioning the wound and zapping bleeders. Over the slurping and buzzing and pops and crackles, he said, "Yeah, just like dying on a dark road with a steering wheel smashed into your sternum." He stopped and looked at Tyronne. "My wife spent the final twenty-four hours of her existence terrified and confused, the last ten minutes running for her life, and the final five slowly dying from a crushed heart. So, in the spirit of an eye for an eye, I've sentenced Andrew Turnbull to suffer through multiple hours of postoperative pain while he waits for his blood to turn to acid and kill him."

"And you sure this is the right thing to do?"

"It's the only thing to do."

"Then I guess I be steppin' out now."

"Before you go, look in the second drawer down." David nodded toward the anesthesia cart. "All that fentanyl and Versed, it's yours."

Tyronne gathered the boxes and left the operating room.

David finished drying the wound and started dividing the muscle layers standing between him and Turnbull's right kidney, but once he gained access to the retroperitoneal space, he stopped. It was unrealistic to think he could excise both kidneys without skilled assistants and an anesthesiologist. No matter. He had cut through all the tissue layers that contribute to post-op pain. He cauterized the remaining bleeders, loaded a suture in a needle holder, and began reapproximating muscle.

When the skin was closed and the wound dressed, David called the guys into the room to help him reposition Turnbull, left side up. After re-prepping and draping, he took his scalpel and reproduced the incision he had made on Turnbull's right side.

- 61 -

Mr. White leaned slightly in his chair so Denise could place a coaster under his coffee cup. She seemed unusually harried this morning. She'd come in late, had noticeable tremors in her hands, and lacked color in her face as if she were ill. But she didn't have the languid manner of someone who was sick. Instead, she was jittery, on edge, quite anxious about something, all of which were out of character for her.

A moment later Cynthia spoke up. "I think we should start without him."

It was 6:20 a.m. and still no sign of Turnbull—no call, no text, no Porsche in the lot. He was now twenty minutes late, and apparently, not only had he never missed a research meeting, but he was always the first one in his seat. And it was somewhat surprising he would miss this one in particular. He himself had touted it as the meeting that would change the world. Mr. White wondered if Denise's anxiety and Turnbull's absence were linked. After all, they had rendezvoused several times in the recent past.

"We all have a busy day ahead of us," Cynthia added, "and we need to get to our labs."

She directed the comment to Sam Keating. Keating deferred the decision to Mr. White with a look that said, *I'm pathetically lost.*

Keating appeared to have finally gone over the edge and was now in free fall. In the wake of the death of Cassandra McBride one week ago, he had become increasingly paranoid and withdrawn. Despite reassurances that the NYPD were honoring the FBI's request to back off the NuLife investigation, Keating was convinced otherwise. He was certain a raid was imminent. Mr. White had repeatedly assured NuLife's CFO that he was monitoring the situation, and neither the NYPD nor the Passaic County Sheriff's Department had any plans, at the moment anyway, to pursue a search warrant. Turnbull, on the other hand, had remained unfazed by the violent death of a young pregnant woman, thus confirming his status as a psychopath. His only concern had been that the incident would draw NuLife farther into the spotlight. So far it hadn't.

For Mr. White, David McBride was the real threat. He had lost his wife at the hands of others and had since fallen off the grid. He now represented a rogue element who could no longer be controlled, a rogue element who was unlikely to sit around and sulk, and men like him were dangerous. The sooner Mr. White could distance himself from the paranoid CFO, the psychopathic CEO, and the specter of a man bent on revenge, the better. But for now, he needed to keep the mission moving forward. Time was not merely of the essence, it was critical.

He turned toward Cynthia. "Yes. We should proceed. Dr. Turnbull can refer to the minutes. Besides, he always knows where each of you stand with your work, does he not?"

This last comment elicited a round of muffled laughter and affirmatory nods from the scientists. It was no secret Andrew Turnbull was an omniscient, micromanaging taskmaster, which made it all the more unusual he would miss a meeting he had scheduled himself. Mr. White felt a twinge of uneasiness take root. "As representative of the scientific advisory board, I'm the one who needs to be apprised of your progress."

"Okay. I'll start," Cynthia said. "I'm pleased to report that since we last met, the synthetic function of the bioartificial livers has dramatically improved. We've seen production of bile, albumin, and transaminase enzymes approaching human physiologic levels. In addition, we sent three separate organs for histologic study, which revealed complete development of their circulatory systems and absence of any necrosis due to lack of blood flow. The stem-cell seed rate exceeded ninety percent in all three organs. In conclusion, we have grown livers that are ready for transplantation into human patients."

Mr. White turned to the lanky young man from Australia who ran the kidney group. "And the kidneys? Are they functioning?" he asked, hearing the anticipation in his own voice.

The answer was yes. The kidneys were making urine and had achieved 80–90 percent filtering capacity. The heart, lung, and pancreas teams reported similar results.

As the scientists formally congratulated one another—they'd been aware of each other's progress all along, this morning's meeting a mere formality—Mr. White leaned back in his chair, buzzing with the enormity of the situation. He had just witnessed a profound moment in the history of mankind's bid to mitigate death and suffering, but more important—

Jeff Abercrombie jumped up and groaned. Denise had knocked over his Double Big Gulp Mountain Dew Code Red while trying to put the cup on its coaster, and most of it had cascaded off the table into his lap. His colleagues offered napkins and assistance, Denise scurried out of the room in tears, and with that, the meeting was effectively over, one of medicine's greatest triumphs punctuated by the havoc of a spilled soft drink.

Denise's reaction to the debacle struck Mr. White as an overreaction. He traced Denise to the women's restroom at the end of the hall, asked if she was alone, and could he come in. "What for?" she answered. He said he needed to speak to her in private. Reluctantly, she said okay. He stepped inside and leaned against the door. It was a small bathroom—two stalls, two sinks. She stood at one of them, tending to her makeup with trembling fingers.

"You are not yourself this morning."

"Everyone has a bad day."

"Yes, but your reaction to a spilled cup of soda seemed quite dramatic."

"What can I say," she said, peering into the mirror.

"Would this have anything to do with Dr. Turnbull's absence?"

She tried to remain unfazed by the comment, but the strain was obvious.

"Were you with him last night?"

She turned toward him. "I could lose my job."

"What the two of you do on your own time holds no interest for me. His safety does."

She lowered her gaze, then raised it to meet his. "We met for drinks. Dr. Turnbull was fine at first, and all of a sudden he was out of it. He could barely sit up, and then this guy comes over to the table and says he's an old friend, and he would take Dr. Turnbull home. It sounded like a good idea, so I helped them to the parking lot, and that's the last time I saw him."

"Was his friend short?"

"No, tall. Maybe six feet or so."

"Fat?"

"Kinda thin, actually."

"And his face? Any distinguishing features?"

"No. Just an everyday face, but his hair was bleached white and almost spiky. It didn't fit the rest of him."

"Was he the same age as Dr. Turnbull?"

"Well, that's just it. The guy made it seem like they were friends from way back, but he was a lot younger. I didn't think about it at the time, but this morning when Dr. Turnbull wasn't here, I started to get really worried. If something's wrong, I feel like I'm responsible. I mean—" Tears streaked down her cheeks. "Dr. Turnbull is a very important man."

"Yes, he is," Mr. White said as he opened the browser on his iPhone. "I'm sure he's at home sleeping it off. Don't be overly concerned." He stepped into the hallway and pulled up a website that monitored the GPS signal from Turnbull's BlackBerry, and had to think for a moment to recall the log-in information. He'd always regarded Turnbull's kidnapping fixation as somewhat paranoid, but maybe not today. He logged in, navigated to a real-time display of the BlackBerry signal, and shuddered with horror. Turnbull was at the warehouse, and had been there for more than eight hours.

Mr. White's world exploded. He had abused his position as a deputy director at the National Security Agency in order to spy on American citizens and coerce them to harvest and implant stolen human organs. He had made himself a party to kidnappings, assaults, and deaths—including the abduction and death of a young pregnant woman, for which he bore an enormous burden of guilt. He had blackmailed Russian mobsters, which might very well cost him his life at some later date. He had done all of this for the sole purpose of saving his daughter, and now David McBride had ripped it all apart. Mr. White ran down the hall and out to his car.

- 62 -

David awoke with a jolt as a siren echoed through the building. He sprang out of the chair, ran over to the windows, and rubbed away the grime until he could see out. Except for swirling trash and a few parked cars, the dark street was empty. He took a deep breath and willed his heart to slow down before it seized up like a car driving too fast in first gear.

As he walked back to the recovery area, he rolled his shoulders and flexed his neck to loosen the knots put there by sleeping in a chair. He squinted at the naked lightbulb hanging from the ceiling—too harsh for eyes that had been closed for a couple of hours. He picked up his blanket from the floor, wrapped it around himself, and sat down. The legs of the metal chair clicked as it rocked on the uneven concrete.

Two-and-a-half hours had passed since David had wheeled Turnbull out of the OR, and still no signs of waking up. His head lay quietly on a pillow. He was propped up to forty-five degrees so his lungs could move air efficiently. White blankets kept him warm. The cardiac monitor beeped at 65 beats per minute, and his blood pressure was stable. Thick leather straps secured his wrists and ankles to the rails of the gurney, reminding David of patients he'd seen on the psych ward as a medical student and resident, people strapped down like animals, people who evoked sympathy. Turnbull evoked only hatred.

David jostled the gurney with his foot. Turnbull stirred and muttered something. David shook the bed again, harder this time. Turnbull opened his eyes, tried to focus, moaned, and closed them.

David kicked the bed. "Wake up, Andy."

Turnbull snapped his head toward David, brought his eyes into focus. "What the hell is this? McBride? Is that you?" He jerked against the straps and tried to sit up. Pain contorted his face. He groaned, fell back and lay motionless, eyes squeezed shut, beads of sweat on his brow, the monitor beeping furiously. "What have you done to me?"

David's veins flooded with adrenaline. His heart pounded as he stood there, waiting for satisfaction. It didn't come, but neither did regret. He tugged on the restraints, made sure they were tight, leaned over Turnbull and lifted the blanket, exposing his torso. "See for yourself."

Turnbull looked at the gauze dressings taped to both flanks. "My kidneys? You removed my kidneys? Is that what this means?"

David said nothing.

"Why would you do that?"

David grabbed the rail and violently shook the gurney. "*Why?* Are you kidding me?"

Turnbull grimaced with pain. "Okay, okay. Back off, for Christ's sake."

David stopped, hands still clenching the cold steel rail, knuckles about to erupt through the skin. "You knew she was pregnant." He shook the gurney and screamed, "You knew it!"

"She was not supposed to be harmed. It was an unfortunate accident."

"Bullshit. I was there that night. I heard what you said when she didn't have a pulse. You were gonna take her heart."

"What do you mean you were there?"

"I was hiding across the road when you pulled up."

"Well, I don't know what you saw or heard, but we had no intention of—"

"You're lying. You've always been a liar, and now you're going to sit here and wait to die, just like Cassandra died on the side of that road. My only regret is that when your heart fibrillates and your eyes roll back in your head, it won't be nearly as painful as a crushed sternum."

"You wouldn't remove life-sustaining organs from a human, not even to save your wife. You proved that."

"Well I guess I've changed, because removing the kidneys of a despicable megalomaniac presented no moral dilemma at all."

Turnbull looked away, stared at the ceiling for a moment, his face a blank slate. Then he turned to David. "Look. I know I've caused a lot of damage, but killing me won't accomplish anything." Turnbull lifted his head off the pillow, wincing as he shifted his weight. "Remember when you worked in my lab, and we couldn't grow anything larger than a ferret organ?"

"Yeah? So?"

"I found a solution. I figured out how to grow adult-sized, fully-functioning human organs from the recipient's own stem cells. We have a lab full of them." Turnbull shifted again, grimaced again. "Think about it, David. No longer will we be forced to violate the bodies of the brain dead, or subject healthy donors to the morbidity of surgery. The horrors of immunosuppression, eliminated. Ventricular assist devices, obsolete. Dialysis machines, collecting dust. These were our goals, right? And now it's a reality. But if something happens to me, all of that will be lost."

"Nothing will be lost. Other labs are doing the same work. Your own researchers will be able to carry on."

"No, they won't. The big breakthrough we've had? I'm the only one who knows what it is. Nobody else has that information. If I die, one of mankind's greatest triumphs goes into the ground with me, and *you* will have the blood of hundreds of thousands of lives on *your* hands."

"I'm the villain here? You think you have the right to fuck over the few for the good of the masses, and I'm the bad guy?"

"It's hardly a new concept. Societies throughout history have sacrificed the few to benefit the many. And we haven't sacrificed anyone. Inconvenienced? Yes."

"Are you out of your mind?" David's voice boomed through the warehouse. "You were stealing body parts, and what about the first donor, the one who bled to death? An inconvenience?"

"An unfortunate complication of the procedure."

"And the heart donor? His death would have been an inconvenience?"

"He was homeless. He had more to offer society in death than in life."

David shook his head. "How do you sleep at night?"

Turnbull tried to sit up. The beeps of the cardiac monitor raced as he struggled to move without the use of arms and legs. Sweat ran down his face. "How do I sleep at night? Like a psychotic on a Thorazine drip. I'm on the verge of making an enormous contribution to mankind. In the end, I will have done a lot more *good* than *harm*. You, on the other hand, with your little revenge scheme? You're indulging yourself with the ultimate self-serving action. No one benefits but you. And remember what Confucius said two thousand years ago: 'Seek revenge, dig two graves.'"

"That's enough."

"At least my actions were designed to help others."

"I said that's enough."

"You're the one who's gonna have trouble sleeping, McBride."

"Shut the fuck up, Andy."

David shoved the gurney and stormed over to the windows. He peered through the grime, at the pink glow edging away the darkness, then he let his head fall forward and squeezed his temples between his palms. His brain was too full, under too much pressure. He could not take any more of Turnbull's twisted logic.

A ringing phone dragged Kate out of a vivid, convoluted dream about a cop who could see into the future. She gave the clock a one-eyed squint—six thirty-five—tapped the touchscreen of her iPhone, and said "D'Angelo" in a groggy voice.

"Kate ... Morales. Sorry to wake you up, but I got a caller on the line insists on speaking to you. Says she's Andrew Turnbull's wife, that you'll recognize the name."

Kate's head cleared as if she had sniffed an ammonia smelling salt. McBride had fallen off the map, NuLife was hands off per the

Feds—even though Cassandra McBride had been found dead less than ten miles away—and the case had gone colder than a cryonically frozen corpse. She sat up. "Put her on."

"Mrs. Turnbull, this is Kate D'Angelo. What can I do for you?"

"I'm sorry to bother you, Detective, but I think my husband's in trouble. I know you recently questioned him about the David McBride case, so I'm hoping you'll help me without insisting I wait forty-eight hours to fill out a missing-persons report."

"Dr. Turnbull is missing?"

"Yes, but I know where he is."

"Then he's not really missing."

"Let me start from the beginning."

As she listened to Mrs. Turnbull, Kate slipped into a robe and went to the kitchen for a cup of instant coffee. Outside the window, the pink glow of sunrise filled the sky.

"Last night Andrew called and said he'd be late, he was stopping for drinks with his CFO, but when I got up this morning he wasn't home yet. At first I was angry. He's had a roving eye for years, and I figured the inevitable affair had finally happened. Then I remembered, I have a way to pinpoint his location. He frequently travels to the Middle East and worries about getting kidnapped, so he signed up with a service that monitors the GPS signal from his BlackBerry. I logged on to the website and found out exactly where he is."

"And where's that?" Kate asked.

"In the city, a building on West 13th. I pulled up a street view on Google Maps, thinking I'd see a nice brownstone or high-rise, but instead, it's a dilapidated meatpacking warehouse."

Kate nearly choked on her coffee. Exposing a warehouse was one of the options on McBride's legal pad. "The signal is real time?"

"Yes, and it hasn't moved for almost nine hours."

Nine hours. Shit. "I certainly understand your concern, Mrs. Turnbull. We'll check it out right away, and I'll get back to you as soon as I know something. Can you give me the web address and log-in information for the monitoring service?"

Kate called Morales, gave him the location of the warehouse. "Get Emergency Services over there now. I want the place sealed, no one in, no one out. And get hold of Scarpelli."

David returned to the alcove, his head throbbing.

"I want to see the kidneys," Turnbull said.

"What for?"

"I don't think you're capable of doing what you say you've done."

"I fed 'em to the rats."

"I don't believe you."

"Believe what you want."

David sat in the chair and wrapped himself with the blanket. Despite the space heater in the corner, he couldn't shake the chill that had settled deep in his core. "Why didn't you save me?" he asked.

"What?" Turnbull said.

"When you were questioned by the disciplinary board, you could've saved my career. Why didn't you?"

With great effort, Turnbull lifted his head and turned toward David. "When you opened your mouth, *you* rewrote your own history. You would have made a brilliant surgeon, and if you had stayed quiet and followed my lead, you could've had a singular career. Together, we could have been titans of the transplant world. Instead, you failed to grasp the big picture, and when you came forward, you made a decision to remain one of the gray people. After that, you were not worth saving."

"I was not worth saving," David repeated slowly.

"Yes, and you will come and go from this earth without leaving a trace. That is your destiny, and that is your fault."

Turnbull let his head fall to the pillow and stared vacantly at the ceiling. He was pale and soaked with sweat, and tachycardic, according to the monitor.

David cupped his hands over his face and rubbed at the exhaustion in his eyes, and the pain in his temples and forehead, still trying to fathom what he had just heard. Before him lay a man he had once revered, a man who had become a father figure to him as his own was consumed by Alzheimer's disease, and even now, after all that had transpired, this man was still incapable of showing a sliver of compassion or remorse. And David's actions were no less despicable. Hatred and vengeance had driven him to do something that would have been unfathomable five weeks ago. Hatred and vengeance had transformed him into a soulless animal. And hatred and vengeance were about to send him into humankind's blackest hole—that of the cold, remorseless murderer. He wondered if it was too late to escape the darkness. He wondered if he should have mercy on the man who lay before him, a man who was still a human being no matter how flawed.

Then he thought of Cassandra—the teary eyes, the dreamy smile, her lifeless head falling into the steering wheel. He pictured the fetal ultrasounds he had seen as a medical student, the fetus a tiny bean, the heartbeat a flicker of light. Cassandra never had the chance to see her own ultrasound or feel the immensity of a new life growing inside her. She'd never get the chance to sit in a sun-drenched nursery and rock her baby to sleep, or change diapers, or pick out clothes for the first day of school. She'd never hear the words *I love you, Mommy*, or softly run her fingertips over perfect skin.

Tears welled in his eyes and ran down his cheeks. He picked up the glass vial sitting on the table. Succinylcholine. The same stuff he had used a few hours earlier to paralyze Turnbull for intubation.

He uncapped a syringe, exposing the needle.

Turned the bottle over, stabbed the needle through the rubber stopper, aspirated 10cc's.

Held the syringe up to the light, tapped it with his finger, and applied just enough pressure to expel a few drops of solution.

"What's that?" Turnbull asked.

Crystalline beads ran down the shaft of the needle.

"Come on, David. We can still fix this. Name your price. One million, five million. I'll have the money dropped off downstairs. And we can get you a new identity, a new life. Mr. White can set you up anywhere you want to go."

David studied Turnbull for a moment. "So we've come full circle. Another offer of large sums of money, and all I have to do is walk away from everything that's happened." David went around to the IV pole on the other side of the bed and inserted the needle into an injection port. "I don't want your money, and I don't want a new life. I'll make do with the one I have."

He applied pressure to the syringe.

"Please—David—at least think about the impact this will have on thousands of lives."

David pushed harder. "Maybe you should think about the impact you've had on a handful of lives."

Turnbull pulled against the restraints. "David, I beg you, please don't do this."

David continued to push, his hands trembling, the tears streaming.

"You'll rot in Hell for—"

Turnbull's mouth kept moving, but no words formed. Then he began to twitch—arms, legs, fingers, face. The succinylcholine was depolarizing all of his muscle cells, except for the heart. It was still beating, a normal rhythm on the monitor.

The plunger stopped, the syringe empty. Turnbull lay motionless on the gurney, his chest still, his eyes wide with fear. David put his mouth to Turnbull's ear and yelled at him the way the French screamed at the decapitated heads during the revolution: "You can't take away everything from a man and expect to live. You just can't!"

The alarm on the heart monitor sounded—ventricular fibrillation.

From up in the sky, the sound of a chopper, coming closer, hovering. From down on the street, cars pulling up, screeching to a stop, doors opening and closing. Outside the dirty windows, lights flashing on the building façade across the street.

David turned and walked toward the elevator, passing through burnt-orange swatches of sunlight that had penetrated the grime on the glass and filled the second floor of the warehouse.

- 63 -

Kate stepped out of the cab and sent the driver on his way. He took his time getting turned around, craning his neck this way and that, trying to take in the spectacle that was unfolding. An NYPD chopper hovered overhead in a sky that had gone from soft pink to flaming orange. Patrol cars and an Emergency Service Unit truck filled the street in front of the warehouse. Uniformed officers were blocking off the area with blue sawhorses. Numerous ESU officers, thick with Kevlar vests and heavy with assault rifles, were positioning themselves around the building. Kate spotted Lieutenant Rick Stubblefield at the same time he spotted her. They met behind one of the patrol cars, not far from the single, windowless door that served as the main entrance to the building.

Stubblefield was tall, about six-five. He stooped a bit so he could be heard over the drone of the helicopter. "What do we have here, Detective?"

Kate, speaking just short of a yell, said, "I believe one of the suspects in the kidney-snatching case is inside. This may be the site of their illegal organ harvests." Having said that, she found it hard to believe such a heap could house an operating room.

"Any reason to think he's armed?"

"Doubtful, but he may be using Russian mobsters as enforcers."

"Since you don't have a warrant, I need probable cause before we break down the door."

"The wife of the suspect tracked him here using a GPS signal. For the last thirty minutes I've been watching the signal myself, and it hasn't moved." Kate took her iPhone from her pocket and showed the real-time-tracking web page to the lieutenant.

"Impressive," he said, nodding. "Possible it's a fuck pad?"

"This dump? Not his style."

"All right. We'll go in as soon as my men are ready."

The lieutenant stepped away and gave a series of commands over his walkie-talkie.

Kate hugged herself, the cold settling in.

Scarpelli appeared next her. "I see you called out the big boys."

"Turnbull didn't come home last night. His BlackBerry's GPS has him at this address."

"Think it's a fuck pad?"

"I think it's the warehouse McBride mentioned."

"So with McBride on the run, Andy's doing his own dirty work."

"I don't know. He's been in there—or at least his phone's been in there—for nine hours. I'm not sure what to expect."

"You call the Feds? And Homicide?"

"I asked Morales to do it."

Four ESU officers wearing helmets and face shields carried a battering ram up to the door of the warehouse. Six more officers lined up behind them. Lieutenant Stubblefield, standing off to the side, flashed a hand signal. The four men rammed the door. It didn't budge. They hit it again, right next to the knob. Hit it a third time, and it flew open. The men with the battering ram stepped aside. The other six went in, repeatedly yelling "NYPD." The lieutenant brought up the rear.

A few minutes later, Kate checked her phone. "Shit," she said with a big, frosty breath.

"What?" Scarpelli asked.

"Lost the GPS signal."

"Wonder what that means."

"Who knows?"

An ESU officer appeared in the doorway and waved them over. Shouting over the hovering chopper, he said, "Lieutenant needs you upstairs."

As they stepped through the door, a paramedic unit flew around the corner and stopped in front of the warehouse. What the hell, did they shoot him? Kate wondered.

Kate stood at the foot of the gurney, dumbfounded by what lay before her. Andrew Turnbull—the handsome, articulate man who quite possibly held the solution to one of medicine's great challenges—was strapped to the bed like an animal, naked from the waist up, eyes gaping open, gauze dressings taped to his sides, no spikes or dips on the heart monitor, only a quivering line. His body jerked as an ESU officer performed CPR.

One of the paramedics—Tom Burnett, according to his ID badge—inserted a breathing tube down Turnbull's throat and started squeezing an oxygen bag.

His partner, Frederico Ramirez, squirted jelly on defibrillator paddles, rubbed them together, and hit a button on the base unit. A high-pitched hum increased in loudness, then plateaued. "Charged to two hundred joules."

"Shock him," Burnett said.

Ramirez yelled, "Clear!" and fired.

The paddles popped. Turnbull's body spasmed, and his back arched.

"He's still fibrillating. Shock him again."

Another pop and arch of the back.

"No change. Hit him again, with three hundred this time."

Ramirez fired. Nothing.

"Let's give him some epi."

Ramirez removed syringes from a tackle box. "One amp of epinephrine going in."

"Continue compressions for two minutes to let the epi circulate," Burnett said.

The ESU officer pumping the chest nodded his understanding, and Kate recalled that all Emergency Service Unit members were certified EMTs as well as cops.

Burnett said, "Can anyone tell me what's going on here? Why we're resuscitating a naked man strapped to a surgical gurney in an old warehouse?"

Kate looked at Stubblefield.

The lieutenant said, "This is how we found him, tied to the bed, not breathing, nobody else in the place."

Kate added, "He may have ties to the organ-snatching case we're investigating. I think it's an attempt at revenge by one of the principle players."

Burnett nodded toward a glass vial and syringe on the stainless-steel table next to him. "Can someone read the label on that bottle sitting there?"

Kate maneuvered herself between the gurney and the table, and with an ink pen, moved the vial until she could see the label. She sounded out the name as if reading from a first-grade primer. "Suck-cin-ul-ko-lene," she said.

"Succinylcholine?" Burnett said with a holy-shit look on his face.

"Time," Ramirez said.

"Zap him, 300 joules."

Ramirez shocked Turnbull again, without success.

"Another milligram of epi. Follow that with 300 milligrams of amiodarone."

More shocks were delivered.

Followed by more drugs.

Followed by more shocks.

The smell of singed flesh filled the air. Turnbull grew increasingly pale, his lips now purple, his eyes glazed.

Burnett leaned over him and flashed a penlight into his pupils. "Fixed and dilated." He looked up at Kate and Scarpelli. "The brain has suffered irreversible injury. Even if we get the heart started again, he'll be brain dead. I'm sorry, but I'm gonna call it."

Burnett instructed the ESU officers to stop compressions and respirations. Freddy Ramirez turned off the IV drips.

Kate said, "This is now a murder scene. Please be careful not to touch or move anything."

Scarpelli came up beside her.

"Find the BlackBerry?" she asked.

"No. I figure our perp has it. Still no signal?"

"No signal."

Kate looked at Burnett. "The stuff in the vial, is that what killed him?"

"Probably. Succinylcholine is a real bad actor. It paralyzes all the muscles in the body except for the heart. If you're not on a ventilator when it's injected, you suffocate."

"Christ," Scarpelli said.

"Execution by lethal injection," Kate added.

"Looks that way," Burnett said. "But the medical examiner will need to rule out other possibilities—other drugs, or a complication of the surgery."

"If the mode of death was an injection, how long ago do you think it happened?"

"When we got here, he was in coarse v-fib. That means his heart had not been fibrillating very long, minutes at most."

Kate turned toward Stubblefield. "You've had all exits covered?"

"Yes. In fact, they're all bolted from the inside with slide bolts. They are not the kind of doors where you can let yourself out and lock them from the outside. And bars cover all the windows. It's like the perp vaporized and floated outta here."

Kate peeled back one of the gauze dressings on Turnbull's side, saw the same blue stitch used to close Jimmy Gray's incision. She looked up at Scarpelli.

"No surprise there," he said. "Motive, opportunity, and means, with heavy emphasis on motive."

Scarpelli went to the car to call in an APB on David McBride, and to call out the Crime Scene Unit, Homicide, and the medical examiner. Lieutenant Stubblefield and his men gathered their equipment and cleared out. The paramedics packed up their stuff and left as quickly as they had arrived.

Kate was now alone with Turnbull. She stood at the head of the gurney and leaned over him. His skin was pale and beaded with sweat, his lips a deep shade of purple. The mucus membranes of his eyes had dried and wrinkled, the line on the heart monitor now flat. She shook her head and sighed, dreading the call to Mrs. Turnbull. On the other hand, she looked forward to finding Jimmy Gray and telling him that, at least in this instance, he wasn't crazy.

She sat in the metal chair at the foot of the gurney and pictured David McBride limping along the icy streets of lower Manhattan, bumping shoulders with the morning workforce minutes after having administered a lethal injection to someone who was once a mentor, a father figure, his fellow man. She wondered how men like Turnbull and McBride—men of intelligence, drive, and compassion, men very much like her father—could become devoid of all humanity. And she wondered if the human race would ever run out of novel ways to brutalize one another. The answer to the latter question was no, not in her lifetime, or the lifetimes of the children she'd never bring into this fucked-up world.

The elevator ground its way to the second floor—Scarpelli.

Kate checked her phone. The red cursor was blinking again. She enlarged the map.

"Got something?" Scarpelli asked as he crossed the warehouse floor.

"A signal from the BlackBerry. It starts on Gansevoort and is now moving up Tenth Avenue. Holy shit. He's only a few blocks away, on the corner of Tenth and West 16th. You call it in. I'm heading over there."

- 64 -

David plodded his way up Tenth Avenue—his shoes and socks sloppy wet after wading through the sewer, his feet and legs numb from the subzero temperature, his right thigh aching after climbing a ladder to the street. But he barely noticed any of that, nor did he care. Pain was now, and would always be, his baseline existence. He expected nothing less, deserved nothing more.

At the corner of Tenth Avenue and West 16th Street he paused, moved clear of the torrent of morning commuters, and studied a Google map on Turnbull's BlackBerry. Four more blocks would bring him to West 20th. A right turn on 20th would take him to the 10th Precinct. Or he could enter Tyronne's number. Either way. It made no difference. Same endpoint. The murder of Andrew Turnbull had carried David over the event horizon and into a black hole from which he'd never escape. Whether sitting in a prison cell, or in a cell of his own design, he'd forever be defined and governed by the calculated action of thumb on syringe. Confucius was right—seek revenge, dig two graves. He put the phone away and started up Tenth.

A half block later, a black Mercedes sedan with tinted glass pulled to the curb. The front passenger door swung open. David was told to get in. He did, and he closed his eyes and let his head fall back against the headrest. "So ... this is how it ends."

"No," Mr. White said. "This is how it begins." He held out his hand. "I need the BlackBerry."

David gave it to him.

Mr. White turned it off and sped up Tenth Avenue.

Acknowledgements

Learning how to write and publish a novel is a long and arduous process, requiring many contributors along the way. The following individuals deserve my immense gratitude:

Scott Driscoll, Pam Goodfellow, Helen Elaine Lee, Dennis Lehane, Sandra Scofield, and Sterling Watson for their instruction and mentorship.

The faculty, staff, and students at Pine Manor College in Boston.

Kathleen Isdith, Patti Arthur, Christine Grace, Karin Wigley, Sig Mejdal, and Jackson Streeter for their early reads and feedback.

Homicide detective, Sgt. Mark Worstman, Seattle Police Department, for bringing my clichéd gang members and detectives to life.

Tom Hyman and the team at Kirkus editorial services.

Kate Race at Visual Quill for her cover and marketing platform designs.

Chris O'Byrne and the staff at JETLAUNCH Strategic Publishing for their design and distribution expertise.

Claire McKinney at Claire McKinneyPR, LLC for her expert marketing and publicity.

About the Author

Richard Van Anderson is a former heart surgeon turned fiction writer. His surgery training took him from the "knife and gun club" of LSU Medical Center in Shreveport, Louisiana, to the famed Bellevue Hospital in Midtown Manhattan. His education as a writer includes an MFA in creative writing from Pine Manor College in Boston, Massachusetts. He currently lives in Seattle, Washington with his wife and two sons.

To learn more about Richard Van Anderson the author, visit rvananderson.com.

Connect with Richard on:

Facebook
Twitter
Google Plus
Goodreads

And finally, the best way for a book to find its audience has always been, and still is, word of mouth recommendations. So, if you liked the story, please consider telling others about it, either person to person, using social media, or (and this is the most effective way) posting online reviews at your favorite review site. Thank you.

CPSIA information can be obtained at www.ICGtesting.com
Printed in the USA
LVOW07s1715040215

425707LV00003B/637/P